COLLAPSE

THE DESPOT CHRONICLES #3

COLLAPSE

ANDY T. HANSON

4 Horsemen
Publications, Inc.

Collapse
Copyright © 2025 Andy T. Hanson. All rights reserved.

4 Horsemen
Publications, Inc.

Published By: 4 Horsemen Publications, Inc.

4 Horsemen Publications, Inc.
PO Box 417
Sylva, NC 28779
4horsemenpublications.com
info@4horsemenpublications.com

Cover & Typesetting by Autumn Skye
Edited by Jen Paquette

All rights to the work within are reserved to the author and publisher. No part of this publication may be reproduced, stored in a retrieval system, or transmitted in any form or by any means, electronic, mechanical, photocopying, recording, scanning, or otherwise, except as permitted under Section 107 or 108 of the 1976 International Copyright Act, without prior written permission except in brief quotations embodied in critical articles and reviews. Please contact either the Publisher or Author to gain permission.

All characters, organizations, and events portrayed in this novel are either products of the author's imagination or are used fictitiously.

All brands, quotes, and cited work respectfully belongs to the original rights holders and bear no affiliation to the authors or publisher.

Library of Congress Control Number: Pending

Paperback ISBN-13: 979-8-8232-1012-6
Hardcover ISBN-13: 979-8-8232-1013-3
Ebook ISBN-13: 979-8-8232-1014-0

ACKNOWLEDGMENTS

For the three legendary Georges: Carlin, Martin, and Miller, for all their lasting gifts.

"To every man upon this Earth, death cometh soon or late."

-Thomas Babington Macaulay,
"Lays of Ancient Rome"

CONTENTS

PROLOGUE ix

CHAPTER 1 1
CHAPTER 2 9
CHAPTER 3 27
CHAPTER 4 54
CHAPTER 5 66
CHAPTER 6 81
CHAPTER 7 95
CHAPTER 8 113

INTERLUDE 132

CHAPTER 9 143
CHAPTER 10 171
CHAPTER 11 187
CHAPTER 12 214
CHAPTER 13 243
CHAPTER 14 263
CHAPTER 15 284

BOOK CLUB QUESTIONS 299
AUTHOR BIO 301

PROLOGUE
HARRINGTON

INFECTION EVENT: GENESIS

Hubert Richard Harrington found himself sprinting through the sprawling halls of AOA's highly secretive and excessively secluded Main Operations Facility for the second time in his life. The first undignified jaunt had come only minutes earlier. Harrington was CEO of the most important and powerful corporation in the world; sprinting was far beneath his dignity, hustling in any fashion really, but propriety had been suspended everywhere throughout the massive production complex nestled deep in the midst of an evergreen forest in central Alberta. A breach had occurred at two ultra-sensitive labs in the far west end of the hidden facility.

The alert system had dropped down on them like a sudden ocean squall. Harrington had been feigning interest as best he could at a resource management meeting in the facility's glamorous corporate wing when the klaxon kicked on, followed by the benign female voice describing the emergency in clipped sentences. The recap alert played on a loop four times over before anyone in the meeting room moved a muscle. To his slight shame, the shock persisted in his own mind a deal longer than in all others, for he knew what they all did not. Hubert Harrington, being chief executive officer for Advancement Operations Alliance, was well aware of what was housed and processed in those specific top-secret outbuildings. A billion fears, dubious rejections, possible plays, end-games and improbabilities had kept him pinned in place at the head of the room's twelve-foot-long mahogany table.

It had been that uncharacteristic delay which necessitated his initial sprint. Harrington needed to arrive on scene first or at least be one of the firsts. He needed to play damage control, no matter what was really going on at the breached labs. His second sprint had been brought about by what he'd discovered when he'd arrived. An unknown strike team of ten to twelve persons had somehow circumvented all subsequent layers of facility security and then blew their way into both of the labs in question. The mainframe had been accessed and downloaded before a virus was then uploaded, erasing everything it had copied. All the research on every project under AOA's ultra-secret umbrella was now gone. But the worst news of all had come when Harrington had shoved through the useless security hatch deep in the production labs to find all twelve Alpha specimens missing from their stasis tubes, along with every last vial of Infection 43 absent from either lab's freezers.

Harrington hadn't known why anyone should come for the Alphas or the manufactured infection, nor could he guess who could've possibly known about them that was also capable of orchestrating such a brazen theft. After all, every government on the planet with the means and motivations to pull off such a feat was already in on the secret. It made no sense that any of them would make such a risky, unsanctioned play, and even less sense to him that they should have their people pick out these two labs in particular. No obvious answers were forthcoming. He knew something catastrophic had just occurred, but he had no idea why, or worse yet, how. He needed answers and knew of only one being who might have them. *She should be here. This is her deal. Ain't this why they sent her in the first place?* Hubert Harrington had asked himself. She was on location, after all, somewhere in the production facility's giant sprawl. *So why the hell ain't she down here? Her precious Alphas are missing. Where the hell is she?* Harrington had known the bitch kept her own schedule, answering to no one, but even still, he had expected her to be there.

The labs were locked down and secured within minutes of his arrival, but he'd wasted a deal of time after, waiting around in expectation that she'd come strolling up all rigid and expressionless at any moment. When he'd finally given up the wait and decided he'd needed to go to her, the pressure and anxiety of all the wasted time had spurred him into this current quick-paced jog. The labs were her responsibility. The ultimate plan was in her mind, not his. Harrington didn't know what the implications of the unexpected breach were as far as future-AOA's timeline was concerned. Everyone had been looking to him for directions, but his hands were tied until the cold bitch told him what she wanted, what *they* wanted.

She should've been on-site right along with him. *Fucking bitch knows she's got me by the balls, knows I can't do nothing without her say. She's making me crawl to her just 'cause she can. Goddammit!* It was all true. Hubert Harrington had been a powerful man nearly all his life. It did not sit right to play the puppet. But, pissed off or not, Harrington still knew he ultimately would dance to the pipes; future AOA was just too powerful, the cold, synthetic bitch being an avatar of that power. And so it was that he was out of breath and sweating when he finally punched in the code outside Liesel Collins' chamber.

Collins' avatar was a long-limbed, pale-skinned woman with an ageless, wrinkle-free face, cold gray eyes and dark shoulder-length hair. Whether or not the real woman from 353 years from then looked anything like her, or at least ever did before transferring her consciousness to a synthetic Alpha avatar, Hubert Harrington couldn't say. He spotted her frosty visage in the small chamber's back left corner after his first step inside the room. The overhead motion light kicked on right away, illuminating the synthetic being hunched inside an information upload/transfer chair. The cramped contraption's widow's-peak-style half-helmet was resting atop her dense black hair. Her long-fingered hands were wrapped firmly around the baseball-sized orbs at the end of each armrest. Her near-translucent eyelids did not flick open to reveal the dark-gray manufactured eyes beneath until Harrington was three paces away from the C-shaped transfer chair.

"You" was all the pale, pristine android said, after a few quick blinks and a slow look around.

"Yeah, me," Harrington agreed with snark.

"What are you doing in here?" Collins asked with flat emotion.

"What the hell do you think I'm doing here? Where the hell you been? Why weren't you down at the labs? The hell you wasting time in here for?" Harrington asked his questions consecutively while Collins lifted the transfer chair's half-helm from her head and slowly climbed out of the cramped contraption.

"What the hell are you blathering about now?" she asked, rising to her full height to look ever so slightly down on Harrington.

"Didn't you hear the alarm? The hell you been doing in that fucking chair? Playing 3D Pac-man? You can't be bothered to notice the blaring klaxons and looping alert message going off for the past half hour?"

"There's no klaxons in here," Collins pointed out.

Harrington realized she was right. Her small, sterile chamber was quiet and still.

"Your day-to-day affairs are yours to handle. I'm here for one reason and one reason alone. You know this," she reminded him.

"Well, maybe if you weren't so keen on only focusing on your business, you would have taken the sensible precaution of not isolating your chambers from the alert system. Maybe if you and your future buddies would have had the foresight to plug you in a bit to our *day-to-day affairs*, you would've saw that the alarm was due to a breach in production labs Kilo and Lima."

Harrington was certain the news of her precious charge being ransacked would illicit some emotion from the robot, but to his disappointment, Liesel Collins simply stretched her back a bit before calmly moving to seat herself in the room's only other chair, a black leather roller.

"Hello, did you hear me?" Harrington almost shouted the question at her. "Someone broke into your labs! They stole the data and then melted the servers! They took every last vial of Infection 43! You hearing me, woman? Your labs have been breached! Hell, they even made off with every last one of your precious Alphas."

Collins' eyes suddenly shot up. This last news had reached her. Her behavior had been so frustrating that seeing the sudden flicker of concern in her glassy gray eyes was pleasing to the point he had to take a breath to fight back a grin.

"All the Alphas?" Liesel Collins asked him.

"Yes," he confirmed with heavy exasperation. "It's all fucking gone."

"You're sure? All of them? You're sure there weren't two left?" she pressed.

"Yes, I'm sure. There wasn't shit left, no data, no Alphas, no nothing," he shot back.

"There should've been two left in their pods," Collins said, though Harrington guessed the statement was meant more for her own sake. Her demeanor had completely changed. The woman had never displayed any emotion before, so Harrington had assumed her avatar wasn't even capable, but the panic and confusion on her face now were as apparent as the top line of an eye exam. "You're sure?" she asked again. "All the Alphas were taken? Every one?"

"Yes," Harrington snarled his answer.

Collins brushed his truculence aside without even looking at him. "Get out," she commanded with a dismissive wave.

Harrington didn't move. Collins didn't seem to care. She was up out of her black leather roller and into the C-shaped transfer chair in the space of a single breath, never looking his way again. Before he could think to protest, the half-helm was seated atop her skull, her eyes were snapped shut, her long fingers gripping tight to the hand knobs, and her consciousness fully linked with the machine. Harrington had never been allowed to be present in the room when she connected herself to the system, and she had ordered him to leave, but he'd be damned if he was going anywhere without some answers. His brain was full of them. If Liesel Collins wouldn't provide, he'd have to take.

He knew full well what the synthetic woman was about. Collins was even now contacting future-AOA and establishing a text chain for direct communication back and forth. Before she'd arrived, or rather before he'd been forced to input her consciousness into an Alpha, it was Harrington who got to make contact with future-AOA. Collins and her fancy chair had usurped that privilege. Contact with the future could only come in the form of data transfer. The cost in power it took to send any physical matter back in time was so prohibitive that future-AOA could only pull off one transfer of that kind. He and his government backers knew they had that big transfer planned for their endgame, but in the meantime, future-AOA relied on Harrington and his current AOA to prepare the ground for their coming arrival.

I can listen in, Harrington realized. Collins was lost to the world, so he used no stealth in plopping down into her vacated roller and pulling himself up in front of Collins' personal computer terminal. Thankfully, his access code allowed him into her system. Harrington navigated the slightly unfamiliar setup with minimal difficulty and had a window of future-AOA and Liesel Collins' current text chain opened up before him within a dozen seconds. He hadn't missed much. Collins had only just achieved a connection, and future-AOA was only just now responding.

...

[Future AOA: Collins, this is Datalis. Your report is scheduled for tomorrow. Power source for Temporal Navigation Pad running low. Why breach protocol?]

[Collins: Had to.]

[Datalis: Problem?]

[Collins: Raid went awry.]

[Datalis: How? Is infection loosed? Explain yourself.]

[Collins: Infection is out, but so are all the Alphas. The two reserves in the back pods were loosed with all the others.]

[Datalis: That's impossible. Why would they do that?]

[Collins: Someone somewhere betrayed us. Only explanation. Rivard Corp., or Blanchard, or maybe even Elicos Corp., one of them knows our plans. One of them has the temporal navigation tech and must've contacted the raiders and made them a better offer.]

[Datalis: Impossible. More likely just incompetence. Were you not the one who contracted the raiders? We consider it impossible any other corp. have a temporal manipulator, and even in the low chance they do, how could they have contacted your specific team? No, CSO, this is on you.]

[Collins: Whoever you want to blame, it happened. Alphas are all gone. We need to handle this.]

[Datalis: We have to have at least one of those Alphas.]

[Collins: I know. Advice?]

[Datalis: Retrieve one. Then advance plan to endgame. Extract the Synthetic Repository Lubricant from the captured Alpha and take it up to Cardinal's Nest. Activate our Alpha avatars as soon as you arrive aboard station. It will take time and draw a lot of power to extract all twenty individual consciousnesses from the captured Alpha's SRL. Let nothing delay you. As soon as each board member's consciousness is isolated and identified, upload immediately into our Alphas... Repeat, advance plan to endgame.]

[Collins: Odds aren't great that we'd find an Alpha now. With servers melted, each ID responder code was lost. I've no way to track them... I renew my request to receive your stored consciousnesses. Upload them now into my avatar's repository lubricant. You can trust me.]

[Datalis: Negative. Your failure today is evident. You're too large a risk. Our trust in you has been greatly diminished. How could we favor you with that responsibility now?]

[Collins: You're risking everything by just hoping to capture an Alpha. Surely, that slim hope is a greater risk to our plans than my competence.]

[Datalis: Considering...]

[Collins: Consider quickly. Each moment wasted is one where Alphas get farther away.]

[Datalis: Very well... Prepare for upload. Our fate is in your hands, CSO Collins. Do not fail us. We've only enough stored power for one chance at this for at least three months. Get it right. We're counting on you... And be wary of infiltrators... Upload commencing...]

The messenger window went blank. Harrington's eyes went to the synthetic woman in the transfer chair. The half-helm was now emitting a red light from the LED fixture embedded in its ridge. Collins seemed to be gripping the hand knobs with all her strength. He could see the artificial muscles in her forearms contort from the effort. *Apparently the transfer's on its way,* Hubert Harrington told himself. *I hope it hurts, you mechanical bitch.* Liesel Collins' conversation with her co-workers from three hundred years in the future had been short, but a lot had been made clear in Harrington's mind by reading those few lines of stilted dialogue. He knew now how well he'd been played.

Truth be told, Harrington figured a group of people from the future who'd mastered time travel would probably be able to keep a few secrets from him, but realizing just how much he'd been manipulated put all his prior beliefs to shame. If these simple consciousness transfers required so much power, then clearly future-AOA was never planning a mass physical transfer. "This infection release was always their plan," he said aloud what he now understood. It all fell into place. He felt a gut punch once he realized how blind to the obvious he'd been. In light of everything he'd pieced together about three hundred years into the future, it was a clearly logical play. Extremely cold but very logical.

Harrington knew future-AOA was one of a dozen megacorporations in their time that effectively ruled every corner of the decaying globe. Famine and drought had turned rainforests to deserts. There was little room for any of the remaining ruling corporations to get ahead, and future-AOA was only a mid-tier corporation in this corporatocracy. But a break came their way, a massive game-changing break. The right scientist, with the right team, studying the right discipline, had serendipitously produced a revolutionary breakthrough: time travel. Future-AOA obviously saw their chance to take it all, and they devised a plan every bit as ruthless as it was genius.

They aren't coming back in anything other than consciousness transfers. That's why they made you add that Alpha printing lab beneath the luxury quarters all secret-like behind that false wall, Hubie. They're gonna kill everyone else and start from scratch and just keep the few of us privy to Cardinal's Nest to run their station. They plan on wiping out the competition before they can even be born. Smart. Cruel and cutthroat, but smart. Start with a fresh Earth, build up the population artificially with their super tech, and then rule everyone as the clear superiors in their near-immortal android bodies. Well, if that's their play, then that's their play. I'll just have to make sure I find some way to get my consciousness transferred into an Alpha so I can live and rule for a thousand years beside them, or however the hell long Collins said the Alphas last. I'll tell the bitch when she wakes up from her transfer that I know everything. I'll tell her only I can keep the workers in line. If she wants to make it up to Cardinal's Nest with their precious consciousnesses, then she's gonna have to cut me in.

Harrington was just about to nail down the opening line he'd deliver when a klaxon of a different octave suddenly barked out from the room's speaker system. A new alarm had been tripped, one that even Collins' private chamber was wired into. No harsh blinking light assailed him though. Apparently, her chambers were only set up for certain sonic alerts. But when he glanced back at the chamber's sliding hatchway, the intermittent red flashing along the corridor was visible through the thin crack at the bottom of the steel door. Hubert Harrington's legs were not responding to his commands. It took a good three seconds before he could get them to carry him back to Collins' computer terminal, and even then, they complied sluggishly at best. Something deep inside told him this new alert would be disastrous.

He bashed the terminal's keypad clumsily but still managed to hail the security room. "This is Harrington. Speak to me. What the hell is going on?"

"Mr. Harrington, sir, this is Watson. I'm out of the security room, sir. We all are, sir," a frantic voice responded. "All security staff are currently engaged with them. They keep coming, sir. They're killing each other, sir. And... and... and some are... some are becoming like the others. It's spreading, sir. A lot of the staff had gathered in the Café after the first alarm. It spread there like wildfire. My men are being overrun there. I'm on my way now."

Harrington trusted his report. The labored breathing of the secret complex's head of security was proof enough for him. "Say again. What the hell is going on, man?" Harrington shouted at the man anyway, despite knowing in his bones full well what the man was describing.

"It's the staff, sir... they... they... they're attacking each other... and... and... everyone in their path. They're... they... they're fucking eating each other, sir!" Head of Security Watson bellowed over the comm.

Harrington said nothing for a long time. The communications link crackled with static. Screams and pleas and other gruesome sounds, muffled and muted over the comm, filled the dead air.

Finally, Watson's strained voice came back over the radio waves. "Sir, did you hear me, sir? Mr. Harrington, are you there, sir? I sounded the evac. Transport choppers are firing up now. Should I rescind it, sir? Sir? Mr. Harrington, do you copy?"

"I copy, Watson, I copy," Harrington barked. "Come to me now. I'll need a security escort to the tarmac. Gather two of your men, and I'll meet ya at the entrance to Beta wing."

"Uhh, what was tha— ...uhh, say again your last, sir?"

"Come get me, Watson. Now!" Harrington shouted the order.

"Sir, I don't think you understand. We're being overrun. My men, sir... my men need me. I can't just leave," Watson explained between labored breaths.

"I understand full well, you dumb shit, and I don't care. Come get me. Now!" he ordered even more forcefully.

There was a pause before the man responded, but it was negligible enough so as Harrington didn't explode on him. "I'm on my way, sir."

"Good. Get two other men too. I want a safe trip to that chopper."

"Yes, s—"

Yes, sir, the man was obviously going to say, but a sudden wail cut short his response.

"Watson, did you copy? Get your ass here!" Harrington shouted into the comm-link in the terminal before him. Nothing came back but fuzz and static. "Watson? Watson? Are you on your way?" Harrington was shouting fruitlessly.

Then a noise so eerie and ominous, like a pride of lions feasting in the dark, leaked through the comm-link. As chilling as those chomping sounds were, the piercing, pain-wracked wail that followed would make any man long for that crunching and chewing symphony.

"Watson?" Harrington asked once more, all the anger drained from his voice.

The connection ended a beat later; the quiet hum of the transfer chair, now all the noise to be heard in the crabbed little room. Then the screams reached his ears, faintly at first, but growing steadily louder and closer. *No one's coming. We gotta go*, he thought, darting his eyes back to the pale woman in the C-shaped chair.

Harrington's shouts for the slender woman to wake up or come out of the transfer lock rose in octave and volume commensurate with the surging screams echoing throughout the corridors beyond. Collins could not hear, or perhaps she simply chose not to; it mattered little. He had to get her up and out of that goddamn chair either way. Harrington ducked around behind the bulky hunk of techno-furniture, searching for a power cord. Several thick black cords protruded from a central hole in the chair's back. None were labeled or obvious, so in the end, he simply yanked the lot of them firmly as he could. The tug pulled none of the cords free completely, but a few moved a smidge, enough to cut the power feed to the uncomfortable machine.

All the various blinking and flashing LED lights along the transfer chair went dark. The low hum of its machinery wound down to silence. Harrington darted back to the front of the chair, thinking he might have to physically yank the woman out of her seat, but instead found her free of the cumbersome seat, alert as ever, though that alert and coherent demeanor was tinged with a furious bemusement. Before he could speak a word in his defense, the long fingers of Collins' right hand wrapped firmly around his throat. With rage-aided ease to go along with the unnatural strength of her mechanical avatar, she lifted him bodily off the floor only to slam him hard against the wall of her small private quarters. Pain radiated through his every nerve, even as her iron grip constricted tighter and tighter.

Blackness closed in around him. *I'm dying. The bitch is killing me*. Harrington assumed this would be his last thought, when, from nowhere, came another, *Kick! Kick the bitch!* He felt a few blows land square. The grip however, stayed firm, right up until the moment it didn't. Collins still held him tight against the wall. Her grip had only slackened enough for the darkness to fade as he drew in a long and painful breath.

"What the fuck are you thinking? How dare you interrupt a transfer?"

"I had to," he coughed in answer.

"Do you have any idea how important that transfer was? Have you any idea what you've done?"

"Yes. But I had to," he managed through searing lungs. "The infection is loose in this facility. We need to evacuate now. They're right out in the halls."

"That can't be true. They aren't to release the infection until 2300 EST, and only once they've touched down at Argos Airport in Belgium. I'm not to have you initiate Emergency Protocol 97 Delta for another eight hours at least. I've matters to handle before then. If it's loose on this continent, the spread could be rapid enough to complicate procedures."

"Haven't ya realized by now that whatever you and your people paid the raiders to do, they obviously had ideas of their own? The infection is loose on these premises. We need to get to the transport choppers before the shit can spread that far." A coughing fit racked him then.

Collins either got tired or took pity on him, he had no way to tell, but she released her grip and let him drop the eighteen inches to the cold tile floor.

"We gotta go."

"I can't leave without completing this transfer," she stated, almost absently.

"Your board members' consciousnesses can be pulled from the Alphas still. We can send a team back for one after we're safe and secure aboard The Nest."

Collins looked him over with a critical eye. Nothing was said between them, but both knew. The synthetic woman understood he'd eavesdropped on her temporal transmission text chain. That much was plain in the creased lines of her normally wrinkle-free brow.

He might've expected her to berate him, or hit him, or kill him even, but instead she said, "There's no guarantee we ever find one. They are programmed to spread out to every corner of the globe. It'll become a needle in a haystack within the next few hours."

"And this place will become a slaughterhouse in a few short minutes. There's no way we could survive here long enough for you to complete the transfer," Harrington pointed out. "Plus, I'm not sure the whole needle in a haystack metaphor works."

"What do you mean?"

"Your people made me install a signal emitter at all seven of our main corporate facilities. I can activate it from your terminal here. It came as an addendum failsafe protocol with last month's temporal data transfers. Don't you remember?"

"I didn't need to be read into every last detail of every last transmission," Collins answered, offended.

"Well, as I recall... 'Once any synthetically printed human avatar, otherwise called Alphas, comes within range of any emitter, their programming prevents them from ever again leaving its limits without direct intervention from its programmers,'" Harrington quoted the emitter file's specifications. "So, we give it some time for the Alphas to spread out and contact an emitter's range; then we limit our searches to areas around our seven facilities where the emitters were installed. Give it enough missions, and a retrieval squad is bound to contact one eventually. What's a few months or years to you people anyhow?"

"Turn on the damn signal then," Collins commanded after a long, contemplative pause. "You can enact 97 Delta on the way to the choppers," she added just as Harrington set to work activating the signal emitters from Collin's computer terminal.

"97 Delta? Shit, you're serious?" he asked. *Of course they'd use 97 Delta to get everyone they need aboard station*, he thought, answering his own question. "Fuck, they ain't gonna be happy," Harrington croaked, rubbing his neck. "Lord knows what I'm supposed to tell 'em. They operate the most sophisticated intelligence operations on the planet. The US will be an especially hard sell, no matter the lie. Odds are they already know everything that's happened here."

"They don't know shit. There isn't a government on this planet who knows a single fact more than we allow them to. So call them up and activate the evacuation. And if they ask any questions, tell them nothing. Tell them if they want any chance at surviving to the end of the week, then they better get their asses to West Virginia, along with every kin-member or support staff they care to corral, or we're leaving without them. Let them know the 24-hour deadline starts now. Remind them how unnecessary and expendable they are. Tell them the clock's ticking," Collins suggested with a hand wrapped around his forearm, guiding him out into the scream-echoing corridor.

By the time they made it to the tarmac and the waiting helicopter atop the northwest pad, Collins was covered shoulder to knee in dark red blood and still holding firm to the bright red emergency axe she'd used to cut their way free of three separate swarms of his flesh-crazed employees. Harrington's face was white and bloodless, his stomach a knot of panic. His throat was so dry, and the trauma of their escape so crippling, that he couldn't even give the pilot the order to take off.

Collins, though, was remarkably unrattled. She shouted for the black-helmeted pilot behind the opaque Aviator glasses to get the chopper in the air before thrusting a pocket tablet into Harrington's chest. "Snap out of it, Hubie. Get your ass on the horn and issue the orders, or I'm tossing your useless flesh out the fucking door."

He got the hint. His breath began to slow. With a sigh so weary it could sink a sailing ship, Harrington took up the proffered tablet and set about following the angry demands of a bloodless android from 353 years in the future.

CHAPTER 1
MAISIE

INFECTION EVENT: DAY 3,167

"Terminal life support systems almost fully restored. Airlock failsafes lift in seven minutes," Roddy Sheffield reported from the lofted central terminal.

Neither Maisie nor Jordana acknowledged the update verbally. Jordana might've nodded as Maisie had, but she had no way to be sure. Maisie faced the Main Control Room's sliding hatchway fronting on the Grand Alleyway while Jordana stood atop the platform to gaze out through the room's massive windscreen, their backs to one another.

"Landing pads should be fully charged and set to receive an E11 in the next few minutes." This last wasn't really a report so much as speculation.

Maisie understood Roddy was talking just to talk. They were all nervous, though of course none had said as much. The thrill of finally getting to speak her mind to a Witenagemot Councilmember had faded almost the instant after she'd disconnected the video communication with Lieutenant Dobechek. Nerves rattled, strained, and panicked killed that momentary high stone dead. Maisie had just sort of drifted to the hatchway after that while Jordana went back to the viewing platform. Roddy had remained at the central terminal, his fingers hardly ever still above the keypad.

Not much had been said in the forty or fifty minutes since that video comm, apart from Roddy Sheffield's infrequent reports. They were simply waiting for the next shoe to drop. Either the sliding hatchway's small window would be filled with the Commander and his cronies, instead of the two confused but alert footmen currently filling up a large portion of that tiny porthole, or a bottle-shaped E11 Transport Cruiser would appear above the lunar horizon carrying Jordana Revere's brothers and sisters in the Bruderschaft. Or the recharging of the Lunar Dock would fail, and they'd be vaporized in the inevitable explosion to follow. A combination of any of those could happen consecutively or all three could even happen all at once. Who knew? Each scenario seemed as likely as the other. All they could do in the meantime was keep their vigils: Maisie at the hatchway, Jordana on the platform, and Roddy at the terminal.

"I'm not sure, but I swear I see something," Jordana abruptly proclaimed, sounding somewhat reluctant.

"What?" Roddy and Maisie both asked.

"It's just a bright spot in the darkness, but I swear it's growing bigger. It's gotta be a ship coming toward us," she said, sounding hopeful now.

Maisie gave up her surveillance of the goings-on beyond the heavy-duty security door. She had to see the truth for herself. Jogging up the platform's staircase, Maisie tried to pin down the spot in the black vastness where Jordana's eyes were currently focused. There were a lot of bright spots out in that cold darkness, and so exactly what had excited the former Royal Air Force fighter pilot was not immediately plain. Jordana settled the search as soon as Maisie arrived alongside her. In a move every bit as graceful as it was unexpected, the svelte beauty stepped up right behind her, took up her right arm with her own, and manipulated Maisie's index finger until it pointed straight at what appeared to be a dull glimmering star. The more she watched the bright spot, the larger it seemed to grow. A flush of excitement coursed through her bones as she gazed upon that twinkling blotch, though Jordana's warm breath washing over her neck in slow, steady pulses might truly have been the chief motivator for her surging exhilaration. Maisie dared not dwell on the specific cause. She had no time for such frivolities. If that truly was an E11, they had a hundred problems heading their way, as well as a thousand hopes. Maisie needed to keep as clear a head as she could for the time being. *There will be time for exploring and adventures later...*

Jordana dropped her support. Maisie's arm fell back to her side. The dark-haired pilot no longer wore the bandage wrap around her head, but Maisie herself had closed the wound with medical glue while she relayed her sad tale in their cozy alcove in the lunar station's maintenance tunnels before storming the Control Room. She knew how nasty a smack and gash the golden-eyed woman had taken. But for all that, her agility and balance weren't diminished in the least. Either that, or she was a superhero before the bash.

Jordana had somehow made it back, standing still as stone alongside Maisie before Roddy Sheffield even had time to turn his head and notice their intimate moment.

"Dock's ready to go. If that twinkling dot really is your pal's E11, they're just in time." No sooner had the words left his lips when a dozen alerts woke with a shriek across every terminal in the Control Room. "Speak of the devil, and she appears," Roddy announced with dry humor in the face of the commotion. "Looks like a ship has suddenly appeared on all the scopes." With a frustrating calm, he flashed his fingers across the digital keyboard for a good ten-count, silencing the alerts one by one before adding any more context, "An E11 Transport Cruiser is currently inbound for Cardinal's Nest. Ship Designate: Morgana 1. Outbound from Casper Station, Casper, Wyoming, eleven hours fourteen minutes ago."

"Casper Station?!" Jordana shouted, vaulting off the platform. "That's them. Hail them, Roddy!" She was shouting as she bounded toward the laconic man with the scraggly black beard and shaggy black hair.

"Looks as though their automatic landing systems are engaged and should have them attain soft dock with Pad 4 in T-minus five minutes, twelve seconds... Morgana 1's cargo bays are at quarter capacity. Fuel cells at minimum... *fumes* might be more accurate... Passenger manifest lists eighty-five passengers, including three crew," Sheffield was saying just as Jordana arrived alongside him, Maisie all but a few paces behind.

"Eighty-five?" Jordana asked in a strange voice. "You're sure?"

It took Maisie a ditzy moment to remember why that number would merit the pilot's sudden crestfallen demeanor. *She said there were eighty-seven others. They lost two, and obviously in an unexpected way, else Jordana wouldn't be so shocked. A horde must have found them out. They left without her report. They musta had to... Oh, god, the carnage... Is it truly endless?* "Jor, I'm so sorry," Maisie said, placing a comforting hand on her shoulder.

Jordana managed a smile of thanks but turned her head from Maisie before any tears could flow. There were still eighty-five of her brothers and sisters on a one-way, automatic trip to Chaos Island. "Patch me into them, Mr. Sheffield, please," the brave pilot requested in a strong voice.

Roddy abandoned his flippancy fast enough, once he caught wind of the sudden mood. "Uhh... okay, here ya go, Jordana. You're patched in," he said after a few keystrokes.

"Morgana 1, this is Cardinal's Nest Station. Do you read me, Morgana 1?" Jordana hailed in her rich and sultry accent.

"Cardinal's Nest, yes, we read you. This is Morgana 1, inbound for Pad 4. Are you ready to receive us?" a voice asked in thickly accented English. "We only just picked you up on our scopes. Automatic systems came online the instant you showed up on our—"

"You're clear for Pad 4, Morgana," Jordana cut in to affirm. "This is Revere. It's Jordana. Arlo? Is that you guys? Kleinert, that you? Merv? Hitch, you flying that thing? Is this the Bruderschaft? Tell me it's you, mates. Tell me I'm not dreaming."

"Jordana!?" an excited British male voice bellowed with a mixture of confusion and elation. "Where have you been, kid? We've been trying to contact the bloody station since back before we even took o—"

"Long story, Arlo," Jordana broke in once again before her counterpart could get lost on a tangent. "You're just going to have to trust me, time being."

"Of course, Jor," the male British voice apparently belonging to Arlo Bailey came back to say. "What are we in for down there?"

"Like I said, Arlo, long story. First things first. How's your landing systems? You say automatic systems engaged as soon as Cardinal's

Nest appeared on your scopes. Have you had any malfunctions with it or any other problems that might jeopardize your landing?"

"No, no problems with the auto lander, I don't believe," Arlo reported. "No real problems at all," he added after a brief round of low muttering amongst a small group of voices in the radio comm's background. "A few scares with some hull tremors along the way, but all in all, we made it through. The damnable thing pretty much piloted itself for the most part. I've adopted a sort of an if-it-ain't-broke-don't-fix-it approach to this flight thus far... Why do you ask? Are you saying we should expect complications?"

"No, you should be good, I think. It's only that... well, let's just say I had the opposite experience on my trip up," Jordana explained with a sardonic flare. "Okay, okay... but good. Yeah, you ought to be good, I s'pose."

Maisie could tell Jordana was distracted, trying to decide their next play after Morgana 1 touched down on Pad 4 of Branch 2's Lunar Dock. "How long until life support systems in the Terminal are up?" Maisie asked Roddy while she had the spare silent moment.

"Airlocks will lift roughly three minutes after their shuttle touches down. Should be perfect timing," Sheffield assessed.

"They need to rush aboard station the instant they can," Maisie urged. "Their shuttle will be spotted by the masses soon enough, and then the Witen will know a minute later. Who knows how they're gonna react? Best to get your friends aboard and their existence plain and undeniable to the people up here as soon as we can."

Jordana drew in a deep breath while her left hand sought out Maisie's right. Jordana squeezed tight, and the two of them locked eyes. Roddy watched but made no comment.

After another breath and tiny grin, the dark-haired, golden-eyed warrior-woman leaned back down to speak into the central terminal's open comm line. "Arlo, I'm sorry. Nothing is as we imagined. We only showed up on your scopes a few minutes back because you passed through the cloaking barrier. All our data on this station and its status were doctored."

"Uhh, say again your last, Jor," Arlo muttered, clearly hoping he hadn't heard correctly.

"It was pure fabrication, I'm afraid. All of it," Jordana sadly reported. "I crash landed and, only by some impossible luck, was rescued by some folks up here who have banded together to resist the gang of thugs that have been ruling this station with an iron fist for the past decade. AOA is out of power. They lost control of the station. But not before they... before... Arlo, the data you saw was all lies... doctored, fabricated, manufactured bullshit, Arlo. Who the hell knows why exactly. Maybe just to fool you specifically, just to mess with your head. Perhaps they took your corporate espionage a bit more seriously than even you dared to imagine... And the worst part is the thugs who've taken AOA's power have found all this cloak and dagger shit quite useful... I'm sorry, my friend. I know this is unwelcome news... The truth of the matter is that roughly five hundred people all made it safely up here on the first day of the infection. There was an uprising shortly after, and some folks up here snapped and took control... It's like I say, long story... So, to cut straight to the point, those thugs in control up here now are likely to be less than receptive to your sudden arrival."

"I see," Arlo Bailey responded after an extensive pause. "Well, you know we can't turn back, Jor. Even if our fuel were not at critical levels, we've nowhere to return to. Casper Station was overrun with them by the time we managed to blast off. We've no way to be certain of finding a properly secluded location to establish ourselves without consulting the thermal imaging satellites. We can't just fuel up and head back and land somewhere on a whim and hope it all works out. We can't go back to a life of running. I've promised our people more than that, Jor. I promised them real hope. We can't just go back. I've got to give them more than that... or bloody well die trying... Jor, we... we... we lost Edgar and Horace in the chaos. The horde, they, they, they came from... from... they... Oh, bloody hell, we should've seen them coming. There's no excuse. My sad attempts won't make a bit of difference. It was only that all our attention was on readying the E11... They crept up on us, and I... I... I lost two more of our brothers, Jor. I'm so very sorry."

"No, Arlo," Jordana immediately responded in a voice heavy with bitter grief and fierce resolve in equal measures. "I'm the only one with anything to be sorry about here," she continued, her sultry accented voice growing steadier with each syllable. "I've failed you all. I lost control of my ship and delayed my report, and now I fear I've only managed to lead you all from the frying pan straight into the fire."

"Nonsense, kiddo. This was a chance we all decided to take, together," Arlo assured Jordana. "All of us were well aware of the gamble. And all of us know that no one else could have gotten as far as you have. We all know that... Just lay it out for me, Jor. You know I trust you."

"Okay, okay," Jordana answered in a choked voice. "Well, I've only gotten as far as this thanks in large part to these resistance fighters I was telling you about, one in particular." She paused there to blush at Maisie.

"I'm happy they were there when you needed a hand. It appears the fates were smiling down on you yet again," Arlo offered with a grin in his voice. "So, this ruling regime, they've been actively trying to keep themselves hidden then?" he prompted, turning serious.

"Correct. AOA were, as I said, the ones who set it in motion. These bastards we've got to deal with now have simply piggybacked the idea," Jordana replied.

"I see. So... we can expect a less than warm reception is what you're trying to tell us."

"Yeah, that's a safe bet. Especially since I'm involved with their enemies," Jordana rushed to add. "I didn't intend to take a side, ya know? Things just sort of ran that way. I made a judgement call in the moment that teaming up with them was the best way to get my report to you. I doubt the Witenagemot would have let me, had I asked. But it doesn't matter anyhow. It's all fallen apart, to the point where I'm now trapped in the Control Room with two of the resistance fighters with absolutely no way to get to you in Branch 2. We did manage to get life support systems turned back on in the Branch, or at least they will be soon, but you'll have to negotiate your own way aboard. I'm afraid you'll have to leave all the rifles and pistols and shotguns aboard the E11. We cannot risk a gunfight in this station. It's far too fragile. If we blow it up trying to shoot them down, it won't do anybody any good, and these brutes might well force that on you should you show up packing. Don't worry too much though. These Witen gents don't have any guns either. They do have axes and baseball bats and everything in between though, and they've a deal more men than us, so do not take them lightly. Just stay calm and let the station residents see you. This ruling Witen has been telling everyone they've been monitoring Earth for any sign of survivors. Maisie, the woman we owe so much to, believes if the people could just see you all, it might go a long way toward undermining their overlords. She thinks it's essential we expose their lie... It's our best play. And sadly, the best I have for now... We'll stay here in the Control Room, so you'll have a big chip to play should they try and keep you all from boarding. We can do a lot of damage from this room. But be warned—these people are unpredictable."

"Understood. Wait, did you say you had to get Branch 2 back online?"

"Yeah, it's like I said..."

"Long story," both Arlo and Jordana simultaneously finished the sentence.

"Okay, Jor, looks like the station is getting pretty big in the window. Docking in T-minus three minutes, forty-eight seconds. S'pose I'd best focus on the task ahead and worry about the next step when it comes time to take it," Arlo informed them. "You just stay strong and safe and know that we're all bloody well proud of you, Jor. We'll be seeing each other soon... 'Til then, my sister."

"'Til then, brother," Jordana ended the communication.

CHAPTER 2
CAPTAIN ALVAREZ

"I just can't even imagine what the little brat thinks she's doing?" Lieutenant Dobechek was saying just as a flustered footman was ushered through the black double doors of the Commander's private office right behind where she paced in the expansive chamber.

Alvarez leaned against the room's back wall, just over his leader's right shoulder. The Steward lurked beside his master, pacing incessantly while nervously gnawing at his disgusting fingernails. The Captain wondered how it could be that the man had any cuticles left to bite. For all his wisdom and organizational skills, the Steward was a weak man at the core, his many nervous tics all the evidence a reasonable man might need to draw that conclusion. As for himself, Captain Alvarez had known as much for years now.

It frustrated and tormented his every waking breath these days that his noble Commander failed to recognize the man's liabilities. Therefore, he wore a smirk this evening, despite the day's unexpected and villainous events. The Captain just knew the Steward would fail to rise to the occasion. And in a situation this volatile, this vital, the Steward's failure could not be unnoticed or ignored. *And then the inevitable rise of Captain Alvarez will soon be at hand*, he professed to himself with a joy bordering on psychosis.

"Whatever the Sagal girl's up to, it's obviously got something to do with that stranger in the flight suit she and Sheffield got in there with them," Lieutenant Masterson surmised from his seat across from Lieutenant Schwambach in the room's two armchairs.

"Maybe," Lieutenant Dirks allowed, fidgeting a bit just in front of the Commander's spotless mahogany desk. "Whatever it is can't be good though. You can do a lot of damage to this place from that Control Room. We're in danger just sitting here."

"She'd never have the balls to detonate the Branch's self-destruct. The bitch would be blowing herself up in the process. She ain't got it in her. No way. She's a fucking Sagal, after all," Lieutenant Woodson added with a lazy flippancy from his half-leaning perch atop the back of Masterson's armchair.

"She could set off the self-destruct on a timer and then just bound on out the same way the bastards got in long before this whole Branch implodes and crumples into the Moon's fucking core with all of us lounging around inside," Dirks pointed out.

"I've organized a detail of footman to don VLSE gear and guard the Control Room's two external hatchways," the Steward removed his fingers from his mouth long enough to report. "Each hatch will have two men guarding it on a rotation. No one is getting out or in that way again, Lieutenant."

"Commander, sir!" The shrill young voice of the flustered footman broke through the Witen Councilmember's idle grumblings. "Commander, a ship! A ship has been spotted. An E11, sir. Footman Caldwell thinks it's most likely making for an auto landing on our Lunar Dock, sir," the pimple-faced, tubby little footman finished informing his ruler just as he arrived in front of the mahogany desk alongside Lieutenant Dirks.

"It's gotta have something to do with the chick in the flight suit, I'm telling ya!" Lieutenant Masterson cried in a tone of vindication.

"It's probably just some ghostship from some forgotten AOA launchpad that went haywire and launched itself on some autopilot course or something," Lieutenant Schwambach added his two-cents for the first time since they'd all gathered in the Commander's office after word of Maisie Sagal's brazen treachery came to light. "That woman in that odd flight suit in there is likely just some resident with a fucking haircut or something. I'm sure someone will recognize her. I mean, how could she really be a visitor up here? How could that

E11—if it even is an E11—be carrying friends of hers from Earth? Huh? Come on, people. Everybody in this room knows that there ain't no humans left uninfected down there. The Steward was the last. We already settled all that shit."

"You're right, Lieutenant," the Commander's raspy growl filled the room. "Odds are it's just some malfunctioning ship, and the stranger in the Control Room has some other explanation that upon hindsight will seem obvious to us, but we gotta deal with the possibilities as well as the probabilities. Better to be prepared for the unlikely than not."

"The Commander's right," Alvarez spoke up, rocking forward from his lazy lean. "Even if that ship does got survivors packing it, we can't allow them to board this station. They could all be carriers of the disease. Maybe in a dormant state or some shit like that, ya know? Who the fuck knows? I'm not a doctor. I'm just saying we can't trust it. We gotta act."

"True, Captain, too true," the Steward agreed. "We somehow need to reach out to the ship as soon as it lands to discover who and what they are and what we can expect from them."

"We need to do a whole hell of a lot more than that," the Commander interjected in a scornful tone, bringing a wider smirk to Captain Alvarez's lips. "We gotta contain this situation. No word of any details we discover about this inbound ship is to ever leave the confines of this room or, least ways, the people in it." He stopped there to glance back at the wild-eyed young footman before him. "You go on back to your post, son, and forget everything you just heard."

"Yes, sir, Commander sir," the little knock-kneed, newly minted footman responded before turning on his heels and marching quickly from the room as if someone held a flame to the seat of his pants.

"Word of this ship has already spread. I guarantee it," the Steward said as soon as the black double doors were closed once more. "We aren't keeping this thing quiet from the people. Once the ship arrives on our dock, folks can just find a porthole in the Living Quarters that looks right down on the docks and see it there plain as day."

"Word of the ship is out. I'm sure you're right about that, Steward," the Commander told his subordinate as he swiveled his seat to face him. "But we can still control the narrative as to who and what might just be aboard."

"Not so long as Maisie sits in the Control Room," the small man annoyingly pointed out.

"She's got that large chess piece to play, no doubt," the Commander concurred, rocking back in his throne-worthy wingback office chair. "So, we must move a powerful piece of our own from the back row into the center of the action."

"What?" the Steward responded, bafflement large as life all over his rosy-cheeked face. "Why not just wait to see what this ship truly means for us before moving aggressively against it? Perhaps it does have survivors aboard. Maybe they could prove useful additions to our Witenagemot."

"You was the one who convinced all of us that such a thing ain't possible all them years back, Steward," Captain Alvarez pointed out. "If word gets out that you was dead wrong about that, it could not only undermine you, but the whole damn Witen by implication. You'd think a man as learned as yourself would understand that danger plain enough."

"I'm not gonna allow anything, regardless of who they are, what they came through to get here, or what truths they may claim to hold about the current state of the Earth, to jeopardize what we have built up here through our own sweat and blood and sacrifice," the Commander growled in a voice that demanded to be heeded. "Our mandate stands, as far as I'm concerned, and that's to ensure the safety and prosperity of this station and its community. I'm not gonna let some bratty little shit, and whatever new friends she might happened to have made, undermine the fabric of our rule... I shoulda dealt with the Sagal-seed long ago. All you who urged as much before, you were right, and I'm sorry. I've been deluding myself to her threat. I see that now. But no longer, my friends. I will crush her and everyone who dared help her just as soon as I can... But... uhh... with that in mind, Captain Alvarez, Lieutenants, I've something to explain to ya'll," the Commander informed his supplicants with unprecedented deference.

"You see, there were some secrets in this Witenagemot to which even yourselves weren't privy. Long ago, at the very beginning, the Steward and I deemed it necessary to hold safe a percentage of the weapons vault's arsenal from the explosion of Gerwitz's Star Hawk all them years back. While we didn't exactly predict this contingency in particular, we figured it was best to keep a few items back. We guessed a day might come when we'd need an ace up our sleeves... But, you see, I think that card could only be effective by remaining a secret. And that meant the fewer people who knew about it, the better. I hope ya'll can understand that much."

"What are you trying to say exactly, Commander?" the Captain asked in a casual voice, hoping to disguise the fact he knew damn well what the man was referring to. He'd known all along, since the very beginning. He'd paid off those engineers to get them to spill the beans about where they'd been instructed to transport the weapons locker during the rec room's transition into Justice Hall. And even before that, the Captain had known the Commander and Steward hadn't blown up all the weapons. He'd been inside the damn vault to see the evidence firsthand. After all, he was the one that had hacked the access chip from the cold, stiff, dead arm of Sergeant Marge Hamill. But he thought it a safer bet not to let on to his supreme ruler that he had gone behind his back. Even though Montrois and Aponyaschefski had lied first, Captain Alvarez failed to visualize any future where the scruffy, scar-faced, milky-eyed gorilla-man who reigned above all others would be pleased to learn he'd been deceived, even if it were by omission alone. *Maybe I shoulda just stayed silent entirely,* he began to think after the Commander stared his way for a quiet stretch.

"We kept back a PRZVL33, as well as a few other choice items. We had to," the shaggy-bearded ruler uttered in a voice as close to guilt-laden as Alvarez had ever heard it. "The Steward and I decided to rip out the weapons locker entirely during the renovation of Justice Hall and install it somewhere secluded in the access tunnel system."

"We can understand your reasoning, sir," Dirks offered with a sycophantic flare. "No need to explain yourself."

"Yeah, no worries, Commander," Schwambach concurred. "I can foresee a 33 coming in mighty handy up here."

"You want someone to set the PRZVL up in the terminal. Ain't that so, sir?" Alvarez cut in to posit, hoping he was right.

"Exactly, Captain."

"Well, I'm your man, sir," Alvarez offered with a grin.

"Okay then, Captain, take five footmen and haul the thing down Branch 2 as quick as you can. The Steward knows where exactly we hid the locker. I'm afraid the location has slipped my mind at the moment," he added, flicking his wrist toward the slack-jawed former lawyer. "Branch 2 and the Terminal beyond oughta have their life support systems rebooted soon," he continued. "The moment the airlocks lift, the Branch hatchway should roll up... Ain't that what you told me, Steward?" He turned to ask the stocky dweeb.

"Yes, sir, th-that-that's correct," the Steward managed in a frazzled, waffling voice. "But, sir, I don't... I'm not sure that... sir, a PRZVL? Really? Are we sure that this situation already calls for such a drastic step? Th-the-the threat that it... a PRZVL could... it could... I'm not sure that we need to... we don't... we... we know nothing about this ship yet, sir. Perhaps it's better to hold that card in reserve."

The Commander didn't answer the man. He left his sunken eyes resting heavy with contempt on the smarmy council member for at least a dozen seconds. When he finally lifted that silencing gaze, it was back to Captain Alvarez that his attention turned. "Be set up with the PRZVL at the Terminal's Nest Gateway before anyone aboard that ship sets foot inside this station. Understand? If they fuel up and take back off, so much the better. We can sell that as a malfunctioning ship, and all we'll have lost is a bit of fuel we don't really need anyhow."

"But you cannot, under any circumstances, actually fire the damn 33," the Steward ignored his ruler's menacing scowl to break in and insist. "Just let the threat of firing serve... Look, gentleman," he added, trying out a more tactful and cajoling tone, "it's just too dangerous to risk blasting that thing off up here. We all know that. Even the goddamn Lunar Dock is vulnerable to catastrophic destruction, should just one bolt go astray. There's enough stored power out there on that tarmac to blow us all to kingdom come."

The Commander didn't bother with the silent stare this time. Before the weak-hearted bastard was even finished with his pathetic entreaty, the Commander had turned his back on him to face Alvarez. "Do you understand your orders, Captain?" the protector of mankind asked him.

Alvarez gave only an eager nod and hungry smile as confirmation.

"Good. Go now then. Get set up fast. You probably only have minutes 'til they land if their ship is close enough to be spotted by eyesight alone."

"Roger that, Commander. Don't you worry, sir. Not a soul will step foot on our turf without tasting the PRZVL's wicked medicine. I promise you that," Captain Alvarez affirmed with a glee in his heart unwarranted by the gravity of the situation. He couldn't help it though. Not only was he being given the opportunity to possibly fire a PRZVL33 at a human target, with its devastating plasma rounds firing off at a ludicrously violent rate of thirteen bolts per second, but also the Steward had just been thoroughly balked by the Commander, and it had been Captain Alvarez to whom their great leader turned in this moment of crisis. If that wasn't cause for a grin, he didn't know what was. "Send me the location of the antechamber housing the weapons locker on my tablet, Steward," he called out to his supposed better just as he flung open one of the luxurious room's tall black double doors.

"Oh shit, wait!" the Commander's call halted Alvarez at the threshold. "I forgot you still need my access chip," he explained, moving out from around his massive desk.

Fuck, I shoulda known to ask as much. Shit, man, they're gonna know you already knew about it and have a key of your own. Why else wouldn't you have thought about how you were gonna get in? The reasoning was sound enough to start his heart into a panic-dance.

"I'll go to the locker with ya to let ya in," the Commander informed him.

Each long, casually honest stride the big man then took toward where Alvarez lurked in the doorway progressively settled his dancing nerves, so that by the time the milk-eyed imperator arrived beside him, the Captain's earlier joy was once again steering his emotional ship. *He don't know shit. He can't,* Alvarez tried assuring himself in order to cling to his contented disposition.

"Send us that location, Steward," the Commander called, clapping the Captain on the shoulder as they stepped through the elegant portal.

"How bad's the recoil, sir?" Footman Fry asked.

The Captain's calm patience had already worn thin long minutes earlier, but regardless, the pudgy, pink-cheeked teenage footman's timidity would've elicited the same vitriol Alvarez treated it with now, no matter his current rushed temperament. "It's mounted to a tripod, you dumb shit. There ain't no recoil," he shouted at the incompetent newbie. "Just depress the two trigger levers on the handles, and the bolts will start pouring out... And pay attention to where you're aiming the fucking thing."

The young footman's uncertain face in response to the Captain's reprimand made him think twice about electing him triggerman. He needed the four older footmen currently spread out alongside him across the breadth of the Terminal's expansive, rectangle-shaped hatchway free to maneuver. But apparently the young footman before him had been promoted too soon. The kid clearly wasn't up to the task. *God, we got no time for this shit,* the Captain thought as he glanced out the cloudy, three-foot-square window beside the giant gray rolling hatchway and saw the newly arrived E11 pulling up to Nest Gateway. The fuel pad the E11 had landed on was only yards from completing its tracked journey from the tarmac to the Terminal along a complex system of shifting fuel pads maneuvered around the dock by a magnetic rail repulsion system under the concrete surface which operated in principle as a direct echo to that of the station's trolly system. They had no more time to waste. Captain Alvarez had flitted away valuable seconds going over each step of the PRZVL33's firing process with Footman Fry, seconds they could never get back. *But if the kid ain't up to it, the kid ain't up to it,* the Captain decided. "Step away from the PRZVL, footman! Report to my office immediately... Now!" He barked when the kid only stiffened in place.

"But... sir, I can... I... I can do this, sir," Footman Fry surprised him by managing to stutter the assurance.

"Then don't be worrying about the goddamn recoil and just focus on pointing that fucking thing down the gateway as soon as this hatchway rolls up!"

"Yes, sir," the footman squealed, stepping behind the red stock of the massive black-barreled plasma gatling gun.

"Footman Childress, you got the feed setup yet?" Captain Alvarez asked the veteran footman standing a few paces to his left.

"All set, sir," the hard, loyal, quick-witted footman responded, turning her tablet toward him to confirm her claim. "Feed is up and running. Lieutenant Dirks is attempting to hail the Sagal girl now. As soon as they respond in the Control Room, she'll patch our feed on."

"Good to hear, footman, 'cause the frickin' ship is pulling up to dock with the gateway catwalk as we speak."

"Are there really gonna be survivors on this ship, Captain?" Footman Weathers, another veteran Witenagemot footman, asked.

Alvarez knew Weathers was a steady fellow. The bulky brawler rarely let his curiosity get the best of him in a moment of crisis. The mere fact he'd said anything now only affirmed the unprecedented nature of this evening's events. The Captain didn't fault him for the breach of mission decorum. He had been asking himself the same question on repeat since the moment Footman Fry had burst into the Commander's office to spill that bit of news. The only time the insistent wonder ceased had been when he and the Commander had first strode into the weapons locker.

Alvarez had been in the room a dozen times before that occasion, and always with a bit of fear lingering somewhere in his mind, but the terror that assailed him on this last visit made the rest feel like a single toe in a vat of ice water versus cannonballing naked into a frozen lake. The fear had seemed warranted at the time. After all, the Captain had the foreknowledge of the obvious depletion of the locker's supply, having done the depleting personally. Alvarez knew that if the Commander had inventoried the arsenal before he and the Steward had moved the locker, then he couldn't fail to notice that, although the PRZVL33 remained in its usual place, the stockpile was light two EMP cannisters, ten shock discs, a minidrone, ten tranq darts, and two video scramblers.

Thankfully, if he ever had done any inventory, the Commander at least had absolutely no memory of the precise number of any of the equipment he may have counted, or so Captain Alvarez surmised when his leader had shown little interest in any of the various weaponry locked secretly away down that cramped and ill-lit little antechamber. The Commander had glanced over everything while his eyes lingered over nothing, neither the clear nor the scarred. He made no indication that the conspicuously reduced supply even registered with him at all, despite the fact that the final tally of missing equipment had wound up being even worse than Captain Alvarez had been fearing. There hadn't just been two video scramblers missing, nor only ten shock discs absent from their display cases. There had in fact been *four* video scramblers absent and *fifteen* shock discs.

The mystery of that unaccounted for equipment had snuffed out all the unnecessary fear from the Captain's heart fast enough. He'd even been puzzling over who could have taken them, and how, for the entire time the Commander had restated his orders to load up a PRZVL33 and three battery packs and hustle down to the Terminal. He hadn't even really noticed the man had been speaking to him until the Commander clapped a massive hand down on his shoulder once more just before stomping out of the cramped vault. He had to give up the inquiry shortly thereafter when he judged his five footmen weren't moving fast enough and needed his specific motivation to get going. His last conclusion on the topic being something along the lines of someone else bribing the engineers to give up the location. Though he had recognized that would only explain how they'd found it, not how they'd gotten in, nor even how they knew there was any information to bribe from the engineers at all.

And so it was that after he'd hushed Footman Weathers and a silence began to settle on the Captain and his hastily assembled band, the puzzle of the unaccounted-for techno weapons was threatening to occupy a hefty slice of his consciousness once more, despite the imminence of the resolution to the constant question of who, if anyone, was on this mysterious E11 Transport Cruiser. A hiss of compressed air suddenly belching out into the freshly oxygenated Terminal put a swift end to that, however. His duty instantly became the sole remaining thought permeating his consciousness, his duty and his ... *opportunity*.

A mere second or two after the blast of air, the broad hatch started slipping up into a thirty-foot-high Terminal wall, painted navy blue for its base coat and adorned with maroon and silver slashes. At no point in its slow journey thus far did the heavy hatch make any noise to speak of.

"Okay, footmen, prepare yourselves," the Captain ordered his crew. "No one makes a move without my say so. You hear that, Footman Fry?" he finished, addressing the member of the squad he trusted the least.

"Yes, sir, Captain, sir," the young footman affirmed, eyes locked down the massive weapon's black barrel. His aim was steady and true, straight down the heart of the slowly revealing Nest Gateway, a forty-foot-long, fully enclosed and climatized catwalk with a twelve-foot ceiling and a fourteen-foot-wide composite rubber floor. The long and sturdy Nest Gateway, its clear and seamless windows taking up the top half of either wall for its entire forty-foot stretch, made it so any craft landing on Cardinal's Nest's Lunar Dock could have their passengers come directly aboard station without having to bother with VLSE gear.

"Okay then. Footman Childress, you keep that vid feed up and running," the Captain reminded the seasoned warrior.

"Yes, sir," the footman declared, a promise in her voice Alvarez trusted completely, just as the gate's hatchway disappeared fully into the gaily painted wall. "The Commander is hailing the Control Room now," the dusky-skinned footman began her play-by-play from her position three paces to the Captain's left. "They're answering!"

"Give me the audio," Alvarez requested.

Childress didn't answer right away, but the shrill voice of Maisie Sagal drifting out of her pocket tablet told him she'd obeyed. "Jasper Montrois, so good to see ya. You and I haven't had a moment to sit down and talk in forever. Is this all I had to do to get you to listen to me?" The bitch needled the Commander from her end of the video call.

"Who's in the shuttle? Who is that with you and Sheffield in there?" Captain Alvarez heard the Commander's calm response clearly from Childress' pocket tablet a few yards to his left.

"I thought you and Harclay got all the answers, Jasper. You figure it out," the Sagal brat's voice answered through the video comm.

"You think this is a game, little girl?" The Commander's growl indicated his barely contained rage.

Captain Alvarez could recognize the warning sign immediately. Maisie Sagal, however, was either too dumb to pick up on a perfectly good hint or too delusional to realize her helpless situation.

Her voice was as sarcastic and disrespectful as ever when it came back over the airwaves. "If it is, Jasper, then I'm just a few moves away from winning. When Jordana's people come aboard, the residents of this station will see the evidence of your lies firsthand. They'll all realize your whole mandate is bullshit, an empty fucking lie, and a cowardly one at that, ever since day one. You hid us away up here for no other cause than your own sick greed. The Witenagemot ends today, Jasper. Enjoy your last hours in power, you rat bastard."

For a stretch long enough for Captain Alvarez to lose patience and stride toward Childress, the video comm feed remained silent. Then the Commander cleared his throat. Alvarez was standing right alongside the footman by that point, so he could clearly see the tablet screen. Maisie Sagal's uncertain face filled most of the space. She had a look that spoke of false bravado masking deep doubt. Panic and fear would flicker across her features periodically, and just for micro seconds at a time, but the Captain registered each one. The young girl's discomfort made him smile.

Then the Commander helped it grow wider. "Keep watching your screen, kid. Captain Alvarez, show her," the gold- and black-clad champion prompted.

"With pleasure, sir," the Captain assured through the medium of the video comm. Tapping Childress on the shoulder, he stepped aside so the hard-muscled footman in her faded, yet crisply pressed, gray uniform could shoot the PRZVL33 with her tablet's camera as well as where it was currently aimed.

"If a single person steps off that shuttle and onto this station, Captain Alvarez will drain all three of the PRZVL's battery packs and turn that goddamn disease-ridden E11 into a pile of slag," the Commander's voice boomed from the pocket tablet. "I don't know what that crazy woman in there with ya might have told ya about these friends of hers, but I ain't letting a bunch of infected monsters loose aboard my station!"

"They ain't infected! Don't be ridiculous," Maisie's voice responded over the comm. "How the hell could they have flown all the way up here if they was one of your Damned? Huh? You can't be serious right now. You can't just go off and shoot them. You can't just do that. They are already here, Jasp—Comm—Commander. The residents already know about the ship. You can't keep this secret. Don't be absurd. You... you can't just... you... you shoulda blew that damn machine gun up when you blew up all the others. You know it ain't safe to go shooting that aboard station."

"Right now it's aimed as safe as it gets up here, straight down Nest Gateway's catwalk and then out onto the wide open Lunar Dock. Whatever breakage happens to come will be a satisfactory tradeoff," the head of the Witenagemot Council responded in his calm growl.

"You can't do this!" Maisie insisted.

"You three come out of the Control Room right now, and we will discuss terms," the calm growl responded.

"What terms!? What fucking possible terms could there be?!" Maisie nearly bawled the questions. "It's over, Commander. There are survivors on Earth and more than just the eighty-five aboard that E11. Your lies are over. At least let those of us who want to go back, go back," she pleaded with pitiable defeat. "Jordana's people are only here to stock up on the supplies they need to start a colony. They just need to find a spot to be safe, a place to live. Let those of us who would return to Earth with them go. Promise me that, and we will come out."

"Step out of the Control Room now, and we can talk about all that."

Maisie's voice responded with some threat, Alvarez couldn't quite make out what it was, something about hitting Branch 1's self-destruct if the Witen blew down the hatchway and stormed the Control Room, which was a clearly empty threat in the Captain's opinion. She broke off her impotent fantasies after a time to chatter with her two other co-traitors in the Control Room. Their quiet bickering remained audible, yet hardly discernable, for a dozen breaths before the open channel abruptly cut out.

"Looks like Maisie ended the video comm," Childress informed the Captain.

"Stupid little shit," Footman Weathers provided his assessment of the act.

"Something is happening at the end of the catwalk, sir," Footman Pontreski called out a breath later from his position on the far-right end of their six-man cordon.

The Captain saw that it was true. The E11 Transport Cruiser's spring-loaded belly hatch was swinging open. "Footman Fry, you ready to fire?" he asked the young lad without glancing back at him.

"Yes, sir," Fry answered. "Got the belly hatch dead in my sights, Captain."

A sandy blond man who, from the Captain's distant view, appeared to be in his forties and maybe six foot tall and two hundred pounds, judging by how much of the hatch his silhouette occupied, stood motionless in the portal.

"Not a fucking step!" Alvarez cupped his hands to shout down the gateway at the distant figure. "Stay in your ship! Not one step aboard, or we will open fire. Return to the tarmac. Refuel and depart immediately! This is a one-time-only offer. Leave now!"

The man at the hatchway threshold was shouting something back. Alvarez had trouble making out exactly what it was. Only broken chunks of his bellows managed to make their way to his end of the wide catwalk. He heard, "Don't shoot" and "Bailey" and "hungry crew" and "coming aboard."

This last made Alvarez irate. The man wasn't listening, whoever he was. "Don't do it. Not one step! I'm warning you! Return to the tarmac!" he shouted back.

The man seemed intent on not hearing him. With both his hands held up like a fugitive finally cornered by the law, the tall figure at the far end of Nest Gateway stepped one long pace from the E11 onto the composite rubber floor of the catwalk. "We just want to talk." The voice came to him unbroken this time. A British accent could even be distinguished in the baritone exclamation.

"Footman Childress, get your tablet back up," the Captain ordered. "Let the Commander know what's happening." Alvarez moved to stand alongside Footman Fry behind the barrel of the black and red plasma thrower.

"All set, sir. They wanna hail Maisie again and patch her back into the feed," Footman Childress relayed.

"Good," Alvarez said, wearing a grin that wouldn't be denied. "She'll want to see this part." He moved two paces to his left then, gaining a better sightline of the individual at the far end of Nest Gateway.

The man had only made it three or four paces onto the forbidden ground, but it was three or four paces farther than Captain Alvarez was comfortable allowing.

"Return to your shuttle now, or we will fire on you. We don't want your infected asses bringing that shit aboard this station. We will not hesitate to protect ourselves. I'm telling ya—last chance—return to your shuttle now," he demanded one final time.

The slow trudging figure responded with some whiny plea. Alvarez didn't even bother listening closely to hear what it might have been.

He simply looked over to Footman Fry. "Blast out the window. Aim close to the fool but try not to hit him. If he's quick, he might just stand a chance at making it back to his ship before being sucked out onto the surface."

"Yes, sir," the chubby teen behind the trigger of the plasma gun answered with a grin tugging at the corners of his acne-strewn cheeks.

"No!!" A voice barked out over the video comm before the kid could fire.

Alvarez assumed it must've been Maisie, realizing the inevitability. So it took him a second to register that the voice was far too deep and haggard to belong to the treacherous young Sagal.

It had been the Steward that shouted. His voice came back over the comm a beat later. "Do not fire that weapon, Captain. You hear me?"

"I made a threat, Steward," Captain Alvarez responded with a snarl as he ripped the pocket tablet from Childress' grasp. "We gotta make good on it. We'd look weak if I don't fire!"

"Do not fire that weapon, Captain!" the Steward angrily shot back.

"Commander? Sir? What... Sir, should I... sir, I have to... to..." Captain Alvarez made a bumbling appeal to the one man who outranked the cowardly ex-lawyer.

"Do what you feel ya have to," the Commander's growl came over the comms a half-dozen seconds later to say.

"Sir! We can't! This is... this... it's too soon." The Steward could be heard needling the Commander on the other end of the video comm. "Just let the man come aboard to talk. We can keep it contained still. We don't need to go blasting gatling guns for no good goddamn reason."

"Hold your tongue, Steward. This is Captain Alvarez's decision. He is on sight. It's his command. I trust his judgement," the Commander could be heard reprimanding his number-two man.

"Just let him come aboard and talk!" Maisie Sagal's voice wailed over the comms.

Apparently the three conspirators in the Control Room were watching the video comm again. *Good. Very good*, the Captain thought. *Watch closely now, you little shit.* "Fry, fire that goddamn PRZVL now!" he shouted, keeping his eyes locked down the catwalk.

The teen footman didn't acknowledge the order verbally. First thing the Captain knew of the boy's compliance was the fizzing burst of the first ice-blue plasma bolt rocketing at hypersonic speed toward the far half of Nest Gateway's right-side wall window. The tall man making the slow progress down the catwalk was only a few yards from where the bolt sheared through the seamless glass. For the briefest of moments that followed, everything seemed to go dead silent. Then the sound of shattering glass filled the Captain's ears, accompanied by three more fizzing bursts of shimmering blue plasma.

Already the vacuum was tugging at the tall man trapped in the tunnel of death. Just before the suction lifted him from his feet and dragged him out into the hellish surface of the Moon, two men made a chain of hands from inside their E11 to snatch the tall blond man by the forearm and haul him back inside the ship. Captain Alvarez could half-see about five or six other shuttle passengers linking arms deeper inside the craft, working together to retrieve their cohort. Alvarez watched on as they somehow managed to pull their belly hatch closed in the same instant Nest Gateway's massive hatchway slammed down in front of him. The rushing air, which Captain Alvarez had all but failed to notice as he took in the action at the catwalk's far end, died away almost instantaneously. Maisie shouting curses and screaming hysterics over the video comm became the only noise to be heard in the vaulted Terminal.

Maybe the brat finally gets it, the Captain was thinking just as her panicked shrieks died off. He was congratulating his small crew on a job well done, the young Footman Fry in particular, when Maisie's voice once more filled the air. Only her voice was louder than before. It seemed to echo all around him. *It ain't coming from the comm*, he realized. Maisie Sagal was tapped into the station's PA system.

"Residents of Cardinal's Nest," the young rebel was saying to every corner of the gargantuan station, "my name is Maisie Sagal. Many of you know me. Many of you are probably aware even now that something is happening out on the Lunar Dock... and now you know too that we have occupied the Control Room. The Witen has been lying to all of us from the start. Now, I know their propaganda is strong, and that some of you will think me a liar merely 'cause they say so, but I ain't asking you to just trust me here. Go to a porthole in Orange Corridor, and look at the Lunar Dock for yourselves. I am in the Control Room right now with an honest to god survivor from Earth. She made it all the way up here herself, and that E11 you'll see on the Lunar Dock is full of her friends. They lied to us about checking Earth for survivors, for signs of the infection's end. It is dying out down there, people. The hordes thin out more and more each day. We can go back. We can find a place to defend, an island, anywhere. We can work on a cure in peace and safety. We could save the few poor souls still trapped by this horrible infection and liberate the globe. We can live free, breathing real air with blue sky over our heads. ...Or not. Go on and stay here if you like. It ain't nothing to me. The point is they hid us away just so they could rule us. They ain't protecting humanity. If they were, they'd let Jordana's people come aboard. They are humans after all. Would they not fall under the sphere of the Witenagemot's *sacred* charge? And don't let 'em lie to you and try to tell ya that they are all infected and are just waiting for a chance to spread the infection up here. It's bullshit, people. They are a group of eighty-five capable and well-equipped *survivors*. They mean us no harm. They just need to come aboard and regroup. Their expertise of the infection could be critical to our future. They know how to deal with the Damned. They've even captured an Alpha and have a sample of one's blood with them aboard that shuttle, a thing that not only did the security staff fail to do, but the very thing they told us was impossible to do, the very basis for them abandoning their missions to Earth in the first place. The good people aboard the E11 currently on our Lunar Dock could help us up here. They represent real hope. Don't let the Witenagemot lie to you any longer. Rise up, people! Rise up and demand they let the Bruderschaft come aboard. Rise up! End their lies. Rise up, my friends. Please, please, it's not too late. We need your help. Please."

The traitor's announcement ended with that pathetic plea. Captain Alvarez was planning to laugh it off. The Commander's furious bellow reverberating over Childress' tablet forestalled the impulse. There were no words there, no clear sentence or instruction, just pure rage, pure fury. Captain Alvarez had a sudden premonition of another gibbet in the midst of the desert's hot white sands with Maisie Sagal's pretty little corpse swinging beneath. He did laugh then.

Time's up, little girl. Time's up.

CHAPTER 3
JED

The tunnels ran all throughout, as well as deep beneath, the eight-million-square-foot sprawl of Cardinal's Nest Lunar Station. Jed knew they were now underground in that tangled substructure. He let intuition be his guide there, that and the fact that they had been walking down a narrow catwalk with no rail either side and a steady downwards slope for half a minute now. Exactly where beneath the station they currently were though, his intuition had no opinion.

Jed had always hated the access tunnels. There were so many twists and turns and loops and dead ends, not to mention the penetrating gloom that would erode even the most practiced adventurer's sense of direction. He blamed Larry more and more with each ill-lit step he took deeper into the cramped maze. This whole day had been a nonstop parade of poor decisions. Not only was his rotund drunkard of a partner to blame, but an endless succession of dreamy-eyed fools had picked up right where the lush left off.

Not twelve hours earlier, everything in Jed Redding's life was comfortable and settled. He knew Larry loved him, despite Jed's avoidance of all things resistance-related, and even in spite of the days and nights his lover would spend at Aziz Patel's living quarters. Jed had come to terms with all of it, even living under a dictatorship. It wasn't so bad, so long as you kept your head down. Jed hated the Witen bastards, but at least he got to do his job. At least he could have some routine, some life. Their rule definitely left a lot of space for life—you had to give them that. Enough to make sharing Larry seem like a trivial matter, anyhow. But now, thanks to fate, and Larry's drunken snap-decisions, he found himself running from the law in the dark and dingy access tunnels with absolutely no future left beyond this inane grazing.

They'd be cornered soon enough. That was the only possible fate left. *Maisie will rat us all out in no time. No way the bastards don't torture her for all the information she's got. They won't take her little message lying down. They'll figure out a way to drag her and her troublemaking girlfriend out of there soon enough. Either that or Harrington and the government jerks spill the beans on the priest and his secret underground network.* One was as likely as the other. What was certain though was that at least one of those parallel fates was imminent. Jed knew it was all over. *Why even bother with this next step?* he asked himself, slowing his considerable gait to a snail's pace.

Carrie Roxanna suddenly rushed out of the shadowed gloom to brush past him, crutches flailing, back up the incline. Jed reached out to guide her by. Though the young girl could boast an innate balance despite her affliction, one slip either way, and she'd take a nasty tumble into a dense nest of grumbling and steaming composite steel piping.

"Excuse me," the fearless genius pleaded once Jed had righted her in the center of the grated path.

"Be careful, kiddo," he instructed her as he returned to his descending trudge, having momentarily forgotten most of his former line of bitter thought. After two or three steps, he broke into a quick-jog to catch up to Dolly. The priest's wife was last in a single-wide line of possible fugitives. Father Boyd, Larry Holderman, Aziz Patel, and Novocaine Barker were strung out just ahead of her, respectively, trudging ever deeper into the chasmal darkness.

"Where are we headed exactly?" Dolly cleared her throat awkwardly before asking.

"Nowhere in particular, love," the priest informed his wife. "We're just putting some space between us and any potential pursuit. Just a precaution, sweetie. There's no reason to think the Witen knows anything about us."

"Not yet, anyways." Larry Holderman skidded to a stop, flask in hand. The others all came to a collective halt a pace later. The catwalk still had no rail to either side, but in the relatively level spot they'd come to rest, massive oblong ducts and fat tubes lined the path for yards unending up ahead, so it hardly mattered.

"Yes, Larry, not yet. But let's worry about the problem before us before the one down the road. We need to keep our heads and come up with some sort of plan to help get Maisie the hell out of that Control Room," Boyd told them, leaning back against a protruding hunk of machinery.

"I hate to break it to you, Priest, but Maisie and her new friends are *our* only hope, not the other way around," Aziz Patel informed the holy man.

"Yeah, Boyd," Larry was quick to concur, so much so that he abbreviated his tug of moonshine and dribbled a bit down his double-chin as he spoke. "They got us scurrying like rats here. Mais is on her own. She knew the risk when she left. Best we can do for anybody now is just stay hidden and pray a real revolution takes place up there. Pray that Jordana Revere and her Bruderschaft can set us free."

"Christ man, you heard her goddamn public address," Boyd exclaimed. "Montrois's been cutting her a break for years, I know, but I'm telling ya, he's done with that now. The bastard is gonna rip her head off for this. He's gonna blow the damn doors down and drag her out of there by her hair. Or Maisie might even set off the Branch self-destruct with her and Jordana and Sheffield still down there before the scarred bastard can get to her. Either way, I cannot—*we* cannot allow that. We have to help her."

"What could we hope to do, my love?" Dolly asked in a broken voice.

Boyd went to his spouse, wrapping his arms around her. Dolly buried her face in the large man's chest.

"I don't know, love. I don't know. But we'll think of something," he whispered. Slowly, they moved together as one back to Boyd's previous leaning spot. "I can't say what just off the top of my head or anything, but if we put our collective noggins together for a bit, we might come up with something. I'm not suggesting we come out of hiding quite yet. Maybe we can organize something with my contacts from down here. I still have my secure tablet. Give me a minute. I think we're pretty well hid away, wherever the hell we are. I'd say it's safe to do some quick brainstorming."

"I'm happy to think, Priest," Patel told him, "but I'm afraid Larry is right. Unless one of us has a miracle up our sleeve, Maisie is on her own."

"Carrie," Boyd suddenly called out with a lightness in his voice that had not been there only seconds before, "you're the wonder-child herself. You gotta have a miracle or three stashed away somewhere we could borrow," he ended, giggling. "Carrie? ...Carrie?" The priest started nervously calling when entire breaths elapsed without a response from the dark-haired child. "Where is she!? Carrie? Cainey, is she in front of you?" he asked the swinish module maintenance worker.

"No," Barker answered, almost defensively. "She wasn't never in front of me. Why would we let a crippled kid lead the way?"

"She was right behind me a minute ago," Dolly said, pulling away from her husband's clutches. "Jed, you saw her, right?"

Cainey's bigoted statement might have received more push-back if the concern for the young girl who had accompanied them on their flight from the priest's Clubhouse weren't so immediate and preoccupying. Jed himself barely noticed the slanderous suggestion, so engrossed with the girl's possible whereabouts was he. Then suddenly, the weight of Dolly's gaze snapped a memory into his mind, one so recent he had no excuse to have forgotten it. *She went back up the incline*.

"Jed?" Boyd prompted. "Did you see Carrie or not?"

"Oh fuck," he muttered. "Damn, you guys... she... she just... I was thinking and... my mind was... she just brushed past me going back up the slope."

"What?!" Larry, Boyd, Patel and Dolly all demanded at once.

"When? Why didn't—Why the hell did you let her g—When did you last see her, Jed?" Boyd finally managed.

"Just a minute ago, just before we stopped here. She's probably just up the path," he declared, turning to jog in pursuit of the wayward youth.

"Wait, wait, wait!" Boyd called, halting Jed in place. "Don't go sprinting off into the dark and get yourself separated from the rest of us too. We'll all go after her together. You can lead the way though, Jed," Boyd added with a flick of his wrist in Carrie's direction.

"How the hell could you just let the kid walk past you, Jed?" Larry asked two steps into their pursuit from his spot on the grated catwalk three rows back.

"My mind... I... it was... I don't... Look, I'm sorry, okay? How was I supposed to know she was gonna take off on her own? I figured she had to tie a shoe or take a look at something, or who the hell knows what. How was I supposed to know she'd want to get away from us?"

"Because you heard Maisie's message too," Boyd answered for Larry. "And you know Carrie. You know how scared for her sister she must be. You know how prone the Sagals are to brave and desperate acts. You should have known at least enough to ask her what she was doing."

"I'm sorry, okay?" Jed said, feeling ganged up on. "I'm not the one who landed us all in this position in the first place."

"Ohhh, don't even say it, Jed!" Larry cut in to shout. "Don't you dare complain one more time about how you were doing just fine minding your own business. We both agreed to pick up that pilot—don't forget that, Jed. I'm serious! You're starting to piss me off a little now."

Jed didn't know what to say to that. He had a thousand thoughts about it, a thousand emotions, a thousand fears, but he had no idea how to respond. "We'll get the kid back" was all he managed to say.

Larry's scoffed response came in the form of a huffed breath that Jed swore he felt on the back of his neck all the way from his spot on the pathway twelve feet ahead of the module navigator. It had a significant effect on degrading his already threadbare spirit, but not as much as when Aziz Patel added a huffed scoff of his own on top of Larry's.

"We'll get her back," Jed said once more, wishing it were something more profound to shut that self-righteous bastard Patel right up.

"What could she hope to do that we'd need to go chasing after her to stop?" Barker asked from his place at the end of the single-file line. "She ain't sneaking down Branch 1 on them crutches anytime soon. At worst, they'll toss her back in her quarters and tell her to stay the hell out their way. This is a waste of time."

"It won't just be her the Witen is gonna have to deal with," Boyd offered in a distracted voice.

"What do ya mean, baby?" Dolly turned back to ask.

"Well," he began with a great yawn as he looked down at the pocket tablet in his hand, "it seems that contacts of mine from all over the station are reporting that a sizeable crowd is gathering right now in the Grand Rotunda, demanding answers and asking to speak to Maisie and Jordana."

Boyd alone among them carried one of the traceable tablets. The rest of them had long followed the protocol of leaving theirs just inside whatever hatchway they slipped into the maintenance tunnels through every time they visited Boyd's Clubhouse, or else they just didn't bring theirs at all. Precautions were necessary for the one-in-a-million chance the Witen had one of the two operators always on duty in the Control Room actually tracking any specific device. Boyd's device was the lone exception to the rule. Well, his stolen encrypted device, to be precise.

His AOA-issued tablet was even now laying in the same place it had been for nearly eight years: hooked up to a charger in the living room of Raymond Boyd's AOA-assigned living quarters and former liquor shop. This new tablet he'd somehow acquired had never been issued to a specific resident and therefore had no ID tag associated with it. For all the Control Room knew, it didn't exist. And even if they managed somehow to track it, by capturing one of his informant's tablets say, they would never be able to read the texts without the decryption code.

Sure, the Witen could beat the code out of said captured informant, but the priest figured he'd have more than enough time before that to discover the informant had been captured and change the code. Jed would have preferred Sheffield and Cainey worked a little harder to churn out more of their little secure comm devices. As it stood now, only Barker, Patel, Sheffield, Larry, and Maisie had one as well as another one which Harrington and his people monitored. But, being that Jed had never fully committed to the resistance, no one valued his opinion on the matter very much. In Jed's assessment, all of Boyd's half-assed security measures were delusional at best really. He was sure the priest had only lasted in his Clubhouse this long due to sheer luck. Boyd was comfortable in his fantasy though, certain he was always one step ahead. So Jed only watched on, lips sealed, as the burly clergyman in the plain black hooded sweatshirt tapped away on his special tablet, careless as a kid flying a kite on a windy beach.

"Looks like Maisie's message might just have worked then," Dolly posited in hopeful melodies.

"Maybe," Boyd allowed. "We'll see how the Witen responds. However they do though, I think it's best we don't allow young Carrie to be present when it happens."

"We'll get her back," Jed meekly told them one last time. Patel's scoff was hard to recover from. In its wake, bitter anger rattled every molecule of Jed's soul. How he found a way to send a clear signal from his brain to his feet, Jed would never understand. But he managed it, never mind how. And after that first step followed the second, and then a plan formed on the third.

He would indeed catch up with Carrie before she did anything foolish. Then, in the midst of that minor victory, Jed Redding would declare himself a full member of the resistance, come what may. If that's what Larry truly required to commit all of himself to Jed, then that's what Larry required. Jed could overcome any fear for Larry Holderman. He knew that, down deep. Patel's jealous scorn would then be doused, and Larry would once more see Jed as a man worth loving, a man far more worthy of his time and intimacy than the skinny little knock-kneed and bony-assed Aziz Patel.

First things first though. Find the kid. Which way did you go, Carrie? Left or right? he asked himself at the first junction he came to in the tunnel system. *God, come on,* he prayed, when no immediate answer seemed forthcoming. *I gotta find this kid.*

ELIAS

He wasn't meant to hear anything inside the Commander's office. Every footman was under a standing order to let anything said, whispered, screamed, or sang, other than a direct address to them alone, go in one ear and out the other. So Elias knew Lieutenant Schwambach's report he was currently offering up to the Commander seated behind his gleaming mahogany desk was not something he should be at all comprehending. Problem was, knowing it was wrong to listen was failing to prevent him from doing so. There were obvious logical truths that only recently had been occurring to Elias, not the least of which being no one else can be in your mind to know if you were really hearing a conversation or letting it drift on by. The awakening had some real-world practical effects. He had been hearing a deal more troubling things than he dared imagine. It nearly turned him back. He wanted to run to the refuge of his former ignorance. Unfortunately, once you know you're pretending ignorance, it gets impossible to exist in that hypocrisy. It's cyclical. Logic traps you into accepting it.

So Elias couldn't help but listen, even if the topic at hand had not specifically concerned him, whereas the one which currently had the station so enraptured actually did. Lieutenant Schwambach's report dealt with a specific aspect of those personally concerning events, a dangerous aspect.

"Commander sir, let me present Miss Arlene Fincannon," the lantern-jawed officer said to the bearded behemoth seated before him.

The Steward stood just behind the wingback rolling desk chair, looking somehow both aloof and attentive.

"She and Roddy Sheffield, the former programmer in there with the Sagal brat, well, it seems they're an item, sir. I knew I saw the little hippie bastard running around my alleyways with some young bimbo in tow lately. So I asked my Green Corridor footmen who this mystery broad might be. The unanimous word came back quick enough. They all fingered Ms. Fincannon here as the guilty party."

"Is that right?" the Commander answered with a venomous grumbling rasp in his voice.

"Apparently, the cradle-robber is extremely smitten with this blonde little cutie," Schwambach informed his superior, holding firm to her dainty wrist inside his large, gnarled hand.

"Well now, that is certainly good to know," Elias heard his Commander declare from his lounge atop his grand office chair.

"Might be pretty useful, I figure," Schwambach proposed.

"I can see it will be, Lieutenant. Good work," the Commander growled with disturbing glee.

What the Steward thought of Lieutenant Schwambach's implied plan, Elias had no way to know. The tall officer's abrupt two-foot shift in positioning before the mahogany desk made it so Elias could not currently see his benefactor. And neither had the second highest ranking Witen Councilmember spoken a word, not a single utterance of protest nor praise, the whole time the Lieutenant presented his shameful prize, or really since they'd entered the Commander's office together five minutes earlier after the Steward completed his daily rounds. The routine had felt somehow out of place, given all that had happened so far that day, but the Steward's silence all throughout had seemed excessive and out of character. So Elias had no way to know how his mentor felt about Maisie's brazen act or the sudden appearance of the impossible survivor or the ludicrous phenomenon of an E11 shuttle suddenly docking on Cardinal's Nest's tarmac. He desperately wanted to know though, wanted some hint at least. It might make it easier when Elias finally allowed himself to try and confront the unprecedented and deeply personal events.

Maisie had finally gone and done it. She stepped too far out of line for the Witen to forgive. Elias had anticipated this day for years now. The accuracy of his prophecies had no effect on lessening the pain when it finally did arrive, however. He had expected it to hurt though. What he hadn't expected was to be so confused when it occurred. There was a strange person in the Control Room with her. A ship did land on the Lunar Dock. Everything she said in her address to the masses sounded almost reasonable, given those facts. Logic told Elias Sagal, Ethling of the Witenagemot, as much. Logic, that cold, uncaring, but also benign, completely neutral bastard of a friend, told him she had a point.

The pain and implications, and all that came with accepting any truth from what Maisie professed, manifested itself in an incessant twitch in his right leg. Not even squeezing it, nor holding it firm, stopped the bouncing. Elias currently found himself seated in one of the room's two armchairs with no memory of sitting nor even moving toward it at all.

Lieutenant Woodson was seated in the twin red-brown armchair across the glass coffee table, staring dead at him.

He sees the twitch. He knows I'm listening, his old superstitious disposition cried inside his head.

Woodson didn't say a word. His eyes moved slowly from Eli's twitching knee, scanning every inch of him like an android calculating millions of bits a data per second. Finally, they came to rest locked firmly with his own. Eli didn't blink. He did not so much as flinch from the scornful gaze.

Woodson did break the deadlock first, but the Commander bellowing an order at him seemed to demand the capitulation. So Elias could not revel in the tiny victory.

"Lieutenant Woodson, Lieutenant Masterson, gather a team of six footmen each and clear out the crowd gathering in the Grand Rotunda," the Commander ordered, rising to his feet. "Give them a reasonable chance to calm down and go home, but if they start giving ya any shit, put them down. Ya hear?"

"Yes, sir," both Lieutenants in question confirmed.

"Lieutenants Schwambach and Dobechek, you're coming with me."

"Yes, sir," both officers affirmed in unison.

"The Steward will stay here and hold down the fort, ready to organize and coordinate as needed. Lieutenant Dirks, you stay here with him in case he needs to send out a quick-reaction force."

"Gotcha, sir," Dirks promised, blowing a bubble from her wad of Cherry Bubblicious, which she hoarded like gold. She even added a wink on top for emphasis.

"Okay, let's move out," the scarred ruler called while quickly stooping down to pull open his bottom desk drawer. When he straightened back up, a silver bullhorn, adorned with intricate maroon slashes, was clutched firm at the end of his long right arm. "Report back here when your missions are complete. Until then, keep the Steward in the loop with quarterly radio checks." The Commander made it across the substantially wide office in little more than six or seven long and rapid strides, speaking all the while and finishing his directives only three paces from his office's tall black double doors. "Lieutenant Schwambach, bring the girl."

"You got it, sir," he called, dragging Arlene Fincannon after the Commander with a meaty paw still clutching tight to her slight wrist.

"You're coming with me, footman," a voice close to Elias suddenly bellowed.

Eli had to drag his gaze from the double doors, and the towheaded innocent vanishing through it, to confront the bellow.

Lieutenant Woodson lurked over him, arms crossed, and mouth crooked in a sneer. "You hear me, footman? I need you for the crowd-control detail," he asserted, turning in place to lock eyes with the Steward still hovering behind the Commander's massive desk.

If the Steward gave a nod of approval, Elias never saw it. The angry officer of the Witen still lurking just to his right blocked his view of that whole side of the room. "You heard me, son? You ain't too good to do your part for the Witen, are you?"

"No, Lieutenant," Elias told the officer, rising to his feet. Once there, Eli topped the crooked-nosed officer and former Integration Program Leader by a good five inches. The fact never failed to piss the antagonistic Corridor Warden off. He pretended not to feel intimidated, but the truth was always plain in his eyes, in the tremor of his hands and in the childhood-bully-like need to attempt to express his dominance over him whenever they happened to encounter each other. "I've never failed to do my part for the Witen, Lieutenant. After all—and don't you forget this now—one day I will *be* the Witen."

Woodson blew a raspberry and shoved him toward the door in response. *Immature old fart*, Eli scoffed as he righted himself from the smaller man's shove after a single pace. If the petulant Lieutenant hadn't insisted on following so closely on his heels through the wide-open double doors thereafter, Elias might have actually been able to discern some emotion or thought on the Steward's face as he looked back just before exiting. But instead, the pushy little lanky-limbed Lieutenant cut short his observation long before any truth, or half-hint even, could reveal itself.

Out in the Grand Alleyway, the threat of chaos lurked but a heartbeat away. The footmen and officers were all still keeping their discipline with straight backs and crisp postures, but regardless, the anxious uncertainty and unsolicited discomfort were evident throughout every ounce of them. Elias could feel it, a palpable tension threatening to envelop every last square-inch of Cardinal's Nest Lunar Station. The Commander's sudden emergence from the Executive Wing had restored some confidence, Elias somehow intuited, but no amount of fear or reverence could account for the unprecedented nature of the evening's events. And so, the general angst persisted. There was the odd exception, of course, Ricky Allanson, Kyle Erkov, and the rest of their sycophantic crew being notable among them.

Lieutenants Woodson and Masterson though, for all their haughty self-righteousness, had been instantly affected by the seething disquiet. Woodson had forgotten Elias entirely as soon as they'd stepped onto the gleaming parquet-pattern tile floor of the Grand Alleyway. The wannabe bully had been keeping a guiding hand on Elias' shoulder nearly every step throughout the Executive Wing. For his part, Elias let it rest there and did not protest. *Let the pathetic man have his small victory*, he had thought. He was surely going to obey the orders in the end, anyway. No sense needlessly defying Woodson to that extreme. Elias might have been Ethling, but he wasn't the Commander, not yet. Only, first step onto the faux-parquet, Woodson's hand dropped away, rendering the whole calculation a non-issue. It had even taken a good three-count before the thin-framed officer and his partner Masterson snapped into gear to corral the necessary footmen for the task they'd been assigned to carry out into a tight three-rank formation. The detail came together quick enough, however, and was ready to move out in lockstep toward the ever-swelling and ever-rowdier crowd gathering in the Grand Rotunda just beyond Branch 1's massive archway in a matter of a few dozen seconds.

Elias had hung back from the assembling formation. Tessa had been one of the footmen milling sternly, yet nervously, in the Grand Alleyway. She'd been standing stiffly at-ease just outside the Executive Wing. As soon as Elias' eyes had located the gorgeous, dimple-chinned, ebon-haired angel, his feet carried him to her side.

Currently, about five yards to their left, Woodson and Masterson were barking orders at their hastily assembled band in the formation ranks before them. Twenty yards down the Grand Alleyway in the opposite direction, the Commander had paused his steady trudge to speak with a shirtless wild man. The Glorifier and he were leaned in close, but it was the Commander doing all the talking, stopping occasionally to poke the gold-legged prophet in the chest with the maroon and silver bullhorn he still held in his right hand. Lieutenants Dobechek and Schwambach hovered a few yards away from the strange pair, Schwambach still clutching firm to the frightened young woman. Behind the Glorifier, five or six of his disciples stood together in a clump of brown and tan skin and tight and tattered gold cloth.

"What's he telling him?" Tessa asked in an unnecessary whisper.

"I don't know," Elias honestly answered.

"What are they doing with Arlene?"

"You know her?"

"Yeah, well, a little. She lives near my parents' place. She's always sweet. Where's Lieutenant Schwambach taking her?" Tessa asked, sounding as if she already knew. "What's really going on today, Eli? Can you tell me?"

"I don't know, Tess. I don't know."

"What your sister said over the PA, was that... is any of that... is it true? There's a survivor in there? That rumor can't be real, right?"

"Oh, the survivor is real, Tess. I saw her through the hatchway porthole with my own eyes. And I'm far from the only one. All of us on the Steward's detail saw her, that's for sure," Elias informed the brave, yet understandably rattled, beauty before him.

"You saw her? And she's not from... She's not someone you just don't recognize... She's not..."

"She's an outsider, Tess. She ain't from the Nest. I can tell you that much for certain."

"But... but then... then what does that mean, Eli?" Tessa asked, demanding comfort.

"I don't know," he said. "Honestly, Tess, I'm a little scared. I'm... I'm all... all confused again," he admitted with unwelcome emotion. "I feel like I'm back at day-one of the Integration Program. Fuck, Tessa, I'm right back there. I'm so sorry. I don't wanna be. I didn't mean to be. But I... I... I'm right back there."

Tessa placed a warm palm, smooth despite the work-worn calluses, upon his cheek. For a while she said nothing, just smiled. The look was as foreign to the atmosphere as snowflakes in volcanoes, but oh boy was it welcome. "Wherever you are, Elias Sagal, I'm right there with you, now and always," she promised him, reaching up on her tiptoes to offer an undeserved, but gratefully accepted kiss, capable of reviving the dead.

"Foooootmaaaan!" The shout marked the sudden end to the intimate moment. "Get your ass in formation! We're moving out," Lieutenant Woodson bellowed at him.

"Roger that, sir," Elias acknowledged the rage-quivering Witen officer with a wave of his right hand. With his left, he gave a final firm goodbye squeeze to Tessa's own. A beat later, he stepped toward the formation of gray-and-gold-clad footmen in order to forestall the order to hurry up and get moving which he was sure the Lieutenant was eager to supply.

It wound up not mattering either way. Lieutenant Woodson was in a shouting mood this night. "Now, Sagal, goddammit!" the crooked-nosed officer screamed. "We ain't got time to be waiting on your special ass. You hear me, boy?! Move!"

Elias didn't dare adjust his speed, for pride's sake, but was nevertheless occupying the last available slot in the rear-rank of the formation within just six quick strides. No time at all, really. Barely even enough to glance back at the Commander to see the Glorifier and him walking away from each other in separate directions; the scrawny, brown-skinned prophet toward Branch 1's archway, bullhorn now in hand and his wild eyes as maniacal as ever, his raving choir following two paces behind, and the scar-faced hulk of a ruler toward the small crowd of officers, footmen, and innocent blondes gathered just outside of the Main Control Room's wide white hatchway. That one quick glimpse was all Elias managed of the situation unfolding behind him. Woodson and Masterson had the detail formation marching inexorably toward the misguided mob nearly the instant after Elias joined, leaving the quasi-mystery of how Schwambach planned to use Arlene Fincannon ultimately unanswered.

Their control was shrinking by the second. The barrier of footmen and officers they'd strung across the archway threshold could not sustain the onslaught. Protesters would be breaching the cordon any moment. Elias was sweating, though not from exertion. The residents were loud and pushy, and there were quite a few of them, sure, but he did not fear any threat they might pose. His perspiration was entirely on their behalf. They were not settling down. They were refusing to disperse, and Lieutenant Woodson was in a bad mood. Elias knew this could get very ugly, very fast. He was begging every face that swam up before him to calm down and be reasonable, desperately trying to get them to see the inevitability in their otherwise understandable defiance. Protests were forbidden by the New Destiny Constitution. Violators were subject to onsite discretionary authority—Lieutenants Woodson and Masterson's authority, in other words. Neither had a reputation for patience. Didn't these people know that? *Shut up and go home*, he silently urged.

Masterson had laid it all out for them the moment their riot-response detail-formation had come to a halt. Elias and the other footmen had fallen out of tight-order to spread out behind the bellowing frog-faced officer. Still, the crowd shouted back, defiant. Woodson ordered the detail to draw a weapon, but even after twelve footmen and two officers unsheathed everything from steel baseball bats to double-bladed axes, as well as Elias' own war hammer—choosing it as opposed to his longsword, thinking it the lesser of two evils and hoping that somehow made it nobler—still, even then, the crowd would not disperse.

When the ratty-haired preacher in the faded skin-tight gold-joggers and black flip-flops had interrupted Masterson's demands to proclaim to the people through the maroon and silver bullhorn the script to which Elias was certain the Commander had laid out for him moments earlier, he dared to hope the bare-chested prophet's wild claims might chasten the insolent mob.

"Hail to the Commander. All glory to him, our great protector," he had begun by saying, his fevered pack of scantily-clad, shaggy-haired acolytes echoing back his words in tandem. "The traitors tried to let them in, good people, but the Commander has stopped them. There is a survivor, yes, my good residents, yes there is. But ... she is *an infected* survivor, just like all those the arch traitor Maisie Sagal was attempting to bring aboard. But give glory, my friends, give glory, for we are protected, my brothers and sisters, for we have *the Commander*. A vision was granted to our brave and wise leader, only last night. Yes, yes, a vision, proof of his great worthiness. I have heard it from his very own lips, my friends. I promise you. This vision, so honorably bestowed upon our Commander, spoke to him of a ship that would arrive on our doorstep. This ship would claim to come only in peace, but it would be a lie. A lie, I say. It's the end of man that ship is here for, the end of us, the last holdouts. So sayeth the blessed vision of our most wise and triumphant Commander, to whom all glory is given."

"All glory to him!" The rabid sycophants gesticulating behind him had called back in ecstasy, forcing the showman to pause his performance.

"Those are not men and women aboard that accursed vessel, my friends," the new-age mystic had continued when the fawning behind him had ebbed sufficiently to suit the purpose of the sermon. "No, I tell you now what the Commander himself saw. They are the last gasp of a hideous curse. In the veins of all those monsters aboard that E11 lurks *the Infection*. It is only *dormant* just now, my brothers and sisters. But once it is invited aboard—if only one creature should make it from that transport shuttle into this station—now, hear me now, listen close, it shall awaken. And that'll be the end. The end, I say, of all of it, of all of us. Humanity is over, ladies and gentlemen. If those monsters on our doorstep are allowed aboard, we will have lost, my fellow residents, my dear, dear brothers and sisters. Think of it—all our sacrifices for nothing. All because we could not trust the Commander. We failed to see the obvious, the plain, undeniable miracle before us. The vision is the truth, my fellow residents, my fellow citizens in the Witenagemot. The vision is our lifeline, our miracle. Do not cast it away. Calm yourselves and fret no longer. Give glory to the Commander. Give glory to the Witen. You are saved," the nut-brown zealot had insisted in his unique and frenzied way.

And yet, even in the face of that compelling exhortation, and despite the ultra-pious fools echoing back his words in absolute ecstasy at points all throughout, the protestors still would not disperse.

Elias knew it was too late for any words to win them when, only a handful of beats after the Glorifier had ceased his clamoring, the first of the rambunctious fools broke through the thin cordon a few yards to Elias' left. He could not move to plug the gap. No one could. All fourteen Witenagemot agents were engaged in battles of their own. The mob would simply not be cowed. Not with words. After three more residents followed the first man through the breach, the ineluctable happened.

Woodson screamed for the detail to "Defend yourselves!" and to "Put the mob down!" just as he swung his black and gold bat into the chest of the panicked woman before him.

Weapons lashed out all about him, black, silver, gray and gold, all blurs whipping this way and that. Screams filled the air, wails and cries, moans and pleas, all laced with disbelief. Residents ran, faster than they'd ever ran in their lives, in every direction, those that could anyways. Others were trampled while others still were bashed and battered, even maimed. A frightened stink invaded his senses, surmounting even the shrieks and screams. All but one. How he picked it out among all others, he'd never know. But he heard it, a heartrending cry from a single fragile voice in the chaos, a plea really. A plea for him specifically.

"Help me! Elias!" he clearly heard. His eyes tracked the cry, only to spot a silver forearm crutch wheeling through the air.

"Help, Eli," the familiar young voice appealed once more in the midst of the madness.

He made it to her side before any terrified resident or rampaging footman could trample her. Bending down on one knee and sheathing his war hammer over his right shoulder to mirror the pommel of his longsword poking up over his left, Elias shielded his baby sister from the violence all about her.

"Elias!" she called, with a joy so surprising it even managed to bring a quick grin to his own lips, given the sheer dread he'd read all over the young girl's familiar face only a moment before.

"Hello, Carrie," he responded just before another bellowed order from Woodson wiped away his incongruous smile.

"Take prisoners! Let the rest flee. Round up what we got," the bloodthirsty officer ordered.

Elias looked down at his helpless little sister before him. He knew he was supposed to bind her arms together with the wrist-straps always stored away in his right cargo-pocket, as instructed by The Footman Code of Conduct, but he hesitated. He imagined carrying out the act. He knew the procedure well enough. But then he also tried to imagine ever managing to forgive himself afterward for subjecting his father's little girl to that injustice. No acceptable scenario revealed itself. Carrie was a kid, just an impressionable kid, worried about her big sister. *They were all just kids, really*, he realized. *All of 'em. They just want answers. This is wrong, Eli. This is so wrong*, he suddenly knew. A massive gray wolf swam into his thoughts then, a monstrous wolf loping toward a helpless child in a custom-made wheelchair to be precise. He saw it as clear as he had in the dream. Its jaws would soon lock around her head. Soon, very soon, it would squeeze. It would bite. But he could stop it this time, he saw. He could save her. The wolf did not have to win.

"Come on, Eli, this way," Tessa's voice, pitched at a whisper-shout, suddenly reached him.

Elias turned from his sprawled-out sister to see his love beckoning him with a waving arm. *Where did she come from*? he asked himself. Tessa hadn't been roped into the riot detail. *She must've been keeping an eye on shit from just down the Grand Alleyway*, he deduced, as though the answer were important at the moment.

"Pick her up. Come on, do it now while nobody's looking."

He glanced around and saw the small window of time to which Tessa alluded. All eleven other footmen and both officers were currently engaged in subduing at least one resident each.

"Come on," Tessa implored more vigorously as their window nearly elapsed.

With no more forethought nor deliberation, Elias scooped Carrie up from the Grand Rotunda floor and darted, sister in arms, behind Tessa.

"The maintenance hatch," the Blue Corridor footman called as he ran past.

Elias followed her outstretched finger and saw the indicated hatch at once. It was placed directly into the Rotunda wall halfway between Branch 2 and 3, at least twenty yards away.

"Go," Tessa implored, understanding his concern at once. "I'll make a scene and give ya cover. Go!" she urged one last time before running toward Lieutenant Woodson while waving her arms and shouting nonsense.

Just what in the hell she planned to tell the man when she finally did win his attention, Elias couldn't begin to imagine. Halfway to the hatchway, he nearly went back for her. It was then he caught Allanson, out of the corner of his eye, abandoning his detaining duties and racing to intercept the dark-haired heroine. Only the weight of his baby sister resting comfortably in the cradle of his arms stopped him. Tessa was on her own. He knew she was a thousand times brighter than Allanson and Woodson combined. She'd think of something. Elias had no choice but to trust that. He had to get Carrie Roxanna Sagal to safety.

His sister had begun directing him through the tangled substructure the instant he'd slammed closed that hatch in the Grand Rotunda. She'd even asked to be let down when they arrived at a juncture of maintenance tunnels somewhere beneath Branch 3. The junctions were as open and bright as any location inside the web of maintenance tunnels ever got. And with railings on either side of the narrow grated path, Carrie assured him she could make do with just one crutch. Elias had let her down with no protest, just as he'd offered no rebuke or course-correction at any point throughout their journey, despite his considerable knowledge of the tunnels and antechambers weaving their way throughout Cardinal's Nest. Elias could think of nowhere in particular to hold up and hide, and Carrie seemed certain she knew where she was going, so why not let her lead? Besides, he wasn't sure he could get his tongue to work properly enough to offer up a suggestion. Carrie's proximity, and the carnage from which they'd fled, rendered him speechless.

He barely thought about where they were headed, in truth. Each step they took, Elias thought more and more about how much of his sister's life he'd missed, so much so that by the first fifty yards into their flight, there was little room remaining in the vastness of his mind for anything else. The crippling shame of who he must be in her eyes left him mute. He had no idea what to say to her. He had no idea how to even begin to communicate what he was thinking and feeling, even if he had the power. For now, it was all he could do to stop the weight of shame from suffocating him completely.

"It's just up ahead," his little sister informed him.

Elias looked up from the grated path at his feet and the tangled rainbow of wires running like a river beneath to see Carrie using her remaining forearm crutch to point to a three-foot-tall gray hatchway embedded into the wall at the terminus of their current trail. Her other hand was gripped tight to a yellow safety stanchion, but Elias was still momentarily concerned the gesture might unbalance her. The trepidation proved unfounded. Despite her affliction and unconventional gait, Carrie had an uncanny knack for moving about and around the tunnels.

"You turn the wh-wh-wheel," she instructed as they arrived at the hatchway within a single pace of one another. "I can do it, but I norm— I norm-normally have both crutches when I do," the undaunted brown-haired child went on to explain. "It's tough either way though. It's always the hardest part of coming here."

"Coming where?" Elias asked as he stooped to his appointed duty. "Where are we exactly?"

"My clubhouse!" Carrie exclaimed. "If Boyd can have one, why can't I?"

"I don't know. I think you oughta have whatever you like, I guess," Elias said, marveling at the fact he was actually speaking. "Wait, did you say Boyd?!" he asked when the content of Carrie's last statement finally registered in his befuddled mind. "As in Father Boyd? He's been hanging out in the substructure too? For how long? No, I would have heard, 'cause the Steward woulda heard, and he isn't aware of anything like—wait... no... are you sure? No, he's shut up in his quarters in Violet Corridor with a beard down to his ankles and lesions all down his legs from lying in bed, night and day. Everybody knows that."

"No, everybody *thinks* they know that. But never mind all that now. We have lots of other st– other st-st-stuff to talk about first. Just come on in," his sister instructed, placing a guiding hand on the frame to help her climb through the now open hatchway. "I have lots of dr-drin-drinks and snacks and stuff." Carrie hobbled along as best she could around the quaint little antechamber, flicking on lamps and navigating expertly around the forest-green loveseat and black leather desk chair, ending up in front of a silver mini-fridge resting atop a ductwork of some sort that jutted into the twelve-by-twelve-square space at the junction of the room's left and rear wall. "I have fresh water in bottles, if you like," she offered.

When Elias failed to respond, beyond a cursory glance around the cozy space, she continued, "How 'bout some coffee?" After two assisted strides, Carrie arrived in front of a narrow end-table resting against the left wall. Atop it rested a percolator with all its accoutrements.

"You drink coffee?" Elias heard himself ask.

"S-S-Some-Sometimes. Not much though. It's not good for bones. Stunts your growth. I only have a cup when I have company," Carrie explained. "You know, to be polite. It's nice to have something to offer."

"You get much company back here?"

"No. Not really. I had some help hauling the furniture in here from the Koppel brothers a few months back."

"The Koppel brothers?"

"Yeah, you probably wouldn't know 'em. They aren't f-f-foo-footmen or anything, not yet anyways. They just live near me and Maisie. They owed me for helping them with some of their Integration Program classwork. They're not the br-br-brightest bulbs. They are tall and strong though. Good for lifting. Easy to manipulate too," she added with a laugh far too mature for any kid her age. "Mais doesn't know about any of that though. She wou-wou– she wou-wouldn't like me helping those guys pass tests just so they can join up with her enemies, ya know?"

When Elias looked away from her instead of answering, the insightful eight-year-old let out a whimsical sigh before reverting back to carrying the conversational burden. "I haven't really had many other guests than those two. Maisie's been a few times, but mostly I come here when I want to be alone. So, no, not much company. But better safe than sorry," she added, setting the percolator running.

"Carrie, I... I..." He couldn't be here. What had he done? He had to go back. Didn't he? Was it all in vain? Had he chosen poorly? Would Carrie even accept him if he dared to stay? The questions were piling up in his mind, sucking all language from him once again.

"What's up, Eli?" the hazel-eyed young girl astutely asked.

"I can't be here, Carrie. What I did... I... I might well should have done something like that much earlier, and even it is probably still way too little and far too late, but I... I... I still gotta go back. I... I... I don't know what I'm saying, kiddo. I'm sorry. I just... I gotta go back. I should go back."

Carrie didn't respond right away. The coffee was ready by then, and so she carefully poured two mugs, adding sugar and cream to each, forgoing any inquiry as to how he might take it. Elias couldn't complain. Lots of cream and sugar would have been his answer, and that's precisely how his sister was preparing them.

After a few quick stirs, Carrie held out one of the matching purple mugs at him. "You don't have to go back, Elias," she told him after he took the steaming java from her visibly shaking outstretched arm and tentatively tried his first sip. "Or rather, you can go back without really *going back*, ya know?" She continued, "You don't have to contem-contempl-contemplate a life of hiding in the access tunnels 't-t-t-'til the end of time versus selling your soul to the Witen. You can just go back without really going back. Go back, if you must, but don't be one of them, not inside anyways. No one ever has to kn-kn-know wh-wh-wh-what's in your head. Remember that. At least not until it's too late for 'em, you know what I mean? Or, i-if-... i-i-if you feel you owe them more than you owe us, more than you owe yourself, big brother, then they don't ever have to know. Just d-d-d-don't go back to them. Don't go back to the man they designed. Find yourself in all this, if ya can."

He had no response. Her wisdom and maturity and understanding froze him in place. Carrie Roxanna was one astounding little girl. *Think of all the time you missed, all the wonders you could have shared*, he angrily demanded of his foolish self. Nothing he ever said or did could make up for all that missed time. Yet still, this girl, who looked so very much like the father he refused to think about, still she had immense compassion for him. She seemed to be holding no grudges. Somehow though, that only made things worse. His soul was in torment, a confused, unmoored and shameful torment.

"Oh, hey," Carrie suddenly called out, snapping the fingers at the end of her crutch-free arm. "I got a few things here for ya. You see, I never lost hope that I-I... that I... that I could show ya my clubhouse someday." She went shuffling off toward the room's opposite corner with that, stopping in front of a small woodgrain footlocker resting atop another jutting piece of ductwork.

"Carrie, I gotta... I..." he mumbled, lost for words.

No matter how intellectually adrift he currently was, thankfully, Carrie was undaunted by the lack of an engaging conversation partner. "They're in here. I ju-just... I just hope I remember the combination," she said, going to work on the footlocker's small silver padlock.

"I'm sure you do. I bet ya never forget anything," Elias heard himself say.

"I wi-wi-wish," she said with a smile in her voice. "So, tell me about Tessa Rodriguez. That was aw-awfully-awfully nice of her to help us out of the Grand Rotunda like that. Are you two married? It's okay that you didn't inv-in... that you didn't invite me and Maisie to the wedding, if ya are. I wish you would have, b-bu-but I'm just happy for ya, really."

"We're not married," he told her, his voice somehow calm in spite of the racing frenzy that was his mind.

"Oh," Carrie said, stopping her padlock twisting to glance back at him. "How come? Seems t-to... seems to me she really likes you. She risked a lot out there for us. She's a lot like Mais. They both are very brave. I think M-M-Mais would l-li-l-like her. Gosh, I hope they don't hurt Maisie. I hope they didn't get to her in the Control Room. I was trying to get to see her before it all went bad."

The sudden digression hit like a knife to the chest, a well-deserved and justly sharp knife. Maisie was in a lot of trouble right now, and Elias damn well knew it. Maisie hadn't been lying. Carrie was no fool. She was bright and honest, and she believed Maisie. Elias knew he ought to take that as gospel. *What's stopping me?* he asked himself. *What am I doing here? Who the hell am I? What the hell am I?*

"So..." Carrie prompted after a few silent moments elapsed, "what's you and Tessa's d-deal then?"

"We were going to get married. We always talked about it," Elias found himself calmly answering his baby sister. "But I... well, I didn't know before... I mean, had they... had they told me... I didn't know."

"Didn't know what?" Carrie broke into his rambling to ask.

"I am the Ethling," he said, by way of explanation.

"Yeah, I know. I was at the cer-c-cer-ceremony."

"The Ethling will one day be Commander."

"So I hear."

"The Commander has no name and no family," he stated, unable to mask his sadness. "I can't marry."

"Oh" was all Carrie managed for a few beats. "Oh, I see."

"Yeah," Eli said, brushing away a tear with the cuff of his sleeve. "I've tried to get her to abandon me. I tell her all the time that she should move on and find someone she can start a family with. She deserves that much at least. But she won't hear it. She's as stubborn as Mais," he added, making both him and Carrie chuckle. "Tessa is very conscientious of her duty. She sees all the women around her having children to help add security for the survival of mankind and she naturally wants to help out where she can. I tell her yes, she deserves all of that, the love and the honor and the reverence. I tell her to find someone to provide that for her. And she comes back with some irrefutable nonsense about the only children fate would ever allow her to have would be my children. She... she... she just won't listen really. Tessa fights for what she loves. And she never quits. She thinks we can have the best of both worlds. That we can make children, and she just won't never tell anybody who the father is. She says it's enough that *she* would know. But it's a foolish hope, really. I mean, who the hell are we kidding here? The whole damn station would know. Oh, shoot. It's probably inappropriate to be sharing all that with you. I'm sorry, kiddo."

"I can hear about babies and lovemaking and stuff. I'm plenty mature," his baby sister assured him, her achingly familiar hazel eyes shining.

"Sure, Ri. Sure you are."

"I am," she insisted, turning her attention back to the padlock. "Got it," she exclaimed as the lock fell open.

"I really should go back," he said, placing his half-full mug of coffee back atop the narrow end-table, "if only to stop anyone seeking after me from finding *you*."

"Wait," Carrie implored, clambering back to her feet, a half-hidden item in each of her small hands. "Let me give these to ya first."

"Give me what?"

"I found this," she declared, reaching out her left hand toward him. In it she clutched a well-worn plain-blue ball cap. "I spotted it atop a piece of machinery in the access tunnels beneath the recycling facility about a year back when I was searching for a good spot to set up my clubhouse. I recognized it from a picture in Maisie's room of you and her and Dad and your mom Joan all smiling at the camera behind your cake. Mais sa-s-said it was on your eighth birthda-d-d-d... birthday."

"I think I know the one," Elias acknowledged, taking the ball cap from his sister. He needed no explanation of where she might have found it, having placed it there deliberately. It was a few weeks into the Integration Program, when he was still confused, but coming around to seeing things from the Witen's point of view. At the time, he had believed the last step he needed to take to grow up and accept his responsibility was to bury his childhood. To move on and start fresh. The ball cap became a physical totem representing his youth and immaturity. He'd thought abandoning his dependence on its memory-inducing comforts would signify in some way his ascension over the weak boy he once was. Holding the dusty cap just now, Elias had no desire to try to explain any of that to his sweet little sister. "Thanks," he managed to mutter without bursting into tears.

"No pr-pro... no problem. There's this, too," she added, offering up the item in her other hand.

Elias recognized it as well. It wasn't quite as familiar as the old blue ball cap, but he knew exactly what it was upon first sight. In days long past, the little red hardcover book was rarely missing from its special place atop his dad's dark-maple end-table between his twin green armchairs. He hadn't seen it, nor even really thought about it, since the day before his father was killed. But now, here it was, in the outstretched trembling arm of his brave and brilliant baby sister.

"The Commander returned it a few years ago," Carrie explained. "He just showed up at our quarters one day. I was sc-sc... I was scared at first, 'cause Mais was out, and I was all alo... all alo... all alone. He was wearing a hood and hunching down, darting glances down the al-al-alleyway the whole time he made his appeal to come inside. I figured he was in disguise, maybe escaping his bodyguards or something. He didn't say, but th-that's the imp-im-impression I got. So then I invited him in for coffee after he handed me the book. I thought it was only polite. He had coffee. I had milk. We sat on opposite sides of the tan couch in the living room, and he told me about how Dad had given it to him the day before they fought. He said Dad made him read a specific poem he marked. Then he finished his coffee and got up and I-l-left without another word. I showed Maisie later, and she told me that book wa-wa-was one of D-Da-Dad's favorites, after scolding me for like thr-th-three hours for letting the Commander come inside when I was home alone. I did read the marked poem myself that night before bed though. It's good. I l-l-like it. Not the best or anything, but I like it well enough. Although I'll admit, I'm probably not the target audience. You, on the other hand," she said, pressing the book on him, "y-y-yo-you might find it enlightening."

Elias stared down at the small red book of poetry, reading its inscription over and over again, *If And Other Poems by Rudyard Kipling*, and remembering all the times his father had studied the faded pages within. He had no words of response. He could not even find his voice to say thank you. He could do nothing but grip tightly and stare at the small book and the plain blue ball cap. "I gotta go," he shamefully muttered.

"Help Mais, Eli. She loves you," Carrie said, just as he made to leave her quaint quarters. "I l-l-l-love you too. Please don't really go back to them."

"Stay safe in here for a while. At least 'til stuff settles down out there," he told her just as soon as he could trust himself to speak without cracking up.

"I'll try," she said with a mischievous twinkle in her eyes. "You just... you stay *you*, Eli... and help Maisie."

"I'll try," he half-promised in a shaky voice after an endless span of eternities. Then, abruptly, he turned from his sister to cover his emotions, using the act to propel him on his way out of Carrie's clubhouse. Although his clipped assurance might well have been offered up in an unsteady and semi-flippant manner, he nonetheless found the resolve behind the pledge grow ever firmer with each step he took toward the chaos above.

CHAPTER 4
THE STEWARD

INFECTION EVENT: DAY 3,168

"Still no response from the transport ship since last contact, sir," the Steward updated.

"How long has it been?" The Commander's question was half-drowned amid all the splashing and giggling, not to mention the maroon and silver cedar-chest speaker mounted high on the wall ten feet away acting as the DJ for the party-like atmosphere by playing Rolling Stone's "Tumbling Dice" much louder than any song deserved, but he didn't dare ask the man to clarify. Context helped fill in any sonic gaps.

"Nearly an hour now, Commander," the Steward said, consulting his pocket tablet.

"They got time still," the Commander managed to say after extricating himself from the groping arms of two of his favorite playthings.

The ginger bimbos weren't actual twins, or even sisters, or relatives of any sort for that matter, the Steward knew, but they looked alike enough so that he could never tell one from the other, had he ever even bothered to learn their names. Jacuzzi party time with two or more willing, or semi-willing, or on his worst nights, entirely unwilling, women to entertain him had become a routine for the scarred giant since far back enough to ever dare hope to spare the Witenagemot the shame of his depredations. The Steward had made an art form of overlooking his council chief's character flaws and otherwise criminal behavior. The discipline was proving as trying as ever for him just now, however.

"Have they at least pinged the Control Room with a fuel request?" The Commander growled the question as he splashed to the edge of the elliptical jacuzzi nearest the Steward.

"No, sir. They sure haven't. Hell, they haven't even detached their E11 from Nest Gateway. No one so much as reopened the E11's belly hatch after the engineers finished welding that steel plate over the shattered window and repressurized the catwalk," the Steward reported, plopping down in a white beach chair beside the natatorium's hot tub and twenty-foot-long infinity swimming pool tucked cunningly away in the far back corner of the Commander's ridiculously lavish luxury quarters.

The Commander leaned his arms out over the ledge of the jacuzzi, peering at the tile floor below tricked out in a mosaic pattern of silver-gray dolphins cresting blue-green waves. For a long while, he said nothing. The Steward had finished his report, for the most part, and was keen on seeking his bed, so he was just about to rise back up from the low beach chair when his ruler raised his scruffy-bearded face to lock eyes with him.

"They'll be gone before the morning," he assured the Steward in a steady, certain voice, plainly discernable over the blaring rock music. "Else they'll wish they had," he added as his face grew dark and his mismatched eyes seemed to fill with a palpable chill.

The sadistic glimmer didn't last long. One or the other of the two bikini-clad lushes splashed up beside him, thrusting a shot glass spilling over with moonshine into his face. The Commander took the proffered drink from the much younger, much smaller woman and tossed the shot back with no visible effect, firmly squeezing her ample freckle-dotted left breast all the while. When he pulled her atop him after and began kissing her neck, the Steward knew he should take the opportunity to rise and walk out.

Only, a memory swam up at him then, so sudden and unexpected, he felt as though his knees had been swapped out for Jell-O. *"Dad, ya can't stay here. We can't stay here. I gotta find Mom,"* his son's voice was shouting at him from ten years in the past.

"Your mother's dead, Wally! They're all dead. I can't go out there! We've more than enough food to survive for weeks now, months even. We can collect all the water we need from runoff and rainfall. We never have to set foot in that deathtrap of a town ever again. We've no need to take one step out this cave. This place... it's... it's safe. We can survive here. We don't have to go back out there, son. We can stay right here. I... I can't go out there," his decade-younger voice feebly responded in his mind's treacherous replay.

"I'm going to find Mom," Wally bravely declared in the face of his old man's gutless response.

"Those creatures will just wind up getting you like they already got her. Or... or... you... or you... you could end up getting chased by a pack of them and lead them straight back here. Then we'd be truly fucked. We'd literally have nowhere else to hide. This place is our little miracle, Wally. Don't ya see? It's the one safe place in the world now. I told you what I saw last week after that last Kroger trip. There were thousands chasing after that girl, Wally. Thousands. No, son, it's far too dangerous now. There are too many of them. There were thousands, kid, right in our little town. Don't ya see? Don't ya get it? They are everywhere. There's just too many now. We can't. You can't. We need to stay here, in the cave, in the dark, until... until..." he mumbled in the poison memory, like the pathetic coward he'd been.

"Until what, Dad? Until when?" Walter Harclay Aponyaschefski asked his dad that cruelly fateful day and now once again in an unwelcome daydream.

"Until it's over," the Steward's past impotent reply rattled through every corner of his present mind. *"If you go, son, I... I... I can't follow. We've no weapons, and no one to defend us. All police and military are dead or one of them. We can't leave,"* he finished from the safety of that cave's dark shadows.

"You'd let me walk alone out there?" Wally's question echoed around the hollow of the half-prison half-castle where, ten years ago, they had ridden out Armageddon.

And then he had spoken words too painful to even tempt a replay in his mind now, let alone the abominable act he had undertaken directly in the wake of those painful words. The memory flash graciously drew to an abrupt end before an echo of that lowly moment could occur. The evil recollection usually only invaded his peace in dreams. That it should plague him now in the waking world was evidence of the not-so-insignificant change in him that had occurred this night. It had been a long time coming, but even still, the Steward did not want to look at it, did not want to face it. He had to keep his mind on the day ahead and the task at hand. The mindset had kept him alive and thriving since the day Wally met his cruel destiny. He feared to lose that focus now. He had no current, nor even periodically recurring wish to confront uncomfortable truths.

Snap out of it, you fool, he demanded of himself. *You have saved humanity, you and your Commander. You've forged your redemption ten times over. Look how far you've made it up here, how long you've endured, and how well the station runs. Think of the justice you've brought, all the good you've accomplished up here, all the wrongs you've set right in Third Days, the Clara Christie fiasco notwithstanding. The Commander needs his pleasures. He deserves them. They all do. Just 'cause I don't share 'em doesn't mean I get to judge them. I don't have to like it, but it's what he and most of the rest of them need to keep the ship running. It's the oil that drives our economy. Be practical and look past the Commander's faults. See his wisdom. Trust him. Trust yourself, goddammit. Don't throw it all away now. You still believe. Don't let some bad thoughts and memories and this one doubtful day cost you everything. Think of all you'll lose.*

"I want to be there when we question the Sagal girl and this pilot friend of hers." The Commander's reminder broke through his tormented thoughts and over The Beatles' "Don't Let Me Down" now blasting out of the cedar-chest speaker.

"Yes, sir. I figure to give them a few hours to sweat before we go down there and have our chat," the Steward told the man lounging in the bubbling jacuzzi before him with a gorgeous, bare-chested redhead clinging to his sides, pressing her soft, pale and freckly skin firmly against him whilst she sensuously stroked his chest and abs.

"Make sure you get a few of the rioters Woodson and Masterson detained ready for questioning too. I want to know just who in the hell were the lead instigators among them, if any," added the cold king simmering in the near-boiling tub.

"They captured thirteen in total, and that's out of the thirty or so at maximum who were actually gathered to protest and riot. I'd say that's a fairly large pool to pluck from, a damn good ratio really. Woodson and Masterson did well. I'm sure if we question 'em all we'll be able to puzzle out the whole truth, no problem."

Thoughts of that short-lived riot were a bit unwelcome at the moment for the Steward. No one had seen Elias Sagal since Masterson and Woodson put down the dissenters. Both of the lieutenants had made some unpleasant accusations about the Ethling's behavior all throughout that mission. They implied, quite heavy-handedly and far more openly and brazenly than any officers ever dared speak to him before, that Elias had turned traitor, that he'd helped one or more of the rioters escape. Tessa Rodriguez, the boy's enduring flame, had even been accused of making up lies to cover his flight.

The Steward had ignored it all, preemptively denying their request to toss Tessa Rodriguez, a Blue Corridor footman, into the brig until Elias resurfaced. He'd shouted them down with a good bit of fiery zeal but also a glaring lack of critical introspection, demanding Tessa be released back into Lieutenant Dirk's authority at once and all pending charges against her immediately forestalled. He had neither the time nor room in his shifting schedule and churning mind just then to entertain any of Woodson and Masterson's slanderous accusations. The Steward had dismissed them with an ill grace before quickly dumping that trouble from his thoughts completely. Nothing much had changed in the thirty or so minutes since that altercation, so he immediately went right back to work, pushing the ambiguous behavior of his favorite pupil onto the deep back-burner as soon as his answer passed his lips.

"Very well. I'll meet you at the brig say ... around 0300 then?" the Commander grumbled, subtly dismissing him.

"I'll be there, sir," the Steward called over his shoulder as he pushed through the natatorium's glass door. Though, given the volume of the music and the friskiness of the man's company, he was positive his assurance had gone unheard by his sovereign.

Regardless, the Commander would want him alert and on the ball for that 0300 interrogation. That meant he had to hustle down the Grand Alleyway to his private quarters to hopefully steal at least an hour of sleep before those festivities kicked off. True, they had already gotten most everything they needed from Maisie and her pair of friends within a few short minutes of custody. They'd been winkled from the Control Room, their one major advantage, rather easily in the end. Maisie's threats of Branch detonation had wound up being no more than that. As soon as the Commander, standing with Arlene Fincannon before the hatchway porthole, wrapped a meaty hand around the tiny little mouse of a woman's throat, Maisie and Jordana Revere, as well as Roddy Sheffield in particular, could all see the tips of his fingers touching before he even squeezed, they had come out quick enough.

The Steward had been in front of the Control Room's main terminal within fifteen minutes of their capitulation, hailing the E11, or more accurately, the Bruderschaft leadership in the cockpit of that E11, as the foxy pilot with the fresh scar at her temple whose full name was swiftly revealed to be Jordana Revere had confirmed her special club called themselves. After Footman Campbell had found the small pistol she was attempting to conceal in a black leather ankle holster, the former British fighter pilot had become quite forthcoming about a great many things.

The Steward had gone on to outline for the European voices on the other end of that pleasant chat an expounded and much more eloquent form of the ultimatum to which the Commander had dictated only moments before contact was achieved. They were to move back to the tarmac and commence refueling, and then to immediately take off and never return. They had until 0800 ST the next morning to comply. A pair of voices had argued back or at least tried to. In the end, it had amounted to no more than desperate pleading. The Steward was having none of it. The Commander had made sure he knew it was a direct order he was issuing to the Bruderschaft. It would be their one and only warning. The Steward was afforded no leeway to play with, no wiggle room at all. The unlucky fools on that transport cruiser needed to understand there would be no negotiation.

Idiots apparently still haven't grasped the real weight of that message yet though, he thought of the uninvited visitors' suicidal intransigence thus far just as he stepped out into the Grand Alleyway's colossal arcade. *Jesus, let's hope the Commander's right in the end.*

It'll be a whole lot easier to explain the ship away as some unaccounted-for malfunctioning anomaly or something if they turn back to Earth before dawn. Either way though, Maisie and her new pilot friend would have to be forced to give up everything they knew about this Bruderschaft, as well as the current state of Earth. If the eighty-five survivors out on Branch 2's tarmac took off only to show up a week later in three more ships, loaded with a thousand more people, the Witenagemot was certainly going to have to know about that ahead of time. The Steward had a mountain of new calculations to add to his current algorithm of authority. He had to keep his edge. *God, I need a damn nap,* he silently declared after tapping the wrong code into his luxury quarter's hatchway keypad for the third time in a row.

He wasn't sure whether or not to bother with pajamas. If he fell asleep right now, an hour and five minutes could be the maximum amount of winks he could snatch before his alarm would be blaring at him. So any wasted time peeling off his uniform and then redressing in precious silks, only to have to wake up earlier in order to strip the silks right back off and struggle into a set of fresh fatigues, all seemed like far too big a bother for his current needs. Although he knew that unless he went all out and got good and comfortable, with precious silk pajama tops and bottoms complete with cushioned eye-mask, he would never fall asleep in the first damn place.

So it was that the Steward found himself midway through pulling his black cotton undershirt up over his head when his bedside intercom buzzed. "Oh, what now?" he muttered aloud as he lurched up off the end of his bed to step toward the end-table where the touchscreen quarters intercom was embedded. "Yeah?" he growled in a venomous voice after tapping the touchscreen even though he knew Mara Ebenfoss, the middle-aged fireplug of a woman on the other end of the comm, in no way deserved his scorn. A Servant of the Witen was assigned to care for private quarters maintenance, prepare meals, and handle whatever other menial tasks a high-ranking officer in the Witenagemot might require. Only himself, the Commander, Captain Alvarez, and Supervisor Chairman Bigelow, the kiss-ass supervisor that had been promoted in the wake of Mikkelson's demise, were assigned one of these permanent personal quarters servants.

Ebenfoss and the Steward did not share a particularly close personal relationship, by any means, but after years of tight proximity, they understood each other's moods. And although the short, flat-faced servant had a deal of deference in her voice, the Steward could tell she took no offense from his snappy tone. "Forgive me, sir. I know you were just about to lie down, but Footman Elias Sagal is here to see you," she informed him.

"Eli? Here?"

"Yes, sir. I have him waiting at the hatchway," Ebenfoss explained over the intercom. "Shall I tell him to come back, sir?"

"Uhh, no, Mara, that's alright. Go on and just send him back," he directed, tucking his undershirt into his gold-trimmed black trousers.

The Steward had been seated once more at the end of his immaculately made California-king bed long before Elias Sagal made it through the labyrinth that was his luxury quarters. The master bedroom was in the far corner opposite his hatchway with a lofted foyer, grand dining room, wide kitchen, and finally, an open space with a vaulted ceiling where his living room and personal office were set up on opposite sides of one another before you could even step into the fairly narrow hallway where three spare bedrooms, two full bathrooms, and his master bedroom were nestled. The boy didn't appear to be in any great hurry either. The Steward didn't know exactly what he'd been expecting, but he assumed some level of agitation at least. Elias, though, had both hands in his pockets as he strolled casually toward the bedroom's red chesterfield loveseat. He did not plop down atop its comfort, per se, but he definitely skirted with that famous phrase, "Take a load off," though the Steward had uttered no such offer.

"Sooo..." he prompted in a voice far softer than the man-child had any right to expect. "Where have you been? I had to contend with some rather unsettling rumors concerning your behavior on that riot detail."

"I left," the tall, athletically muscled footman said from as comfortable a position on the loveseat any person with a three-foot war hammer and a three- and a half-foot longsword sheathed across their back could possibly attain.

"You just ... left?" The Steward knew how incredulous he sounded despite his best efforts.

When the footman he had mentored for nearly a decade merely nodded his head in answer, the Steward had to push off his pillow-soft mattress and stumble to the bar he maintained inside the rotund globe beside the chesterfield.

"Why?" he asked after the first shot of harsh moonshine was down his gullet, and his glass was refilled with the second.

"They didn't need me." Elias offered up the weak explanation after rising to help himself to a tumbler of the nasty stuff. "None of the protesters were any real threat. They just wanted some answers. And I guess they got a few, didn't they? In some form or another."

The Steward didn't acknowledge the boy's last tossed off blasphemy. Elias Sagal had been a trial to keep on the true path since the very day he'd met him. Of course, the kid had proved himself worth the effort, time and again. The Steward knew he allowed the Ethling a deal more insolence than he would tolerate from any other footman— or supervisor and officer for that matter. Though, that might have had a deal more to do with his guilt over Wally than the kid's particular skills or usefulness, not to diminish the latter by any means. But their dynamic was what it was at this point, so he merely released a long, disappointed sigh before asking his next question, "So you just up and excused yourself from duty?"

"I guess," Sagal responded, tossing back the dregs from the bottom of his tumbler.

"So then, I suppose it's also true that you helped some rioters escape justice too." His hopes for an adoption of a more contrite manner from the footman after his sudden shift in tone were squashed to pieces when Elias only refilled his tumbler as he softly chuckled a few incongruous giggles.

"*Justice?*" Sagal finally responded after downing his fresh glass in one deep gulp, spicing the word with as much sarcasm and incredulity as any one man could.

The Steward didn't really trust himself to speak just then. His favorite footman's attitude was as irritating as it was surprising. The footman had always been capable of a bit of cutting wit and laconic sass, but even still, his behavior was coming as a genuine shock. So the number-two man on the Witenagemot Council said nothing as he went back to the bottle for a third time to pour out two fingers of his clear moonshine into his crystal tumbler.

Sagal waited until the Steward's glass was full before breaking the silent stretch, "I need to talk to Maisie."

"What?" Truly, the Steward was unprepared for this conversation.

"I'd need you to let me into the brig to speak with her."

"That can't happen," he scoffed so emphatically he about dropped his glass.

Elias didn't acknowledge the dismissal of his request. He downed one more drink before stepping away from the globe-bar beside the chesterfield loveseat in the center of the wide, low-ceilinged master bedroom. At length, with his back to the Steward, Sagal broke the silence, "What made you so certain, Steward?"

"Excuse me?" the Steward asked, positive he'd misheard.

"Why were you so certain you were right all them years back?" Sagal turned around in order to further clarify his query. "You were so sure of yourself, so sure about the curse and humanity's failure to share the tech, as well as AOA's complicity in it all. You seemed so certain about all of it. Why?" he finished, ending up right back beside the couch and globe.

The floor beneath the Steward's feet suddenly shifted. If he had not been so close to his bed by that point, he might've wound up on the floor. As it was, he managed to squat back down on the edge of his California king. Another unbeckoned memory flashed into his mind as the troubled young man finished his questions, one so real he could nearly feel Chief Greymoor's hand holding his forearm flat and firm to his pinewood desktop in his office on Main Street in Millstone, West Virginia. He could see Brent Ashly leaning close across the desk with a lit Camel Turkish Blend cigarette held delicately between thumb and forefinger as clearly as he had that lamentable morning.

Oh, what the Steward wouldn't have given for the power to alter the past, if only in dreams. He longed to reach across that pine desk and slap the mocking look off the pretentious prick's condescending face. Not for the first time, the Steward reflected on his disappointment to discover neither Brent Ashly nor Chief Greymoor had made AOA's guest list aboard Cardinal's Nest Lunar Station. He had to let the mere fact that, although Ashly surely had a high opinion of his value to his evil corporate masters, his omission from the resident roster was apparently deemed no cause for concern. The Steward had to let the simple indifference to Ashly's particular well-being by the shallow souls for whom he shilled be a satisfactory vengeance for the pathetic excuse for a lawyer's bestial treatment of Harclay Aponyaschefski on that long ago day.

Is that why I was so certain? The sudden thought smacked him hard as a bullet train into a bird as he stared his pupil dead in the eyes. *Oh, god, could he know? Is that why he asked? Did I make it all up just to punish AOA and their fatcat government backers? Did I lie so well, even I was convinced? Oh god, no more of these thoughts, please.* "Eli, why... why are you asking me this now?" He managed the question after a long and labored breath.

"I'm going for a walk" was the footman's strange answer.

"A walk? What? Wh—where?"

"Is Tessa okay?" Sagal asked, trudging toward the bedroom hatchway.

"Woodson and Masterson, with a deal of encouragement from Footman Allanson, all wanted me to toss her into the brig. They seem to believe she lied to them to cover for you."

"She didn—"

"I made them release her immediately," the Steward cut in before Sagal could work up a good protest. "She was sent off free as ever the last time I saw her. She probably went home. She's most likely sitting there now, worried sick about ya. Maybe you oughta include a stop at her quarters on your walk."

"Are you suggesting I pay a visit to the woman that the oath you talked me into swearing forbids me from ever satisfying with the life she deserves?"

The Steward felt gut-punched. He had to drop his eyes from the intimidating young footman before him.

"I might pay her a visit, boss, I might. I'll let my feet take me where they will. Just do me a favor, sir, if you would. Don't let them hurt my sister. If Maisie refuses to talk, which you and I both know she will, then let me take on whatever torture you would mete out for her defiance. Let me stand as her whipping boy. Please, sir. She'll talk quick enough if she knows I'm being hurt for her silence. You know she will, sir. Please, sir," he begged in a reverent tone of voice that had been wholly lacking earlier. "Please promise me that much, sir. Please don't hurt her."

"You know I never would, kid," the Steward managed, not looking up from his bedroom's rust-red carpet.

"Don't let *him* hurt her either," Sagal added, catching the Steward's deliberate omission.

His eyes stayed on the carpet. Long, awkward silent moments ticked by. Finally, he felt more than saw the footman continue on his way out of the master bedroom. When he was certain Elias' back was to the room, the Steward allowed his eyes to rise. They came up just in time to watch Sagal step through the hatchway portal. He could read little from the young man's body language, beyond a general exhaustion. What did catch his eye, however, was the bill of a blue ball cap sticking up out of the back right trouser pocket of Footman Elias Sagal's crisply pressed and extensively decorated gray footman's uniform.

CHAPTER 5
CAINEY

A visit to the Billiard Lounge had been a long time coming for Nate Novocaine Barker. He had resolutely avoided the place since that bullshit game of pool he'd played with Sergeant Marge Hamill, Gillian Gerwitz, and Barry Calvin over nine years back. The self-imposed prohibition made stocking up on alcohol a hassle, to say the least, but Cainey was content with bartering his supply from third parties. Every resident had their own stockpile to trade with, so really, one need never actually visit that saloon-style Billiard Lounge. But, despite his flawless record of abstinence from the Cardinal's Nest main drinking hole—a considerable feat when you factored how plugged-in to the residents and their various moods he always was—Cainey nevertheless currently found himself crossing the threshold of that dimly lit drinking hall's gaping archway.

He'd been everywhere else first, everywhere within sound reason anyway. After all, it wasn't as if he were likely to uncover the current tenor and atmosphere among the veteran residents by snooping around the cattle farm or air recycler facility, not this time of day anyway, if ever. Cainey had strolled through the Central Hub instead, pausing to casually eavesdrop whenever an opportunity presented itself. Once that location was exhausted of relevant information, he'd made his way toward the Main Cafeteria, where he'd nibbled at a pulled-pork sandwich as he attempted to snatch a few words of private conversation from the limited stock of scattered folks nearest his table. From there, he'd moved ever deeper into Branch 4. There was always someone doing something somewhere in the Rec District. The theater was a ghost town though, likewise the IGS pods and casino. Cainey had known what that meant. Nine years of work, nine years of incredible discipline would have to be wasted. Clearly, everyone was doing what folks in crisis always do: drink and talk, and they were obviously doing it in the Billiard Lounge. If that Calvin bastard's shitty little face smiling that shitty little smile even momentarily floated up into his mind while he was in here, then the priest could be goddamned. Cainey had learned more than enough already. He wasn't about to linger in a place that might spark some reminder of the shame of that night. Not after the hours of focused meditation he'd poured into erasing those early days from his mind altogether.

Boyd had called an end to the search for the Sagal brat after one of his contacts messaged him on his secure tablet, saying the protesters had been dispersed or detained, and Carrie Sagal had definitely not been one of them. The priest had insisted they still seek the girl out since they had little better to do just then, but he had put an end to the urgency. They agreed to take a minute to catch their breaths and find their bearings. A juncture where three tunnels converged afforded them all a bit of space and plenty of pipes, tubes, ducts, and bulky hunks of some humming piece of machinery or another to rest against or atop. Boyd had been getting pings on his tablet for a solid fifteen minutes straight before the halt, and after he'd resurfaced from reading and responding to them all, he lifted his head to display a toothy smile that, although it irritated the hell out of Nate Barker, he had to admit was an encouraging sign.

"No one is buying the Glorifier's bullshit," the priest had said, that pretentious smile growing wider by the instant.

"What's up now?" Dolly had asked when the grinning fraud seemed uninterested in elaborating.

"The Glorifier gave the crowd of protestors some line of garbage about the Commander having a dream or a vision or some shit, telling him Jordana's Bruderschaft friends are secretly carriers of the infection in a dormant state. It wants to finish off humanity for good and all, the Glorifier tried to tell 'em. Like it's got a frickin' mind of its own or some shit. But they ain't buying it. Well, most aren't anyways.

From the reports I've read, that seems to be the consensus. We gotta jump on this while it's hot. One of you has to go up there and keep the pressure on the Glorifier's bullshit. Spread the word around about what we know about Jordana and her people. I need some eyes and ears up there. We have to rely on Maisie's plan now. We've no other choice. We have to try and convince a critical mass of the population to petition for the Bruderschaft's invitation aboard station."

"But... but they just locked up half of the last group of protesters, didn't they, hun? Ain't that what you said a few minutes back while we were walking?" Dolly asked in a reticent manner. "Are you sure it's a good idea to encourage more people to try the same thing? Maybe they don't just haul people to the brig next time. I know you said they were using axes and bats and hammers and everything else last time too, but maybe next time, they don't use the blunt ends. Maybe they won't be satisfied with drawing a bit of blood and raising a few bumps and bruises."

"Maybe, Doll," the priest had allowed in a voice that had lost all its momentary mirth, "but what choice do we have? If the Witen gets away with destroying that E11 or sending it back to Earth, which amounts to the same thing in the end, then all hope is lost. If the people can accept an atrocity that great, that heinous, what won't they accept? Our days will be numbered, with *small* numbers, the kind that we'd be lucky if it took two hands to count to. Our plans for the long haul down Branch 2 are foiled, and Maisie is locked up down Branch 1. We got no options left, my love. We have to push the people now. We have to get all of them if we can, but most of them at the very least, to believe the Bruderschaft is here in good faith. Now, I'll do what I can on that end down here, through my handy tablet and reluctant contacts, as well as keep the search up for Carrie since she wasn't at the protest. Odds are she stayed down in the tunnels. Dolly, you're with me, and I'll not hear a word about it."

"I wasn't going anywhere, Boyd," Dolly's voice called out with a deal of cheek.

If Boyd said something back or smiled that obnoxious smirk of his in response to his wife, Cainey Barker had no way to tell in the gloom. "I'll go up," Cainey barked, sending an echo bouncing off in three directions.

"You?" Boyd had asked with a condescension that made Cainey want to scream.

"Yes, me. No one knows those people better than me. If you want to know how they feel about the Glorifier's line or the Bruderschaft's intentions, I'm the only guy to send," he said, thinking they'd all surely have to agree.

"No one up there is gonna give two shits what Cainey Barker, of all people, has to say. You need more than some creepy snoop. You need someone who can lead up there." Of course, Larry's bitch-ass couldn't dare admit Cainey's superiority. He always had to challenge everything he said or did. The fat bastard thought just because he was a navigator and Novocaine was relegated to grease-monkey that somehow made him better. Truth was, Larry was a liability at best and a drunken oaf at worst.

"You volunteering, Larry?" Boyd had asked.

"Nah, that ain't me. I'm just saying it ain't Cainey neither," Larry Holderman slurred.

"You just don't want to lift your fat ass back off that duct, more like," Cainey told the red-cheeked sot. "I can handle it, Priest," he then assured Boyd before Holderman could thunder back.

Jed was working up some indignant defense of his hairy lover from somewhere close by in the dimness as well.

Cainey bowled right over whatever limp insult or contrived threat the module pilot might have been attempting. "I'll catch up with ya'll over the coded comms once I'm done. Patel, you still got your comm device, right?"

"I've got my comm, yes," Patel confirmed begrudgingly.

"Good. I'll catch up with ya later then," he'd said, darting down the middle of the three branching tunnels where he knew a connecting path spoked off, leading to an access hatch near Branch 6's archway. Cainey hadn't wanted to give the waffling, doddering old priest a chance to protest. He knew he was the right man for the mission. It didn't matter what those cowards scurrying below ground might think. The priest was right about this being their best and final chance to overthrow the Witen. Cainey wasn't about to let some drunken blowhard like Larry Holderman, or some reluctant yellow-belly like Jed Redding, or some pencil-neck dweeb like Aziz Patel screw things up.

He was muttering low curses about the cowardice of his cohorts as he made his slow way through the crowded lounge. So much so that he almost didn't hear the Control Room operator speaking in hushed but emphatic tones to three off-duty footmen. The priest had been right, for the most part, so far as Cainey had gathered. The station wasn't buying the Glorifier's bullshit, though he and his disciples were relentless in their attempts to sell the wild yarn. Even here in this neutral ground, where, to Cainey's understanding, neither the Glorifier nor the disciples often preached, they could be spotted among the masses. He heard a bellow burst from one or the other of their lips all throughout the expansive space in a fairly rhythmic pattern. They were selling hard, no doubt about it. Most folks ignored them even in the best times though, so their animated states weren't really any more drastically impactful than usual. In fact, Cainey was fairly certain their incessant proselytizing was as unwelcome now as it ever was. He hadn't been in the lounge for long, but the vibe was the same as in the Central Hub and Cafeteria.

Cainey was just about satisfied he'd heard all he had needed to when the operator's voice broke into his conscious line of thought, "...that's when that fucking cunt slapped me. And that was all after her British bitch strapped me so tight to a chair it cut off all circulation to my fingers," the operator Cainey finally recognized as Marty Stiveson was telling the footman. "Fucking rugmunchers are in for it now though. The Commander's gonna be smacking 'em both around all fucking night."

"Rugmunchers?" the footman leaning on a rack of pool cues to the right of their tight little circle asked with a chuckle. "Please don't tell me that tight piece of ass Maisie Sagal is a dyke."

"What do you care, Tito? She wouldn't give you the time a day either way," the short footman beside him put in with an elbow into the side of the guy apparently nicknamed Tito.

"Fuck you," Tito came back with the classic dopey response.

"Oh, she's spending her nights down in the carpet, for sure, boys. I promise you that," Stiveson piped back up to insist. "Her and that apple-bottom bitch pilot were making googly eyes at each other the whole time I was in there, stealing winks and blushing red like fucking teenagers. It was pathetic."

"Maybe we oughta see if we can peer into their cell after the Commander has had his fun with 'em," the third footman suggested. "Might be quite a show, watching them two comforting each other all through the long night."

"That idea ain't half bad," the short footman said as he and Tito drunkenly giggled.

"You boys can count me out there," Stiveson cut through the humor. "Them chicks don't deserve another moment of pleasure in this life. I certainly don't want to have to witness it. You boys just don't get it yet, do ya?"

The three idiot footmen exchanged baffled looks, finally shrugging their shoulders at the older operator.

"Maisie and her fucking girlfriend done kicked over the applecart. The Glorifier's preaching ain't gonna change that. The Witen has been exposed, boys. All the Commander's power, all *our* power, yours and mine, it comes from the people. That big black axe can't cut everyone down, not if they all stand together. And proof of healthy humans surviving down there on Earth for the past decade has got the potential to unify the bastards. If you boys value your positions up here, you ought to be helping the Glorifier and his shabby disciples spread the Commander's cover story."

"Bullshit," the short footman scoffed. "These fucking people are terrified of the Commander. They don't gotta buy his story. One demonstration with that big black axe of his, and everyone who can't swallow the Glorifier's tale about some sacred vision will be more than eager to at least pretend they do."

"Yeah," Tito concurred, still mirthful and giggly. "You freakin' worry too much, Stiveson."

"More like you're just hoping the people stand together," the third footman said. "You know the Commander and Steward are gonna blame your ass for Maisie and her girlfriend taking you hostage and fucking with Branch 2's hatch and shit. You're just hoping to be spared from the punishment you know is coming."

Tito's giggles turned to roaring chuckles. "I think Kenny's got you pegged, Stiveson."

"Think what ya like. You shitheads oughta know enough to respect your elders," the operator told them, wearing a scowl as he emptied the mug in his right hand of its last two swallows of brown beer. "I've been an adult from the start of this shit. I remember how it began. I remember the power of the mob."

"You know, Stiveson, that kinda talk sounds an awful lot like treason to me," the short footman said with some steel in his voice.

Stiveson just stared at him for a while. Then all three. No one spoke. The footmen all sipped at their assorted drinks.

Finally, the operator waved his hand and said, "Ahhh, you go on and think what you like. I'm going to bed."

The words did illicit a few more chuckles, especially from Tito, but Stiveson seemed to be forgotten by the three footmen within a span of a few short breaths. They tightened their little social circle almost like a reflex and transitioned right into a conversation about the Main Cafeteria's lobster bisque getting nine people sick last Thursday.

Cainey quickly lost interest in the young soldiers. Stiveson was the reason he'd eavesdropped on them in the first place. What he might've hoped to hear from the operator about his brief detainment, he couldn't remember. It didn't seem to matter now. Maisie had stolen his love right from under him, if Stiveson could be believed. *Why would he lie about that?* Cainey asked himself. And when he drew a blank about a possible motivation to spread such a slanderous rumor, his hatred for Maisie and sense of betrayal flamed brighter than a thousand suns.

That bitch. She knew. Everyone had to know. Our connection was obvious. What, did I have to slap a purchase tag on her? he asked himself incredulously. *There ain't no way anyone in the priest's Clubhouse could not have understood that Jordana Revere was crushing on me every bit as much as I was her. But nonetheless, the Sagal bitch still betrays me. Well then, Nate, what are you gonna do about it? You gonna lie down and let your soulmate be stolen out from under ya? No. Fuck no. If Maisie is gonna make me fight for Jordana, then I best start swinging*, he thought, settling on a course of action.

He fled the Billiard Lounge the same way he'd entered, unnoticed. The alleyways beyond were all but empty. Cainey may have walked past a couple of residents on his steady slog to the Nest's small brig at the far end of the Grand Alleyway directly opposite the Commander's luxury quarters. He couldn't say with any certainty. His mind was off in other places. Truth be told, lost in lustful anticipation as he was, he may well have dodged a stampede of hundreds of citizens along the way, for all he knew. Jordana Revere's gold-flecked eyes and her long, sensuous, curvy body permeated every conscious thought, leaving room for little else. But were he forced to guess, considering the crowd in the lounge, Cainey would assume the two footmen who spotted him across the line of flowering hibiscus bushes halfway down the vaulted arcade were the first folks he'd encountered since leaving that drunken madhouse.

Their shouts broke through his all-encompassing visions of the angelic pilot. Cainey had come to an immediate stop as soon as he'd realized who was speaking. Despite his anger at Maisie and how fervently he desired vengeance for her betrayal and regardless of how nervous he was to see his Jordana and profess his undying love or how anxious he felt over how best he might approach the Commander with his planned offer, a part of Nate Barker knew that immediate deference to any Witen official was a necessary element to success. That acutely aware corner of his mind had ordered an instant halt to his pumping legs and a shot of present clarity to his thoughts.

He stayed right there, frozen to the spot, as the pair of guardsmen made their way between a break in the median planter boxes ten yards up. Cainey even tucked his chin into his chest and kept his eyes locked on the fancy tile floor. Clearing the floral divider, the pair hurriedly yanked matching steel clubs from leather sheaths strapped across their backs. Shouts for him to fall to his knees with his hands atop his head came blaring past both sets of lips the instant steel weapons were firm in hand. Their agitation was understandable. Random residents didn't just take casual strolls down the decadent alley. Not even on normal days. The heightened state of security being as it was, Cainey took no issue with the rough hands the pair of wide-bellied footmen laid upon him.

"I need to see the Commander," Cainey calmly told them.

"Why the fuck would the Commander want to see you?" the female footman of the pair asked, standing over top of his sprawled-out figure as her thick-bearded male counterpart held him firmly to the floor with a bony knee in the center of his back.

"The Commander is busy. He ain't got time for your bullshit." The male footman's voice was pitched higher than Cainey would've guessed.

He knew them both, as he knew everyone, but he'd never actually had a full-blown conversation or interaction with either. Apparently, they knew him though, "You're that fucking Novocaine guy, ain't ya? He's on the watchlist, ain't he, Murph?" the chubby female footman asked her associate.

"He sure the hell is," Murph concurred. "Lieutenant Dobechek is always telling us to keep an eye on the guy and report his movements when we spot him in our alleyways."

"Yeah, Lieutenant Masterson has told us Orange Corridor heroes are pretty much the same," said the female footman lurking above him as she tapped her wicked club in her open palm. "The bastard must be here to break out his child-boss."

Murph laughed a bit and then said, "Not a very smart plan. You ain't too good at this hero shit, are ya, Barker? You couldn't come up with no better scheme than walking right down the Grand Alleyway like nobody would notice?"

"I'm not here to help that bitch. I've come to help the Commander, to help the Witen," Cainey told them from his uncomfortable position flat on the cold floor.

"Bullshit," both footmen chorused back.

"I can help the Glorifier's story catch traction. I know who's working the people up against him. Somebody's manipulating things from the shadows."

"Bullshit," they answered back yet again as Murph pressed his knee harder into the small of Cainey's back.

"Nobody needs manipulating. The pathetic idiots doubt shit just for the fun of it. They ain't got nothing else to do but complain. They'll all be towing the line before long though, you'll see. The Commander sure don't need help from your dumbass, either way," Murph surmised while Cainey released a long and shameful groan.

"Just hear me out," he wailed in pain. "Just hear me out, and if it's bullshit and not something you think you oughta waste the Commander's time with, then you can kick my ass after. You don't have anything better to do just now, do ya? C'mon, what've you got to lose? I promise, the Commander will be rewarding you for taking me to him before you can say, 'Maisie's a lying bitch.'"

"Okay, you're right. We ain't got nowhere to be but here. You got our attention, for the moment. So, go on, start squealing, little piggy," the female footman prompted with a sarcastic giggle in her voice.

It took longer to convince them, in the end, than Nate Novocaine might've hoped. The pain from Footman Murph's stout frame directed into the small of his back through his rather sharp and fleshless knee clouded his thinking skills rather more than Cainey would ever admit. Finally, when he'd stuttered and moaned through enough anecdotal hearsay to convince the pair of guardsmen that it was at least possible he was telling them the truth, they pulled him to his feet and marched him, one to either side, toward the brig.

The female footman—whose name still continued to elude him despite no longer having a fat man's knee grinding into his spinal discs—stepped away as they'd approached the plain, run-of-the-mill hatchway that led to the modest prison. Cainey heard her attempting to hail someone on her tablet, her watch-commander no doubt. A clipped conversation followed. He heard no more than a handful of soft sounds. Not one word came clear to his ears. Still, he figured whoever was on the other end had given their permission to enter the brig and approach the Commander. When she brushed past him a few seconds after her quiet conversation ended to punch a code into the hatchway keypad, Cainey figured his intuition knew what it was about.

Wasting no time, Footman Murph shoved him into the jailhouse's narrow hall as soon as the hatch slid halfway open. Raised voices came to his ears, muffled greatly by the thick cell walls.

"They're in the last one on the right," the female footman informed her partner.

Murph latched a firm hold to Novocaine's right wrist and tugged him along toward the origin of the muffled commotion. Two footmen stood either side of the tight hall just inside the hatchway. Neither looked him in the eye. Just as neither acted as though any of the ambient muffled commotion was reaching their ears. Perfect sentries, in other words. *On their best behavior, I'm sure, being so close to their Witen's top two councilmembers*, he thought, before forgetting them entirely and refocusing on the cell at the end of the hall.

Cainey could guess what was happening behind the thick sliding hatchway of that prison cell, and the supposition brought a grin to his lips. He thought he could clearly make out the Steward's voice now, though what he was saying remained a mystery. The small, petulant voice that sporadically responded to the muffled demands was plainly Maisie's. His mind raced every step of the short trek down that thin hallway, imagining the backstabbing bitch crying and pleading for mercy. He wished he'd heard more than the two muffled thuds to accompany the shouts, but he was disappointed on that end. *She's probably already battered to hell*, he consoled himself as the female footman with the pressed uniform adorned with a fairly impressive array of commendations stepped past him once again. She merely knocked on the slender cell hatchway this time, completely ignoring the keypad embedded into the wall three feet off the floor to the door's right.

The pounding did not draw an abrupt end to the shouting inside the prison cell, but the Steward's indecipherable jabbering did tail off within a few short seconds of her knuckle's first contact. When the hatchway swished open a dozen seconds later, the eyes of both his guides snapped immediately to the buttercream composite-material floor at their feet. The Commander filled the dainty portal. He even had to duck and twist to step through. Once he did, however, Cainey could finally see into the cell behind him. Maisie was indeed strapped to a steel chair, just as he imagined, and she did in fact have a fat lip, a black eye, and a bit of blood dripping from her Grecian nose, but it was only the one black eye and the barest trickle of blood. Maisie deserved far worse. Enough at least so as to make the defiant look that was still shining brightly in her eyes never dare show itself again.

His disappointment was quickly forgotten when the Commander of the Witenagemot stepped within a foot of him with his arms crossed and clashing eyes fixed firm upon his brow. "Cainey Barker," the massive man sneeringly grumbled his name after a time.

"Yes, sir," Novocaine muttered back.

"This better be good," the Commander said, another long pause later.

CHAPTER 5

"I promise it is, sir—"

"Shut the fuck up," mankind's emperor cut off his assurance. "I wasn't talking to you. I'm gonna talk to you as little as I can. You know you fucking disgust me, Barker. So just stand here and shut the hell up until I directly address you. I was speaking to the footmen." He stepped a pace to his left with that, giving Cainey a bit of breathing space. "Lieutenant Masterson tells me this'll be worth ya'll interrupting important Witen business. Let me tell ya right now, it damn well better be, or it'll be your asses."

"He says he can bring us to the priest, Commander sir," the decorated footman defended her actions with a slightly quavering voice. "Barker has long been a suspected associate of Maisie Sagal, sir."

"I'm aware, footman," the Commander said, sounding dangerously irritated.

"Yes, sir, I'm... I'm... I'm certain you are, sir. I was just... I—"

"Just spit it out, footman!" the grizzly bear before her roared.

"Yes, sir, sorry, sir. It's just that... well, sir, Barker claims Father Boyd has been living somewhere in the access tunnel system for years now and has been secretly coordinating a network of spies within the Witen. He says Maisie and the priest and some of their friends have been plotting for a long time now to escape this place on one of your E11's, sir," the footman paused there to lick her plump lips and swallow her nerves.

"Barker claims this survivor that was with Maisie in the Control Room was discovered by some of the priest's cohorts, and they all entered into a conspiracy to bring her people aboard and then bring the Witen down," she elaborated. "It all sounded fantastical, sir, to us too, but he said the reason why the Glorifier ain't having success convincing folks about your vision is because the priest is using all the connections he has throughout the Witen and among the residents to tell them it's all a lie, sir," she paused there, clearly wary that she might've overstepped her bounds.

After the Commander said nothing, only stared her down all the harder, she continued, "He says they spent time with the survivor and know for a fact that she ain't infected. His people are spreading it around that the Bruderschaft are just here for help and that they have a lot of experience that could be useful. Ya know, basically everything Maisie said over the PA. I thought Barker's story was intricate and surprising enough to maybe have a bit of truth to it, so I called up Lieutenant Masterson, and he agreed. We could prove it easy enough with your help, sir. We just need the master code for the quarter's hatchways, and we can storm Boyd's place and find out for sure. I wish we didn't have to interrupt your work in order to make sure, but I... I... I thought that we didn't... there wasn't much to lose by checking, and there was a lot to gain if Barker wasn't bullshitting. I mean, if the priest really ain't in his quarters and really is manipulating people from the shadows... well then, I thought that might be something you should... it seemed like something it was our duty to bring to you, Commander sir," the woman finished without her eyes ever once rising from her black tennis shoes.

"Is all that true, Cainey?" the Commander asked him, still staring down the two much shorter footmen before him.

"Yes, sir, it is," he croaked through a dry throat.

"Why tell us? Why now?" the Commander asked the obvious.

"The pilot," Cainey offered the simple response, hoping it was enough of an answer.

"*You* and *her?*" the Commander asked with the brow above his milky eye arched so high it nearly reached his hairline.

"Yes, sir," he said, keeping his responses short so as to leave no room for a blunder of the tongue.

The Commander gave up his scowling inspection of his subordinates to step back in close to Cainey. He leaned in, breathing his hot, stale breath straight into Novocaine's face. "You really believe that?" the bearded brute asked, chuckling.

"Cainey!?" The confused exhortation stepped on the toes of his defiant response. Maisie Sagal had noticed him from her open prison cell. "What are you doing here? Did the pr—are you here for... Who... who... Why are you... What are you doing here, Cainey!?" Maisie finished her blabbering by sounding as if she'd puzzled it out.

"There, you hear that, sir," Barker called, pointing to the helpless woman. "She was about to ask if the priest sent me. You heard it yourselves. You see?"

"Cainey, you son of a bitch!" Maisie shouted, realizing her error. "You slimy fucking bastard! Don't you dare help these assholes! Don't you fucking dare! Cainey! Cainey, look at me, you fucking worm!"

"Steward," the Commander called to the man still standing in the prison cell beside Maisie.

"Yes, sir?" prompted the Steward, stooping through the open hatchway.

"Send a footman to Boyd's quarters. Give 'em the master code and tell 'em to drag the bastard the hell out of there and straight here to me, kicking and screaming if you have to."

"On it, sir," the Steward stated while squeezing around them.

The Witenagemot's lawgiver pulled out his tablet as he rested against a cell hatchway two-thirds of the way down the austere hall. The man methodically set about complying with his orders just as Cainey felt the Commander's powerful gaze fall back upon him.

"Okay, *Novocaine*," he prompted, putting a scornful emphasis on the nickname, "say you aren't lying and my men storm Boyd's quarters to discover the man ain't home, what is it you expect for this information?"

"Just a few moments alone with Jordana Revere," Cainey answered, knowing he sounded like some lovestruck boob but not caring about appearances, even before the might of his overlords.

The Commander laughed a bit before clapping a hand down on Cainey's shoulder and shaking as he spoke. "What for?" he managed to ask between chuckles.

"I can convince her to join us, the Witen I mean. She and I will be the most loyal citizens you got. I promise. Once she knows the only way for us to be together is by giving up everything she knows about her people, as well as whatever else you need from her, she'll come around fast enough. I know that, given a chance, Jordana and I could provide humanity with offspring worthy of the Witenagemot. Just give me a few minutes alone with her, sir, please. That's all I ask."

The Commander was all done laughing, but a smirk still remained beneath his tangle of dark facial hair. "We'll see, Barker. We'll see," he said, before moving past Cainey to regroup with the Steward now at the far end of the narrow hall.

Some sort of excitement was happening somewhere in the station. The low chatter emanating from the number-two man's tablet certainly indicated as much. Cainey only prayed it was the footmen sent to find the priest in his Violet Corridor quarters. He knew the search would come back negative, his rational mind did anyhow, yet a finger of panic tickled at his spine the whole time he watched the Commander and Steward receive their report. *Jordana is all but mine. It will all work out. You got this*, he counseled himself. Hopeful flashes of the gorgeous pilot pressing her firm body hard against his own manly, muscled frame made convincing himself of both the former and the latter all the easier, as well as helped him find his smile once again.

CHAPTER 6
JORDANA

"Never give up your pistol without firing it empty first," had been one of the last pearls of wisdom Barrett Hitchens imparted upon her just before she'd sealed herself into that deathtrap of a Star Hawk. The advice had been received no more than thirty or forty hours earlier and had still been fresh on the mind even as that handsy footman discovered the Colt 380 at the end of his pat-down body search. But, despite her never being less than aware of the wise words of her dear friend and brother, Jordana hadn't squeezed off a single round before they'd taken it away. She hoped Hitch would be sympathetic to her particular circumstance, though she knew none of it would've ever prevented him from making every last bullet count.

Even the knowledge that it had been that particular character distinction which prompted Arlo to elect Jordana over Hitch for this mission, more so than her slightly superior piloting experience, was no salve for her frustration. Jordana longed for that pistol now; she needed it. Or lacking that, at least a club or a knife—anything she could inflict some pain with. Oh, how she longed for something to swing or throw. But no, here she was, the Bruderschaft's one last hope, hogtied to a steel chair, stripped of every last item she'd lugged up here with her, battered, abused, and berated, completely helpless to stop the psychotic American macho wankers from destroying her brothers and sisters. *My god, have I utterly failed them?* she honestly asked herself, hearing Hitch's voice on endless replay, just one among a chorus of her closest and dearest kinsman.

What good is a knife or club with no one to swing it at anyhow? She reflected on her solitude inside the lunar station's cold prison cell. *Face it, Jor: you're bloody well stuck with nothing but your torments and no way to release the stress.* She couldn't even scream in the hopes of a therapeutic release. The bastards had slapped a thick strip of duct tape across her mouth before locking her up inside the oppressive buttercream cell.

Her eyes were on the slab floor when he entered. She heard the hatchway's whoosh and saw the shadow of a pair of legs grow closer, but she never looked up to see her visitor. Not until he dragged the small room's only other piece of furniture, a black steel chair to match her own, two feet in front of her did she lift her head. Initially, her eyes rejected the apparition before her. The Commander had walloped her upside the head at least five times—three of which brought on the fabled "stars"—so it was entirely possible she was a deal more concussed than she might realize. Only, after a deep breath and a fairly lengthy stretch of softly pressing closed her eyelids so as to wipe clean the etch-a-sketch of her mind, the ugly little man with the strange nickname who'd leered at her nearly every second they had occupied the same space was still hunched in the steel chair before her, scratching his head and pouring sweat from shoulders, chest, belly, and everywhere else she dared not think about.

After he'd leaned forward in his chair to slowly and agonizingly rip the tape from across her lips, Jordana posed each new half-thought as it popped in her head. "What are you... *you*... You're Cainey, right? Are you here for... Did Mais... did... did... Why are you... How did you get in here?" She glanced at the hatchway after this last to see it locked in the open position. "Where are the guards? How did you get in here?"

"I worked out a deal," the short pigman cryptically answered.

"A deal? What deal? What in the bloody hell are you babbling about? Cut me loose. We need to move."

"We won't be disturbed."

"*Disturbed?*" she asked, thinking it an odd choice of words. "Did the priest send you here to free us? Did he manage to distract the guards or something? I remember seeing the Commander and the

Steward walk past the hatchway's small window only a small while back. Did he make a distraction for all of them to respond to then? What's going on, dammit? Are my people alright, the Bruderschaft? Why haven't you started cutting me loose?"

"I will. I promise I will. I want to—believe me," Cainey squeaked.

"What do you mean you want to? Just do it now before they all get back."

"I told you we won't be bothered until we're ready to walk out of here."

"What?" Jordana demanded, exasperated. His eyes, those dark beads empty of all character, told her everything she needed to know. *He ain't here to free you. He's here for you. He ratted out the priest, and I'm the barmy bloke's sick prize.* "What have you done, Cainey?"

Far from being shamed by the question, he seemed only to be pleased by his name having passed her lips. "I did what was best for us, Jordana. I had no other play. I'da saved your people too, if I could, but no way would he allow that. I was lucky just to convince him to give us both a second chance. The man doesn't compromise easily, ya know? But... I... for you, I... you see, I knew that, even though I had to face down a giant to do it, I would, for us to be together. I wish I coulda saved 'em all, even Maisie. ...maybe. I knew the only way we could vouchsafe a bit of happiness in the middle of all these mad events was if I confronted the Commander and cut us a deal. He knew better than to refuse me. He saw my strength, a strength he's feared for years. Now, maybe one day you and I can set the Witen aside, but right now, our only play was this deal. You... you... you gotta tell 'em everything you know, Jor. You gotta. It's the only way we can be together."

Her tongue was unresponsive for lifetimes. "What in the bloody hell are you talking about, you goddamn ugly, treacherous, two-faced, wormy bastard?" The indignant question finally burst free. "Are you mental? When did I ever, even for one bloody moment, give you the impression that I had even the slightest attraction to you, much less one that would ever make me betray my Bruderschaft? How dare you?!" Jordana was incredulous. Cainey Barker had only really registered on her radar long enough to mark him for a perverted creep. To think the oblivious bloke could actually believe she was even the least bit interested in him, much less that they shared some unspoken love-at-first-sight connection, tattered her already threadbare respect for American men. "What have you told them, Cainey? What have you done? Where is Maisie?"

This last snapped the blushing smirk from his lips. "Don't talk about Maisie!" he shouted with a flash of rage. "Never mind her. She's nothing to us," he went on, quickly adopting a puppy-dog manner. "I know you did what you had to for your people, but you don't need to coddle up to that bitch anymore. You got me. I worked out a deal for us. You're safe. You just... you gotta tell 'em everything they want to know. You already proved how brave you are. You took their beating, and you're still defiant. You kept your honor. I'll make sure no one ever dares say otherwise. I'll look out for you 'til the end of time... my... my love."

Can anyone truly be this delusional? she asked herself, still not believing despite the proof right in front of her. "Cainey, I... I... I don't even know where to start. You... you're..." She cut short the torrent of insults churning through her mind just before a single one could burst loose. The hatchway, still locked in the open position, caught her attention, piercing through the madness of Novocaine Barker. "Where are the guards?" she asked him.

The off-topic question didn't rattle the man, "I told you they won't dis—"

"Disturb us. I know, I know," she interrupted. "But what does that mean? Where did they go? ...I guess," she said, with a clear and hopefully obvious flirtation in her eyes and tone, "what I'm asking you is how much privacy do we really have?"

The light that brightened his eyes and body language was an encouraging sign. When he had to lick his lips before responding in a dopey lovestruck voice, Jordana knew her ploy was off to a good start.

"I requested total privacy. The Commander knew not to haggle with me. It's like I was saying—he could see my eyes. He knew I deserved you. He knew not to try and bargain."

"So... we're alone then? No footmen down the hall?"

"Nope. It's just me and you."

"Ohhh," she said, stretching the word into a seduction, "I think I like the sound of that."

"What do you mean?" the moron sheepishly inquired.

"Oh, well... you see, I'm not good with this stuff, but I... well, I... well, it's possible you were right, and I was a bit harsh earlier," she explained in her best damsel-in-distress imitation. "I might've been lashing out due to my shock with coming to terms of not being able to help my people. I feel a little dirty even thinking about giving up what you and the Witen want just for my own peace of mind. But... well, dammit, you're right. The Witen has won. Might as well accept it. Might as well take advantage of the handsome man in front of me who has so bravely faced death just to profess his love," she finished with a shy smile.

"Are you..." Cainey began with a puzzled brow. "I mean, I think I can trust you. I'm looking into your eyes, and they're telling me to believe. I know we shared a connection. I know that's real, but... I don't know... I want to trust you."

"Then trust me... Please," Jordana begged, stretching her smile.

"I want to. I... I... I do. I do. It's just... maybe I oughta call the Commander in here so you can give them what they want. I hate to leave you tied down 'til then, but... but... I think it's best you tell them first."

"Oh, come on, *Novocaine*," she purred, linking his strange nickname with as much eroticism as she could muster without gagging. "Let's not waste this private moment right here and now. It's just you and me, remember? Cut me loose and let me show you how good I'll be for you. Let me show you what I'll offer for a lifetime up here. Come on, Cainey. Please, cut me loose. Please, Nate. Please, my sweet, sweet *Novocaine*, cut me loose."

Barker was thinking. She could read that plain. Jordana did not want him thinking. She wanted him acting with that surely tiny mushroom in his trousers. So she tried a new tact, "Wherever did you get yourself a nickname like Novocaine from, anyhow?"

The thoughtful expression ran away, just as hoped. A playful grin filled with genuine surprise replaced it. "Promise you won't get jealous?" he asked.

"I'll do my best. That's all I'll promise," Jordana agreed, grinning through the unpleasant charade.

"Well, it was my very first girlfriend that give me the name actually."
"Do I dare to wonder why?"
"I told you not to get jealous."
"And I made no promises."

The perverted little man's fetid breath invaded her sinuses as he creepily chuckled. Somehow, she flirtatiously smiled through the pain, even though she would have gladly endured a few more of the Commander's smacks or even hours more of the Steward's belittling interrogation than suffer this particular torture.

"Well, you asked, so I'm telling ya. If it drives you wild, so be it," he said, leaning back in his chair to her great relief.

"I can handle it," she told him, still light and airy and in love. "I really am interested to know. It's a unique name."

"I'm a unique guy."

"No arguments here."

"It isn't no big story or nothing really. She just used to tell me that she ached whenever we was apart, and that I was like her novocaine. You know, 'cause I like, eased her heartache or whatnot."

"Of course. I can understand her pain," Jordana Revere told the idiot across from her. She didn't believe the story for a second. More likely, the moniker had a far less flattering origin. Clearly, everything the man had ever said or done was not to be taken at face value.

"I'm thinking maybe you do," the creep declared suddenly. A beat later he was on his feet. "Tell me that you'll be with me. Promise me you'll give the Witen what they want. And I'll... I'll... I'll cut you loose," he finished by withdrawing a pocketknife from his front trouser pocket and flicking it open.

"Cut me loose so I can wrap my arms around you. Please, now, cut me free. Do it. I need you," she seductively begged.

Cainey bent close, his hot, nasty breath once again washing over her. In a flash, the plastic tie holding her hands firmly together behind the chair's back was sliced through. Jordana stood as soon as Novocaine had clipped both ties clasped around her shins and the chair legs. Barker was still crouched low, rising slowly from freeing her. The treacherous worm wore the most enraging grin on his dumb face when he finally reached his full extension. Jordana used it as fuel for the knee she drove like a jackhammer into his groin just before he could wrap his grubby paws around her.

Barker dropped like someone had opened a trapdoor in the floor beneath him. He looked so pathetic, writhing and squealing within a matter of milliseconds, that she couldn't bring herself to drive the toe of her boot into the side of his miserable head, as she had planned. Instead, Jordana Revere merely stepped over the delusional dickbag and made her way softly to the open hatchway.

Cainey had said there were no guards currently in the brig, but she knew far better than to trust the man. She paused just inside the threshold, trying to hear what, if anything, lurked in the hall beyond. She realized the exercise was useless within a few wasted seconds. Cainey's pathetic moaning was plenty loud enough to travel all the way out into the Grand Alleyway, not to mention the crash that accompanied the chair his writhing had knocked over. If anyone was out there, they knew something was amiss.

And they woulda ran in to investigate by now, she reasoned. *Perhaps the creepo wasn't lying about the guards at least. Now, which room did they put Maisie in? And how in the bloody hell am I supposed to open up her cell?* Jordana was asking herself as she stepped out into the brig's narrow hall. An idea was bubbling up but died stillborn the instant something solid smacked into the back of her head. Crashing to the cold floor, Jordana saw stars and her failure, and nothing more, for a long time.

When the stars receded enough so as to allow a bit of her environment to be processed by her waking mind, she found herself sprawled out on the hall's hard slab floor. A pair of legs stood one to either side of her.

"Drag that jackass out of there," a voice she guessed belonged to one of the pair of gray legs near her said.

The legs to her left marched off a beat later, back into the cell to get Cainey, she assumed. When the pathetic man's high-pitched protests pierced her head fog a moment later, Jordana knew the crack she'd just taken, though heavy and painful, hadn't totally damaged her reasoning skills.

"What are you doing!? Get off me! The Commander ordered this place cleared out. Let me go. I was supposed to get time alone," Barker whined from somewhere close by.

"You got your private time, Cainey. Quit your bitching," the same voice that had spoken before said.

"Looks like the Commander was wise to send us to watch over you in the end," the other pair of legs pointed out. "You promised to get her to confess all she knew. But instead, me and Footman Wallace find you in there cutting the prisoner free. God knows who you'da tried to break out next."

"Damn good thing we was here, Jake," the footman apparently named Wallace put in as though the comment were scripted. Even in Jordana's current haze, she understood the whole thing had been a game. Cainey was only playing the part the Commander wanted him to, though the creep acted unwittingly. Jordana remembered Maisie's stories. She knew the Commander had a grudge against the porky module maintenance tech. The Steward at least was smart enough to know Jordana would see her chance and manipulate the clueless stalker. They could try Cainey's ploy of convincing her to capitulate merely to secure a life beside him, and if it worked, so much the better. They had next to nothing to lose. And when it didn't work, as they clearly guessed it wouldn't, they could claim Cainey betrayed them and have a gold-plated excuse to lock him up and throw away the key with all the rest of the poor souls trapped behind the array of sliding steel hatches.

The footman apparently named Jake spoke up to confirm her suspicions, "The Commander knew you'd betray us, Novocaine. We were sent back here to witness your treason. You do not disappoint, my man. I'll say that much for ya."

"No!" Barker squealed in protest. "No. She tricked me! She said she'd give the Commander what he wanted. I was only... I was just... she... she was gonna give it all up. She was!"

"Sure, Cainey, you go on and believe that, if it gives you comfort. You'll need plenty as you rot in here, you weaselly little fuck," Footman Wallace told Barker with a sick glee in his voice.

Jordana never saw them drag her craven admirer to a vacant cell, though she heard it clear enough. She couldn't lift her head to watch. That unseen sucker-punch bash to the back of her skull had been a big one. Blackness was once more clouding the edges of her vision. The cold floor flush against her cheek was the last thing she clearly remembered before the bursting stars and suffocating blackness washed away the conscious world.

JED

"Where the hell is this junction?" the priest asked from his point position in the strung-out line of meandering resisters.

"Should be just up ahead," Patel supplied the ambiguous assessment from his position on the grated footpath directly behind Jed.

"You sure about that?" Boyd asked, clearly unhappy with the vague answer.

"Well, I haven't been down here in a long time myself, but from what I remember, at some point soon, this path comes to a T-junction beneath the center of the Module Garage with a path branching left and another going right," Patel explained between breaths. The priest had been keeping a brisk pace. Even Jed was a touch winded, and he kept in excellent shape.

Cainey's call had been as encouraging as it was cryptic. Why exactly he couldn't just supply his report over the comm was still unclear, even after the hundreds of meters they'd walked since hearing it. Jed had a lot of questions after that call. He'd even tried to voice a few. Boyd was single-minded, however. He was so eager to hear Cainey's assessment of the station's mood that he irrationally dismissed any conflicting concerns. In the end, Jed chalked up the module maintenance tech's odd request to meet him in person for the report as some sort of flex. Cainey loved showing off. Jed had never known a man with a larger opinion of himself than Novocaine Barker, much less one that had so little to base that view upon.

Still though, something about the meeting spot in particular nagged at him. Why there? It was far from where either he or they had been at the time. It made no obvious tactical sense, none at least that a layman like Jed could see. No matter how often he turned it over in his mind throughout their near-jog from searching for Carrie Sagal beneath the air recycler all the way across the station to the substructure junction beneath the Module Garage, he could not make rational sense of the choice. But then, as they all were well aware, Cainey was not a rational man. So, he kept quiet. The priest was wise enough to have seen the oddity in the swinish grease-monkey's instructions on his own. Plus, Jed's voice would not be welcome now, no matter how prescient or wise its content. They still had not found Carrie. Jed could feel a palpable pity and derision from his fellow searchers over this fact. Larry would not even look at him. *I gotta find that kid*, he thought for the millionth time since the elusive rascal had fled.

"That's the junction there. That bright spot just ahead," Patel's baritone boomed past his ear.

"I see it," Boyd said, reaching the outer limit of the junction's halo of bright light. "Spread out. Find someplace to flop," he instructed as the gang bunched up behind him in the center of the forking paths.

"So... where in the sam hill is the little bastard?" Larry wondered aloud as he leaned his bulk against a series of thick gray pipes.

Jed plopped down on the footpath, hunching against the rail just across from his best friend and lover. He wanted to look up and share his similar concerns about this strange meetup and Cainey's suspicious absence, but he knew they'd be greeted with an icy chill, and Jed could not cope with that kind of confrontational rejection, not now, perhaps not ever. So he kept his eyes on the grated path at his feet and the rainbow stream of wires running beneath. Larry could be cold, and even a bit cruel, when angry. The alcohol could really elevate the rage on occasion, as well. Jed seldom upset his lover though and never to the extent he had this night. Still, he knew it would be a few hours, at the very least, before Larry was ready to engage civilly or work toward some sort of reconciliation. Jed would just have to wait him out.

Or better yet, Jeddy old boy, you could find that damn kid, he urged himself, rising to his feet and stepping a few paces into the dimness to his right. The goal had been driving him since they'd discovered little Carrie had left them, but the longer he spent in the vicinity of Larry's scorn, the stronger the imperative became. Instead of growing angry with his partner for getting him caught up in this life-risking madness, Jed found himself feeling guilty for letting Larry down. And the colder Larry acted, the guiltier Jed felt. It scared the hell out of him. Who did he have up here, if not Larry Holderman? What good was a life without the embrace of his scruffy cuddle-bear? It was enough to make a man weep. *God, I gotta find that kid.*

"Get Barker's ass on the comms, Aziz," Boyd directed. "Tell him to hurry the hell up."

"On it," Patel affirmed.

Jed assumed the saturnine engineer snatched his rickety little comm device from his pocket, but with his back turned on the rest of his unfortunate allies, he had no way to be certain.

Until Patel started calling, "Barker, you there? Barker, come in. Cainey, you there? You coming?" and other such similar hails, all spaced with a nice even rhythm.

Jed was contemplating setting out on his own in search of Carrie as he turned back to the junction. They didn't all need to be here for Cainey's report, he figured. If Jed took Patel's comm after the man whom Jed was trying very hard right now not to call an adulterous snake contacted Cainey, they could reach him if anything came up that made his search unnecessary or impractical. Barker and Larry would still have their comms, after all.

He'd all but decided to ask for the small, duct-tape-laden radio device and head off when he heard the low thump behind him. No one else heard. Patel's calls were too loud for the soft noise to have reached them. In fact, their unified lack of reaction made him doubt whether he had truly heard the isolated bump. So he turned to where he thought the thud originated. The junction was well lit with respect to the rest of the substructure. The sound though had come from the shadows just five feet from where Jed now stood. Taking one long step, Jed leaned his head around a bulky black tube on the right side of the grated path. A fist flew out of that darkness to crash between his eyes harder than an asteroid into the moon.

Jed went wheeling back. The wallop had lifted him completely off his feet. He never really felt the crash of his back smashing into the steel footpath. The first thing he felt, heard, or saw after that fist came flying at him fast as an AOA rocket was someone heavy stepping on his chest. Multiple ribs cracked under the booted foot. He tried to curl up around the pain, but at least two more people came crashing past his sprawled-out bulk. One stepped on his hand. Another stomped down on his right calf before clipping the back of his head.

Shouts rang out from three directions. "Everybody freeze! Nobody move! Down on your knees!" the booming chorus demanded.

Jed was dazed but still understood what was happening. Cainey had betrayed them. Footmen were rushing up from all three spokes. Jed's friends were in a line before him. Three footmen were now between him and Larry. Beyond the navigator were Patel, then Dolly, and then the priest. The central footpath of the T-junction opened up in front of Patel. Two gray uniforms filled the narrow trail. To the priest's right, the Commander and a tall black-bearded footman closed in. It was a shock to see the scarred visage of the Witen's supreme ruler in these rough tunnels, but in spite of Jed's current position flat on the path and his blurred, unfocused vision, there could be no mistaking the man.

"Run, Priest!" Larry shouted as two of the three footmen that had waylaid Jed set about subduing him.

The look on Boyd's face in response to the desperate plea spoke volumes. He was boxed in and knew it. The priest and his wife were slowly backing from the approaching Commander and his henchman, but within another five or six steps, they would be bumping into Aziz Patel. They had nowhere to run. Larry was raging against his captors. Patel was dodging as best he could in his limited space to avoid the two footmen closing in on him from the central path. It would all be over in a matter of seconds.

"Run, Boyd. Run," Larry implored from beneath his attackers.

"He's right, Boyd," Dolly said, taking her husband's hands into her own. "It's you they're after. It's you they need. Run! Go... Now!" she demanded after he did not budge.

Boyd only shook his head, as if lost in a mushroom haze. He couldn't understand what they expected of him, clearly. There was nowhere to run.

But there could be. Jed's perceptions coalesced into perfect order in that moment. The pain in his ribs and hand faded to nothing. Suddenly he saw it: his chance. It was clear what Larry wanted. Even Dolly was demanding it. They could not risk the priest's capture. If Jed could facilitate his escape, that would go epically farther toward winning Larry Holderman's sole attentions than finding Carrie ever could. *Do it, now, for your man. Make him all yours, forever. Get up and make Aziz Patel a thing of the past. Do it, and he'll never stray from your bed again,* Jed urged himself. In a flash, he was back on his feet. "Priest, run!" he shouted.

The three closest footmen were busy with Larry and Patel, their backs to him, leaving just enough space on the left side of the pathway to dart by.

Jed dashed into the gap, shouting, "Run!"

A peripheral glance at the priest was all he managed before he was on them, enough to notice his wide-eyed expression and little else. Jed launched himself through the air, colliding into the two footmen on the central path with enough force and violence to make any linebacker envious. His arms wrapped firmly around both men as their heads whiplashed into each other. The intertwined trio went crashing to the floor as one. "Run, Priest!" he implored from atop the surprised pair, waving his arm to indicate that he wanted him to jump clear of them and take off down the path.

He was busy begging the man to seize the fleeting moment with both insistent eyes and flailing gestures, and so didn't see the fist the footman beneath his right side launched until it smashed flush into the bridge of his nose. Blinding pain radiated through him. And no more than two breaths later, a river of blood was spurting from the shattered appendage.

Boyd caught on to the chance in the end, but his initial shocked delay cost him. The priest was in the process of leaping over Jed and the two footmen beneath him when the Commander's massive right hand caught a clutch of his shirt. Jed was trying to roll off and away from the irate soldiers, but neither would loosen their grasp upon him. He had to watch helplessly as the Commander slammed the priest down on the path just ahead of him.

"Nooo!" Dolly screamed, frantic as a buzzing fly. "No! Please don't hurt him!" she begged over and over again.

"Shut her up," the Commander growled.

Larry and Patel were tied up by then. Two of their captors moved to Dolly to give her the same treatment.

"Don't you fucking touch her!" the priest screamed at them from his back.

A slap from the Commander cut short his indignation. "We told you to freeze. That was an order," he told them all in a strangely soft voice. "But you folks think ya'll are above my law. You think you can defy me, even to my face. You think you can attack my footmen, in my presence, with no consequence," he added, locking eyes with Jed.

A shiver rolled up and down his spine like waves on an EKG. Jed's blood ran cold.

"Well, you're wrong. You're dead fucking wrong," the milk-eyed madman said, bending down to grab him.

A thick, impossibly strong hand wrapped around Jed's throat before proceeding to lift him bodily off the footpath. The tyrant then pressed his back flat against a section of steel ductwork lining the tunnel. The reality of his circumstance didn't immediately register in Jed's rational mind. Something was preventing him from actually believing that the Commander of the Witenagemot was truly squeezing the life from him, breathless second by breathless second. It was too contrived almost. Or too surreal, but in an inevitable premonitional sort of way.

Jed's eyes sought Larry's, hoping they could convince him that this feared fate was really just some ludicrously vivid nightmare. Instead, the panic and helpless sadness he saw within his lover's eyes only confirmed the horror. These were indeed going to be his last moments. It took that understanding to get him kicking, as well as punching and chopping and hacking and pulling and herking and jerking. Jed emptied his arsenal, giving every ounce of reserve energy he could muster to the effort. To his tormentor though, all his bashes and thrashes were no more than the soft tickle of a feather duster. At no point did the Commander's inexorably tightening grip slacken in the slightest.

He's killed me, Jed knew when all strength had fled. The understanding brought his eyes back to Larry. "I love you," he meant to mouth. Whether or not he had completed the sentiment before death's cold kiss swam up to embrace him was only one of many parting consolations denied to Jed Enoch Redding in the end.

CHAPTER 7
ELIAS

He hadn't gone far after leaving his mentor's lair. Elias had been close enough to spot each of the four footmen dispatched from the Steward's quarters, clearly tasked with tracking him. He'd expected nothing less, really. Plus, he was more than ready to be found, provided it was to stand as Carrie's whipping boy. As soon as he saw a footman dispatched from the brig, Elias would step out of the hidden little cubbyhole of an alcove just inside Newton Hospital's archway where he currently basked in anonymity. The location was more than adequate for his needs just then, having a relatively clear view down all but the nearest third of the Grand Alleyway and almost perfect concealment by shadow and niche.

From this well-conceived vantage point, Elias had plainly seen the Steward and Commander both exit their luxury quarters and stroll across the wide arcade into the tightly restricted brig within minutes of one another. Maisie was in there too. If the Steward was truly the honorable man of his word Elias hoped him to be, a footman would emerge from that crabbed detention center looking for Elias. He knew he had to allow time for some necessary logistics, as well as Maisie's natural truculence, but it ought not be very long before that messenger emerged.

So he waited and waited and waited and waited some more, and when he'd grown too impatient with the waiting for comfort, he tried to imagine plausible scenarios and excuses for why he had been kept waiting. But the small hatchway at the far end of the Grand Alleyway stayed resolutely closed for a long, long time, for far too long for hope to withstand. Finally, Elias cursed the man and spat. Then immediately felt guilty for spitting on a hospital floor, which very quickly led to thoughts of Perry Sagal, which in turn brought on the tears, rivers and rivers of tears, puddling with the spittle. He fell to the floor after the well ran dry and used the sleeve of his uniform blouse to mop up his guilt and pain.

All at once, he had to get out of there. He needed to be as far away from the brig as possible. He was no better than the lowest coward in the end. He needed to run. *Tessa*, he needed Tessa. Bouncing to his feet, Elias used his remaining clean shirtsleeve to dry his eyes. *Now's as good a time as any*, he told himself, knowing the two footmen on patrol in the Grand Alleyway had just set off away from the hospital. Their circuit wouldn't bring them back around to spot Elias slipping out for at least five minutes. Rather casually then, he strolled back through the low hospital archway, straight toward the Grand Rotunda. Elias checked the time on his tablet as he crossed Branch 1's threshold. He knew Tessa had duty tonight but wasn't quite sure when her shift ended. *She's most likely hanging around Blue Corridor either way*, he reasoned. Branch 4 felt sufficiently far enough from the brig for Elias, so he made its alleyways his destination.

Elias received a bit of a fright when he looked up from his time-check. Cainey Barker nearly barreled straight into him. The tiny old-timer had his eyes glued to the floor and never even noticed him, not even after Elias near pirouetted around him to avoid a collision. He let it go though. Barker seemed to him like the kind of fellow who'd report seeing Elias to the first person smart enough to ask. No reason to cause a scene over such a creature as he. It never even occurred to Elias to wonder where the ugly troublemaker was headed.

Blue Corridor had one of the more straightforward layouts among the six color-coded corridors. Elias took a methodical approach to sweeping its grid, strolling down the center of Alleyway IV and scanning down each cross alleyway as it came. He found his gorgeous gift from the gods embarked on a solo patrol down Alleyway VII. "Tess," he stage-whispered from ten yards behind. "Hello, my love." A smile was spread wide across his lips when she turned to face the call.

"Eli! Oh, sweetie," she softly wailed, before throwing up her hands and closing the gap between them with a two-second sprint. "What happened? Where have you been? The Steward's got people looking for you. It's in our shift notes to report if we see you."

"I know. It's alright," he assured, softly cupping her face between his rough hands. "He and I had a chat a while back. They won't drag me in or nothing. He let me walk right outta his quarters. He's pretending to trust me, for his own sake more than anything else, I figure. For now, he just wants an eye kept on me. He ain't sure what I'm gonna do."

"Well, I'm sure that's just it," Tessa allowed, withdrawing from the embrace, "but what *are* you gonna do exactly?" Her wry smirk showed she'd never let him off the hook so easily.

"I got no idea," he admitted after a time.

"Well, where you been? At least tell me that much," she demanded without sounding hurt nor harsh. "Is your sister okay?"

"She was fine when I left her. So long as she didn't leave her clubhouse, she oughta still be that way."

"Her clubhouse?"

"Yeah, she uhh, led me to it after you helped us get out of there... I was relieved to see whatever line you fed 'em was good enough to throw off suspicion," he said, changing the subject. "I was so scared. I saw Allanson going after you just as I stepped into the tunnel. I nearly went back."

"Yeah, well, it was a close thing," Tessa admitted. "If Allanson and Lieutenant Woodson had their way, I'd be under heavy suspicion, let me tell ya. The Steward rescued me in the end, but he didn't even bother to hear my bullshit. And that sure pissed Woodson and Allanson the hell off," she explained with a mocking giggle. "They went off muttering after that. I ain't seen 'em since, but I know they got their eyes on me. How those two dishonest pukes have as many friends as they do in the Witen is beyond me. Luckily for us, the Steward's got more... hopefully," she added, still mirthful.

The Steward, ugh. The name alone was an agony. "I can't think about him just now. Or any of it. They... they... they got my big sister, Tess, and they're... they're hurting her. And I can't do nothing about it.

Worse yet, I'm not so sure I have the courage or strength to save her even if I could. I have *been* the Witenagemot for so long. All of me is in all of it. I am its legacy. ... At least, that's what he told me... Do I really have to make the choice between Maisie's truth and the Steward's Witen? Why, Tess? Huh, why? I didn't ask for any of this shit... Did I?"

She only looked at him in response, but it was more than enough. Tessa Rodriguez loved him. He knew that was so. Not every aspect of his reality need crumble. The notion was as comforting as it was needed. Tessa stepped back in to wrap her strong arms around him once again. They stayed locked like that for a long time.

"Come with me," he heard himself saying into the peaceful silence.

"Where? I'm on duty?" Tessa mildly protested.

"We'll go see Carrie. We can rest up there and... and... and figure out a way to get Maisie and her friends outta the brig, and... and... and how to stop the Witen from sending the Bruderschaft away."

"You and I and your baby sister are going to do all that?" she asked with a playful scoff.

"We gotta try, Tess," the solemnity in his voice was new and sudden, but it was not false, for he could deny the obvious no longer. There could never be true joy in the poison light. He saw clearly and could not go back. The Witen was rotten and corrupt, its light harsh and unhealthy. There was no crack nor crevasse of his peace it could not seep inside and tarnish. He'd given his soul to a lie. Whether redemption was possible now or not, he needed to try and stop them. Elias Sagal was the last man of his family line; it was his duty to protect them, to love them. He had to save Maisie.

"If I leave right now, my name will be on the detain-on-sight list within the hour. Then both you and I will never be able to show our faces up here without having a horde of footmen come chasing after us." Tessa withdrew from their embrace yet again to sound the warnings. "I'm not saying you're wrong, Eli. I think your sister did tell the truth today, but... but... the Witen is everywhere up here. It will be all or nothing from this moment on."

"Yes, it will," he reluctantly agreed.

"My parents, Eli, they... they might... we won't be able to protect them."

"Not if it's just you and me," he said, taking her soft hand into his own. "So... we uhh... we'll just... we'll just have to figure out a way to work real fast or else get a lot of help."

"You make it sound so easy," she sarcastically said, brushing the back of one hand over his stubbly cheek.

"I'm sure it'll be anything but," Elias answered with an equivalent wit. "I'm committed either way, Tess," he added when he was sure he had her full attention.

"Okay," she said, nodding her head and drawing in a sharp steadying breath. "I trust you, Eli. And I told you wherever you went, I'd be there too. And I mean what I say," Tessa declared, unbuttoning her tactical blouse.

Elias wasn't sure what she was doing, and he certainly didn't expect her to slam the starched gray top to the floor and then proceed to stomp on it three or four times. He was smiling by the end of the display, nonetheless.

"Let's get outta here while we still can then," she said, leading him off by the hand toward the nearest tunnel system access point.

They flipped positions almost immediately after stepping through that access hatch in Alleyway III. Tessa had been in the tunnels a time or two but always with Elias as guide. And since only he knew where Carrie's hideout was, it made perfect sense for her to yield to his expertise. Whether or not she could have done any worse definitely merited debate. Elias would be so certain he'd taken the proper fork, only to smack up straight into a dead end or somehow wind up making one big circuit. Tessa, to her credit, and god bless her, made no effort to point out these blunders. Elias felt her irreverent pity despite her silence.

"Goddammit!" He finally threw up his hands and admitted defeat. "I'm sorry, sweetie. I got no idea where the hell we are right now."

"Yeah, I kinda figured that out," she said, strutting in close with both hands on her hips. "Where is this clubhouse at exactly?"

"Her place is under Branch 3, kinda near the processing plant, but for the life of me, I can't remember which tunnel it was."

"You do know we're under the Greenhouse right now, right?" Tessa asked.

"What? The Greenhouse? Are you... No, we can't be." How could he have led them so far astray without noticing? Tessa was clearly mistaken. He knew it had to be so, but he stepped up to the placard riveted to one of thousands of steel stanchions that held the footpath in place. Every third of these were stamped with a placard of a convoluted map of the tunnel system and its precise location within. "Goddammit!" he bellowed yet again. "How the hell did I get us this frickin' lost?"

"You got a lot on your mind, Eli," Tessa pointed out. "You gotta take a breath and drop the weight of the world from your shoulders, for a few minutes at least. You can only solve one problem at a time. I suggest you focus on the task at hand, not the battles down the line."

It never ceased to amaze him just how she could read his mind with such pinpoint accuracy. He was indeed worrying about the battles to surely come. In fact, he had no clear memory of any specific turn or decision he'd made the entire excursion. *Focus on the path at your feet, Eli,* he scolded himself. "Well, c'mon then, babe," he called, waving over his shoulder for her to follow. "Let's backtrack a bit. I'll get us there."

"I believe in you, big guy," she said with a lightness in her voice, for which he was monumentally grateful. "You get one do-over; then I'm steering the ship. Fair warning," she caveated her support before running up to plant a kiss on his cheek over his shoulder from her tippy toes.

Tessa never had to make good on her threat. With a one-foot-in-front-of-the-other approach, the small gray hatch sealing off his little sister's hideaway was within a stone's throw in a matter of minutes. There may have been one wrong turn along the way, but Elias remembered a shortcut that made up the distance right after and so felt it shouldn't count against him.

"That's it up ahead," he called over his shoulder.

"That hatch up there?"

"Yeah."

"How does she get that thing open all on her own?"

"With some difficulty, so she tells me."

"She sure is something, your sis," Tessa marveled as Elias went to work on the hatch's wheel.

"No arguments here."

The hatch popped loose a beat later. Swinging open, it revealed Carrie Roxanna Sagal a foot inside her clubhouse, leaning heavily on one forearm crutch and wielding a steak knife with her free hand. She slashed the air before her, shouting, "You won't take me! You won't take me!"

Elias had to duck in close for the light from her clubhouse lamps to touch his face before she dropped her defense tactics.

"Eli!" she squealed in a complete 180. "You're back!"

"I'm back," he allowed.

"And you brought Tessa!" In a flash, Carrie was pulling Tessa by the hand into her clubhouse. "Let me show you around." His sister was gushing as she started pointing out the various furniture pieces in the small chamber.

Elias went straight to the percolator. "Mind if I make a cup?" he asked over Carrie's tour-guide spiel.

"Of course. Make one for Tessa too."

"What about you?"

"I've had one too many since you left, I think."

The innocent brilliance Carrie imbued into her every word was intoxicating. His sister had the power to change his mood with one perfect sentence or one wise look.

"Coffee drinker, are ya?" Tessa asked Carrie as she took the seat the young child offered her.

"Only on occasion," Carrie explained.

"Only with company, I thought," Elias said, needling his sister as any good brother should.

"Well, today's been stressful," she defended herself before climbing into the dining chair across from Tessa. "I've been shut up in here, helpless as a b... helpless as a-as a-a-a baby. It's no fun at all, trust me. Alls I can do is listen in on the resistance's private comm line. I can't even speak to let 'em know I'm fine. They've been roaming all over l-loo-looking for me, and I didn't want to leave and go chasing after them. We might end up walking circles around each other. They're headed someplace clear on the other s-s-side of the station to meet up with Cainey right now. I f-f-figured there was no way I'd make it there and catch up with them. I'm gu... I'm guess-guessing the meetup won't last very long, and they'll be moving again right after. I-I-I don't get around thi... around thi-thi-this place as quick as most. Maybe now that you're here though we can all go f-f-f... we can all go find them together. It'll be a whole lot easier with three, I think. I could even hop on your b-b-back, Eli, if you guys th-think I'm h-ho-holding you back."

"Whoa, whoa. Slow down, kid." Elias threw up his hands. "Who's looking for you?"

"The priest, D-D-Do-Dolly, all of them. They sent Barker up to check on the station's mood, and he's reported back a couple times. They t-t-told him they were still searching for me when he asked for a sitrep."

"A 'sitrep'?" Tessa asked, smirking.

"A situation report," Carrie specified, as though Tessa had been genuinely curious about the phrase and not pointing out how cute it was to hear an eight-year-old girl using radio jargon.

"I'm still confused, Ri Ri," Elias said. "How are you listening to the priest and Cainey and all them?"

"Well... well, y-y-you-you see... it's kind of a long story, but basically Maisie and the priest's resistance established an encrypted comm system independent from Cardinal's Nest's communication lines. They've only f-f-fabricated a few comm devices so far though, and I was always being left in the d... left in the d-d-dark by Maisie, so I tried to make my own. I bartered with Roddy Sheffield for access to his for a while and tried to re-re... tried to reverse engineer it. I could only figure out a way to tap in and hear the tr... the tr-traffic though. I can't communicate on it."

"You built a comm device?" Tessa and Elias both asked.

"No, I built a stupid l-l-l-listening device, if anything," she humbly answered.

"You're amazing, kiddo," Tessa said, ruffling Carrie's dark hair.

"So, what's going on with Ma-M-Maisie? Did you get to see her, Eli? I been so wo-wor... I been so wor-w-worried about her. I thought maybe the Commander had gotten her to tell him where my clubhouse was. I was afraid you guys were a couple footmen he sent here to take me in. That's why I was swi-swi-s-swi... that's why I was swinging the knife like that. Funny that you did turn out to be f-f-f-footmen after all. The gray uniforms were all I saw at first. You can probably im... you can pro... you can probably imagine how happy I was when I finally recognized you as the only two footmen in this station I didn't need the knife for," she ended with a smile over the irony.

The words added weight to the light mood, despite the grin. He did not want to tell her the truth. Right then, Elias would have sooner disappointed the Commander, the Steward, and even God herself rather than his baby sister. She deserved the truth though. He could give her that much. He could give her what had been denied him for oh so very long. If he really loved, respected, and wanted the best for Carrie Roxanna, he would shoot her straight from here on out.

"I tried," he finally began, unable to avoid qualifying his explanation with a pathetic attempt to excuse his actions. "They wouldn't let me see her. I tried to take her punishment, but they... I didn't know... I couldn't... I didn't know what else to do, Carrie. She's still in that brig. I'm so sorry."

"That's okay, Eli," she assured. "I never expected you to fight 'em all to save her or nothing. Then you'd just end up dead too. That's n-n-n-not... that's not how we're going to get her out of there."

"How are we going to get her out of there?" Tessa asked, making the issue sound hopeless.

"Together," Carrie fired back with a confidence they could not help but find uplifting.

The coffee was ready then. Trying not to show Carrie his wide, admiring smile and tear-brimming eyes, out of an unconquerable sense of discomfort with emotional expression, Elias went to work preparing his and Tessa's drinks. A burst of crackling static filled the small room as he brought the mugs to the table. Carrie set her aforementioned contraption down on the tabletop and began twisting a tiny red knob on the side of the far-too-impressive-looking slapdash device. The crackling grew louder as she fiddled with its controls.

Abruptly, the static cleared, and a thickly accented voice came clearly to Elias' ears, "Barker, you there? Barker, come in. Cainey, you there? You coming?..."

The calls continued on like that for a bit. Barker never responded. The voice speaking perfect English in a thick Indian accent suddenly stopped mid-sentence. A choir of authoritative voices started echoing through Carrie's device in its absence, growing louder and clearer by the second. Right up until the moment a harsh crash of plastic on metal screeched through the speaker. The muffled demands came back at once, and with their return came an understanding. The comm device had crashed to the grated footpath amidst the sudden commotion. The priest and his people had been set up. A flash of Novocaine Barker strutting obliviously into Branch 1 confirmed it without a doubt.

Why Maisie and her people had ever trusted the incompetent bastard in the first place was still a mystery though. Cainey, for whatever reason, had clearly led his supposed allies right into a trap. Elias could hear it even now. The struggle was plain through sound alone. Carrie and Tessa recognized what was unfolding on the other end of that radio just as he did. It was plain in their crestfallen expressions and panic-stricken eyes. When a series of successive voices rode over all other sounds to encourage the priest to try and flee, a flicker of hope did flash across their faces. But after a short tussle that must've sent the comm device crashing against the rail, judging by noise alone, the Commander's voice filling their speaker with menace in his every word doused their spirits before they could truly lift.

There was no way to be sure. All they could discern were a few choked gasps after the Commander said, "You think you can attack my footmen, in my presence, with no consequence. Well, you're wrong. You're dead fucking wrong," but they all seemed to accept that their giant ruler was throttling Jed Redding to death.

All at once, Carrie lurched into Elias, wrapping both her arms around his torso. "He's killing Mr. Redding!" she exclaimed, horrified and helpless.

He had no idea what to say. He could think of nothing better than simply hugging her back.

Tessa rose and joined the embrace. "He'll pay for it. We'll make him pay for it," Tessa comforted in a soft whisper.

"They're taking Boyd! They're taking Dolly! They're taking all of them!" Carrie screamed, pushing back from their group hug after the noises still muffling over her listening device suggested as much. "They're taking the priest away. They'll tor-tor-t-torture him. He'll tell ever-ever-everything, in the end. We can't let them take him! We gotta save him. It wa-wa-was bad enough they had M-M-Maise. If they ge-ge-get the priest too... We have to save them both. We have to save all of them. We can't let them have the priest. We can't, Eli. We ha-ha-h-h-have to do som... we have to-t-to do something!"

He and Tessa locked eyes after Carrie's screed. They both agreed she was right with facial expression alone.

After a simultaneous breath and sigh, Tessa said, "Well, we can't do nothing for them down here."

"If I told you to stay here, would I have any hope of you obeying me?" Elias bent down to ask his sister.

"I think you already kn-kn-know the answer." Flipping moods in a blink, Carrie added an achingly innocent smile.

"We'll need help—a lot—or we won't last ten minutes up there," Tessa pointed out.

"Yeahhhh," Elias agreed, dragging out the word as he thought. "So, we bring our appeal right to the people. It's late, but I bet the Billiard Lounge is still at least half full, and everyone there at least half in the bag. That could be good for us or bad, depending on how good we are at recruiting."

"Well, I'm no talker," Tessa said, waving off the responsibility before he had a chance to saddle her with the task.

"Neither am I," Elias argued.

"I'll talk to them," Carrie boldly declared, her bright and pure voice ringing with undaunted determination. "I'm serious," she insisted, after neither Tessa nor Elias were able to fend off their knee-jerk skeptical reactions. "I want them to exp-exp... I want them to explain to me how they can sit around g-g-getting drunk while real innocent human beings are begging for a place among us, be-be-begging for their chance at a go-g-good life. We have the room, more than enough. I will ask them how a group of adults could be sc-scared enough to let a madman send eighty-five healthy people to their hor-horr... to their horrific deaths back on Earth."

"That ... might ... work," Tessa allowed in a begrudging, stilted sort of way.

"You can come with us, Ri Ri," Elias decided, "but if some footmen come for me and Tess, you gotta promise you won't get involved. If that happens, I expect you to come straight back here, swift as you can, and don't come out until I come get ya, or until you run out of food."

"Okay," she said, too fast for Elias' concerns.

"I'm serious, Carrie. You may well be the smartest person left alive, but you're still just a kid. If we come into some trouble up there, you better just run away. Promise that. Promise you will, and you can tag along with me and Tess."

"Say it like you mean it, Ri," Tessa instructed. "Your brother and I are serious about this."

"I know. I know," Carrie assured, throwing up her hands in surrender. "If you tell me to run, I will. I promise."

"Good. Okay then," Elias said, grinning at his sister now, "do you, uhh, happen to know the fastest way to the Rec District from here?"

"Follow me," Carrie directed with an eye roll and an ever-widening smirk as she deftly hobbled toward her clubhouse hatchway.

Guiding the last half of the journey from her piggyback perch on Tessa, Carrie had them standing just outside the Billiard Lounge in under ten minutes. Elias would've gladly been the one to aid his little sister, but the sword and hammer still sheathed across his back were too prohibitive. Tessa never complained though. Carrie was still a small child, maybe 60 pounds at best, Elias guessed, so it required no real exertion. Tessa was fit for far worse.

"You guys good?" he asked, nonetheless, after Carrie clambered down from Tessa's back, narrowly avoiding smacking her head into the shaft of the morningstar the Blue Corridor footman always carried. "Remember what you promised now, Ri Ri," Elias reminded his sister after she and Tessa both rolled their eyes at him before assuring, in tandem, that they were perfectly ready.

"I remember," Carrie indignantly assured.

"Okay, stick close, both of you," he told them before crossing through the archway of the still significantly crowded drinking den.

Elias guessed there were at least two hundred Witen citizens spread across the massive square chamber. Some were even still engrossed in games of pool, though most were bantering in small clusters along the two side walls and back. Bottles passed from hand to hand. Glasses sloshed their contents in the reckless grips of tipsy drinkers. The Glorifier stood at the back of the room, preaching nonsense. His disciples could be seen everywhere, half-clad and irate. And dotted around and among the social cliques, prophets, and gamers were near an entire squad of armed and alert footmen. Elias spotted all seven of them before he made it two yards into the lounge.

It was impossible not to be noticed by one or the other of his fellow footmen. There were a lot of drinkers in the place but not that many. After three of his gray-coated brothers and sisters had looked their way only to keep their eyes fixed firmly as they snatched up their tablets to report their discovery, Elias gave up on the idea of stealth altogether. *We gotta get everybody's attention somehow*, he knew. *But how?* Best he could come up with was running to the center of the room and then hopping up on a billiard table to shout at them. If he got the people's attention and interest quick enough, they could prevent the room's squad of footmen from pulling him down and hauling him and Tessa before the Steward, or worse. He was not at all looking forward to that next part of his incredibly weak and unanalyzed plan. Elias Sagal had never given a speech in his life. He avoided such situations like a billionaire avoids death.

Having no idea what he would say did not slow his pace, however, as he led Carrie and Tessa to the lounge's center. Still, his gait was not blistering, by any measure. Carrie was down to just the one forearm crutch, after all. Tessa held Carrie's free hand with her own, helping her along. Elias focused on clearing the way before them. Thirty feet from what he judged was the center table, Footman Conover and Footman Baines converged to block their path. Elias halted in place and felt Carrie and Tessa follow suit two paces behind.

This is close enough, he told himself, hopping atop the table two feet to his left. "Don't believe his vision junk, people!" he shouted. "That crazy bastard wouldn't know a line of bullshit from a hole in the ground," he declared, pointing a steady finger directly at the Glorifier. "Listen to me, folks, please. My sister told you all the truth today."

Baines and Conover reached him then. They stood to either side of the billiard table, trying to pluck at his arms and pull him down. Elias dodged as best he could and tugged free when captured.

"Ain't that the Ethling?" He heard a man ask from somewhere close.

"Yeah, that's him. Check out the sword," a second male voice confirmed.

"Hey, let the man speak," a third, barely audible voice called out from the back of the lounge.

"Yeah, the Glorifier and his annoying ass minions have been running their traps all night long. Give the Ethling a turn, why don't ya?" a woman shouted from four billiard tables over.

The priest's influencers in action, no doubt. The quick support only made sense in light of what Carrie had explained on the journey to the lounge. Elias wasn't sure he believed it when Carrie first insisted the priest had connections all over the station or that the failed holy man had sufficient leverage over each and everyone so as to assure their compliance. The half dozen other concurrences that rang out for the footmen to allow Elias to speak settled his doubts though.

The other five footmen in the Billiard Lounge were closing in fast. Elias couldn't avoid all of them forever. Soon enough, the morons would wise up and stop trying to grab him from the floor. Once they jumped up on the tabletop, it was all over.

"Blasphemer!" the Glorifier wailed, pulling at his hair and pounding his chest. "Do not doubt!" he implored with dramatic sorrow.

The golden prophet's shouts had at least stopped the footmen in their paths, all seven of their heads turning the Glorifier's way.

"Not you, Ethling, please. Do not doubt our Commander. He has seen the truth of those monsters on our dock. Do not deny the gift. Do not deny the holy vision. Your fall may doom us all. Please, I beg, do not lead these good people astray. No, please, not you. Only reach behind your shoulder and touch the hilt of your fabled sword, and you shall remember yourself. Remember the feat you accomplished to win that sacred blade. Remember the wicked foes of our mighty Witenagemot you felled. It was your faith in our great purpose alone which allowed you to prevail. Three against one and you survived, with only scars as testament. Touch those scars now, good sir. Remember who you are. Please, Ethling, I implore you, climb down from there. Do not betray your courageous deeds. Do not lead these good citizens astray," he finished, falling to his knees beside Elias' table.

Sometime during the Glorifier's pleading, Carrie had climbed atop the table one aisle over. "They have taken the priest," she shouted into the silence that pervaded the immense space. All eyes went her way, Elias' included. "They took him."

"The priest is rotting away in his old shop, kid. Come on down from there. This ain't no place for you. Go on back to bed," a condescending male voice shouted from somewhere in a crowd now pressing close to the two tables with Sagals atop them.

"He hasn't been in his quarters for years, you bl-bli... you blind fools," Carrie shot back, spinning as fast as she could manage to find the asshole. "The priest is the only reason the Commander hasn't burned this whole station to the ground yet. He has been keeping supervisors and footmen off your backs from the shadows for years. You all surely know my si... my si-s-s-sister has been resisting the Witen since the start. Well, I'm here to tell you that the pr... the pr-pr-priest has been right there with her nearly this whole time. Every day he dances on a tightrope to protect this place. Whatever you have suf-suf-suffered under the Witen, know that if the priest were not acting behind the scenes, your suffe... your suff-suffering could have been much worse. Father Boyd even has some influence among the Witen Council itself. He is all that is preventing them fr-fro-from passing their most extreme and fasc-fascistic g-go-goals. It's only thanks to him you have any freedoms left. Count yourselves lucky you still have this place, a-a-a-and the booze to go with it. If we don't demand they release him now—and all the others—the last ch-ch-check on the Commander's madness will be gone. We are running out of time up here, p-p-people."

"Silence, child! Come down from there," the Glorifier ordered.

"Speak to them, Carrie," Elias encouraged with a nod and a smile.

"Pull them down!" the prophet screeched. "Now!"

"Can you prove any of this, kid?" a woman in the front of the compressing crowd asked as many around her did their best to hinder the footmen and disciples trying to carry out the Glorifier's orders.

"If I have to. I can lead you to his clubhouse right now. But we don't have time. I kn-kn-know that just asking you to tr-trust me isn't fair. I know it's all the Witen ever gives us, but we really need to act now. Not only can we not allow them time to tor-to-tor-torture Boyd, but the Commander could force the Bruderschaft away at any moment."

"Well, if they's infected, then maybe they oughta be sent away," a male voice drunkenly slurred.

"They aren't," Carrie responded with an exaggerated eye roll, her third in the last fifteen minutes.

"The Commander's vision tells us otherwise," the Glorifier boomed.

"When did he become this infallible god for you, Glorifier?" Carrie asked, sage as a tenured philosophy scholar.

"Silence, child!" he screamed, marching toward her table with a wagging finger. "You have no place here. Get her down from there!" he demanded of two Silver Corridor footmen whose names Elias couldn't immediately remember.

"Oh, just let her speak. What are you afraid of?" the woman who had spoken from the front of the crowd earlier asked the Glorifier.

After a wave of concurrences streamed out from all around her, Elias could see a foreign uncertainty in the shirtless preacher's eyes. The footmen tried to comply with his commands anyway but were rebuffed by the inebriation-induced courage in most of the gathered crowd.

"Come down!" the Glorifier demanded once more, trying to reclaim some semblance of authority.

"I think I'll stay up here for a bit, if you don't mind," Carrie told the man through a wicked grin.

The Glorifier's dark face flushed beet red. The footmen struggled to reach the billiard table.

Carrie smiled, naturally understanding how to cultivate a captive audience. "Do you have an answer to my question, sir?" she prodded the prophet. "When did he gain this status of perfect human in your mind? Was it after the third head he chopped off or the fourth? Huh? Which display of wanton bru-bru-brutality convinced you exactly?"

The crowd, and Elias in particular, were enraptured, hanging silently on her every word.

"When did all of you turn into these selfish cowards before me?" she demanded of the residents encircling her.

No one answered. None could meet her eyes, but neither were they turning from the message.

"Life is good up here, I know," Carrie continued. "And I know it isn't pleasant to thi... to th... to think about things on Earth right now. You all can remember the infection. I wasn't alive yet. I have no memory of any of that horror. I have no memories of Earth at all. Maybe tha...

maybe th-tha-that's why Earth is all I ever think about. Maybe my hope of go-go-going there one day is why I'm not so easily blinded as you folks."

She shamed them all, yet no one present protested.

"I'm not willing to drown my responsibilities and accept that it's just too much to ask to allow eighty-five perfectly healthy people—whom this station has mo-mo-more than enough room for—to come aboard and contr-contri... come aboard and contribute. None of us would go hungry if that were to happen. No one up here wo-w-would lose a single meal. Our output in the farms and Greenhouse will only increase when we have more people to chip in and work. As of now, a good b-bi-bit of each ha-ha-harvest is wasted. My m-mo-m... my mother worked in the Greenhouse before she was kill... before she... I've just always been inter-interested in everything about it. I read the reports they make available on the pocket tablets every m-m-month. I was just I-loo-looking at the data last week, but I can't recall the exact percentage. It's high though. I re-remember that. High enough that we shou-should all be ashamed of so-s-some of the hoarding we do up here... Bottom line is, more l-l-laborers means fewer fr-fruits and vegetables withering and rotting on the vine and in the Greenho... the Greenh-Greenhouse soil. More re-re-residents could only be a n-net positive for everyone."

"The kid's gotta point," a deep male voice called from the middle of the gaggle.

"I'm going to Branch 1 now," Carrie told them all. "I'm going to demand the Commander be reasonable and let those innocent human beings out on our Lunar Dock join our civilization. They-th-th-they've as much right to be here as any of us. If I have to face the Witenagemot all on my own to do it, then I-I... then I will. But if you would all just come with me, none of us would have anything to fear."

She paused there to let the statement settle on the two hundred-odd intoxicated minds all about her. "The Commander is only one man, in the end, with only one axe. And the br... the bri... the bri-br-brig is already overcrowded as it is. It won't be as if we are demanding anything unreasonable. We need not violate any bylaw of the Ne-New Des... New Destiny Constitution. We have a right to demand answers of our Com-Co-Com... of our Commander. If we go there as one and ask that representatives of the Bruderschaft be allowed to come aboard and negotiate so we may learn the truth of them, as well as demand the priest be freed from his un-unlaw... from his unlawful arrest, then how could any rational and honest person deny us? The Steward, at least, is a man of reason, isn't he?"

"He's always saying as much, anyways," a light and tipsy voice joked.

"Then let's go to them now. Come with me and let's ask them to be reasonable together. Please, my fellow res-res-residents, please," Carrie appealed to them with a burning sweetness in her voice and manner that could melt glaciers. "Let's just ask for a chance to talk. Just a chance to find out if those are our fellow hu-hu-humans out there or not. Stand with me, and we've nothing to fear."

Silence was her only answer. It lasted for eternity, it seemed, long enough to send Elias' heart plunging into his stomach anyway.

Then a man's voice bellowed from the back of the room, "Lead on then, kid," he said, with a near-full beer stein raised up high over the crowd for emphasis.

Agreements poured in like someone flicked a switch. The Glorifier's deep, anguished wails were drowned out in the chorus. Elias leapt down from his billiard table and strode over to help his little sister off hers. Footman Baines managed to get a hand on his shoulder, but Tessa shoved him away before he could get a firm grip. The suddenly excited and redemptive crowd took care of him and the other six footmen after that. Tessa and he strode one to either side of Carrie every step from the Billiard Lounge to just outside Branch 1's archway, lending her a hand all the while to compensate for her missing crutch.

CHAPTER 8
THE COMMANDER

There had been more action aboard station over the last twelve hours than over the previous five or six years combined. The Commander hadn't needed to make so many decisions or interrogate so many prisoners or plot so many ambushes in any one week since the Witen's dawn as he had on this day. So he needed his music. He needed a few minutes of privacy to find the right headspace. Father Boyd was not a man to take lightly, clearly. The clergyman had managed to convince the Commander and every last one of his underlings in the Witenagemot that he'd become an ailing shut-in. Not even the Steward had any notion that the man was hale and healthy and running some shadow resistance right beneath their noses.

Or maybe the Steward does know, and he's been keeping information from you? The doubt suddenly bubbled up over even the frenzied strumming crescendo of "Lazy Eye" by The Silver Sun Pickups blasting directly into his ears through the noise-canceling headphones currently covering both. The Commander had never fully trusted the Steward. The man was a lawyer in his old life; the Commander never forgot that. But for so long their goals had been aligned. They were useful to one another, and the Commander was content. But lately, for months really, years even, the Steward's ambitions and ideas had been a lot closer to perpendicular to his own as opposed to parallel. He never expressed these thoughts though. How could he? To whom? The Steward himself was about the closest thing he had to a confidant. The rest of the Witen were only too eager to pounce on any weakness they saw in leadership. They all had power designs of their own. He knew that. The Commander wasn't nearly as blind as they all hoped. So, for the most part, he'd just let the Steward be.

Only now, his procrastination was coming back to haunt him. The Steward had made his contrary opinion on how to handle the Bruderschaft known early and often. And he'd been of no real help in any of the interrogations so far. He seemed to be merely going through the motions. The Commander had no idea where the man's head truly was. He even allowed himself to imagine mutiny on the smarmy little clerk's mind. The Commander had thought he'd made his displeasure with his reluctance plain enough so his number-two man would at least start acting as if he was on board with the Commander's plans but apparently not. When the Steward explained that he had some vague work to attend to and wouldn't be participating in the priest's interrogation, the Commander knew the man was no longer to be trusted. He knew he was truly all alone then.

So, he needed his jams and his privacy. A love of music was just about the only characteristic that had transferred from Jasper Montrois into the Commander. It wasn't so much the lyrics anymore that did it for him; hearing about all those bullies getting their come-uppance in Jim Croce songs, for instance, wasn't exactly moving his needle these days. It was more the emotions in the chords and melodies, the passion in the rhythm. The lyrics to any song might well be skatting gibberish for all he cared anymore. But when he needed to straighten himself out, tapping into the emotional memories entangled into each note of his favorite tunes was the one surefire way he knew of accomplishing the task.

Therefore, when he spotted Supervisor Addison leaning his thin frame against the wall of the Grand Alleyway across from where the Commander currently paced and swayed along to his music just outside the brig, he was instantly annoyed. He shot the interloper a scowl to show his displeasure. It chased the loitering supervisor away the instant the gangling fool felt the glare, but the mood was ruined. The Commander ripped his headphones off and tossed them to the parquet floor. *Fuck this bastard anyway,* he thought of Father Boyd.

If he tries to get smart, I'll break his fucking face, he decided while punching in the code to the brig's hatchway.

Six footmen snapped to attention when the hatch swished open.

The Commander marched past all six in no more than ten strides, arriving in front of the second to last cell on the left-hand side of the narrow hall. "Has he spoken at all?" he asked his footmen while staring down the closed cell hatch.

"No, sir, n-n-not that we heard, anyways, Commander," the tall hawk-faced footman nearest the cell nervously answered.

Giving the smallest of nods, he set about dialing the cell hatch code. Father Boyd's girth made the room beyond look even smaller than it already was. The big bastard was locked down tight to a steel chair in the center of the otherwise empty cell, his hands strapped atop each armrest and his shins tied to the chair's front legs. He wasn't struggling, but his eyes were sure wild. The Commander was glad to see it. The man was clearly nervous. He obviously had a lot of secrets to protect. *Well, well, well, I wonder just what I'll learn about my station tonight*, he pondered silently as he stooped through the low hatch.

"Hello, Father," he said, after moving to within a foot of the priest and standing silently before him with crossed arms for at least a full minute. "Been awhile."

Boyd looked up then. His eyes were no longer frantic, no longer calculating, but neither were they nervous nor afraid; they were petulant and pitying. The look begged to be slapped from the traitor's fat face, but the Commander resisted. He only stared down in silence, waiting for his prisoner to speak.

"Jasper," Boyd finally said, inclining his head in polite greeting.

The Commander did slap him then. He could not let the interrogation start off with such disrespect. Boyd would give the Commander his proper dues. He would say his name, or he'd never speak again. "That ain't my name," he told the priest before another slap clapped down on the sinful holy man's opposite cheek. "Say my name," the Commander demanded, after the priest's eyes rolled back down and lost their glaze.

"Why?" Boyd asked a question instead of complying. "What the hell do you get out of it? When did you become so vain? Huh? When did the monster overtake you? I mean, for god's sake, Jasper, you just murdered an innocent man. You strangled a good man to death with your bare fucking hands no more than thirty minutes ago, and you expect me to offer some respect for you after this? Do you think I'm anything like you, anywhere near as broken? Huh? Really, please tell me. I truly want to know. How does a man ever become as pathetically broken as you?"

A mere slap would not do. A stronger response was necessary. The Commander stepped into a jab straight into the clergyman's thick gut. Boyd crumpled around the blow as best as his restraints allowed. After two follow-up jabs that the Commander managed to land in just about the same exact location, the priest was spitting up phlegm between moans and gasps.

"One way or another, you're gonna wind up telling me everything you been up to these past years, and you ain't gonna leave out a single detail," he explained in a reasonable voice to the pitiful resistance leader bent over in the chair. "Now, I'm happy to keep punching and smacking and snapping bones for as long as you like, but you *will* give me everything in the end. Know that. Defiance is useless. You'll fold in the end. They all do. There is always another bone to break, another nail or tooth to pull, or eye to gouge. So just save yourself the useless agony, why don't ya? Let's not waste time here. I want names. Tell me everyone who knows about you, everyone who's been lying to me, every last son of a bitch you've ever even so much as thought about plotting or scheming with. I want them all... But first, say my fucking name."

"Fuck you, Jasper," the priest croaked through his pain.

The Commander lost it then. He saw red and started swinging. When he finally stopped his assault and his crimson fog lifted, the full extent of the damage he'd done left him a bit shocked. Boyd's face was battered and torn. Both eyes were swollen. Gashes dripped blood from both cheeks and two separate wounds on his forehead. He couldn't tell if he'd knocked loose any teeth from the man, but a bloody fat lip was more than evident. Boyd hadn't lost consciousness, however. Even as the Commander watched, the battered man spat blood between groans.

"Wow, what a witty response from such a brave man," Boyd spluttered between spits and wheezes. "Untie me, why don't ya, you fragile fucking fascist bastard? Let's find out just how tough you really are."

"Oh, you think you're so brave, do ya?" the Commander shot back. "Hiding away in the tunnels don't sound too brave to me. I don't remember you making any attempt to stop me from strangling that treacherous module pilot friend of yours. You barely even protested the entire time I was squeezing the life from your laughable little rebellion's foot soldier, not near loud enough to catch my attention and make me stop, anyhow. You let him die. *You* got that man killed tonight, not me. You had your chance to fight me during the Final Tournament too, but you stayed silent because you're the one true coward in this room, and both of us know it. So quit your fucking petty defiance and... Say. My. Name!" He ended with a shout and a slap.

"Okay, *bitch*. There, I said it, your true name," Boyd sneered through his pain.

"You want more, Boyd? Really?" the Commander taunted his prisoner. "I'll beat your ass up and down this cell all day and night and never break a sweat. If that's what you want, keep running your mouth."

"You are nothing. Just an ignorant bully snatching lunch money because Daddy's mean at home. You're a goddamn blundering fool," Boyd told him, spitting a thick glob of phlegmy blood at the Commander's feet. "Where is your sidekick? Huh? Don't you normally leave the thinking to the Steward? All you understand is violence. All else is a mystery to an ape like you. You're out of your depth here, Jasper, 'cause nothing you could ever do to me will get me to talk. All your strength is useless here. You are nothing. So go on now, run and find your little pet so he can do your thinking for ya."

The Commander snarled then, though he wished he hadn't. He had no desire to let the man see that his taunts had affected him, but Boyd's cocky, undaunted disdain was simply more than he could stomach. The rage had to go somewhere. If he aimed it at the bound clergyman once more, he'd end up killing him before he'd learned a damn thing. So he shouted and snarled and smacked the cell walls.

"You've lost the station, Jasper," Boyd told him as he raged. "No one buys your vision bullshit. No one believes you anymore. The people are wise to your impotence, Jasper Montrois, husband of Carrie and father of Roxanna. You have lost. Beating me won't change that now."

Bellowing, the Commander grasped the ring and pinky fingers of Boyd's left hand. With a squeeze and a jerk, he snapped both appendages. The priest wailed in pain.

The Commander leaned in close to get a good look at the torment in the man's eyes. "How many more?!" He shouted the question an inch from Boyd's bleeding and swollen face. "Huh?! How many more shall I break?!"

With that, he moved on to the middle and index fingers. Before the priest could capitulate, he snapped both of those as well. Boyd's pain-soaked wails grew louder. The Commander moved in closer, nearly touching noses with the tortured traitor. Tears began welling in Boyd's eyes as the Commander gripped his left thumb and prepared it for destruction as well.

The Commander was certain Boyd was about to beg for mercy. He would have bet the farm that the man was less than a heartbeat away from calling out, "Please, Commander, stop. I'll tell you everything. Please."

Unfortunately, the footman poking his head into the room and clearing his throat forestalled the confession. "Commander sir, the Steward says come quick," the hawk-faced footman explained his intrusion in a rush. "There's a crowd gathering in the Grand Rotunda again, sir, a big one."

"What do they need me for? Get some fucking footmen together and clear them the hell out," the Commander shouted with seething frustration.

"They won't disperse, sir," the footman said, his eyes fixed on the slab floor. "The Steward don't want to give the order to use weapons. There's too many of 'em, he says, sir. They're all drunk too, Commander. The Steward thinks they marched straight from the Billiard Lounge."

"Of course it's a bunch of drunks," the Commander snapped back. "Who else would be up this time of night?"

The nervous footman plainly didn't know how to respond. His bewilderment sapped some of the rage from the Commander's shoulders, and a great deal more calmly, he asked, "How many of these drunks are there exactly?"

"Not sure, sir," the young footman answered. "The Steward was saying an estimate of two hundred to two hundred fifty over the comms earlier. Could be more by now, Commander."

"*Two hundred?*" the Commander skeptically inquired. "That's nearly a third of the goddamn station. There can't be two hundred of the bastards."

"Well, reports all night long have said that the Billiard Lounge had at least that many in there. Word was most hadn't left yet either. If they all came down... well..." The footman trailed off, leaving the Commander to grapple with the implications.

"Very well, footman," he said, turning from the priest with a sigh. "Inform the Steward I'm on my way." He could let the man know personally with a simple call on his pocket tablet, but he preferred not to speak to the Steward just now, if he could avoid it. Plus, it was better to delegate orders as often as possible, especially now. The people had to know who made the commands. They had to be eager to jump if and when the Commander snapped his fingers.

Sparing not a single glance back at the whimpering priest, he stooped through the cramped cell. "You six, with me," he called to the footmen standing at attention in the hallway. Close that cell." He stopped to point back from whence he came. "Ensure the rest are secured as well. We'll be back soon, I expect, but close 'em all up anyhow."

"On it, Commander," two of the six footmen responded in unison, though all six went about the duty.

It was a quick housekeeping chore, and once done, he led them out into the Grand Alleyway. The Commander had wanted to berate the Steward for inflating the size of the gathered crowd, and so, arriving at the threshold of Branch 1's archway, was disappointed to discover that the footman's relayed estimates were most likely an undervaluation, if anything. With no overt reason to unleash his venom on his number-two man, he offered up a simple silent nod.

"They're demanding to be heard, sir. Calling for you specifically," the Steward explained in a raised voice barely discernable above the drunken roar of the mass of citizens before them. "We've issued order after order, command after command, but they just won't listen. They've only grown rowdier and rowdier, even in the short time since

I've arrived on site. I've been reluctant to give the footmen the order to start taking prisoners and swinging their clubs. We are vastly outnumbered here, Commander. Things could go bad for us very fast."

"Is this every last footmen we got?" The Commander growled the question without looking the Steward's way, instead keeping his eyes fixed on the pulsating mob before him. The quick headcount he tallied while striding toward the madness in the Grand Rotunda had come up with no more than two dozen footmen onsite.

"The rest have all been put on emergency alert and ordered here immediately," the Steward explained the discrepancy. "But most will be coming from their quarters across the rotunda. It could be half an hour before we are fully staffed, and even then they'll have us three to one, sir. I... I... sir, I think it's time... Well, they want to speak with you, sir, and I... I... I think that's our best option now, Commander."

"Give in to their demands?" The Commander scoffed, still staring straight ahead. "That's your advice, Steward? Perhaps you need some sleep, my friend," he suggested, finally turning to face the squat little man.

"Sir?" the Steward managed through a mask of confusion.

"Your advice all day today has been suspect, Steward," the Commander told him plainly. "Perhaps you're not thinking straight. Perhaps you push yourself too hard. Maybe you oughta go take a nap."

"I'll not deny I need a good long rest, sir," the Steward said, his face now composed. "But I fail to see how any amount of sleep will ever get me to believe it is in humanity's best interest that the Witenagemot end here and now in a shower of blood. These people have been drinking all night. They've been riled up somehow. They've got nearly a decade's worth of claustrophobic anxiety built up and begging for a release. We cannot win here, sir. Not by force. Just speak to them. Find out what they want. We need not hand over the keys to the Branch. We can give an inch and still be on firm ground. Perhaps their demands aren't all that unreasonable. Please, sir," the Steward shifted to more conciliatory tones, "please, for the sake of the Witen, just hear them out."

The Commander stared down his second in command, the architect of the Witenagemot and the New Destiny Constitution, for what felt like a long time. The jumbled voices of the inebriated crowd melded together, fading to nothing so much as soft white noise in his mind.

When the beads of sweat pouring down the Steward's face became evident even from where he stood six or seven feet from the man, the Commander finally answered him, "I will hear them out, Steward, I will. But know that I can imagine how this night could've unfolded very differently, if only you would have woken up and offered me your unquestioned support from the damn start."

The Steward seemed to shrink. His eyes went to the parquet floor. His shoulders hunched and twisted away. The Commander forgot him altogether, striding two firm and dignified strides toward the crowd and crossing the imaginary boundary that had sprung up between the line of footmen across the Branch's threshold and the two hundred-plus residents facing them in the Grand Rotunda. A hush rippled through the drunken mass. The crowd parted before him. A child came hobbling down the opened lane.

He knew her. A memory struck him, one as often buried as it treacherously resurfaced. It had been a day of weakness. A day worth forgetting. From nowhere, a trapped anxiousness had suddenly struck him one average day some years back. He'd found himself compelled to escape his own security detail. On a whim, he'd snuck back to his quarters to collect the book, the tiny red book of poetry that Sagal had given him before he... *before*... *No, I won't think about that*, he silently declared. But he couldn't stop the memories now. He saw the young Sagal girl as clearly in his mind's eye as he did in the flesh before him. He even remembered the feelings, the melancholy and the confusion, the need to return the ratty old book, the need to meet Perry's child, though he recalled no clear rationalization for the impulses. *Why her? Why this child? Why now? Why is she even among these alcoholic morons?*

"We've some concerns, Commander, and we demand you hear us," Carrie Roxanna Sagal freed him from his troubling and distracting thoughts after hobbling on one crutch past her sea of supporters to face him down in no-man's land.

"You'd all have a child speak for you? Ya oughta be ashamed. You are the last human beings alive. Don't be such an embarrassment. Show some goddamn spine. Put this kid to bed and send out your true representative. C'mon, I won't bite. I promise to hear you. I have no wish to upset any of you. It's my duty to protect you, and I've been doing nothing but since the day I won my title. I'm more than happy to listen to your concerns. I ask only that you try and trust my answers. I don't know how you've all allowed just one strange day to corrupt your hearts and assume I'm not forever acting in our best interest, but I'll forgive your weakness. You're only human, after all. We all are," he qualified when a low groan murmured forth from the crowd. "I will listen. Just stop being cowards and send forth someone I can truly deal with, on level terms."

"I am a citizen of your Witenagemot, Commander," Carrie said after no one in the crowd moved to comply. "I have as much right to be heard as any other. I've read your Constitution enough to know that much, Steward," she added with a scathing glance at the shrunken clerk. "We w-w-w-want to know about the Bruderschaft. We demand you let representatives from their sh... from their sh-sh-ship come aboard. Let them come before us and tell us face to f-f-face who they are and what they've seen. We all deserve that much. And we demand you do this now, b-b-before it's too late for those poor people out there on our Lunar Dock. And w... And w-w-we demand you release the priest. He has been an unsung champion for all of us, the forgotten citizens of your despotic Witen, for years and years. We demand you give him back to us. We demand you give all of them back," the child finished with a confidence that brought on a cheer of approval from her supporters.

"I really, truly do not understand this. I'm actually hurt," he told the crowd as he stepped away from the child to face the rambunctious drunks. The Commander realized, begrudgingly, that the Steward was right; if they started bashing skulls and taking prisoners the temporarily courageous residents would overwhelm them eventually. He wasn't ready to throw his rule away quite yet. So, he had to play this just right. He was never much for speeches, but he knew he'd have to walk a tightrope with this one. *Where the hell is that lunatic bastard Glorifier when you need him*? he asked himself, just seconds before spotting the bare-chested wild man lurking at the back of the mob, surrounded by his disciples, all of whom were hanging their heads. *The zealous nut already tried and failed to convince 'em. Well, shit, that don't bode well for me*, he thought before mentally shrugging his shoulders.

"How can you all still doubt me?" He began with a question that shifted the guilty burden onto them. "Our glorious Witenagemot is the fairest and most honest government ever devised by mankind. It holds the purest, most indisputable authority. You all were there, I'm sure. You witnessed me win my imperial right. It was I whom the fates chose on that long ago day. I was the one left unchallenged. Don't forget so easily, my friends, my brothers and sisters, my people. Don't be led by some mere child into forgetting that, since that righteous day of days, I have treated you all like the treasures you are. I have protected you, given you every luxury you could possibly want, and all the while demanded little more than a few hours work a week and a bit of respect for the sacrifice of every Witenagemot officer, supervisor, and footman. That you could believe that I, or any other representative of the Witen, would lie to you all through the Glorifier about the sacred vision the fates bestowed upon me is simply shameful. It breaks my fucking heart!" he shouted at the silent sea of boozers. "But sadly, obviously you do have your doubts. I mean, here you are voicing them, after all, albeit through the shield of a poor small child, but here you all are, nonetheless. So, despite my foreknowledge and despite my better judgement and the judgement of the Witen council, let me propose a compromise. If you agree, you need say nothing, only turn and head on home, and I can forget you ever defied me."

"We aren't here for compromise," Carrie screeched over the rumbling voices.

The Commander ignored her, only raised his arms for silence. They were still his flock, he saw with heartening certainty. He was still their shepherd. Quick as ever, all murmuring ceased.

"I will allow three representatives from this Bruderschaft to come aboard so we might learn the truth of them. They will be heavily guarded with an enforced quarantine of ten feet around them at all times though. I will not risk the security of this station for your drunken whims alone, no matter how many of you stand before me. If it turns out they aren't carriers, that somehow I misinterpreted my vision, then I will indeed let them all come aboard."

A burst of cheering came swift on the heels of that pronouncement. Another raised hand from the Commander cut short the jubilation.

"Provided, they all agree to become law-abiding citizens of the Witenagemot," he stipulated. "If they prove dishonorable and decide they value their useless freedom more than a secure sanctuary in which to live and grow a family, if they feel submission to the Witenagemot and its New Destiny Constitution is just a bridge too far for them, then I have an alternative solution I'll propose. But I won't just send them away. I promise you all that. I see that you all will never believe anything I tell you about their intentions now if that were to happen."

"You're goddamn right," an unsettlingly familiar male voice, young and strong, boomed out from somewhere amidst the tightly compacted crowd.

"Very well, very well," the Commander said, somehow staying calm in the face of the wildly insubordinate shout, "I understand you are all a bit lost and full of doubts. But hear me, please. What I say now I will hold to. You have my oath. If these Bruderschaft folk are fully human, I will propose they come aboard and live in lawful peace as citizens of the Witenagemot, same as every last one of you," he said, waving his arm to encompass the entire crowd. "But, as I say, if they aren't partial to disbanding their pathetic little brotherhood, if they feel that it's only fair that they get the same shot to rule up here that we all had, then I will offer them that chance as well."

Bemusement mingled with a bit of fear in the crowd's murmuring now. Each were coming to realize the implications of his words in their own time. He let their agitation stew for a bit but broke in before he lost them.

"Fear not, I'm not imagining another Final Tournament, if that's what you're all thinking. The Final Tournament was the *final* tournament, after all. How could there be another? No, I've something different in mind. So, as I was saying, if they aren't infected monsters and the past nine years on Earth hasn't ravaged their wits, they will see the good sense in coming aboard as honest and productive citizens of the Witen. If they aren't monsters but are nonetheless still mad though and they feel the Bruderschaft should rule this station, then

I'm sure they will see my counteroffer as more than fair. Whatever they decide, we will broadcast their response to the entire station. I swear it. Perhaps after you see the three reps come aboard with your own eyes and hear their response over the station's PA, this madness of drunken doubt that has gripped you all today will end, and you will trust me again. For now, know that you have my word, as well as clear and obvious markers that will indicate whether or not I lie. Let this be enough to satisfy you and go on home. Sleep it off."

"And what about the priest and Maisie and all the others?" Carrie asked with desperate pleading.

"What about them?"

"Welllll," Carrie stretched out the word, clearly thrown off her game, "what do you mean t-t-to do with them?"

"The priest and his friends, as well as your sister and her fellow terrorists, along with every last one of the rioters taken into custody earlier this evening are no more than simple criminals," he added, staring the young Sagal girl bearing his infinitely lamented wife's sweet name square in the eyes. "They will remain where they are until we have time to organize their trials."

"No, you can't! They just wanted you to talk to the Bruderschaft, and you've agreed t-t-to do that. So you can let them go. They are n-n-no more threat to you now, surely."

The Commander said nothing, acting instead as though she hadn't even spoken. The crowd got the hint.

"Wait, don't... he's... h-h-he hasn't... wait..." Carrie harangued a thoroughly cowed crowd now steadily drifting toward Branch 4 in large droves, all the while grumbling barely snatched acceptances of the Commander's eloquent compromise.

The Commander didn't wait around to make sure they all indeed dispersed, leaving said task to his underlings. After calling to the Steward, "Gather the council in my office in thirty minutes, the officers especially," he turned around and marched back down the Grand Alleyway.

Having no desire to return to his interrogation just then, he set his sights on his private office, or more precisely, the full bottle of dark-red wine in the bottom drawer of his mahogany desk. He should have twenty or thirty minutes to drink in peace before the councilors arrived, if he hustled. *Maybe I could even kick back with a bit of music*, he hoped, pining for just a few minutes of pressure-free me-time while knowing all too well that the Commander of the Witenagemot is forever fated to be denied such simple pleasures.

BOYD

The pain was not ebbing. Raymond Boyd was certain it would last forever. *Or at least until I set these fucking fingers*, he thought, bemoaning the futility of the hope. The priest knew his mental energy would be put to much better use meditating on redirecting focus from the four busted fingers on his left hand, but it didn't stop him from praying for some cessation from the torment. Even knowing with every last fiber of his rational mind that there had never been an omniscient deity listening to mankind's trillions of prayers over its expansive existence couldn't prevent a man from crying out in a moment of true agony in the hopes that somewhere, in some tucked-away corner of the infinite cosmos, there was some agent with the means and desire to both hear and respond to his plea.

The pain was that large. He didn't even realize he was no longer alone in the tiny cell until Supervisor Addison bent down in front of him to lock eyes with Boyd's hanging head.

"Fuck me, he sure messed you up," the scraggle-bearded gold-coat croaked.

"My f-f... my fingers, y-you-you gotta set my fingers," Boyd pleaded as best the pain allowed.

"Your *fingers?* What the hell are you... Oh," Addison huffed, finally spotting the priest's mangled hand. "What am I... I don't know nothing about setting fingers... I... What am I..."

"Just grab the fucking things and set them straight!" Boyd shrieked his impatience.

"Okay, okay, jeez. What the hell am I supposed to know about first aid, for god's sake?" the supervisor muttered, reaching a hand out to attend the task.

"Just grab 'em and pull! Please."

With the timidity of a 60's prom queen touching a cockroach, the supervisor squeezed all four fingers at once and gave a strangely high-pitched yelp as he snapped them all back into place. Immediately on the heels of the snap, Boyd released a stream of profanity between spits of bloody phlegm.

"I'm sorry. I'm sorry. What the hell am I supposed to know about first aid? I only did what you said," Addison defended himself.

"Oh, just shut the hell up already!" Boyd snapped after running dry of curses. "What the fuck took you so damn long? I heard the bastard take all the brig's footmen with him. I've been sitting in here in pure agony for hours."

"The Commander only left to deal with the protesters five minutes ago."

"Well, you try telling time with four dislocated fingers."

"I came when I could," Addison said, crossing his arms. "I shouldn't have even risked coming to see you at all. The Commander saw me all by myself loitering down by the brig with no conceivable reason for me to be there. Hell, he probably already knows. Me coming in here all alone is probably just some fucking trap," he babbled in a nervous rush, darting glances behind him every other word. "The bastards are probably about to come storming in at any moment."

"I said shut the hell up," Boyd ordered, sitting back in his chair after taking his first pain-free breaths in minutes, relatively speaking. "I don't want to hear your whining, Jeremy. I told you long ago I never want to hear you whine ever again. Nothing's changed."

"I've never failed you. I've given you everything you've ever asked," Jeremy Addison indignantly relayed. "You have no idea how close I came—how close *you* came by implication—from being caught. You would never believe me if I told ya how many times our fates rested on some chance bit of luck. You've been sitting down there in your comfy Clubhouse while I'm up here taking all the risks."

"You ain't alone. You've never been alone."

"Oh, yeah? Well, where are the others then?" Addison asked, spinning in place and shrugging his shoulders at their apparent absence. "You talk a big game, Priest, but here you are, with only me to help you. And you start by telling me to shut up and quit whining? Why don't I just walk right back out of here then, if you want to act like that?"

"Do that, and I sing the Commander a sweet song of every last one of your mountain of treasons, going all the way back to you and that pedo-bastard Mikkelson colluding together to kidnap Maisie behind the Witen's back," Boyd threatened.

"You don't know nothing about that! It's all lies, whatever you might've heard. You oughta know better than most by now how much everyone up here lies."

"Yeah, the rumors are just wrong when they concern you, right? Just like you and your pal Naughton had nothing to do with Clara Christie's murder."

"What? Wha... wha... I... That wasn't... She drowned. The woman was just some fucking alcoholic jackass who wandered too close to the damn river."

"Bullshit."

"That's what the official report says."

"I wipe my ass with you and your Witen's official reports!" Boyd shouted, growing both angry and distracted. They had no time to tread this old ground. Boyd understood full well the man was lying with every other word. He knew, as strongly as a man can ever know anything without being able to outright prove it, that Addison had played his part in that poor girl's epic demise. Right now though, Boyd did not care to be reminded that he had to work with people he'd sooner see rotting in some dungeon somewhere for all eternity. Boyd needed this jackass now. So he took a breath.

"Even if there was foul play there, it didn't have shit to do with me. I've told you that. My alibi for that night is airtight. You already dealt with the man you guess had some involvement. So let it end with the *accident* you arranged for Supervisor Naughton. I don't really care either way. I just don't want to have to listen to this shit about that stupid drunk bitch ever again. I had no part in it. And anyways, you would never rat me out," Addison said, defiant as Boyd had ever seen him. "You would lose 'em all then. You know that. All your other contacts would be cutting deals to save their own skin once they hear you've turned on me."

"Maybe," Boyd allowed after a considerable effort fighting back a shout. "But if it gets to the point where I see it all burning down no matter what I say, then you best believe I will give you up. I've had to grub pretty low in the dirt often enough these past years, I'll not deny it, but protecting your sicko perverted ass is the thing I am least proud of. So, tempt me, Jeremy, taunt me, go right ahead. There is only so much shit a man can stomach."

"Fuck you, Boyd. You're just some failed preacher-man, probably even screwed a bunch of young altar boys yourself. Don't play high and mighty with me. Especially not now, not when you need me," Addison countered, a petulant grin hinting on his lips.

"Just cut me loose already," Boyd said, looking away from the slimy supervisor standing before him.

"I can't do that."

It wasn't the answer Boyd was expecting, despite the man's petty posturing. "Why the hell not?" He growled the question.

"Because then they'll know someone on the inside helped ya. Only councilmembers have the brig codes. They'll just check the ID log on the door codes, and I'm dead ten minutes later."

"You're dead faster still if you don't get me the fuck out of here."

"I can't," Addison said, almost squealing, "not now anyways. I only came to talk. I figured you might have a plan in mind, one that ain't as stupid as the two of us just strolling out the fucking front door. Oh, Christ!" He did squeal then. "Your fingers, I... I shouldn't have... oh god, I shouldn't have fixed 'em. They'll know someone came to see you."

"Relax, Jeremy. The Commander's mind is far from here. The man won't notice. I doubt he'll be back tonight, anyhow. If he asks tomorrow, I'll say the medic set them. I'm sure the evil bastards have one set to make a house call on us poor doomed souls in these here cells before the morning."

"Ya think?" Addison gushed. "He really won't be back tonight? But... but how can... You can't know that for sure."

"No, I can't," Boyd agreed, "but you and I are gonna take the risk. So, go on, sneak back out of here and find Carrie Sagal for me."

"The little crippled kid?" the greaseball incredulously asked.

"Yes, you fucking dim-witted sleazeball, she's the brilliant little girl that incidentally happens to be afflicted with cerebral palsy."

"What the hell do you want me to find her for!? I can't be running off on any stupid time-wasting nonsense errands now, Priest. The Commander will have you and your pals hanging from a desert gibbet sooner than you think if we don't think of a better plan, and fast. I'll do what I can to get you out of here, within reason anyways. I'll do that much, but then you and I are even. I'll be square then. That's more than a big enough favor to pay off whatever I owe you, no matter what you think I might've been a part of. After you're out, getting off this station is up to you. I suggest you beg the Bruderschaft for a lift home. I don't really care what you do, so long as you don't get caught again. Even though, if you do, if you really want to stay the man of honor you pretend you are, then you won't rat me out after the Commander drags you right back here."

"Fine, Jeremy, fine. We'll be square, though I'll never take an eye off you. I'll never trust you. Maya Angelou taught me to believe someone when they show you who they are. I'll never forget what you are, Jeremy, but I'll keep your name secret, provided you get me and my wife and Maisie and everyone else in these cells the hell out of here." Boyd stopped to spit out the blood that seemed to be filling his mouth on a constant loop. "And to do that, Jeremy," he continued, taking a deal of joy in the sneer that crossed the face of the man in the black-trimmed suit coat nervously pacing before him, "to do that, first, I need you to find Carrie Sagal. She knows how to find my Clubhouse. Tell h—"

"Ya know," Addison cut in to complain, "I would know how to find the place too, and we coulda saved ourselves a fucking step here if you weren't so high and mighty and ever invited me in there for one of the thousand meetups you've made me sneak around for over the years."

"I chose right not to trust you that far, Jeremy, clearly." The retort increased the pathetic man's pacing. "Now, as I was saying, have Carrie go to my place. Tell her to find the list I keep in the green notepad on the far left of the top shelf of the bookcase. In there, she'll find the names of everyone who owes me anything. Tell her to use her wits. I trust her completely. Tell her that. Tell her to use whoever she needs on that list to organize a prison break. Tell her not to dare come herself though, ya hear?" he demanded. "That's important now. Tell her I don't want to see her anywhere near this place when it goes down. You tell her I said that's a goddamn order. Make sure she understands. I'm holding you accountable if she disobeys. Ya hear?"

"Yeah, yeah, I hear," Addison confirmed, ceasing his nervous pacing.

"Good. Go on then, run off, and do as I say. I'll be in here warming up my singing voice in case you decide to fail me."

"I'll find the brat, I swear it," Addison promised unconvincingly.

"Tell her to act fast. You're right about the Bruderschaft. That might well be our one shot. And they could be gone any moment."

"Alright, alright, I'm on it," Addison said, turning to duck out of Boyd's cramped cell.

"Wait!" Boyd shouted the man to a halt. "Tell Carrie to meet me and her sister and the others in Branch 2. Tell her to wait just inside the access hatch outside the Terminal until one of us opens it. Okay? You got all that?"

"Yeah, I got it," the Witen councilmember whined.

"Don't forget now: the access hatch just outside the Terminal."

"Okay, okay, I got it," Addison said, stooping out of the cell. "You best be one damn good liar, if they ask ya about them fingers," he insisted from the narrow hall with a self-righteous disdain wholly lacking in either his tone or body language only seconds before. "And you best keep that tongue of yours inside that fat mouth. If I suspect, even for a moment, that you've sold me out, I'll toss that crippled little shit out an airlock."

Slowly, Boyd's head turned toward the supervisor lurking beneath the harsh lights of the jailhouse's lone hallway. His gaze pinned the gangly rat-faced creep in place. Boyd never said a word. The look was enough. Addison's knees seemed to buckle, and only then did he march out of sight, presumably to find the eight-year-old genius to whom Father Raymond Boyd had tied all his hopes.

INTERLUDE
DORIS THE DAMNED

INFECTION EVENT: DAY 57

Doris Demeter, that had been her name. She remembered everything about the fast-paced life Doris Ruthann Demeter, DDS, had lived, except the feeling of warmth. For months and months now or centuries perhaps or infinite eternities even, she had been cold. Her body did not display the signs, however. There were no frostbitten fingers, no white pallor to her flesh, and though it had been some time since last she'd accidentally glimpsed her reflection, there had been no red flush on her puffy cheeks. Instead her skin was gray in color. Her fingers, though missing several nails, showed no sign of rot nor black decay, and her once beautiful face had no color beside the same ash-gray as the rest of her body, or at least those parts exposed by torn and missing clothing.

For the first eternity trapped inside herself, Doris had fought. She struggled, unceasingly, day and night, to run away and find a fire and a thick blanket; she struggled just to move a damn muscle really, to exert any of her own will over her body. Never once did she come close. Never did so much as a finger twitch at her command. The battle might have been worth fighting; the struggle against the ungodly torment might have been endurable, if only she ever even slightly felt herself gaining any ground. All her efforts had proved useless though. Dr. Doris Demeter was locked out of her own body. Though, sadly, not from the pain and the cold, nor the thirst and the hunger. No, those regrettable attributes of the human condition remained to her.

True hope vanished for Doris some time ago now, hope for warmth and an end to pain anyway. Now, in this second endless epoch of her awful existence, all she dared long for was the foreign intelligence in her mind and controlling her body to elect her as the next group sacrifice. She did not kid herself. Days of endless torture trapped inside one's body as it was taken over and used for horror and violence sufficient enough to make the devil blush would make anyone a realist. She knew being selected for the sacrifice promised pain, ludicrous, excruciating pain, but it also promised an end. Nothingness, sweet nothingness, had become a prize beyond measure to Doris Demeter.

She had been forced to gulp down the bodily fluids and choke down chunks of flesh and organs of a sacrifice enough times to know that at least when the feast was through, there was not enough left of the poor soul to rise and rejoin the horde. It didn't work that way. They weren't mindless undead zombies. Whatever they were was far worse. They were still alive, all of them. Doris felt every last cool breeze and hungry gnashing bite and was completely cognizant of everything happening around her. She just simply had no control over her experience.

Doris had heard the invader in her mind, had felt it call to her, felt her body respond to its commands, and she assumed, from context alone, having no way to speak or even look any other of her counterparts in the eye, that the same went for the others. She thought they must too feel the pull to be near the invading intelligence and that they too recognized the intelligence's source as emanating from a bull-chested middle-aged guy with wispy flaxen hair. Doris would've noticed the man even if her foreign body-driver had not radiated a sense of absolute loyalty throughout her mind upon first sight of him. Of all the unfortunates attached to her roaming horde, only the beefy blond man's skin was free of the gray tinge. His clothes alone among the vast group of infected remained intact and even relatively clean. Doris and the rest were covered in mud and filth and blood and guts and gristle and things that did not bear thinking about. It was only the clean blond man among them who ever abstained from the putrid sacrificial feasts. Nor had Doris ever seen him drinking the bodily fluids of one of her horde's countless innocent victims.

She knew the clean man with the smooth, unlined face and strange gray eyes was not human. Doris could taste the artificial flavor of his presence on the back of her tongue. Almost immediately though, she had known he was the driving force behind the infection, the bane of mankind. She knew the man who wasn't a man was evil incarnate, but she could not stop herself from obeying his every command. So, for going on a seeming millennia now, Doris had given up resisting his unconquerable control altogether. This was her new existence. There was no escaping. So, instead, she prayed for a dearth of uninfected targets to seek and destroy. The unman, the general of her horde, would have to select a sacrifice then.

Doris knew humans could live without water for about three days. The infection changed that, as it changed so many things. She knew it had turned the blood in her veins to a dark-red sludge, for instance. She'd seen her infected brethren's spilled enough to understand that much. Whatever other changes to her composition the infection made, it somehow increased the length of time a person could go without sustenance. But even still, Doris knew her thirst was reaching its maximum limit. The clean, pale-skinned leader would force them all to drink blood and bodily fluids and ingest some meat soon. And she fervently prayed to be the one chosen for that sacrifice.

Turning it over in her head as she swayed in the driving rain somewhere in the midst of her horde all grouped together in a small weedy park in some hick town in West Virginia, Doris even thought the invading intelligence may, in fact, actually have to select several sacrifices. No one in her horde had eaten or gulped fluids in days and days. They would all need to be fed, or else the mind-invader would see his precious horde start dropping dead en masse. Which might seem like a scenario worth hoping for, but Doris knew better by now. The inhuman invading intelligence did not make those types of mistakes. He might wait until the very last minute, but he would not let his horde die off. So, *the sacrifice*, that was her one last hope.

Her horde did have things a little easier of late, but easy was a relative term. They had stopped roaming. The mind-invader had started slowly pooling them together in a tight huddle in the modest park at least a week ago, though, admittedly, her grasp on the passage of time had been thoroughly skewed. But, for sure, they hadn't moved in several sun-cycles, unless she counted the gently rhythmic swaying the intelligence was forcing each of them to mimic. True, she was still cold in that park, and doubly so thanks to the fat drops of rain currently plopping incessantly atop her skull, but the bodies pressing close around her did lend some small measure of warmth. All such had been otherwise absent ever since that infected woman had clawed her across the belly three days after the infection began to spread. She and five friends had been caught by a horde of dozens as they were making their way on foot to what an emergency radio broadcast had told them was a makeshift refugee camp in D.C. Her friends had been killed while Doris had been made cold. The meager calefaction from the diseased bodies of her fellow hordesmen provided a minuscule improvement on that end. However, none of this relative relief was near enough to stop her wishing to be chosen. Right then, Doris Demeter was certain she would rather endure several bouts of being eaten alive by thousands of human automatons than another single second trapped inside herself in this never-ending hell.

The half-dozen-odd gunshots that suddenly echoed off the buildings surrounding the small park at the center of town eradicated that extremely tenuous and frail fragile hope for an end to her suffering. Doris had been a gray monster long enough to know that the crackle of gunfire meant healthy people; it meant live prey. The clean, unhuman leader of her sick horde would have them investigating those shots, as well the shrieking wail of one of her fellow infected that faintly reached her ears a few beats after the whizzing bullets' diminishing twang.

A shiver preceded his invasion. The intelligence seeped its invisible foreign presence into every last corner of her mind and body. She clearly registered the command it issued for her legs to start pumping but could do nothing to influence the appendages against the order. Dangerously dried muscles in her thighs and calves resented the instruction but obeyed regardless. The cries of pain they screamed into her useless mind with each step the invading intelligence demanded of them were powerless to stop the persistent tormented march. Doris could not even scream to release the agony. She could not so much as grit her teeth. She was paralyzed in a moving body and could do no more than simply endure. The torture would last until they found them, or until the untiring mind-invader gave up the search, or the sun exploded. Doris did not like to bet on which would come first.

She could not scream, but she could moan. They always moaned when hunting. Doris didn't know if it was their one limp exertion of will spewing out the lamentation or if it was some kind of byproduct of the invading-intelligence's unhuman mind connecting simultaneously with the entire horde; perhaps some overload glitch that forced them all to vocalize the electric fuzzy background noise of their unwelcome leader's strangely lifeless mind. Who could say? All Doris knew was she moaned and groaned every hunt and never at her own pace nor design. There was even some music in the miserable cacophony, if she listened close. A melody seemed to pop out after a time, like the sonic version of a magic-eye poster.

Doris tried not to listen close. She tried to take her mind somewhere else, anywhere else, it hardly mattered. The hunts were the worst. Knowing that all too soon she would have to feed. Soon the evil entity inside her skull would force her to strip the life from some poor soul a single bite at a time. No one ever fought back, least ways they were always done by the time Doris was forced to push and shove her way into the gory feast. Their screams were the worst part. Before any of Doris' fellow hordesmen got to them, when they still believed they had a chance to get away, their screams could bruise worse than any of the agonizing motions the invading intelligence put her body through.

Doris had no teeth left. She'd felt every last one break off, each as painful as the last, though it never stopped her biting just as hard on the next bite as the one before. She was reduced now to sucking the foul fluids of their prey, to slurping down ropes of intestines whole and never gagging despite desperately needing to. She in no way looked forward to her upcoming meal. *But at least I can stop walking when I eat*, the morbid thought crept up through the pain. She needed to cry but couldn't. Marching forward, step by excruciating step, was all there was and ever would be.

INTERLUDE

The unhuman commander of their consciousnesses drove his horde from somewhere in its center. Doris couldn't say where exactly; she couldn't turn her head to seek him out, but she felt he was close. Having nothing else to do but think about her endless pain, she counted the tightly compacted rows of her fellow infected ahead. They stretched out across the entire breadth of the city street. Doris figured she was somewhere in the fifteenth or sixteenth loose row of the cramped gaggle. She had no way to be sure, but based on all the people she'd glimpsed over the past days in that weedy park, she assumed there was something like another fifteen rows of her fellow infected behind her.

So many had joined them there that Doris had nearly been able to convince herself that infected humans were all there was left on Earth. It had been so long since they'd last seen any prey, especially not in anything like the groups they used to find them in. Today's gunshots told against that assessment, however. The horror of the hunts were not over yet. *Gunshots could be a good sign too though*, she reflected through the unceasing torment. She'd heard folks taking potshots at their horde more times than she could count, many of the luckier hordesmen had been killed by the firing, in fact. Not her though. Doris was condemned to the center of every pack. The bullets always ran dry by the time she reached the prey. There was no escape for her in that route.

Most folks were too terrified to think straight when the horde was on them, much less shoot straight. And there were just too many infected. Their feeble resistance never lasted long. Only, reflecting on the specific pacing of the shots, Doris could not recall an analogous confrontation exactly. *It could be a bunch of people with guns*, she thought, hope bubbling within her despite her best efforts at tempering expectations. *Maybe they'll have machine guns and bombs and... and... maybe there will be hundreds of them with thousands of bullets. Maybe I'll get to die today after all.*

When she got her first clear look at the fleeing healthy people responsible for those gunshots, some of her hopes were squashed. Though, by now, she was a veteran of disappointment, enough so as to refocus on what was actually encouraging about the seven racing souls spread out down the length of the cracked road before the horde. There weren't near as many as hoped, but they were well armed. They appeared professional, too, in a way Doris and her fellow hordesmen had never encountered. Six of the seven wore matching black trousers and blouses with identical black boots. The seventh was different—hunched, scruffy, and covered in filth, nothing like the others.

One of the black-clad six carried a corpse over one shoulder. Another jogged but a pace or two behind. The closest of their small crew faced the horde while sprinting backward up the road. Unaccountably, even as she turned the corner to gain a clear, unobstructed view, the smallest of the matching armed warriors ran full speed into a clothesline smash delivered by the largest member of the martial band. The last of the six stopped to gawk at the strange spectacle as the huge brute in the black tactical outfit placed a boot on the tiny man's ass and kicked. The clotheslined man scraped across the asphalt a good foot or two. The big man went in for the kill, but the whippy warrior woman beside him pulled him away before he could plant his fifth kick into the bleeding and rain-sodden little man's side. Shouts passed back and forth between the soldiers. Doris heard none of it, only saw their lips move. The moaning all around her, coupled with the pattering rain, drowned out all other noise.

Her horde closed in. The man hauling the corpse began to lag. The two pulling security behind him stopped to lend a hand when the bearer attempted to readjust his grim baggage. One even went so far as to transfer the load to his own shoulder. *Why don't they start shooting?* She screamed inside her head. She could get lucky. God knows she was way past due for a bit of good fortune. A bullet could clip her before they ran out. It wasn't impossible. The mob would still be numerous by then, for sure, but maybe enough of her fellow infected would be killed so that a path straight from one of the soldier's guns directly into her forehead could open up before the poor bastards were overtaken. It could happen. It was something, some hope at least. She did not want to have to eat these people. *Please, just start shooting already.*

She got her wish. A mass of infected emerged from just up the road. The invading intelligence had split the horde. This splinter group was appearing from a cross street twenty yards ahead of her and cutting off the three soldiers and their one dead friend from the rest of their crew. The three must've realized there was no outrunning the mob. As if in response to an unspoken order, the corpse bearer dropped his precious baggage as all three took up their semi-automatic rifles to fire precision shots at the horde closing in from front and back.

Her hordesmen fell one, two, even three at a time. The press before her was thinning. *Please just shoot me. Please*, she begged. *Get to the front!* Doris uselessly implored her paralytic limbs. The desire had no effect at altering her speed. Steady as ever, the mind-invader had her trudging relentlessly toward the trapped trio. Doris knew the fates existed merely to mock her when she finally made it to some open ground only to see the three black-clad soldiers cease their sporadic firing and take off toward a ransacked party store on the south side of the wide lane.

Turning to follow, by way of a will alien to her own, she was actually pleased to wind up in the middle of the chasing horde once again. Doris saw what the mind-invader had made those nearest the fleeing men do. She had no wish to shatter glass windows through relentless forward motion, no desire to feel the massive shards left in the wake of the demolition ravage deep gashes into her infected gray skin. She knew she would never avoid pain until the hunt was done and she was back swaying in the park, or a stray bullet burst its way through something vital, but if her misery could be minimized to the simple agony of walking, she would count herself lucky, well luckier than some at least.

She ended up stomping through the gaping expanse that had once been a shop window at least a dozen seconds behind the fleeing soldiers. The party store was tiny, enough so as to create an instant bottleneck. She pressed firmly into the backs of infected before her for another dozen seconds before her turn came to funnel through the narrow alley behind the cash register the men had fled through. Bursting back into the dim daylight of this rainy autumn day, Doris nearly lost her balance, or rather the entity controlling her body nearly lost *its* balance as she trampled over a door that had been knocked off its hinges and now lay askew atop a concrete alleyway.

The snake of strung-out hordesmen before her led her through a dingy, puddle-strewn path. Emerging from the cramped alley, Doris swore she felt the rain's intensity increase. She saw the horde before her flowing west, chasing the three battle-ready soldiers 70 yards up the street. Had she the choice, she'd have turned east and headed back to the overgrown park where she had swayed for days now. There were only three of them left, and they had to be low on ammunition. She would never catch a bullet now, not with dozens, or even possibly hundreds, of her fellow hordesmen between herself and their prey. But of course, she had no will of her own. The mind-invader wanted her to chase the soldiers, same as all the others. So, she headed west.

Doris could not see what happened next, but she sure heard it. The pained wail of a man in convulsive agony was unmistakable at this point in her life. The ululating groaning of her fellow drones ticked up commensurate with the soldier's bellow. Doris was not exempt from the vocalization. *They've got them*, she knew, hope flickering out of existence as fast as ever it blossomed. *It won't be long now*. The evil entity controlling them would be sure each of its puppets had enough to eat and drink, enough to carry on their miserable existence. She would be feasting on steaming intestines soon. Oh god, how she wished she could cry.

Doris heard no more gunshots, but intelligible shouts were still evident. *Someone's still alive*. Steadily, relentlessly, she trudged forward. The healthy bellows grew louder with each step. She expected a hideous shriek of pain to replace them soon. They were obviously down to fighting with clubs and bats now. Her horde was far too large to be stopped by such. She could almost taste the copper tang of human blood on her tongue now. The soldiers' end was surely imminent; she'd suffered through enough hunts to know that much.

Therefore, when a flash of fire and thunderous explosion suddenly burst to life twenty yards ahead of her, sending a semi-spherical shockwave rippling outward from its zenith, Doris' hope for finding her end on this wet and gloomy day sparked anew inside her once more. These men had hand grenades, clearly. Maybe bigger bombs even. All she had to do was keep walking toward them to find out. And the mind-invader was obliging. Not even the jagged scrap of shrapnel that embedded itself three inches into her right forearm diminished her hopes for total destruction by way of a massive explosion. The pain was there, one point of torment among many, but each time her arm swung into her peripheral vision, the sight of the warped steel protruding from her bloodstained gray skin only encouraged her. Not even slipping in the soupy mess of her once fellow hordesmen, now lucky dead, left in the wake of the grenade's blast tarnished the hope.

She held it firm for at least eight blocks. There were only two soldiers left at the head of the chasing horde now. Zigzagging from street to street, the prey stayed just out of reach. Whenever the mass of infected would surge close, one or the other would drop another hand grenade. Always though, Doris remained just out of death's range. She collected a few more painful chunks of shrapnel, but the fragmentation explosions never engulfed her fully. She had to watch others be propitiously ripped apart in the deadly shockwaves and shredded by shards of white-hot steel. Dozens of her fellow infected were blessed by the grenade's loving kiss, but not Doris, never Doris.

When the pair of soldiers made it to the outskirts of town and ducked into the dense mountain forest, Doris assumed her chance at blissful nothingness had passed her by. The mind-invader made her pursue, nonetheless. Apparently, the black-clad healthy humans felt no more grenades were necessary to secure their escape, or perhaps they had simply run out. All Doris knew was that no explosions burst to life for the entire trek through that thin strip of forest.

Stepping clear of the tree line, she saw a new chance at death. A Humvee sat astride a two-lane highway. The pair of soldiers were only fifty yards from their getaway car. She knew she would never reach them in time to prevent them climbing aboard and taking off. It hadn't been the two running men that renewed her hopes though. It was their two teammates taking potshots at the pursuing horde from their comfortable positions in the bed of the tactical vehicle. Even as the mind-invader had Doris take off toward the waiting Humvee, she watched hordesman after hordesman taken out by the pair of marksmen with headshot after headshot.

Oh please, God, if you're real, me next. I'll forgive the neglect of the past months. I'll look past the suffering you unfairly put me through. Just please, let them shoot me, she screamed in silence.

Doris had just enough time to take back the prayer, just enough time to wonder who in the hell these well-equipped professional soldiers were and what their existence might mean for her impossible dream of being cured of her awful ailment before her head burst apart in a painless flash of misty red.

CHAPTER 9
ELIAS

INFECTION EVENT: DAY 3,168

He'd left them both in Carrie's clubhouse. He hadn't wanted to, but there was simply no arguing with either. Elias couldn't be sure if Carrie and Tessa's charisma had the same convincing effects on others as it had on him, but he guessed it was likely. The way they shut down any rebuttal before Elias could even get it halfway past his lips was quite remarkable. He had faced some tough challenges over the years, but he knew ever saying no to either girl was the one he would never conquer. They were right too. That helped. Elias might well have wished to never let Carrie or Tessa out of his sight from now until kingdom come, but they did need ears in the Witen's closed-door meeting with the Bruderschaft. All of them knew full well that any plan they devised to liberate Maisie, the priest and all the others in the brig would be hugely impacted by whatever was agreed to in that fateful meeting.

They needed to know their time scale at the very least. If the Bruderschaft were to immediately take off after the sit-down, Carrie, Tessa, and Elias needed to be aware of that fact. Hopefully, whatever the outcome of the meeting, they would have a bit more time than that dreaded scenario entailed. Either way, they needed to know. So Elias had to go. Only he among the three of them stood any chance at getting into that meeting. He was still Ethling, after all. The title afforded him some respect, enough at least to merit an invitation to the momentous discussion.

Of course, that was before he had confronted the Steward and abandoned his duty in order to whisk Carrie away to safety. That was before he helped organize the huge crowd from the Billiard Lounge to confront the Commander. His status could not help but be diminished in the face of all that. Word had to have reached the top by now. The Commander had to know it was Elias and Tessa that organized the mob. That fact alone was enough to have him shipped off to the brig the moment he showed his face.

Elias' only hope, and therefore Carrie and Tessa's only hope, which also meant Maisie and Father Boyd and Dolly and all the other prisoners' only hope, was that the Steward was still battling his guilt to the point where he would not confront Elias for his insubordination, and that the Commander still respected his number-two enough to defer to him in matters concerning his protégé. The odds were high on the latter hope, he judged. The former, however, was a toss-up. The only way to find out was to walk straight into the lion's den. If they swarmed him, he'd know. If they merely gave him reproachful glares, then too, he would know. One way or another, he was about to find out.

The die is cast, he thought, emerging through the same maintenance hatchway in the Grand Rotunda he and Carrie had escaped through mere hours before. *C'mon, lady luck, be with me*, he silently hoped, despite hating to gamble, at any odds. The Grand Rotunda was all but empty. Even as he watched, a few pairs of residents were making their way through Branch 4's archway on the opposite end of the rotunda. Elias pegged them as the most zealous gawkers, the most starved for entertainment among the folks who'd come to witness the Bruderschaft's three representatives being escorted from their E11 to Branch 1's executive office wing. The way they kept looking back over their shoulders showed just how hungry their curiosities truly were.

Elias had plainly heard all the commotion, even through the thick composite steel hatch. Nearly a decade trapped inside the station had a way of driving one mad for any sort of spectacle, no matter how mundane, so long as it was rare and new. Under that paradigm, newcomers, survivors, genuine healthy human adults coming aboard station was an event worth turning out for. Judging by noise alone, Elias would guess that at least half of the station's residents agreed with that assessment. He could pinpoint exactly when the Bruderschaft's three had come into sight of the gathered crowd as the frenzied conversation beyond the hatch reached a pinnacle before tapering back down again. Elias waited until he could make out no more voices before finally pushing the hatch open.

The spectacle was indeed past. He was a little afraid he'd actually waited too long when he got his first clear glimpse down the length of Branch 1's Grand Alleyway. The cordon of footmen escorting the three Bruderschaft members was only a dozen paces from the Executive Wing. He didn't want to sprint, no reason to draw unnecessary attention, especially given his ambiguous status. Beads of panic-sweat began rolling down his cheeks over whether he could reach them before they made it to the Commander's office and thus have the black double doors closed before he could slip in. The pace of the escort dried the perspiration quick enough, however. Elias need do no more than slightly extend his already lengthy stride in order to overtake them.

The footmen were wary of the Bruderschaft, clearly. The Commander had promised a ten-foot cordon at all times, but none of the six surrounding the Bruderschaft's three were within twenty feet. The Bruderschaft had sent two male representatives, one tall and sandy blond, the other squat and dark, as well as one female representative that looked a few years older than her two forty-something counterparts. All three of them seemed to recognize the footmen's reticence to get near them. Elias was sure they were all deliberately straying closer and slowing their pace, forcing the wary footmen to adjust accordingly. The whole process made for slow forward motion, to the point where Elias was actually able to overtake the loose gaggle just inside the Executive Wing. The slow-moving escort was a good ten yards behind by the time he made it to the elegant double doors of the Commander's private office.

The doors were flung wide open, a rare sight indeed. Unlike the pair of footmen flanking the open portal. Childress stood at attention beside the left-hand door. Weathers was similarly posed beside the right. Both stared him down the moment he entered the lobby and hadn't taken their eyes from him yet. Elias was sure they'd stop him, sure they'd say something. Instead, their eyes found the approaching escort behind him and forgot Elias altogether. *Lady luck is holding up so far*, he told himself, fearing a jinx for acknowledging his good fortune.

Crossing the double-door's threshold, Elias beheld every officer and supervisor in the Witenagemot spread all throughout the spacious office. Two chairs had been added, one to either side of the red-brown armchair that faced away from the door in the center of the wide room. In the matching regal recliner across the coffee table, facing his wide doorway, sat the Commander, stoic as ever. The Steward leaned on the mahogany desk behind him. His eyes locked on Elias, along with all others. No one spoke. Elias' heart stopped beating.

Lieutenant Woodson stepped off the wall where he had been leaning to point an angry finger in his direction. "What the hell do you think you're doing here?!" he demanded. "How the hell did you even get here?! I gave my goddamn footmen an order for you to be taken into custody on sight."

"You've been AWOL, footman," Masterson added with a menace equal to Woodson's. "You have a lot of shit to explain—that fucking mob you arranged for one. We've been looking for you. Just where in the hell you been?"

"He'll explain himself to me after," the Steward said from his lazy lean. "You've no place to issue orders concerning my detail. I'll handle my people, thank you very much. You issue the orders I tell you to issue. Don't forget yourself, Lieutenant. All this hardly matters right now, anyhow."

"Of course it does," Masterson barked back. "No one invited him here. This is for councilmembers only, even if he wasn't a damn traitor. If he hadn't been hiding like some scared little girl, he would know this here sit-down is strictly members-only. Go off and sit in the lobby until we can deal with your ass," he ordered Elias. "Footman Childress," Masterson then shouted at the guard just beyond the doorway, "get in here and hold this son of a bitch in custody until we can deal with him."

"You have no authority over my detail, Masterson," the Steward said in a voice as stern as Elias had ever heard it. "I say who comes and goes here, not you. Understand that. Take a breath and calm yourself the fuck down. I will deal with the Ethling on my own terms. You got me, Lieutenant?!" he shouted with a pointed finger of his own.

"Your boy betrayed us, Steward!" Captain Alvarez screamed, taking three large steps in the Steward's direction. "We have it from the lips of the damn footmen in the Billiard Lounge, every last one of 'em. They all say your boy turned a mob loose on Branch 1. Your boy pressed the Commander's hands. He forced this cordial fucking meeting with those infected fucks on us. He has fucking betrayed us, and you… you… you want him to stay for this goddamn meeting? Are you kidding me? What the hell happened to you, man? You've lost it, gone soft. You ain't got the commitment to humanity anymore."

"Fuck you and your ignorant, opportunistic, greedy, self-interested fucking opinions," the Steward snapped, standing his ground. "You haven't the first fucking clue. I know it all, you dumb shit. You think you're subtle? Remember your place and shut your lip. Keep your foolish dreams close, if it makes ya feel better. I don't care. Just dream 'em quietly. You got me, Alvarez? You catching my drift?"

"My name is *Captain* Alvarez," the Captain petulantly insisted.

"And mine is the fucking Steward! Now, you try and remember the weight of that word when next you say it. Remember your fucking place, *Captain*," the Steward implored, making mock of the title Alvarez so coveted. "I said I'll deal with Ethling Sagal on my own terms, and I will. If that ain't good enough for you, Captain, if you find minding your business when it comes to your betters just too much for you to handle, you can go ahead and resign your post. I see it is you whom the stresses of the job have fatigued. Everyone here can clearly see a man who has lost his goddamn mind, a man who has stepped in some shit and better start showing some fucking contrition if he wants any hope at ever getting clean again."

"Drop it, the both of you," the Commander growled. "We've bigger fish to fry," he added, flicking his wrist at the Bruderschaft even now being ushered into the office. "Sagal," he said, locking eyes with Elias, "stand against the wall for now. You, me, and the Steward are gonna have a long talk when this is done."

"Yes, sir," Elias muttered, looking for an inconspicuous spot to take in the meeting. He sought out the Steward's eyes after he picked a fairly secluded patch of office wall to lean against.

His mentor's head stayed down, however, his eyes fixed on the carpet. Elias had nothing to read. He would like to imagine that the Steward had fully come around to seeing the hypocrisy of his creation. Elias definitely wished the man had come to see the error of his ways. He'd like to imagine that the Steward could be his ally in rebellion. Unfortunately, although he'd stood up for Elias and fought for his right to attend the meeting, he could not read the thoughts that might currently be rattling around the Steward's mind.

Odds were the man loved Elias and simply did not want to see him punished, rather than he'd become a full-fledged freedom fighter. The Steward was the creator, the architect of the Witenagemot, after all. He might well think of Elias as the son he'd lost, but the Witen and the mission he'd assigned himself, those seemed to have the potential to be stronger motivators guiding the man's decisions. For now, Elias decided to set the mystery aside. For now, he thought he'd merely count himself lucky the Steward had helped as far as he had and not waste time overanalyzing. He needed to pay attention to the upcoming meeting. Elias could not imagine either Tessa or Carrie being very understanding of any gaps in his memory over any point in the proceedings.

"Please, sit," the Commander invited the Bruderschaft representatives with an open hand indicating the mismatched trio of seats across from him.

The hush in the office was profound. Elias swore he could hear each of the Bruderschaft's footfalls as they were led to the three chairs, despite the room's plush carpet and their six rubber-soled tennis shoes. The blond male Bruderschaft member's throat-clear was the first verifiable noise in the room since the Commander's semi-polite/semi-hostile invitation. The man plopped himself down in the central chair directly across from the Commander immediately on the heels of the clearing. The other male slowly took the chair to the blond man's left while the female rep sat down in the right in as dignified a manner as the situation allowed.

"You sure you want us this close?" the blond man asked in an unpretentious yet imperious English accent. "Aren't you afraid we might cough on you? We are infected in your eyes, are we not?"

"I feel safe anywhere in my station, with anyone surrounding me, near or far." The Commander's signature menacing growl was in full effect. "There's nothing you could threaten me with."

"Have you some divine protection then?" the blond man asked, sarcasm evident in every syllable. "Same ain't true for your men though, eh?"

The Commander didn't answer. Leaning forward, he snatched his tumbler of moonshine from the coffee table's glass surface. "I'm detecting a fair amount of hostility," he stated simply before sipping from his tumbler.

"Bright fellow, you," the blond man pointed out laconically.

"I hardly see how that attitude could be in any way useful just now."

"You... you," the man muttered, utterly flabbergasted, "you don't think my attitude is warranted? Are you a serious person? Really?"

"I'm very serious," the Commander's growl assured.

"My people have done nothing to you. We haven't even asked you for help. We had data that indicated we would find this place barely hanging on. We thought our arrival would be welcomed, if anything. But we certainly didn't arrive with our hands out looking for charity. We were hoping for a bit of cordiality at the least, though. I thought you'd at least let me come aboard the bloody station to negotiate and explain ourselves before you started blasting off laser bolts at my head. We want nothing from you, sir. We've brought our own seeds. We planned to grow our own crops and stock up our supply from that growth alone. We certainly did not believe in our wildest dreams that any man would begrudge us a few months recuperation, especially not a man with more than enough room to accommodate us. We foolishly assumed to be treated like bloody human beings, but it seems that was too much to expect from you chaps. If you can't understand my attitude, sir, in the face of all that, then I don't foresee this little chat being very beneficial."

"The cordon was for the residents' sake," the Commander responded to the rant only after finishing his moonshine.

"Excuse me?" the female rep asked in an accent very similar to the blond man's.

"I know you all ain't infected," the Commander explained.

A murmur rippled through the office. The scowl on their ruler's face quickly silenced the whispers.

When he had a quiet sufficient enough to suit him, the Commander continued, "You obviously ain't one of the Damned. I'm no fool. I saw as much from the start. You are a disease, however, a cancer on this station. For almost ten years now, we have existed up here on the edge of a knife. My Witenagemot and I have fought, day in and day out, to keep the balance. It ain't been easy, let me tell you. This haven," he said, indicating the station around him, "this is a gift that humanity ain't worthy of. The infection should have ended us. It was our fate. But somehow, up here, we've defied fate. We persist in spite of reason, in spite of logic or nature or the will of the gods. We had to change our reality to do it, but we, the Witenagemot, we persist. We're a blip in the system, a glitch in the software. We shouldn't be, but we are. We have endured up here only because I have sold my soul, only because I gave up my humanity. One of us had to. We had to rule this place with an iron fist. I have to keep the fragile egos and grand dreams of hundreds of fallible human beings in check. The people need the lies. They need something to fear, something to keep them putting their own selfish desires behind the best interests of the society. We can't have them distracted with hope of cures or some ill-advised and ultimately doomed return to Earth. We settled all those distractions the first time around. The old world, as we like to call it, died. And so too its morals and ethics and naïve notions of freedom and liberty and right to truth. So yeah, I told the people I had a vision that you were all infected—to protect them. Your brotherhood might well have been beneficial in your survival on Earth, but up here, it will destroy us all. I can't have you spreading your ideals around. The people need to stay focused. This station has to stay in balance. You and your brothers and sisters in your Bruderschaft, you all would tip the scales. Just one hour of neglect, and this place blows up all around us. I cannot allow that. I swore an oath to never let that happen."

"Then why bring us in here at all? Why not just leave us to suffocate on our ship?" the blond man asked with a shocked and incredulous cadence.

"I was all set to. Circumstances changed," the Commander explained, filling his tumbler anew.

"What circumstances are those?"

"We'll get to that. Right now I think we should get on with introductions. I am the Commander of the Witenagemot. You may call me the Commander," he said, smiling over his glass of moonshine. "The man behind me is the Steward. That is Captain Alvarez. Around the room in the gold coats are my supervisors. Those in black are my lieutenants. You can learn their names later if you like. For now, it's enough to address them with their titles."

"*The Commander*?" the blond man skeptically stressed the name. "Commander what?"

"Just Commander."

"Okay, just Commander, my name is Arlo Bailey. My brother and sister beside me are Barrett Hitchens and Janessa Fussgood, respectively," the sarcasm in the blond man's voice hadn't left.

"Pleasure meeting you," the Commander said unconvincingly.

"The pleasure is all yours," Bailey snarked back. "Now that all of that is out of the way, will you please tell me just what in the bloody hell you want from us? We were perfectly happy suffocating together out on your Lunar Dock. So if you just dragged us in here as a means to deceive your people, then we will get up and go back to our E11 right now. I'd much rather spend some agonizing minutes with the people I love than another second stuck in this room with a gang of impotent fascist thugs," the man declared, rising to his feet.

"Sit down, Mr. Bailey," the Commander said in a reasonable voice. "I can't just let your people die on my dock, not now anyways. My residents have risen above the propaganda. It's reached a critical mass, I'm afraid. What we could have done better, or how we might prevent future failures of this sort is something me and my Witen council will have to work out after this is all over."

The Commander's eyes found Elias. The rest of the councilmembers present were induced to follow suit. Only the Steward's eyes did not seek him. Elias' mentor was still staring resolutely at the carpet. He found the Steward's reluctance to even lift his head far more troubling than the menacing glares of the councilmembers. They had lost their ability to influence Elias. It wasn't a deliberate act of will. Elias just simply could not go back to the man he'd been less than a day before. The mystique was gone. The wizard behind the curtain had been shown to be no more than an ordinary man. He recognized that getting out of this hostile environment at meeting's end would certainly prove a trial, but as far as being intimidated by the scowls and empty words of the councilmembers, those days were gone forever. So he never broke, never so much as flinched.

Finally, after a laughably long attempt to cow him, the Commander cleared his throat and turned back to the Bruderschaft reps. "As I was saying," he began with a lame attempt to dismiss the moment and regain his menace, "my people won't accept us just sending you away, not without being seen to speak to you first. I had your escort keep the cordon around you to... uhh... well, to save face, I guess you can say." He grinned a foreign, self-deprecating smile. "I was forced to invite you aboard for this meeting, but I couldn't be seen to completely abandon my previous conviction. It's like I was saying, I gotta keep the balance."

"Are you ever going to get to the point?" Barrett Hitchens grumbled in a cockney accent. "Like Arlo was saying, our people have an hour's worth of oxygen left on our E11. If you don't plan to kill us off, someone better start letting them aboard or else resupply our oxygen in a bloody big hurry."

"That's precisely what I mean to do. In fact, Mr. Hitchens, I have my people in the Control Room topping off your O2 tanks even now," the Commander said, once more using his reasonable voice, much to the Bruderschaft's undisguised irritation.

"Why?" Bailey finally managed through gritted teeth.

"Why what, Mr. Bailey?"

"Why refill our oxygen if you don't mean to let us come aboard? What's the point of keeping us out on your dock? You know we can't return to Earth, not without a few harvests at the very least, even if you were to give us the necessary fuel. So you know we are just gonna sit there until this new supply of O2 runs dry. Why then? Just to earn some points for your clueless residents, to prove you offered some small measure of charity? If that pathetic ploy is what you've pinned your hopes of regaining the people's confidence to, and this meeting is no more than a show, then why bother speaking to us at all? If this is mere charade, then do us the kindness of dropping the whole act. I'd much prefer to simply sit here in silence until we're allowed to go back to die with our brothers and sisters."

"Oh, I'll let your people come aboard... eventually, with one or two caveats," the Commander told him after polishing off the second tumbler since Elias had entered the office. "All of you, even you three," he added with a dangerous grin, "are very welcome aboard station, provided, every last one of you swears an oath of loyalty on your very lives to come aboard as loyal citizens of the Witenagemot, subject to its authority alone. I shall also require that you three, as well as every last Witen councilmember in this office, swear, until the very end of time, to never speak of anything said or agreed to in this meeting, under pain of torturous death. You all hear me? Not a word leaves this room," he ordered, staring down the councilmembers spread out around him. "Anything gets back to me, I'll know who to blame, won't I?"

"Yes, sir," a collection of voices chorused.

"We got you, Commander." Lieutenant Schwambach slyly smirked.

"Your secrets are ours, sir, you know that," Captain Alvarez concurred. "If there's ever a leak, all of us will know who to blame," he added, staring Elias down.

When the Captain's lone glare had no more effect than the collective did minutes earlier, the Commander cleared his throat and refilled his glass.

"Suppose we weren't keen on joining your merry little band of autocrats. What then?" Bailey posited as the Commander gulped two fingers worth of moonshine in one sip.

"Tell us what you've done with Jordana Revere and perhaps we will contemplate maybe thinking about possibly considering your ludicrous demand," Barret Hitchens cut in.

"Jordana Revere is being held in custody in our brig for violations of the New Destiny Constitution," the Commander explained after a mighty belch.

"And what in the bloody hell is the 'New Destiny Constitution'?" asked Janessa Fussgood.

"You care to explain it, Steward? She's your baby, after all," the Commander turned to ask the man leaning atop his desk.

"By all means, sir, I yield the floor to you," the Steward responded in a voice simultaneously insubordinate and reverential.

The Commander wasn't pleased with the response. Obviously, he wanted to put on a bit of a show, a little good-cop bad-cop, but his number-two stepped all over the moment. Another gulp of moonshine righted the gorilla-man. His scarred face quickly cleared of all signs of frustration.

"The New Destiny Constitution is our law, more or less. It stipulates a citizen's rights, outlines various regulations and rules, as well as detailing punishments necessary for violations thereof. Now, since Ms. Revere holds the status of non-citizen, her crimes are classified under the terrorism clause. The penalty for all infractions under that umbrella are death by hanging. Now, I'm willing to spare Ms. Revere that fate," he quickly added before any of the three could explode, "if she swears the citizen's oath. She too can join our sacred society. If she don't, she hangs. And if you all don't, you slowly suffocate to death in your spaceship."

"Join you or die? That's your ultimatum?" Bailey asked with a pitying disgust.

"What, not fair?" the Commander wondered with an innocence that even Elias wanted to smack off his grizzly face.

"It's bullshit is what it is," Hitchens answered for Bailey. "This whole meeting has been one big bloody fucking waste of time. I'll not spend another second of what time I have left in your rancid company," he stated, rising to his feet.

Bailey and Fussgood joined him, but before they could turn to leave, the Commander spoke, "There is another way."

"Of course there is," Bailey said, throwing up his hands in sheer bewilderment. "Okay, I'll bite. Lay it on us. What is this other way?" he finished back in his chair, his counterparts following his lead.

"Your arrival has exposed some assumptions that we in the Witenagemot have passed off as facts," the Commander began with a quick glare over his shoulder at the Steward. "As I was alluding to earlier, doubt has gripped my people. No amount of sermons from the Glorifier nor threats from me and mine will wipe them away again. The Witen has grown too comfortable, too lazy. I blame myself. Be that as it may, complacency has allowed our grip on what is and what is not truth to slacken. Our constructed reality has been pierced. We need to give the doubters something to believe in again. A time has come for the Witenagemot to prove its righteous provenance. Your arrival has exposed the problems that have been simmering below the surface for years now. But, blessed as I am, I recognize that your arrival also is the answer to those simmering problems. Your arrival has provided us with a means to prove our right to rule."

"What are you talking about?" Fussgood asked, sounding genuinely perplexed. "How can we possibly 'prove your right to rule,' especially when none of us believes any one man should ever rule another?"

"We'll prove our right the same way we earned our titles," the milky-eyed emperor told her.

"That being?" Bailey asked after it seemed the Commander might never speak again.

"Through blood and battle," he casually informed them as he poured himself yet another tumbler.

"Speak sense, man," Bailey implored, rubbing the bridge of his nose.

"You might not believe this, Mr. Bailey, but I am a fair man," the Commander insisted.

"You're right. I don't believe it."

"Well, it's true. We all are," he said, indicating his subordinates. "We're honest. We make oaths, and we keep them. Don't we?"

"Hell yes, Commander," every Witen voice other than those of Elias and the Steward shouted, as though they'd been waiting for the call and response.

"Get to the point," Hitchens demanded with crossed arms and a furrowed, impatient brow.

"If you all don't wish to come aboard to live as loyal Witen citizens and also prefer not to suffocate to death in your ship, then you can compete for your chance to rule this station. If you feel your hippie-commune, danger-fleeing sort of lifestyle will benefit the folks up here, then I offer you the chance to install that system. I'm offering you a fair chance to not only survive, but to take over this station and do with it whatever you please. If you defeat me and my team, you can stay and rule or stock up and leave. There will be no one to stop you either way. Just a few minutes before you three graced us with your presence, every councilmember in this office swore a sacred oath to honor the will of whichever side comes out on top. And, as I was saying, oaths are things we hold dear. If any of us are left after it's over with your side the victor, they won't stand in your way. We are true to our words here in the Witenagemot. Perhaps you wouldn't understand the ways of honorable men and women, but we all see our integrity, our *word*, as the pearl beyond price. We know once it's gone, you never get it back. And if we could be said to fear anything, that would be it."

"What in the fucking bloody fucking hell are you fucking babbling about?" Bailey bellowed. "'Compete'? 'Defeat your team'? What fucking team? What, do you propose we play a pick-up game of baseball to decide if you'll let my people live or not? Is that it? You think us ignorant foreigners will just wind up trying to kick the bloody thing to home plate or something?"

"I'm not talking baseball," the Commander disabused him.

"Well, what are you talking about then?"

"Like I said, battle, real battle," the Commander explained with a sinister lilt in his growl. "You know, combat? Fighting, scratching, clawing to kill your enemy. I'm talking your best thirty against my best thirty. No guns, no grenades, just simple axes, bats, and spears and any other non-projectile weapon you can devise, along with whatever armor you can improvise. We line up on either side of the Meadow and meet in the middle. Whichever side comes out victorious will have been proven worthy of control over Cardinal's Nest Lunar Station. I'm talking the one and only truly impartial and just way to decide humanity's fate."

Elias had seen it coming, in truth, almost since the instant the man first spoke of a third option. All the Commander understood was violence. *Might don't make right,* his dad always used to say. The Commander took the opposite view. Elias had felt the man itching for a fight for years now. It emanated from him like electricity, the need to swing his battleaxe. His lack of surprise over what this third option would be did not diminish Elias' frustration and anger with the Commander and every other councilmember, the Steward especially, over the fact that they would all collectively agree to devise a plan to kill the strangers who turned up at their door looking for a bit of help, a bit of understanding, a bit of common decency and solidarity. When he reminded himself that he was one of them only a few hours earlier, he wanted to scream. Flashes of Perry Sagal casually recounting his grueling days to a sleepy eleven-year-old Elias on their old tan couch snapped again and again in his mind. *Would I have gone along with this shit if Carrie had not been in that crowd*? No immediate answer came to him, only a sense of bitter shame.

"You're mad," Bailey said, shaking his head.

"No. I'm sensible, for this age anyhow."

"My people are not soldiers."

"Well, you always have the other two options available to ya."

"You're mad," Bailey repeated.

"I am no more or no less than humankind currently requires."

"What if our people can't decide? The Bruderschaft isn't a monolith. What if some would rather die or fight and others feel taking your oath is something they could stomach?"

"I won't play any nickel and dime shit," the Commander growled. "You people are a package deal, as far as I'm concerned. Either all of you come aboard or none of you do."

"And the refueling option: is that still on the table?" Arlo softly queried.

"No," the Commander answered simply. Then casually sipped another finger of clear liquor.

"Why?" Arlo asked, sounding as though he already knew the answer.

"You had that chance but chose to spit in my face and stroll aboard my station anyway. Negligence has consequences, Mr. Bailey, in negotiations as in all things. It's far too late for all that. The bell has tolled. I can't let you just return to Earth. My people would naturally create legends around where you might have gone and when you might return again to liberate them. They've seen you. They all know now, beyond the power of any piece of propaganda to influence them otherwise, that there are people out on that ship on their Lunar Dock. I can't just let you limp away, not now. You have three fates to choose from; don't go fishing for any more. You might find my patience, as well my tolerance to be influenced by my flock, only extends so far."

When Arlo only shook his head as though he pitied the mammoth monster before him, the Commander pressed on, "I'm not expecting an answer here and now. Go back to your ship; talk to your people. You all decide in your democratic way which option to choose. Your O2 will run dry again in eight hours, so you've some time to grapple with your choices. Think hard, and don't doubt either our resolve or our loyalty to our oaths. If you choose to die together, then just keep your asses in your ship. If you decide to be reasonable and swear oaths of loyalty or to be giant fools and demand a battle, we will contact you an hour before your oxygen runs out, and you can tell us your decision then."

"My brothers and sisters will never accept living under your tyranny."

"Well then, if you want to save them, if you're the leader you present yourself as, you better convince them to fight, or else ya'll can fucking rot in that E11."

"You expect me to pick thirty of my brothers and sisters, folks who have been through hell and back again more times than I have fingers and toes, to fight some medieval hand-to-hand battle? How can I do that? You're a leader. Somewhere deep inside your crusty soul you must know how impossible that will be."

"You need not pick. If it's the chance to rule the station they all want, you oughta have plenty of volunteers. Hell," the Commander added, smacking his knee, "if your people are too cowardly to fight for their convictions, you can even appeal to my citizens to join your cause, though you might find that any of 'em worth a damn at swinging an axe will be beside me on the battlefield."

"I'll volunteer," Elias heard himself say. To be sure, he'd meant to speak, but his heart was beating so fast, and his mind was buzzing so loudly that he wasn't certain he could control his voice enough to actually enunciate the words. The thundering silence that gripped the room fast as a hummingbird beats its wings and the dozens of eyes that fixed him firm with menace and incredulity confirmed that he had indeed spoken.

"What?" the Commander asked, though his face immediately after showed the question had escaped his lips without his permission.

"I will be one of the Bruderschaft's thirty, if they'll have me," Elias defiantly declared.

Arlo Bailey spun halfway around in his chair to lock eyes with Elias. What the man might have read there, Elias couldn't be sure, but it was enough to get him to nod his head in acceptance.

"Traitor!" Captain Alvarez's scream was so angry it drove his voice hoarse. "You see, Steward. We told you what he was. Lieutenants," he called to Schwambach and Woodson, the two lieutenants nearest Elias, "take that fucking piece of shit out of this room. Hold him in the brig until I can join you."

"How very honorable," Arlo Bailey cut through the room's ambient tension to sardonically state. "One minute you tell me how sacred you hold your oaths and that I may accept any man willing to join my thirty, and the instant one volunteers, you threaten him with imprisonment. What is a truly honest man to make of that? Why should I put thirty of my brothers and sisters through such a violent trial if we can't even be sure you'll honor your commitments when it's over?"

"You doubting my honor, you limey prick?!" Alvarez roared, stepping toward the center of the room. "You can have any idiot who joins ya, but that traitor behind ya is no more than a common criminal. We'd be locking his ass away right after this anyhow."

"Sure, of course I trust the word of an arrogant American bloke screaming at me like some petulant toddler. That makes perfect sense," Arlo scoffed, eyes rolling into the back of his head.

"You got some lip, you British bitch," the Captain mocked, stepping even closer toward the Bruderschaft with an angry finger leading the way. "You best drop it before I smack the fuck out a ya before the battle can even begin."

"Oh, I bet. I'm sure you've so little honor you might even sneak aboard our ship and slit all our throats in the middle of the night so you wouldn't have to face an honest battle."

"Fuck you!" Alvarez screamed, charging in.

"Control yourself, Captain!" the Commander boomed, freezing Alvarez in place two paces into his charge. "Get back against the wall!"

"Is this display representative of the sort of *honorable* behavior we should expect, should we fight tomorrow?" Bailey asked, staring the Commander down, Captain Alvarez all but forgotten.

Bailey had him. The Commander knew it. He wasn't pleased, but he knew it. In the end, he could do no more than scowl at Captain

Alvarez until the number-three man lowered his head and stepped back to his spot against the wall. Even then he obviously did not trust himself to speak. His eyes flicked between Elias and the Steward. Elias gave as good as he got, but the Steward never once looked up to play the glaring game.

"Sagal is yours. He won't be touched until the battle begins, if it's battle you choose. You have my word," he said, daring Bailey to doubt his promise. When the Brit stayed silent and merely crossed his arms, the Commander continued, "Tomorrow morning, 1000 ST, if your people agree to the fight, send out your warriors. They are to exit your ship empty-handed. If any of your battle-team sneak so much as one firearm aboard station, the deal is off. All thirty will be taken into custody while your remaining fifty-five brothers and sisters will be left to suffocate in their ship. If you attempt a mass breakout, your people will be mown down by our PRZVL33. I believe you two have been introduced," he added the dig with a small taunting smirk. "You will be provided weapons when you reach the Meadow. I suggest you make a banner for yourselves to fight under and to wave in the event of surrender, though I'll not make that a stipulation. Me and my people will know the fight is over when there isn't one of you refined, pretentious European bastards left alive."

"A *banner?*" Fussgood scoffed. "How fitting for such feudalistic madness."

"Be ready to announce your decision when we contact you in seven hours," the Commander said, ignoring Janessa Fussgood. "I will broadcast that communication to the station so all can hear your decision firsthand. The whole human race will know then if we were to betray our deal. Take that for whatever assurance you may. I really don't care. We are done here."

He stood up abruptly with that, snatching his tumbler from the glass tabletop. Turning his back on the trio to stroll to his desk, the Commander flicked his wrist by way of dismissing them. Bailey, Hitchens, and Fussgood got the hint. Without flinching from any of the various glares the councilmembers fixed upon them, the trio marched steadily out of the office. Elias felt the gazes shift from the Bruderschaft to him. Only the Steward's mattered just then though. His mentor's eyes were still on the carpet, however. Elias willed him to look up and wanted desperately to stay until he did, but he knew, despite the Commander's promise, he would not survive long in that office.

No one barred his path. A few spat at his feet. But he made it to the double-doors quickly enough. Just before he stepped through into the lobby, his eyes locked with those of a skinny supervisor with a pencil-thin mustache. Elias couldn't immediately place his name, but he thought the man oversaw the Module Garage. What caught his attention was not that a man he barely knew was staring at him, but rather it was the way he was staring that was strange. Every other glare that fixed him in that office was full of vitriol and spite. The look in the skinny supervisor's eyes was altogether different. It was almost like he was trying to tell Elias something. He couldn't be sure, they'd locked eyes for less than a half-dozen seconds, but that was certainly the impression he carried with him as he strode out of the elegant executive office wing.

ARLO

Their escort slammed down on them the instant they left the office, corralling them on the same journey as before, only in reverse. The return trip played out much the same as the first, right up until a strong young voice hailed them. They were almost to the Terminal. Arlo could even then see the big laser gatling gun that had nearly killed him earlier still aimed down the center of Nest Gateway. The same pimply teen that fired off those near-fatal *warning shots* still had a greasy fat finger wrapped around the trigger as well.

The voice called from halfway down the long alleyway cutting straight down the heart of the Branch. All three of them stopped and turned toward the shout, as well all six members of their escort. "Wait, please. Just a minute, Mr. Bailey, sir." The young man who'd volunteered to fight for the Bruderschaft in the insane battle the arrogant asshole calling himself the Commander had proposed came jogging into clear sight.

Barrett "Hitch" Hitchens and Janessa "Nessa" Fussgood exchanged a look before each turned to him. Neither of them knew what to make of the kid any more than he did, clearly. Shrugging his shoulders, Arlo offered the lad a short welcoming wave to hurry him along on his jog. Before Arlo or Hitch or Nessa could acknowledge the mysterious man-child verbally, the escort's lead footman broke ranks.

"Hold it right there, Sagal. Stay back! You need to get lost, and I'm talking right fucking now, in a big damn hurry," the tall footman with the strange chalky blue eyes and wormy lips screamed before planting himself firmly in the middle of the alleyway halfway between them and the young man. "You have no place anywhere near this Branch, traitor! We may have just received orders over our tablets to ignore you and not give you the beatdown a phony little bitch like you deserves, but that don't prevent me from following protocol. If you impede me in any way on my detail's duty to escort these three straight from the Commander's office to Nest Gateway, then the New Destiny Constitution instructs me to 'eradicate with extreme prejudice any and all elements involved with the aggression.' That's Article 6, Section 11. Your daddy the Steward is the man who wrote the damn rules, and he has clearly outlined my duties in that section. Shall I pull it up on my tablet and show ya, or do you maybe want to turn your backstabbing, baby-dicked, spineless traitor ass around and get the fuck out of this Branch?!" he finished with an inflective rise to punctuate his point.

The young man from the meeting was not impressed, barreling right past the tall footman without breaking stride. The footman turned, jaw dropped open with incredulity, to clap a hand on the young man's shoulder. The kid from the meeting let the hand stay there, ignoring it completely to drive a backfist square into the chalky-eyed footman's twig and berries. The leader of the escort dropped to his knees, clutching his crotch, only able to produce the tiniest of whimpers. No one moved until the footman toppled over on his side to curl up around the pain. Only then did the other five footmen snap into action.

"I got no wish to fight any of you here now. I only need a few seconds with these people is all," the young man explained to the five who froze, unsure of themselves, as he made his plea. "I doubt the honorable Commander would deny me that much. Do you? I mean, a soldier has a right to confer with his commanding officer before a battle. Right?" He barked the question at the footmen. All five recoiled a step from the shout in tandem as though a pack of hounds before the kennel master.

"Well, tomorrow, if it's to be battle, that there will be my commanding officer," he said, finger pointing straight at Arlo. "So step aside and let me speak with them. Five minutes. That's all," he added when the footmen remained reluctant.

None spoke to the young man, but two of the five gave him a small nod and stepped over toward the still writhing wormy-lipped footman.

"Tell Allanson, when the pain eases enough to let him think straight again, that if he is a real man, he can volunteer and get his chance at revenge tomorrow."

The two who nodded scowled at that but ultimately acknowledged the task.

Turning back to Arlo and his friends, he said, "Hello, Mr. Bailey, Mr. Hitchens, Ms....?"

"Oh, uhh, it's Mrs.," Nessa clarified.

"*Mrs*. Fussgood. It's a pleasure meeting you all, despite the circumstance," the young man finished.

"You'll forgive me, son, I know," Arlo said, taking up his proffered hand with some reluctance, "but I'm not quite sure what to make of your intentions. Or even what those might possibly be."

"I only want to see the Witen fall," the gray-clad young man explained.

"Why? Are you not one of them?" Nessa asked.

"I am... or I was... I mean... it's a long story."

"Oh, I'm sure," Arlo agreed, "but we are going to need to hear some of it at the very least. If we were to agree to your madman of a king's medieval demands and fight a hand-to-hand battle to the death, then I am going to need to know, absolutely, that I can trust the people around me. Why should I waste one of our thirty spots on you? I've many capable brothers and sisters I know I can count on."

"I have to beat him. I have to burn it all down," the man said after some thought. "He has my sister. But more than that, it's... it's the only way I may ever achieve any sort of redemption for all I've been a part of, for all I've personally done and been responsible for. I am their Ethling. I have been the Witenagemot, inside and out, for so very long, too long maybe to ever actually be redeemed. But I gotta try. It took me a while to see that, but now it seems so obvious. You see, sir, I... I... I abandoned my family for nearly a decade. I have to fight for them now, one way or another. If the Commander wants to willingly line up across from me in open ground, well, sir, Mr. Bailey, I think that's just about the best opportunity I'm ever gonna have. I gotta take it for both my sisters' sakes and their mother's and for Carrie Montrois and her daughter Roxanna and for all the billions of others. I have to try and finish my father's work."

"Your 'father's work'?" Hitch queried the strange statement.

"He tried to stop all this, back in the beginning. He would have too. He... he... he did—in another life, a just life. It was my fault then, and it's my fault now. I have to stop them. I have to fight them, all of them, the Commander and... and... and even the Steward too, if he makes me. And though I don't know much of you and your people, but from the honesty and courage you displayed in that meeting, I believe if... if, that is, you all decide that a battle must be fought, if I were to be allowed to fight that battle beside you, I would be most honored."

"Noble words, son," Arlo responded through a smirk that wouldn't die. "I'm afraid I'm not so eloquent. But if we decide to fight, you'll have your place on our side." He couldn't say exactly why, something about the look in the man's eyes did it, but he believed him, every word.

"What's your name, kid? We oughta know that much if we're to die together tomorrow," Hitch asked as the young man turned from them.

Stepping back, with a smile, he told them, "Elias Sagal."

"Nice to meet you, Elias," Nessa said, stepping in to shake his hand.

"I'll be in the terminal waiting tomorrow when you all come out, should you choose to fight," Elias informed them with a final nod of his head before marching back down the arrow-straight alley.

"We've got it from here, chaps," Arlo called to the footmen as he stepped through their now extremely loose cordon.

Before any could react, Hitch, Nessa, and himself were all past the bulky bolt thrower and its pudgy triggerman. The scrambling escort gave up their lame attempts to corral them and simply watched Arlo and his friends stroll into Nest Gateway.

"Better get everyone together on one of the decks," he said to Hitch and Nessa both as they marched down the wide catwalk.

"Deck 3 would be best. It's just open space. We'll have to repressurize it, but we shouldn't be in there long enough to impact our O2 all that much," Hitch muttered in an offhand manner. "The bottom two decks below are full-up with cargo, and the passenger decks have too many seats taking up space to allow everyone to attend."

"Fine. Deck 3 then." Arlo had larger issues on his mind. He had to decide just what in the hell he was going to tell his people. *Best start with an apology for failing them*, his shame silently screamed at him as he stooped back through Morgana 1's belly hatch.

The deck stayed silent for a long while after he'd laid it all out. A few of the smaller children muttered and whined as toddlers do, but the rest were in shock, or so Arlo judged. He felt the embarrassment and impotence, knowing they all must be pondering how they'd gotten this far only to have the man they trusted to bring them peace utterly fail them in the end. His knees were rubber. Cold sweat trickled down his spine. He loved these eighty-four souls around him, as much as he had ever loved any of his family. Most had been beside him for over nine years, since the very first months of the infection, others they had collected along the way, but all were precious to him. Every last one was truly his brother or sister. And yet still, he failed them. The guilt that stabbed at him was as unrelenting as it was painful.

"This Commander, he is serious then?" Helmut Dittmar broke the still silence to inquire in his thick German accent, turning the *th*'s into *z*'s.

"Afraid so, Helmut," Hitch answered for him. "That was the warning we received from Jordana as well. She has spent time with some of the residents. Their reports are not encouraging, I'm afraid."

"You saw her? Jordana? How is she?" Luca Clijsters, a thirty-something man who'd been a newly minted Belgian Army cook before joining the Bruderschaft, eagerly asked.

"No. Not this time. Not at all really. We only heard her voice just before we landed," Hitch answered.

"Oh," Luca groaned, obviously disappointed with the report. "Did she at least sound alright?"

"She did then," Hitch answered bluntly.

Nessa stood off to Arlo's left while Hitch flanked his right. Their remaining eighty-two brothers and sisters sat around him in a loose circle filling the empty cargo deck.

"How long have we to decide? Did you say?" Kathy Primrose, a relative latecomer to their band, having been found by them hiding in the basement of their vacation home in Switzerland with her two young children, asked in the wake of the awkward silence following that news. Jordana was a popular member of their brotherhood, loved by all. It was easier not to speak of her than to dwell on what the Witen might even now be doing to her.

Arlo was definitely thankful for the change in topic. "The man said seven hours, but really that depends on how much O2 they actually gave us," he managed somehow to answer Kathy, despite the megaton weight laying atop his heart. "The bloke is a complete psychopath, I'm afraid. For all we know, everything he said was a goddamn lie, just some game he is playing with the station residents."

"I wouldn't put it past him," Nessa agreed.

"I was in the cockpit right before you called us here. The O2 gauge was back to reading around a quarter full," Mustafa Roland, a trilingual Sudanese-born Frenchman and early member of their tight-knit band, pointed out. "I don't see how they could fake that."

"Well, we'll know if we start running short of air whether the fool really wants to go through with this whole *honorable battle* madness," Hitch stated dryly.

"Should we just turn back then, Arlo?" Mary Coppersmith, a shy woman, not one to often voice her opinion in their open meetings, asked from the back of the circle. "I mean, if it's really submit to a psycho or fight a battle to the death or suffocate on this ship, then landing on some island and hoping it's clear of monsters and can sustain us doesn't sound like such a bad option anymore."

"I'm not going back down there, not if we have to keep running," Cora Lindross flatly declared. "We've talked about this and talked about this, Mary. We have to be sure to find a place where we can set up roots. We have to give ourselves time to build a compound, to cultivate land, to find peace again."

"Well, that was our dream, yes, mine too," Mary Coppersmith answered her, "but that hope seems lost now. If you all won't agree to head back, then... then... then at the very least we oughta, maybe think about... about... about joining."

"You really would have us join this Witenagemot? Shall we willingly allow all the effort we put in over the years to keep the Bruderschaft a free brotherhood, to keep our dignity in this dystopia, be for nothing, just because our lives got threatened? Is that really how you think we ought to honor our fallen?" Cora put the questions to Mary as kindly as she could. In stronger tones, they could have come across as condemnation.

Arlo knew Cora did not mean it that way. She loved Mary as much as everyone else, and she certainly didn't think less of her. Honest open discussion was simply how they maintained their humanity amidst the daily horror.

Mary didn't take it as a harsh rebuke either. She instead hugged her daughter close and said, "I don't want to give up on our goal. I don't want to sell my humanity to this madman, Cora. I just know I can't watch my baby suffocate in this ship. And I'd rather not go back without the supplies and information we would need to ensure success... I just... I... I'm worried about my child, Cora, about all the children."

Arlo could certainly sympathize with that concern. He knew he could never just sit by and let them suffocate, even if he did talk tough about that option in front of the Witen. Really, Arlo knew that the battle was the only option. He'd gone through it all in his head, over and over again, from the minute the Commander had spoken of it until this very second. The battle was the only answer—their only real chance at keeping the Bruderschaft alive, of keeping precious hope alive. His people needed to come to that understanding on their own terms, in their own time. So he said nothing while others supported Mary's points and others Cora's while others still spoke of unrealistic chances or possible plays.

Finally, before the discussion could escalate to argument, as he had so often done in the past, Arlo broke through the cacophony, "We can't go back, even if we could bring ourselves to face another day of fleeing the hordes. The Commander won't give us the fuel. I'm afraid, my brothers and sisters, that the son of a bitch wants this battle to happen. I recognized a thirst for blood in the twisted man's scarred eye. I think... I think... I'm sorry, but I think we are going to have to fight them."

A burst of anxious and high-pitched discussion rang around the deck in the wake of that statement. Arlo and Hitch and Nessa let it flow and naturally ebb. He took comfort in their presence beside him. They too had known that any return to Earth was a non-starter but, like him, knew the people needed to work it all out before that bomb was dropped upon them.

"Please, my brothers and sisters, please, calm down," Janessa Fussgood, the mama bear of their Bruderschaft implored. "I'm afraid Arlo is right. We have to fight this battle. He won't accept half-measures. We, of course, won't force anyone to do anything but know that the Commander won't let just a few come aboard and join him; it's an all-or-nothing package deal sort of thing. Now, I recognize how unwelcome the prospect is, especially for you Kathy and for you Mary and you Michael and Florence and all of you others with children and blood kin in the Bruderschaft. But there are only fifty-three adults among us. Not enough of those are single to choose our twenty-nine from that pool alone. A few of you with family will have to volunteer as well. I'm sorry, you guys. I'm sorry, but we have to fight this battle. We've no other viable option."

"Who's to say the bastards bow down to us if we come out on top? We'd have to put every last member of this Witenagemot to death when the battle's done or else never know a night's peace up here. They'll want their revenge. And then we'll want ours for their reprisal. And on and on it'll go. Where the hell will it end, I ask?" an exasperated and defeated Collier Streamlight wondered from a few rows in the circle just in front of Arlo.

"There isn't a guarantee, Collier," he told him, shame turning his voice to gravel. "There is no good option here, no easy choice, and no guarantees. We could risk everything, half our damn people, in this battle only to have the bastards renege at the end. I have failed you all. I promised you a regular life again. I promised peace. I promised so many bloody things. But I have failed. I have only this battle to offer you now. I'm sorry."

"Not your fault, Arlo," Terry Yves, an original founding member of the Bruderschaft, said. "It was impossible that you even got us this far. If it's a fight before us for all our dreams and hopes to come true, then I say bring it on. These Witen bastards haven't a clue what they've got themselves into."

"Here here," the chorus rang out from dozens of voices.

"Did you say twenty-nine volunteers?" Helmut Dittmar asked when the chorus faded.

"Yeah, well, twenty-eight actually," Arlo confirmed. "I'll be in the front of the melee, Helmut, just try and stop me."

Helmut smiled at that but still held the confusion about the numbers in his eyes. "Okay, you're one, but who is this other volunteer? Hitch, you fighting this battle?"

"You best believe it, Helmut," Hitch declared with an incongruous anticipatory grin. "But I believe Arlo's math included Elias Sagal rather than myself."

"Who in the bloody hell is Elias Sagal?" Rick Powys, another early addition to the brotherhood, asked, leaning his lanky Welsh frame against the deck's far wall.

"He is the Ethling of the Witenagemot. And he's volunteered to fight beside us," Nessa told them all.

"*The Ethling*, eh? Can he be trusted?" Cora Lindross asked.

"I believe so," Arlo answered, remembering the look in the young man's eyes. *God knows we need all the honest help we can get*, he thought wryly. "We're all agreed then? Battle?" he asked his people, spinning slowly to look as many in the eye as he could.

No one shouted their enthusiastic agreement, but neither did anyone protest. Arlo had his answer.

"Very well then, so be it. Before we get on with the volunteers, I thought we'd lift our spirits a bit. We are instructed to provide a banner for tomorrow's horror show. I believe we should take the opportunity to tell these cocky American bastards just what we think of them. So, with that in mind, what shall our sigil be? What emblem shall the Bruderschaft fight for its existence beneath?"

Smiles alighted on faces all about him, warming his heart before the treacherous cold could finish off its glacial freeze. There were plenty of ideas among them. *God, I love these people*, he thought, allowing a single tear to fall.

CHAPTER 10
LIESEL

INFECTION EVENT: DAY 3,169

This next leg of her excursion would be the slowest. Liesel Collins had known that long before she slipped away to embark upon it. Her unnatural strength and agility had propelled her through the tangled substructure all the way from Branch 4 to Branch 2 with a graceful ease. Even when she first popped out of the airlock on the other side of the terminal, she hadn't needed to control her pace as much as now. Liesel Collins' avatar required no oxygen. Her artificial skin cells did register the cold of the airless void but only as a bit of data advising she not persist long in that climate or risk damage. They even registered the extreme heat as she passed from shadow to sunlight while scaling Branch 2's outer wall and reaching its wide flat roof. She disregarded the data, knowing she wouldn't be out long enough to cause any lasting damage to her flawless mechanical body. Her only concern was not being spotted by some lucky operator. So as soon as she'd crawled down the outer wall that faced Branch 1, and the rectangular Control Room resting at its end in particular, she judged it wise to slow down.

    Liesel had long ago mastered her new body's strength and agility. She may have stumbled a time or two that first week, but only Harrington noticed the awkward imbalances, if anyone. This was her first time with her new body in light lunar gravity, however. She could not risk a stumble. There was nothing to conceal herself behind for this part of the journey out toward the Bruderschaft's E11. She had only shadow as ally from prying eyes for this fifty-yard stretch. It would be too cruel an irony for her to misjudge her strength and leap out into the sunlight just as some bumbling operator happened to stroll up on the Control Room's observation platform to take a gander at the Lunar Dock. She still did not see any such operator up on the platform through the room's huge stanchioned window, but Liesel Collins wasn't about to risk it, not now.

After nine and a half years of utter drudgery, after hope of ever recovering an Alpha and, more importantly, its Synthetic Repository Lubricant, had seemingly faded to oblivion, suddenly, from nowhere, the fated liquid was brought straight to her door. Collins had never been a superstitious person, in her old worn skin nor her new, but she couldn't stop herself from repeating a heartfelt thanks in her head on a continual loop to whomever or whatever was responsible for her unimagined luck.

To have it all fall apart before she could sneak aboard the Bruderschaft's vessel and then into the Alpha printing lab in the substructure below the executive office wing to extract her board members' consciousnesses and upload them into the Alpha bodies that had been printed months before the infection and were now held in cryo-stasis would be too much. She feared the artificial brain inside her composite steel skull might just overload and melt in such a cruelly unfortunate circumstance. So, she was going slowly, her back to Branch 2's outer wall, always in the shadow.

Harrington might mock her should he see her creeping and skulking like some scavenging rodent instead of owning the light, as was only just for an advanced being such as she, but Liesel didn't let the thought bother her. She had danced to his pipes for years now, enough so the big-headed ignoramus probably actually believed she was loyal to him, but that time was almost past. She would cast it all at his feet, all the failures of the past decade. If her fellow board members demanded a scapegoat for their delayed ascension, Hubert Richard Harrington and his government pets would make the perfect foil. *Let him make all the snide remarks he wants. It'll be me laughing in the end,* she thought with delight.

Liesel had been forced to stay close to him this whole time. He alone knew her secret. Her avatar was impressively strong and quick, but she couldn't fight the whole Witen. If they came for her, they'd take her. She'd had a chance at changing things back at the beginning. Harrington had talked her out of it somehow. She still couldn't forgive herself for listening to the bastard. Fair, he had points, good points even. For instance, if she were to fight in the Final Tournament, there would be no way to control her strength so it resembled anything human, and if by a miracle one of the contestants actually managed to land a cut, the crowd couldn't help but notice the dark-red sludge that trickled from the wound. The idiots might well interpret the sight as confirmation that she was infected somehow, rather than a synthetic avatar, but either way, they'd know something was up. Harrington wasn't wrong there. Liesel just didn't agree that it would have been as big a problem as the CEO predicted.

The fools might well have worshiped her as a god, regardless of whether or not they figured out that the infection was entirely AOA's fault. It seemed to her practiced eye that the sheep aboard station were capable of being manipulated into swallowing any conviction in order to keep on living the good life up in the cozy bosom of Cardinal's Nest Lunar Station. But despite her beliefs, she had listened to Harrington. She'd heeded his advice and bided her time and resented the hell out of him for it. Her reward for not strangling the man and burning the other corporate execs and government leaders to death in their quarters had come only yesterday in the form of an offhand statement from Maisie Sagal about the Bruderschaft capturing an Alpha and having a sample of its blood aboard their ship while she made her desperate plea to the station after storming the Control Room with two accomplices.

Harrington and the rest were thrown into near chaos by the girl's announcement. They couldn't understand how anyone was left alive on Earth, much less how they found one of their E11 Transport Ships. Almost the instant the girl's message faded from the PA, Harrington had ordered an emergency meeting at his quarters. Harrington's cramped, one-bedroom living quarters wasn't even next up on their rotation of meeting spots; they liked to mix it up in case the Witenagemot ever cared enough to listen in and find out what the folks they evicted from Branch 1 were up to. Protocol be damned though, Harrington needed to control the speculations. So while they all gathered to drone about who these visitors on the Lunar Dock could be and just what they planned to do about it, Liesel Collins made plans of her own.

She was all set to scale the Branch and break into the Bruderschaft's E11 late last night, but fortune was again smiling on her. Word of the massive protest of drunkards from the Billiard Lounge and what the Commander had promised reached them just minutes before she planned to slip away into the substructure. The delay had her anxious, to say the least, but she deemed it optimal to wait another night, after the Witen met with the Bruderschaft and the situation had a chance to settle on everyone. Her sneak and snag scheme would benefit from the operators in the Control Room growing complacent. Another day of getting used to the big E11 on their Lunar Dock could only help. The Bruderschaft wasn't going anywhere, after all.

So its pluses were clear and obvious. Its minuses negligible. Though all that hardly made the wait any easier. She had to endure a whole day of endless speculating in one meeting spot after the other.

With his subordinates, Harrington argued whether or not some ex-employee of theirs named Arlo Bailey had anything to do with the newly arrived ship. "We disabled his access codes the day he was fired, weeks before the infection spread. There is no way he could know about the evacuation!" he'd shouted at them.

"Well, sir, he was the only other person not on this station who was aware of the alternate launchpad facility in Wyoming, and word is that's where that E11 came from," one or the other of his fickle underlings would point out.

"But how could he know about our evacuation, even if he somehow survived ten years on Earth during a zombie apocalypse?" Harrington would demand on cue. Then get even more frustrated when all he received for answer were shrugs and mutters and hairbrained postulations.

Once those fruitless brainstorming sessions ended, Harrington and Collins then were corralled by the government leaders into explaining where the ship had come from. None had been privy to the alternate launchpad's details and were thus very confused. Harrington tried lie after lie, most involving the satellite platforms that the Steward had claimed they'd destroyed. None of the lies pleased the bureaucrats any. Neither did Collins' silence. Their reproachful looks had no effect on her, however, not then. Liesel knew after tonight she would never have to play her pathetic role ever again. She knew their reproaches and snide comments would turn instantly to fawning gazes and zealous praises.

Liesel paused at the end of the Terminal's outer wall. She would have to be exposed for at least five bounds before she could hide herself behind the E11. Another glance through the Control Room's massive window told her she had all the time in the world to make the short trip. Regardless, she was tucked away on the far side of the transport ship in less than ten seconds. "There you are," she said aloud, though no sound reached her ears in the vacuum. Liesel had spotted the hatch she was after. Just above the refuellable rockets on the first of the ship's cargo-decks, the wheel of a manual hatch only just poked out into space.

"Let's hope these Bruderschaft people aren't complete morons and don't have the deck pressurized," she once more silently said aloud as she began scaling the rockets, finding purchase difficult on their smooth surface. She knew the bastards had no reason to waste oxygen. They had to have depressurized all of their cargo-decks to reduce waste. Nothing was certain in this world though. Liesel Collins had learned that the hard way. So she braced herself against the sudden rush of air as she turned the small white wheel.

The spring-loaded hatch popped open with no surprises though, just as planned. *Another phase of the mission down*, she self-reported. A smile wouldn't be denied. She felt it stretch her synthetic cheeks as she pulled herself through the open portal. Pulling out the flashlight from her back pocket, Liesel went about seeking her prize. Somewhere in this tangle of wares, the Bruderschaft had a vial of Synthetic Repository Lubricant, more specifically, a sample which contained the consciousnesses of her employers. *It's gotta be in a chilled storage system of some kind*, she reasoned, flicking her light all about her. Two aisles over, she found what she was looking for: a refrigerator with a transparent door sat at the far end of the cargo shelves.

The Bruderschaft had themselves ten blood samples from infected people: five children and five adults. They also had samples of various animals' blood. *Why?* Collins couldn't begin to imagine. It was a continual point of humor for her that AOA's dopey, unenlightened scientists thought they could ever devise a cure for the infection. Liesel knew there was no going back once the infection was in your bloodstream. It irreversibly changed organic material to synthetic, essentially turning blood into SRL. What it did to organs in order to prolong them in spite of minimal sustenance was above her paygrade. She was no scientist, but she knew enough to mock the hopes of all the fools who thought they had any power over the infection. They were about a century and a half shy, technology-wise, from even understanding the basic science behind the infection, much less the Alphas.

"Ahh, the Alphas," she reverently chanted as she located the vial she sought. It was a small thing to hold so much power. She knew she held the future there in her pale hand. Turning over the three-inch vial, Liesel's mind raced. *I could smash it now*, she tempted herself. She did have the wrath of Datalis and the other board members to deal with if she were to go through with her plan. She could avoid any possible punishment from them right here and now. *I could smash it. I could*, she once more thought.

Following that action through to its conclusion, Liesel understood she'd be right back to what she was earlier today—Harrington's lackey. *No, I'm done with those ancient, ignorant, backward bastards*, she decided. After all, she still had the option of throwing Harrington under the bus if her board members needed someone to punish for their delayed arrival. Tucking the vial into the front pocket of her trousers, Liesel Collins shook her head and told herself, *Come what may, the true AOA return tonight.*

Closing the manual hatch behind proved a minor trial, but she was back on the Lunar Dock's concrete tarmac less than a minute after stuffing away the precious vial. Peering around the rounded hexagonal rocket, she scanned the Control Room's wide window. Still, no operator strolled the narrow viewing platform. Within the same ten seconds as before, she was once more in the shadows, back to Branch 2's outer wall, feet pressed a good two inches in the powdery soft moondust. *Now comes the hard part*, she told herself, scooting slowly in the shadows along the outer wall. Somewhere along the outer wall of Branch 1 that even now faced her there was a small innocuous button she needed to find. Liesel knew roughly whereabout the hidden-in-plain-sight button was, but she hadn't ever entered the Printing Lab from its concealed outer hatch.

She'd been up to the Nest a few times before the infection to print the Alphas and make sure the facility was manufactured to the proper specifications, but each of those times, she'd entered the lab through the hidden hatchway in the CEO's luxury quarters. Liesel knew what she was looking for though, so kept a high-level of optimism in the face of the difficulty. Keeping her back ever to the outer walls, she slowly bounded from Branch 2 along the Grand Rotunda's outer curve before moving up Branch 1's arrow-straight wall. When she made it halfway down the Branch's length, she slowed her already slow pace even more and turned around to scan the wall.

It caught her eye like a blaring neon sign, but only because she knew what to look for. The simple AOA logo imprinted on a three-inch oval plate would appear to any others as no more than some oddly placed decoration. Liesel knew better. Bounding in close, she depressed the small plate with her thumb. With a click, it slid a half-inch back into the wall. The rumbling beneath her feet came two beats later. *Oh shit*, she thought, remembering the process as she leaped six feet to the left of the small button. Looking back to where she'd been standing only seconds before, she saw the moondust begin to vibrate. With a groan that was felt as opposed to heard, a slit in the soil slowly opened. Widening, it revealed a set of stairs leading below the Branch. Liesel stepped back when the retracting doors below the surface reached their limit.

Groping once more for her flashlight, she descended the hidden staircase. An automatic hatchway embedded into the station's substructure rested at the stair's end. Approaching the keypad embedded in the wall beside the hatchway, Liesel had to stop herself from doubting whether her code would still work. *Calm yourself, you fool. You know damn well your override code cannot be locked out of the system.* The Witenagemot kept operators in the Control

Room, but not a one had a clue. They were basic-level 21st century programmers at best.

The code will work, she told herself, almost like a chant, as she punched the keypad. Nerves can't always be tamed by reason though, and when she failed to hear the hiss of compressed air that heralded the opening of an automatic hatchway, the pulse of panic shooting through her wouldn't be denied. Though it died less than a second after blooming as she saw the hatchway begin its slow retraction. *Fool, there's nothing to hear out here,* she admonished herself, stepping into the dark room beyond.

Moving by architectural logic alone through the pitch blackness, she found the inner keypad. A few keystrokes and the hatch was closing as the lights popped on. Liesel found herself in a small airlock anteroom. Another hatch, very similar to the one she'd just closed, was carved into the wall directly opposite. She would not be granted access to the printing lab beyond until she pressurized the anteroom. Liesel had some difficulty recalling the procedure, but after a few wrong turns, she dialed up the proper protocol. Instantly, she felt the rush of air flowing over her synthetic skin. A red light above the hatchway leading into the lab went from solid to blinking before ultimately cutting out altogether. That was the cue. Liesel could enter the lab. Before opening the hatch, she patted the vial in her pocket almost subconsciously. Its minor bulk proved a comfort as she punched in her code.

The lab beyond was bathed in dim red emergency lighting from an LED band running along the top of the walls the entire circumference of the wide square space. In that dimness, her synthetically enhanced eyes could perceive twelve cryogenic-stasis tubes spaced out along the far wall. Beside her, on either side of the door, twelve more tubes lay perfectly spaced out atop the austere white slab floor. All but four of the stasis tubes were occupied by an avatar, though even her keen eyes could pick out no faces from this distance.

Having been in the lab multiple times before, Liesel knew where the operations terminal was located. She let her feet carry her to the terminal through muscle memory alone. Cracking her knees into a hard, unyielding surface, she knew she'd arrived. Bending down, she found the terminal keypad and woke up the computer. Instantly, its two-foot square screen brightened, displaying the system homepage. Within moments, Liesel had the facility completely lit and humming. The only thing that interrupted her steadfast focus on preparing the SRL sample for extraction was when she happened to step over to fire up the homogenizer and spectrophotometer and caught her first glimpse at one of the synthetic faces inside the stasis tubes.

Virgil Datalis bore an intimidating visage in his true skin and had seemingly ensured that element of his character transferred to his avatar as well. A tall, broad, chestnut-complected man with a solid belly and long limbs was her company's CEO. His angular face seemed to cast shadows wherever it looked. He'd even made sure his avatar sported the same perfectly lined mustache and goatee. It was eerie seeing him there after all this time, looking as though a moment hadn't passed since her consciousness had been sent through the temporal portal. Liesel had to remind herself that she hadn't changed either. It was strange to think about. It wasn't ground she often tread.

Angered over the distracting thoughts, she huffed and marched back to the operations terminal. *Twenty distinct consciousnesses located. Do you wish to proceed with isolation?* the computer asked her. She smashed down the enter key without hesitation. The homogenizer began to spin, and the program went to work. Liesel went about looking for a chair to squat atop while she patiently waited for the program to run its course when a voice crackled over the PA.

"Ladies and Gentlemen, residents of Cardinal's Nest and citizens of the Witenagemot," the Commander began, "on the line with me now is Arlo Bailey, leader of this *Bruderschaft* attempting to force their way upon us and disrupt all we've worked toward over the last decade. I offered Mr. Bailey and his two colleagues a more than fair choice. They are welcome aboard, despite our legitimate concerns, provided they swear an oath of loyalty to the Witen and the New Destiny Constitution. Which is no more than every last one of you have done. Why should they hold themselves above you? Ask yourself that. Now, as I say, if they decide to spurn this gift, the Witen, being the honorable and righteous and *fated* governing council that we are, offered them, in a way, the same chance each of you had in the early days. You all could have challenged in the Final Tournament, just as they can defeat us in battle. If they choose not to come aboard as faithful Witen citizens, then we shall meet tomorrow morning at 11 ST in the Meadow. Thirty of our best will face thirty of theirs in a hand-to-hand battle on that sacred turf. Whoever yields the fight first or loses all its warriors, loses ... everything. If that's the fate these impossible people choose, then I encourage everyone to come out to the Meadow to witness destiny firsthand. First shift shall be placed on skeleton-crew protocol. So, Mr. Bailey, speak your choice loud and clear so all my people may hear."

Bailey's voice took a while to reverberate back over the PA, but when it did, Liesel Collins had to marvel at humanity's bloodlust. "My name is Arlo Bailey, and though my brothers and sisters and I don't doubt most of you folks are fine people indeed, we cannot come aboard to be a part of your morally repugnant regime. We choose battle, Commander," Bailey stated in an admirably steady voice.

The Commander came back with some response just a few beats later, but Liesel Collins, Chief Security Officer for Advancement Operations Alliance, circa 2379, was no longer listening. She was grinning. Good fortune kept right on showering gifts upon her. *The stupid bastards will leave Branch 1 all but empty just when the avatars are ready to emerge. My god, it's almost too easy,* she laughed. Liesel decided she would wait until the last minute to call Harrington and whoever he trusted most among his executives to join them before they presented themselves to the station. The bigger the crowd of supporters around them, the better. Although she really wasn't very nervous about how the Witen, if there even still was one, would react, but a bigger group couldn't hurt any. Liesel smiled as the hum of electricity radiated around her. With a nonchalance she didn't need to fake in any way, she plopped herself down on the slab for lack of a chair.

CARRIE ROXANNA

"But, Eli, wait. I just thought of something. If you're at the battle, then... th-th-then you'll be left behind," she exclaimed from her seat atop an island-counter stool directly across from her big brother. Carrie had come to terms with why he had to fight soon after he'd first explained to her and Tessa what he'd done, but somehow this crucial point hadn't quite registered yet. She'd been enjoying the one-on-one time with her long-lost sibling, staying very much in each moment. They must've had at least an hour alone in the priest's grand Clubhouse after her, Tessa, and Elias' brainstorming session. In all that time, the obvious point never once registered. She did not blame Tessa for returning from her dangerous trip back up to the station-proper for bursting the happy bubble, but her arrival two minutes earlier did start Carrie on the line of thought that highlighted the glaring flaw in Elias' plan.

"That's just the way it's gotta be, kiddo," her older brother responded to her panicked observation after a lengthy pause. "I'm sorry, Ri Ri. It's... it's just... it's the price I owe, is all. It's gotta be."

Tessa stepped back from Boyd's refrigerator then, recycled bottle of water in hand and approached the island countertop. She was still a bit winded. Knowing as well as any of them how little time they had to waste, Tessa had jogged through the access tunnels all the way from deep into Branch 4. "You'll come back for us one day, I'm sure," she told Carrie after a hefty swig. "When the infection is all eradicated, and you and the Bruderschaft are powerful enough to defeat the Witen. Which, with your help, I'm sure they're likely to be in no time."

"You're staying too, Tess?" Carrie screamed when she deciphered Tessa's winded statement.

"No, Tess," Eli flatly declared. He hadn't sounded so serious since he'd made Carrie show him and Tessa the priest's Clubhouse. Shortly after they'd pushed through the manual hatch, Elias had told them of all that had happened at the meeting between the Witen and the Bruderschaft. Resolutely, yet always with a tear in the corner of his eyes that never fell, Elias had explained to Carrie and Tessa why he'd made the choice to fight.

Neither Tessa nor Carrie really pushed back all that hard. They both knew what a gamechanger of a warrior Elias was. They both saw the chance, small though it may be, to slay the Commander. Only after the two girls before him nodded their approval did his manner soften.

It was then he'd told them of Supervisor Addison tracking him down in the Grand Alleyway and passing on the message he'd received from the priest for Carrie to go to his Clubhouse and find his list of associates to plan a prison break. "Tessa, please," Elias tried again after his girlfriend silently ignored him as she polished off her bottle of water. "You have to go with them, baby. After the battle... if we lose... if... well, I... I... well, goddammit, I won't be able to protect you."

"I'm staying, Eli," Tessa told him, climbing atop one of the six stools encircling the black and white island. "Don't even start. Not only because of how much I love your dopey ass, as well as my promise to always be by your side, which I affirmed only a handful of hours earlier, but I have my parents to worry about too. My family is here, Elias. I'm staying, come hell or high water."

Carrie was doubly devastated. She wanted to cry but felt the cathartic act might sway her brother to look on her as an emotionally immature child and convince him not to let her help with their plan. So she bit her lip and looked down at the countertop as she said, "But I j-j... but I just... but you both only j-just joined my life. I can't lose you both now."

Elias loosed the tears Carrie had refused to let fall. He smiled all throughout though, so Carrie knew they were good tears. "Well, Ri," her brother managed through a wide grin, "I guess you'll just have to do like Tessa says then, won't ya?"

Carrie smiled back at her sibling, though she understood full well how hopeless that dream really was. She'd only just gotten her big brother back. Her heart was breaking knowing they'd be separated again soon or, worse yet, that he might be cold and dead in less than twelve hours. Not spoiling the moment was more important than pouring her heart out and making useless pleas, so she smiled and held her tongue.

"So, shall we go over the plan one more time then?" Elias cleared his throat and asked.

"Lay it out, Eli," Tessa invited with a grand prompting gesture.

"Okay, okay. So, first things first," Elias crossed his arms and began the rundown. "You're sure these codes Supervisor Akino gave you will work?" he asked Tessa.

"I laid out to him the exposure he risked in fairly detailed fashion should he provide me the wrong ones," Tessa explained with a what-are-you-gonna-do shrug. "We chose him specifically because he has the most to lose by the priest ratting out all his contacts, remember? The man knew where he stood well enough, I think. Most of my threats were only stated because I found it such fun to watch the self-important jerk squirm."

"And where were you exactly while you were having all this fun?" Elias asked his girlfriend.

"I cornered him in the Rec District's minicaf. Boyd's sheet said the guy lingers there nearly every afternoon. Apparently, he's got some probably perverted crush on some cook who won't show him the time of day."

"So the priest's intel is good then?"

"Uhh, yeah, from what I saw, I guess it was."

"How long were you in the minicaf?"

"Like two or three minutes maybe," Tessa answered with impatience. "Relax, Eli, I did only what we agreed to before I left. I took no unnecessary risks. It's lucky for us that tiny cafeteria is almost always empty. I made it in and out with Akino the only soul to spot me. There's an access hatch I remembered right between the minicaf and IGS pods. And, before you can worry about my other meetup, Footman Leroy was at his quarters in that zigzag alleyway in the far back of Blue Corridor. I just popped out the access hatch twenty yards from his place. I was in and out of there just like the minicaf. Shit, I doubt if I was actually out of cover of the tunnels or Leroy's quarters for more than five minutes total. It all went just like I said it would, Eli. I told ya I knew Leroy. The guy is always shut up in his quarters whenever he ain't on duty. He don't do nothing around the Station for fun. It was actually a fairly uneventful mission, all in all."

"I shoulda never doubted ya," Elias allowed with a wry smile.

"And yet, you'll surely do it again." Tessa winked back. "Anyways, I stayed there in Leroy's stale quarters until he finished a few phone calls and traded a few shifts and favors to get himself on the skeleton-staff for tomorrow. He'll be the lone footman posted in Branch 3 during the battle. From there, he'll call for help from the two footmen on duty in the Grand Alleyway."

"Any word on who that might be?" Carrie's big brother wondered.

"Leroy didn't know. Could be anyone really."

"Not Allanson."

"No, probably not him."

"Although, who knows, the coward might well have faked an injury rather than volunteer for the Commander's thirty."

"I wouldn't put it past him."

"Whoever it is, you sure this call from Leroy will be enough to bring 'em both running?" Elias asked, getting back on topic.

"So the man assured me, anyways," Tessa qualified her answer.

"Addison's dumbass shoulda just gave me his code when he tracked me down."

"That woulda made things easier, for sure. But who knows where that ugly worm is hiding right now? Just be glad Boyd's book included info on where one of the supervisors hangs at least," Tessa pointed out.

"Yeah, you're right. Best not dwell on all the shit we can't change. Okay, okay, good," Elias muttered, rubbing his chin. "So the two footmen pulling duty in Branch 1 run off to help Leroy, leaving you and Carrie a gold-plated window to make your way down the Grand Alleyway and use Supervisor Akino's code to get into the brig and free the prisoners."

"We still better move quick when that window comes, Ri Ri," Tessa said, placing a hand atop Carrie's resting on the island. "Whatever Leroy comes up with, his alert will be bullshit. The two Branch 1 footmen will figure that out pretty fast."

"I'll hustle," Carrie promised. "I can move when I need to."

Smiling at her, Elias cleared his throat one more time to reclaim control of the conversation. "Okay, so, you girls open the cells and cut everyone loose. Then you tap into the terminal beside the Brig's lone hatch. Watch the monitor and wait for a good moment to jump out on the two footmen who will have returned to their posts by then. Remember, be as quiet as you can when you subdue them. You can use one of these shock discs from the priest's serendipitous supply," he added, pointing to the five gray pucks on the white countertop. The priest's list, and the accompanying green notebook, had directed them to his stockpile of super-tech. Boyd managed somehow to collect five shock discs and three video scramblers, all of which were discovered squirreled away in a seldom used kitchen cabinet beside his massive stove. "No reason to waste 'em if you don't explicitly need the things though," Elias continued. "You're gonna need all you can when you take the Control Room. However you take out the footmen, just don't alert the operators in the Control Room."

"We know, Eli. We got it. Trust us," Tessa told him in lightly exasperated tones.

"I do. I do," he quickly assured. "I'm just nervous leaving you alone on such a risky mission."

"We got it, Eli. You just wo-worry about that scary battle you g-go-gotta somehow survive in a few hours," Carrie implored.

"I will. I will. Let's just finish going over the plan before I occupy my mind with that pleasant proposition," he responded with cheeky snark.

"Okay, so... we've taken out Branch 1's guards..." Tessa prompted.

"Right, then you gotta get in the Control Room. And that's when Carrie's brilliant idea comes into play," Elias said, a proud look in his eye as he smiled at her. "You guys contact the operators on one of the footmen's pocket tablets. You'll use their thumbprint to open their tablet and ping the Control Room for help. The operators will see the request as coming from the on-duty Branch guards and will come out to investigate. Most likely both won't come out, but you only need one. All you need is that hatch to open. Have some of the prisoners wait beside the hatch out of sight. As soon as it swishes open, you guys storm in. Toss out a shock disc into an empty patch of room and set it off. Then show the operators—shouldn't be more than two—show them you have four more to use at leisure. That should stand them down quick enough. Tie them up as soon as they throw up their hands. Who knows what kinda hijinks they can get up to on those terminals? Now, there are only four VLSE suits in the Control Room at most, so you all will have to take several trips. So work fast. Suit up four, exit out the emergency hatches that Maisie and her friend used to get in. Hustle to the Bruderschaft's E11. Make sure you stay close to the Branches, now. You don't want the footman manning the PRZVL in the Terminal to see you. Make for the manual belly hatch on the E11's first cargo-deck. It won't be easy getting up there, but after the first trip, you can set up a rope or a ladder or something for everybody else. Once you make it into a pressurized area of the ship, one of you returns with three suits, and you continue the process over and over until you're all aboard. Have those folks in the first waves be your most persuasive. They gotta convince the Bruderschaft to take off and leave their thirty warriors behind. Be blunt. Tell them if any of their brothers or sisters survived the battle, they'll be put to death soon enough anyhow. And if we win, then we will contact you all later somehow. We will track where your ship lands and send word. Tell 'em whatever you need to. Just make them agree to leave. Then, as soon as you're all aboard, you take the heck off. That's important now, Carrie. Promise me you'll leave as soon as that ship is ready. Oh, wait!" he shouted, smacking his knee. "Before you depressurize the Control Room, you gotta have the operators refuel the Bruderschaft's E11. Don't forget that now."

"Don't be like you?" Tessa needled her boyfriend through a teasing grin.

"Yes, by all means, keep your heads. Be better than me," Elias agreed, returning the grin.

"I'm gonna m-miss you, Elias," Carrie said into the silence that followed the rundown. "I wish you we-we-w-were coming with us."

"I wish I was too, kiddo, believe me. But you'll have Maisie with you. You won't be alone."

"And you're coming back to get us, remember?" Tessa pointed out.

"Yeah," Carrie managed, after a time. "Yes, I'll be back. I swear I will."

CHAPTER 11
THE COMMANDER

BATTLE'S EVE

The tub was warm. He hadn't meant to slip off. Within the steam, sleep had crept up regardless. Not even the giggling ginger twins sandwiching him in the oval jacuzzi prevented him from drifting off to dreamland. He knew he'd arrived there once he saw them atop that rust-rotted bus. The Commander hated it here. No matter how many times his subconscious planted him on that cracked and Damned-crowded street, he never got what he wanted. He never saved them. He only ever joined them. *Wake up!* he demanded in an unheard voice from some far-off corner of his shadowed mind. If he'd heard, the dreaming Commander only mocked him, charging yet again into the horde, swinging a black battleaxe that had not been there only moments earlier.

"Carrie! Roxanna! I'm coming!" the dreamer screamed, edging ever closer to the vine-invaded city bus.

His wife's face was bright and hopeful, anxious for their reunion. Its every curve and delicate wrinkle was as clear and well defined as when last Jasper Montrois had seen her. Roxanna's sweet innocence was likewise staring back at him with the same realistic resolution. He did not want to see them, despite how much he missed them. They were the eternal pain pressing heavily upon his heart, and he could not afford to be compromised by longing, not now. There was to be a battle tomorrow, his shadowy consciousness knew, if not the dream-walker. He needed to keep his focus. His family's faces could only complicate things. Waking up before he reached them was imperative.

Instead, he found himself vaulting atop the bus's flat roof with the ease and grace of an Olympic gymnast. *No, not again. Wake up, goddammit!* His shadowy awareness was silently screaming when, abruptly, he was no longer standing atop a rusted steel roof but in his own office—Branch 1's executive office inside Cardinal's Nest Lunar Station, more precisely—a place his wife had never been. Yet still, there she stood across his mahogany desk. As he rose, the image before him shifted. It remained his wife, though she'd suddenly appeared fifteen years younger. Coming out from around his massive desk, he stepped up close. Carrie wore a white gown and veil; he recognized her wedding gown. He looked for Roxanna but realized where he now was and understood his daughter would not be born for another few months.

It was their wedding day. Carrie was reaching out her hand to cup his face. A dob of vanilla frosting from the cake they'd only just cut together as man and wife had stuck in the corner of her lips. Jasper Montrois leaned in to kiss the sugar clean. "I so love you," Carrie whispered in a voice he somehow heard clearly above the cheers of their many guests all about them.

He'd meant to say it back. Jasper Montrois had done so that day; he clearly recalled it. But instead, his mouth stayed closed, and his hand went around her throat. Cheers turned to shocked screams as he lifted her, tightening his grip all the while. *Stop! What the hell are you doing?!* His shadow awareness's scream rattled around his mind. It reached the dream-walker, but it did not stop him squeezing. *No! This isn't how it happened. Stop! Stop! Wake up!* he begged himself as his wife's eyes met his. There was no shock in them, as might be expected. They bore no dismay nor horror, only pity, only scorn, only utter distain. The dream-walker hated the look. Raging, he snapped the twig of a neck beneath his mighty fist.

The neck cracked and the head lolled, but it was no longer his wife's. A woman with features very similar to Carrie's now hung limply in his grip. Stevie Hyun's head dangled loosely off the end of her snapped spine. She was dead, yet somehow she was looking at him. Her tongue drooped from her mouth. Her chest did not rise and fall. But still, she looked at him. Her dead eyes saw. Silently, they accused him. Her voice rang out with charge after charge, though her lips never twitched. With a bellow of despair, the dreamer released the long-dead redhead in his outstretched arm. Stevie's body quickly crumpled into the foggy, unformed floor, sending up a spray of water in her wake as though she'd plopped into a deep puddle.

He bent down, uselessly clearing fog to discover where the body had gone, and a wave rose up out of the mist to crash full into his face. Giggles followed the splash. When he recognized who they belonged to, the Commander awoke in his jacuzzi. Francie and Dianna, his two favorite tub-mates, flanked him either side. Dianna was even then playfully flicking water in his face. "Hello, Mr. Big Bossman, what do you think about Francie's plan for the evening? Do you think you could even handle all that?" Dianna asked, rubbing his chest. Having no idea, nor care, what she might be talking about, he ignored her while extricating himself from their clutches and splashing over to the far side of the enormous tub. "It would be fun, don't ya think?"

"He ain't listening to us, Di. What's the matter, sir? Don't you wanna play today? C'mon, my big sexy Commander, what's got you so distracted? Huh?" Francie asked in her sexy pouty drawl.

"Never you mind. Just shut up and drink," he barked at the pair over his shoulder. "Where the hell is the Steward?"

"Your servant just rang over the intercom to say that he just arrived at your hatchway like ten seconds ago," Dianna told him in a confused voice.

"How could a man drift off to sleep with you and me beside him, Di?" Francie asked, still in her pouty voice. "I think I'm a bit insulted," she added with a splash and a giggle.

The Commander continued ignoring them, climbing from the tub to seek his flip-flops and a towel. He located a dry one lying across the back of the pool chair where his flops were placed just as the Steward shoved through the glass door to stumble into the natatorium.

"Follow me, Steward, if you would," he immediately called, stepping past the man and exiting through the very door through which the Steward had just entered. He never looked back nor said another word, trusting the man to follow. When he'd made it to his kitchen and stepped up to the coffee maker, he was pleased to know he could indeed still trust the architect of the New Destiny Constitution at least that far.

The Steward leaned against the pantry across the kitchen's island counter, but his eyes were on the floor when the Commander finally turned from the coffee pot to face him. For a long while, neither man said a word. Neither hardly so much as moved, unless breathing counted. The Commander would be damned if he'd be the first to speak, so let the silence stretch. The Steward had some explaining to do if he wanted to reclaim the confidence of his sovereign. He needed to remember his place, to remember that he was a supplicant, that he answered to the Commander. So, he stared the small man down as the coffee boiled. Only after the Commander shoved a mug of straight java across the island did the Steward finally look up from the floor.

Still, he stayed silent, however. It wasn't until two sips in that the Witen's number-two man finally spoke. "You wanted to see me," the Steward prompted, eyes on the black liquid in his thick mug.

The man's truculence was galling. The Commander had to fight the urge to lean across the marble countertop and smack the ungrateful jackass. For months now, the Steward had been drifting from his righteous purpose. The Commander had ignored it, hoping it was simply a phase. Then the last two days happened, and the man had been of no real help. Their Witenagemot, the thing the Steward constructed with his very own hands, was in mortal threat, and the jerk couldn't be bothered. He'd hardly done or said anything, apart from protecting his treacherous little protégé. And now, the boy he'd trained and mentored for nigh on a decade was going to fight to destroy them, and the Steward acted as though he didn't know why the Commander wanted to speak with him? The reckless insubordination was bordering on criminal. The Commander tried to tell him as much through glare alone, but the Steward kept returning his gaze to the floor between sips.

Finally, he felt calm enough to speak. "Yes, Steward, I wanted to see you. And you know damn well why," the Commander told him in his signature grumbling growl. "Look at me, goddammit!" he shouted, adding a fist-pound atop the marble counter to punctuate the order.

Slowly, the aging lawyer raised his eyes. "You made the rules, sir. You said they could choose from among our people," he meekly defended himself.

The insolent retort forced the Commander to step away from his number-two and begin to pace along the length of the expansive island counter. "He woulda never thought to volunteer if you hadn't been slipping lately," he pointed out, still pacing, steaming mug in hand.

"I had a different idea of how best to play the Bruderschaft's arrival, I'll not deny that," the Steward appealed, finally standing up straight, "but I have never fostered in that boy any resentment for the Witen. I tried to make him ruler after you're gone, remember? You think I'd encourage mutiny?"

"I don't know what to make of you lately," the Commander said, halting his impatient pacing. "I'm wondering, quite frankly, whether or not I can trust you anymore."

"Of course you can," the Steward answered quickly. "I am the Witen, through and through. I've never been anything but."

"You forget yourself in front of the men. You question me. You show your doubts in your mannerisms. The people see it. You used to tell me of the fawning deference you needed to display in public, and how important it was, so that the people would adopt the same."

"And they did. I had thought the job done, sir. Forgive me."

"Bullshit, Steward. That ain't it. You're different. You've changed. You seem ashamed of your own creation," the Commander accused, stepping back directly across from the much smaller man.

"I'm not ashamed," the Steward tried to assure. His flimsy, half-whispered voice gave proof to the lie though.

"You are directly responsible for all of this, Steward," the Commander told him, leaning across the countertop. "You took humanity's fate into your own hands. You created this present reality. It was you who crafted it from the ashes of the old world. You were the one who molded it into what we've become today, like so much putty in your hands. Its successes are your successes, same as its failures. You cannot avoid your responsibility now."

"I'm not trying to, sir. I swear," the Steward answered, his voice gaining conviction. "I know we can't stumble now. I apologize if I've failed to offer a proper example. My mind has just been racing. I've a thousand scenarios zooming in and out. If I've been distant, it's only because I'm thinking how best to save the Witen, how best to keep this station safe and running, of how best t-to... to save... to save humanity. My thoughts are only there, Commander, I assure you. I'm sorry about Elias, I really am. I'm sorry I didn't see that coming. But you can still trust me, sir. I am still the Witen. My head is here now. I promise."

"So you are gonna fight beside me tomorrow then? And I can trust you will have my back?"

"Of course, sir."

"Very well, Steward, very well. Tomorrow decides all," the Commander growled, partly satisfied anyway, and allowing that to be enough for the moment. "You will be banner bearer then. I didn't want you fighting at all, but you volunteered in front of the whole Witenagemot, so I can't very well stop ya. Though it woulda been in our best interest to give your place to someone who actually has warrior training."

"I know, sir. I... I... I thought about that before I volunteered, but I judged that twenty-nine of our best would be more than enough, and... and... and I... I guess I have felt the doubters lately too, and I judged it worth the trade-off to put any lingering doubts or resentments to rest by having me clearly volunteer to fight for our existence," the Steward nervously explained between sips of coffee.

"Just stay out of the action tomorrow as best you can," the Commander said, forcing himself to accept all the man's explanations. "Hold our colors high and do not let them fall."

"I won't," the Steward promised with his eyes once more fixed on the floor.

"Fine, leave me then. Be in my office ten minutes before the others arrive tomorrow morning," the Commander instructed with a slight scoff and a flick of the wrist.

CAPTAIN ALVAREZ

"The Ethling is mine. I'll tell ya'll that much. I'm gonna be dancing on that fucking traitor's mangled corpse before noon tomorrow, ya'll hear?" Footman Allanson informed them, unprompted.

They were gathered in Lieutenant Woodson's luxury quarters. Six of them stood around the man's square dining table. Woodson had invited them over to help polish off a few bottles of his vast stockpile of wine after the impromptu Witenagemot gathering had wrapped up. The Commander had ordered all officers and supervisors, as well all fifty-three footmen, to gather in the Grand Alleyway just outside the executive office wing almost immediately after Sagal had scurried, hot on the heels of the Euro trash trio, out of the big man's office. Forty-five minutes later, the entire Witen was gathered in a ring around one of the median planter boxes of the spacious arcade.

Their ruler had wasted no time laying out the choices he'd offered the Bruderschaft, nor in asking for volunteers to represent the Witenagemot as one of its thirty warriors, should the Brits and Krauts choose battle. It took Captain Alvarez shouting his desire to be one of the thirty before the silence that gripped the Witen in the wake of their leader's recap and call shattered. All five lieutenants then declared their intent to fight before the echo of the Captain's bellow could fade from the air. The volunteers came pouring in after that, Footman Allanson being one of the first of that latter group to offer up his services.

The footman's eagerness to fight had been evident in the red flush of his otherwise pale face, along with the ruffled state of his normally pristine uniform. Clearly he'd been raging at Sagal's betrayal before the gathering. The young veteran's enthusiasm for justice seemed to make the Silver Corridor Warden proud. The Captain knew Allanson was a favorite of Woodson's. He could hear it in the man's voice even now as he responded to the brash brute's promise to do Elias Sagal in, "No need to take him on yourself, Allanson," Lieutenant Woodson cautioned through a wide smile. "Sagal will be the only bastard the Bruderschaft will have with any sort of weapons training to fear. The smart play is to team up and take him out early. It'll be a cake walk after that."

"The Lieutenant's right, kid," Captain Alvarez concurred. "We'll cut the head off the snake together. But then... that limey prick running his mouth at me in that meeting *is* all mine, ya all hear that?" He emphatically mimicked Allanson's earlier language, looking each one of the other five Witen members around that wide room in the eye to make sure they understood.

"That Hugh Grant-looking motherfucker is all yours, Cap." Lieutenant Schwambach laughed, seating himself in one of the dining table's six tall chairs.

"Refill, boys?" Woodson asked Allanson and Erkov. The two young footmen were plainly nervous to be in such lofty company as Lieutenants Woodson, Schwambach, and Dobechek, not to mention the Captain himself. They managed, though, to nod their heads and hold out their glasses as Woodson stepped over to pour.

"You boys did well today," Captain Alvarez told them, claiming a chair alongside Schwambach. "I saw you. You were some of the firsts to offer yourselves up. That's noble shit. I just hope that after the Bruderschaft's declaration over the PA, you haven't begun to second-guess your decision."

"No, sir Captain. I'm ready to fight. I can't wait," Footman Erkov puffed out his chest to hotly declare.

"I never had a doubt that the pussy European shits would choose to fight," Allanson insisted. "They had to. Karma wouldn't allow Elias Sagal to get away that easy. I knew they'd fight, 'cause I believe it's my fate, Captain, to kill that treacherous toad tomorrow."

"Well said," Woodson told his favorite pupil with a concurrently deferential and approving head nod.

"Words come easy, boys." The Captain poured cold water on their sweet little exchange. "We'll know the truth of all of us come noon."

"That we shall," Dobechek agreed, still leaning against the back of one of the room's tall chairs. "Anything can happen in a brawl like tomorrow is gonna be. Even the greatest warrior in the world can stumble into a pothole or have his weapon break at an inopportune moment or fucking anything really."

"Listen good now, fellas," Schwambach lazily implored. "Lieutenant Dobechek is a woman who would know. You two was probably no more than snot-nosed punks when she fought in the

Final Tournament. So let me sum it up for ya... That there, boys," he said, pointing at Dobechek, "that's the toughest bitch to ever walk the Earth. And yet even still, she needed a bit of luck to win her match."

"That's right." Dobechek slammed her cup on the table to both call for a refill and punctuate her concurrence. "I'm still counting my lucky stars about my weapon winding up within my reach just before I blacked out. Wasn't nothing more than blind luck coupled with a refusal to quit, which is the attitude you're gonna need tomorrow, by the way. And yet even then, there ain't no guarantees. Hell, not even the Commander himself is guaranteed another night in the Nest now that these damn idealistic European pansy ass morons have chosen to fight. So don't go getting cocky now, footmen. That's all I'm saying."

"They know the risks, Lieutenant Dobechek," Woodson assured her, filling her glass. "They'll make it through. I trust our training."

"I just want 'em prepared for whatever," Dobechek answered after a long sip. "Tomorrow is gonna be a hell of a day. Best to prepare them for the truth, for the Witen and humanity both. We need to bring our fucking A games, all of us."

"I won't let ya down, Lieutenant," Allanson promised her.

Tomorrow was sure to be chaotic—that much was plain to read in the fog of future possibilities at least. Captain Alvarez was actually counting on it. Dobechek was right about battle; nothing would go exactly to plan. And somewhere, at just the right moment, in the midst of all that controlled chaos, the Captain would seize his chance. Ever since the Steward had surprised them all by shouting his intent to join the fated thirty, Captain Alvarez had thought of little else. Immediately, or rather as soon as his shock and frustration had ebbed enough to have clear, rational thoughts, he plotted scenario after scenario, contemplating how best to kill the Steward in the height of battle so as to make it look like an honest casualty of war.

The opportunity seemed almost too good to be true. He knew he wouldn't sleep tonight. The temporal proximity of his greatest hopes acted as a pseudo caffeine, sending jolt after jolt of energy racing throughout his every nerve. Captain Alvarez had long surmised that the Commander had been subtly pulling for the Captain to supplant the Steward. When the man sided with him over the Steward concerning the whole matter with the PRZVL and firing at that uppity

British bitch, the Captain felt it confirmed all his suspicions. *He might even have allowed the Steward to claim a spot in the thirty that could have been filled by someone actually useful just so I can get the chance to rid the Witen of the cowardly clerk's poisonous presence*, the Captain posited to himself, growing more certain it was true with each successive word. *The Commander has been afraid the Steward has been plotting to destroy him ever since he made Sagal Ethling. I'll bet he'll thank me with a promotion to be his number-two right after the battle, before that weaselly bitch is even cold.* The more he turned it all over in his head, the more certain he became.

"What are you planning to do, armor-wise, Captain?" Dobechek was asking him.

Snapping out of his hopeful deliberations, the Captain answered, "Not sure yet. What are you thinking?"

"I don't got much. I probably should be back at my place right now actually, cobbling something together. I figure my old Kevlar helmet could deflect a blow or two. Same goes for the vest. Beyond that, I haven't a clue," Dobechek said.

"That's more than we got, Lieutenant, no offense," Footman Erkov added, growing bolder under the influence of the dark-red. "Think about what those of us without the Kevlar vests and helmets are left with."

"You know Dirks has got an engineer buddy," Schwambach offered around a belch.

"And ... what of it, man?" Woodson demanded after a silent stretch, softening the frustration with an exasperated levity over Schwambach's seeming contentment to refuse elaboration.

"I've been back in that workroom of theirs. They got stacks of those lightweight super steel sheets forty feet high in there," Schwambach answered, casual as ever. "They melt the bastards down one at a time in their massive forge and then pour out the molten metal into molds of different types for repairs around station and shit. I seen 'em do it before."

"We ain't got time to make everyone a molded suit of armor, Lieutenant, if that's what you're thinking," Captain Alvarez disabused the dreamer.

"No, no. I ain't saying that," Schwambach assured, after polishing off his tumbler of dark-red wine. "I bet it won't take Dirks' buddy long to cut up a few sheets though. Alls we gotta do, seems to me, is strap a few sheets around our thighs and shins with some tape or something. The footmen can all strap a few sheets around their chest and shoulders too, I guess. The Kevlar vest and helmet oughta be enough for the top half, as far as us officers go. Probably should fix a few squares of steel atop our boots with a bit of tape too. If it comes down to the thirty of us pressing up against the thirty of them, it'll be best to protect what's vulnerable, namely our feet. And, now that I think on it, a steel cup might be worth the time to fabricate under that circumstance as well," he added in his usual flippant, laugh-at-the-world manner.

"We'll see what Dirks' whiny engineer bastard can do for us on that end, Lieutenant Schwambach, but you know what they all are like. You might just have to watch the low blow when the steel starts flying, I'm afraid," Captain Alvarez told him with humor in his voice for the first time all day. "The rest sounds pretty promising though. Not bad, Lieutenant."

"Thank you, sir," Schwambach belched.

Woodson and Dobechek burst out with belly laughs, and when Captain Alvarez only grinned back at their technical insubordination, the two young footmen added a few chuckles of their own. "Erkov, Allanson, gather up your pals, the ones who volunteered, and meet us at the engineers' workroom," he told them, swapping his grinning lips for a thin pressed line. "We'll get everyone set up before the morning. Schwambach, hail Lieutenant Dirks and tell her to get a hold of her engineer buddy."

"On it, Cap," Schwambach affirmed, reaching for his pocket tablet as Erkov and Allanson ducked out of the dining room.

"Maybe we could pound some sort of shield out of these steel sheets or something. If we all had spears too, like a proper ancient Greek or Roman infantry phalanx, we could keep the bastards off us while we spear 'em down one at a time at our leisure. Shit, we could even sharpen the edges of the shields and use them as a weapon too, if the bastards manage to close somehow. You know how well

AOA's fancy future space steel holds an edge. Whadya say, Captain?" Dobechek asked him.

Yes, I've seen its bite, the Captain thought, recalling the infamous black battleaxe the engineers had long ago fashioned for the Commander, and how, in one smooth stroke, it had sheered the head of Abner Hyun clean in half. "Sounds like a promising strategy, if we can get the right gear," he concurred with a caveat. "I guess we'll just see what the bastard can do for us before the battle starts. I wouldn't hold out much hope for miracles or nothing though."

"Well, shit, we might as well rouse all the engineers and put 'em to work then," Schwambach reasoned with a superior chuckle. "We fire up that forge and get all eleven of 'em working up a sweat and earning their pay, as it were, and might be we could have a shield for everyone come the morning. Who knows? Maybe even ones with Dobechek's sinister sharp edge could be included. I imagine we can move mountains if we push the bastards hard enough. There's gotta be enough spears in the Witen's armory to arm all thirty of us by now, don't ya think? If there ain't, we'll gather the spears of those footmen who have 'em and didn't volunteer. If the Captain puts out an order over the tablets, I'll bet we could gather enough to come awfully close to thirty at least."

"I'll see what I can do," the Captain said. The lieutenants' ideas were promising. Any advantage one could claim was an advantage one ought to. The image that flashed in his mind of the Witenagemot thirty armored head to heel, axes and clubs strapped to their backs and spears and shields gripped tight in their hands while marching through the Bruderschaft like tissue paper, gave him a warm and fuzzy euphoria. Captain Alvarez had a feeling he wouldn't be remaining a mere *Captain* for very long. The belief put a spring in his step as he left Woodson's quarters, typing orders into his time-worn tablet.

ELIAS

The weight of the last few sleepless days, the last few restless years really, seemed to hit him all at once. He had told Carrie and Tessa that he needed some moments of solitude to help wrap his mind around tomorrow or some such half-assed excuse. Really, he just couldn't fight back the nervous shake in his hands a second longer and couldn't bear for either to see it. He had put on as brave a face as he could muster while he laid out his reasons to his vibrantly gorgeous love Tessa Rodriguez and his precociously brilliant little sister Carrie Roxanna about why he felt he had to risk the exposure and volunteer to fight alongside the Bruderschaft. He'd even kept up the calm deception for a good few hours after while they'd formulated their plans.

    He and his sister's hour together alone in Father Boyd's secret Clubhouse had indeed proved a great distraction from his worry while it lasted, but reality had come in to burst the happily-reunited-family bubble. Tessa and Carrie had both decided, independent of any suggestion from Elias, to prepare him a proper suit of armor for the upcoming battle. They surmised the Witenagemot could arm themselves quite impressively and effectively, given their resources, and so judged it necessary to get to work immediately on preparing something that could be at least somewhat comparable to the Witen's. Well, comparable to what the footmen of the Witen would likely be wearing anyway. The officers should all still have the gear and equipment from their security staff days, Kevlar gear to be precise. Nothing they could cobble together for padding which also would not limit his range of motion would ever compare to that. The girls were extremely determined to try, nonetheless. Both were clearly as greatly worried as he was about his prospects of surviving the bloody melee just hours away.

    Elias guessed that was why they gave little pushback to his pronouncement. Both had merely uttered some reminder not to stray too far as he stooped out of the priest's cozy chamber. All of them understood full well that there were many in the Witenagemot who would kill him on site for his betrayal should they stumble across his path, regardless of orders. Captain Alvarez may even be inclined to send out men into the access tunnels deliberately seeking him for assassination. The Captain, as well as Lieutenants Woodson and Masterson, and a good deal of footmen, including his constant nemesis Ricky Allanson, had never made their distaste for Elias a mystery.

Despite the fairly strong odds of one or the other of that rather large pool of suspects taking matters into their own hands, Elias figured the tunnels were extensive and convoluted enough that a chance encounter was highly unlikely. So he roamed around in the gloom a bit, searching for a way to slow his heart rate. Finally, leaning against a stanchion bar somewhere beneath the Module Garage, the lack of sleep and unyielding anxiety sucked away his strength to fight off the sandman all at once. He didn't even remember if he'd made it back to the footpath before he'd slipped off.

One moment he was imagining the various spears and axe blades shearing past his face in the morning's battle as he stared off into a shadowed alcove of the station's substructure, and the next he was riding atop a giant gray beast, familiar to him in every way, right down to the musty scent of his thick gray pelt. It had been years since he'd been astride the gargantuan canine. The beast had visited in dreams here and there, but Elias had never once ridden the wolf since stabbing that great bull all those years ago. Yet there he was, as comfortable as an old-hand cowboy in the saddle.

Bounding all about a freshly planted farm field, they even howled in unison at the mighty moon hanging low in the star-speckled ebony sky. It all felt so familiar, like a straight replay, yet also brand new, like a movie viewed through a new perspective lens. He gloried in the baying and running, in the freedom of knowing he was king. This world was theirs, Elias and the wolf's. There was no one they ever need fear.

The warm security that came with being pack leader was intoxicating. It made him want to howl even more. Elias didn't know if it was his own thought or the wolf's, but somehow he felt that if he could only just bay loudly and powerfully enough, it might push the rogue, mocking moon back into its proper place in the night sky. The thought became an obsession. And so he tore up the neatly planted rows of crops in his frenzy to defeat the massive gray-white orb.

How any noise could penetrate their ferocious howls was a mystery Elias' dreaming self seemed not to care about. He only knew he desperately wanted to turn to see the shouter as soon as the soft words saying, "Elias don't go back to them, not really," reached his ears.

Elias turned, but the mythical beast he rode atop did not. No matter what Elias did to get the wolf to budge, still, it would not acknowledge the young girl on crutches standing behind the farm field's post-and-rail fence calling for Elias to stay with her. Not until he had the thought to leap off the wolf's back and run to her did the shaggy gray giant give up his truculence and turn around to face the little girl. Elias knew it was his sister Carrie there, leaning heavily on the old failing fence, a part of him did anyway. Another part of him, the wolf half, saw only an enemy. It saw prey. That part did not know the girl. It would not even learn her name when the other half spoke it. Elias felt its hunger and tasted the anticipatory copper tang of fresh blood and raw flesh on the back of his tongue.

"No!" he screamed aloud, but the beast was not listening.

Elias had no more control over the massive wolf beneath him than a random passenger in coach once had over their 747 from Denver to Dallas. Just as they had been, Elias was merely along for the ride. Screaming "No!" louder and louder wasn't helping any. Pulling hard on the beast's thick gray pelt did not slow it. Kicking his heels into its flanks had no effect. And the wolf was nearly on the sweet, gentle child now. Elias was going to have to feel the glory of a fresh kill simultaneous to the horror of destroying his sister. The terrible understanding awoke something within. He felt himself sever from the beast. At long last, his will was his and his alone.

The wolf, though, still had its own will. And it was still charging his innocent baby sister. Bereft of better options, Elias dove forward, wrapping the creature's enormous gray muzzle in a bear hug. The wolf bucked and growled. Elias only clung all the tighter. Slamming down, he crashed to the turf over and over again. The beast was bashing its head trying to shake him free. Still, he clung—until the paws and claws came raking in. The wolf scratched itself free. Elias was left with bloody arms from wrist to shoulder and deep gashes across his neck and cheeks. He felt them, but the pain was far away. The drive to save his sister muted all else.

"Here," he heard the hazel-eyed angel beside the fence say, "you may find it enlightening," she finished when he turned to look at her. Still leaning against the rickety post-and-rail, Carrie held a worn red book toward him in an outstretched hand.

Before he could think to reach for the little hardcover, the wolf growled low just above him. Elias watched as it bared its teeth, glistening slaver from the ends of pointed fangs. Growling low, it reared back to pounce. Carrie stood but six feet away, well within the range of the beast's considerable leap. Bellowing with fear and rage, with sorrow and despair, with courage and conviction, with cowardice and hopelessness, Elias lurched up from the dirt to snatch the mighty slavering jaws in either hand. A strength was with him then, a supernatural strength that he dare not question. Straining, he pulled the jaws wide open but did not stop there.

Whether or not Carrie was still there behind him, Elias couldn't say. All there was now were the quivering jaws wrapped firm beneath his torn, blood-slick grip. A veil of darkness had cloaked the rest of the world. Elias knew he had to act fast. He could not give in to the savage pain, muted or not, in his lacerated hands—not now. He had to keep pulling. So that was what he did. His bicep and shoulder muscles tore. Blood vessels burst in both eyes. But still, he pulled. The snap of thick bones followed by the whimper of a defeated predator finally came as music to his ears. The sweet sounds even ended the pain, though it might have been his confusion numbing his senses. Mere seconds after the break, sparks came shooting out of the unnaturally wide maw of the dead wolf within his clutches. Its eyes burst, running like white rivers down its furry cheeks. Glowing red mechanical eyes were laid bare below the organic false ones. He felt the sparking monster shudder back to life, and a wave of its hot ammoniated oily breath washed over his face.

Then, clap, the whole universe was black. The beast in his grasp was once again unmoving. *Dead again*, he knew, though he could not see it. Collapsing from exertion, Elias crumpled atop the shaggy corpse of his former canine friend but awoke with his cheek plastered with sweat to the cold metal grating of an access tunnel footpath. He didn't have his pocket tablet on him, not since first entering the tunnels with Carrie hours and hours ago, so he had to get up and stumble to a tunnel junction to locate one of the many communication kiosks embedded into each junction's central stanchion just to check the time. Elias wanted to see just how long he'd been out. The dream was as quick as it was enduring, but that meant nothing in realtime. He calmed and allowed himself a yawn when the timestamp on the kiosk homepage indicated that he couldn't have spent more than a half hour drooling on that footpath.

"Good," he said aloud in the yawn's wake, thinking what an irony it all would be if he overslept and missed the battle because he couldn't be found. *It would be fittingly poetic though*, he joked with himself, thinking back on the time he nearly slept through his father's fateful match in the Final Tournament.

The irony reminded him of what he still had in his back pocket. Simultaneously, he saw his sister both in the dream, leaning on the old fence and holding out his father's worn red book, right alongside a superimposed memory flash of Carrie smiling in her clubhouse, the same hardcover held out to him in the same small pale hand. Slowly, he reached back to tap his pocket. He felt the old blue ball cap first. Its bill was crumpled, but he could clearly feel it through the fabric of his tactical trousers. The idea of it balled up and compressed into the bottom of his pocket was somehow heartbreaking in a way he hadn't the time to analyze. So he set it aside and patted his other pocket. The book was indeed still there. A part of him wanted nothing more than to whip it out and flip to his father's favorite poem. Another part knew how painful the act would prove, and so he was hesitant.

In the end, his need to read aloud the words his father had so often recited to him won the battle of wills. Though that's not to say his hand wasn't shaking as he held the Kipling poems before his eyes. Very delicately, Elias thumbed through the yellowing pages, coming at last to "If." The poem's title was nearly rubbed clean from its oft perused page. He might have missed it, if only he hadn't committed the page number to memory years and years ago. Perry Sagal's sage and contemplative voice came alive inside his head as he began to read aloud the worn words,

If you can keep your head when all about you

Are losing theirs and blaming it on you,

If you can trust yourself when all men doubt you,

But make allowance for their doubting too;

If you can wait and not be tired by waiting,

Or being lied about, don't deal in lies,

Or being hated, don't give way to hating,

And yet don't look too good, nor talk too wise...

Elias was bawling by the time he'd reached the end. All his father's wisdom, distilled into those thirty-two lines of bluntly beautiful advice, unleashed a decade's backlog of emotion. He had not been the man advocated in the stanzas, not by a long shot, but he had not completely failed his father quite yet. Tomorrow was a gift. He must have recognized as much hours earlier, or else he wouldn't have agreed to fight. The words and memories had simply made obvious what he'd only barely understood in a passive, subconscious kind of way before: a chance to prove his honor, an opportunity to stand up and fight for true virtue. Redemption had kindly come knocking.

Perhaps he could never make amends for abandoning his sisters for so long, nor for participating in a corrupt and solipsistic lie. He knew what the Witen was all along, the part of him his father had trained had known, anyhow. That part of Elias Sagal was reawakened now, and he could no longer deny the underlying thrill-chasing and simple power lust that had kept him happily blind for so long. The recognition increased the tears, but Elias considered them a blessing, washing his fears clean. The release seemed somehow necessary, as if he were making room for the iron determination that was swimming in to replace the crippling guilt and fretful doubts.

Clearing the salty mess from his surely red eyes with his shirt sleeves, a sudden whim took him. His fingers began tapping and swiping at the junction kiosk. They knew what they were about, even if Elias' present self did not. Before pressing send on the communication request link though, he reclaimed control of his digits and paused to think the action through. *He'll most likely be alone in his quarters this time of night*, he tried assuring himself. *And if he ain't, then he ain't*, he mentally shrugged, before clicking the enter key and establishing a video chat with the Steward.

The dainty, dusty screen displayed a spinning progress wheel. An old 90's style phone-ring chimed lowly from the kiosk's tiny speaker. Elias got lost in the repetitive sound. So much so that the Steward's face suddenly filling the screen took him off-guard. "I had forgotten I'd given you my private access number. It took four rings before the memory of that day resurfaced. As soon as it did, I knew it was you," the Steward said in a tired voice that Elias guessed wasn't only due to lack of sleep.

"It was the day of my ceremony," Elias told him, remembering the private moment they'd shared. The Steward had sat down with him at a table in the Main Cafeteria after the short service where Elias had been dubbed the Ethling by the Commander's own axe. It had meant the world that such a lofty councilmember would share a public meal with him. The Steward had always treated Elias kindly, far more so than most, but he'd never dealt with him on equal terms before. Elias felt seen as a man for the first time in his life. The pride he'd felt had burned away any concern about all the wary, jealous eyes that had studied him ever since. It was during that publicly private dinner that the Steward had given Elias the code for his private vid chat line so that he might call the Steward anytime... *"Whenever something is troubling you, day or night... within good taste"* had been the Steward's exact words, rendered in companionable tones.

"I remember it vividly," the Steward said of that auspicious day. "I thought you might call, some small part of me anyway. Perhaps that's what kept me awake."

"I didn't know I was going to until I had already dialed," Elias told his old mentor.

"Alvarez's men tracked your tablet down hours ago. I told him you'd ditch it. The fool thinks everyone is as dumb as he is. So where are you calling me from exactly? Some kiosk in the access tunnels?" the Steward asked after a huff and sigh.

"I'm sure you can do a quick trace and find out exactly which one. I'll be long gone by the time you send someone to it though," Elias declared in a voice he hoped had sufficient scorn to discourage the man from even bothering.

"And why would I do that? Are you planning to avoid tomorrow?"

"There's no avoiding tomorrow, for either of us," Elias sadly stated.

"Perhaps not," the Steward allowed. "What is it you called me for, Elias?" he asked after a lengthy silence.

"I don't know," Elias answered honestly.

"Something you want to say to me, maybe?"

"I won't apologize, if that's what you mean," Elias said, unable to stop his lower lip from quivering and spoiling his defiance. "I can't. I'm not sorry."

"I know."

The Steward's quick acceptance threw him a bit. Elias didn't know how exactly the Steward would respond to his refusal to show contrition, but the man's instant two-word answer was not at all like what he'd been imagining. "You... you... are you saying... you... you understand?" he asked, confused and hopeful.

"I didn't say that," the Steward cautioned. "You betrayed us, kid. You betrayed me," the number-two man in the Witenagemot told him with a piercing glare.

Elias said nothing.

"I nearly lost the Commander's trust," the Steward continued, stern disappointment in every syllable. "I had to volunteer to be one of our thirty. You put that weight on my shoulders. Your actions did that. I... I gave you cover, and you betrayed me. The rest of them sensed a weakness in me, because of you... and maybe they were right. Either way, I had to volunteer to fight a battle I have zero skills to fight, all because you made them doubt me."

"I won't apologize," Elias restated.

"I didn't ask you to," the Steward said, dropping the scornful edge in his tone in the span of a single breath. "I won't apologize to you either. I took you under my wing. I saw greatness in you."

"You saw your son," Elias shot back. "I was a tool to fill a hole in your heart. Just like the Witenagemot was your tool for exaltation. I don't know if you still believe yourself, or even if you ever did, but don't lie to me now. I didn't call for that."

"Why did you call?" The Steward's voice was more sad than indignant, despite Elias' bluntness.

"To say goodbye. You were good to me, in your way. I don't hate you. I should. I know I should, but I don't. I just... I ... just wanted to say goodbye, I guess."

"And what happens tomorrow then, should you and I come face-to-face amidst the carnage?" the Steward asked with anguish plain in each begrudged word.

"I'll ... do what I have to," Elias told his narrowly wise teacher, his flawed master, his dear and true friend.

"So will I," the Steward finally managed in a cracking voice while wearing a bittersweet smile.

"Goodbye, Harclay."

"Goodbye, kid." The Steward ended the video chat. Elias stared at the black communications window for a long time after. He might've cried again, had he any tears left. Instead, he sighed, shaking his head at the madness of life. At length, he got his legs moving again. *Suppose I better go see what the girls have cobbled together for me*, he thought.

DOLLY

"It's gonna be alright, sweetie. My husband won't let me go out like this. You'll see, honey. Boyd will get us all out of here before too long," Dolly told a nearly hysterical Arlene Fincannon strapped tightly to the chair beside her for the eighth time.

The younger woman had been battling fits of panic since Dolly, Larry Holderman, and Aziz Patel had been strapped tightly to chairs of their own in one of the brig's larger cells alongside her. On top of that, Arlene had been blubberingly pleading for forgiveness in between the bouts of fear. She'd mumble about some footmen sneaking up on her during her shift in the IGS pods to snatch her before she even had a chance to run, as well as continually begged Dolly and the others to excuse the fact that she didn't demand Roddy Sheffield let them kill her rather than open the Control Room hatch. "I was just so scared," Arlene would weep. "He had his hand around my neck, and... and... I could see his axe slung across his back. I kept imagining it covered in my blood. I... I... I was just so scared. Please forgive me, but... I begged him to open up. I begged, and they did. And now..." The newest member of the resistance's inner circle would always break off then to sob.

Larry and Aziz stayed silent in the face of Arlene's nervous ravings. Dolly had been forced to set aside her worry over what they were doing to her husband in that cell they had thrown him in all by himself. A friend needed her just then. So she'd done her best to comfort the woman, even though it had been little more than repeating her assurance that her Ray would save the day somehow. Larry's silence she could excuse. After all, he'd only recently witnessed his longtime lover and closest friend strangled to death before his eyes. She had a harder time forgiving Patel's effort though.

Unless he was involved with Jed as well, Dolly suddenly pondered, feeling her right eyebrow shoot up. That might explain the awkward waves drifting off the two men tie-strapped to steel chairs on the opposite side of their buttercream prison cell. Several times over the past—however the hell long they'd been locked up together, Dolly had no sense for that sort of thing—she had watched Larry pull his knee away when Patel had stretched his out. *It could all be explained by Larry Holderman's guilt*, she tried to tell herself. *Perhaps he just doesn't care to be reminded that he'd been two-timing the man who'd just risked his own life for the very cause he'd spent years trying to convince him to join.*

That was certainly possible. Men from her and Larry's generation weren't known for their expertise in properly processing and expressing feelings. But something about their behavior made her believe there was a little more at play. Either way, she just wished one or the other would get over their shit and give her a hand.

"It's gonna be okay, Arlene. It is. You'll see. Boyd will get us out of here," she assured for the ninth time. Dolly had to grit her teeth to do it. Her hands had gone numb under the tight straps, and it was all she could do to keep from screaming.

"My god, Dolly, will you stop saying that already? Please," Larry Holderman spoke for the first time since they had all been left alone in the cell. "The ditzy broad don't need to hear your bullshit right now. None of us do. Might as well be honest in our last hours. Nobody's coming for us, Arlene," he barked at the emotional woman.

"Stop it, Larry!" Dolly ordered. "If you can't be useful just now, then just keep on sitting there in silence. Same goes for you too, Aziz." Patel looked at her with confusion in his eyes, but Dolly didn't give in to the innocent charade. "You two both know full well all the friends my husband has got around this place. All of them got a whole lot to lose if Boyd starts talking. They aren't gonna want that. Someone will be breaking us out of here soon enough. And that ain't just bullshit, Lar. Now, I'm real sorry about Jed. I loved that man. And that bastard Commander will pay for all he's done. But for now, best we can do is keep our heads and not lose hope. Arlene, don't you listen to them. You understand me, darling? Boyd is coming for us, I promise."

"I believe you, Dolly." Arlene managed a smile. "I'm sorry I been so difficult. I know you all have plenty of worries of your own, and here I am bawling and showing you I wasn't good enough for the resistance all along. I'm real sorry I let you all down. And... and I'm real sorry that alls I can do about it is stupidly say sorry over and over again. I know that don't help any, but I... I just can't help it. I fucked things up so bad."

"Don't say that, honey. I'da begged Ray too, had it been my neck in the Commander's hand and him the one behind the hatch. You're a brilliant coder. Your father taught you well. And now you're far better than he ever dreamed he could be. I know too that Roddy don't give you the credit, but you had a big hand in the secure comms network. My Ray knows that too, honey. He knows your worth. The resistance is far better for your help than we could ever really know. So enough of this beating yourself up crap. Okay?" she demanded with a soft grin.

"Okay," Arlene managed, trying to wipe some of the tears from her cheeks onto the shoulder of her sweater.

"And as for you two," Dolly said to Larry and Aziz, talking now only to distract from her tingling hands, "whatever you think you're proving by ignoring each other in a moment where comfort and love is required, it ain't worth it. Grow up and forgive yourselves. Jed is gone, but he wouldn't want any of us to punish ourselves for it. He risked himself for a noble cause. Now let's honor him by keeping our focus, by keeping our hope. It ain't foolish, Larry. Raymond Boyd will die before he ever lets me down."

Larry had his chin in his chest as she spoke but now slowly raised his head. His eyes were mean when they met hers. Dolly was not expecting that. She'd thought it likely to see disbelief there, or stubbornness, or even scorn, but not out and out anger. "Your husband is probably already dead," he told her as calmly as if someone had asked him the time.

Aziz gasped. Dolly tried to tell herself she hadn't heard the man properly. No amount of recent trauma permitted one to say something so vindictive. Arlene started sobbing again. Larry just kept up his barbarous stare. Finally, Patel broke the tension. "That was cold and unnecessary, Larry. Take it back," he demanded of Holderman in his accented baritone.

"It's the truth. We ain't never leaving this place," Larry said, shifting his menacing gaze to Aziz. "And I ain't just talking about this station. I mean we ain't ever leaving this prison, not in one piece anyways. Don't you remember what they did the last time they had prisoners? You remember when they marched 'em all into the desert? Each one looked like they'd had the shit kicked out of them for the whole month they was locked away. That's our fucking fate now, ya'll. So spare me your foolish fucking hope, Dol. Your husband ain't coming to the rescue. He's dead. Maisie and her girlfriend too. It's all over. All of it."

"I remember the prisoners in the desert, Larry, quite well actually," Dolly said, slowly, so as to maintain her composure. "Gabe was one of them, in case you've forgotten. So yes, I fucking remember what they did to him. Don't tell me to lose hope. I had to watch my husband strangle to death at the end of a rope. If any of us has an excuse to give up, it's me. But I still believe. And it ain't foolishness. It's righteousness. Giving up is easy. Thinking the worst and grieving about it before it's even confirmed is easy. But I still believe. So, you just sit there quietly, like I said. I understand your pain. But you just sit quietly, and don't tell me to give up hope. Raymond Boyd is coming to save me. He's coming to save us all."

THE STEWARD

Sleep was no longer in the cards. Such had been the case even before Elias' video call. The Steward certainly felt drained; a weariness had crept into his very bones, but sleep would never come, no matter how long he lay in bed, darkening the world around him with his silk sleep-mask. So the Steward didn't even bother. Only seconds after he'd ended the chat, he'd allowed his feet to carry him to his bar-globe in the middle of his spacious master bedroom. He was surprised, though, to see his hand shaking as he filled a moonshine tumbler nearly to the brim.

"*I'll... do what I have to,*" he heard the boy's recent words in his head, followed by his own reply of, "*So will I,*" as he gulped half the glass in one swallow. It had been simple enough to say; he'd managed it without breaking, anyway, but thinking about what exactly it really was he would have to do tomorrow was far more difficult. *Could I really kill that boy?* he asked himself. His brain responded with images from nine years before in that dark damp cave. A knife was in his hand, its point deep in his son's young belly.

"No! That's not how it happened!" he castigated his faulty memory. The tumbler fell, discarded and forgotten, to the carpet. Both hands went to his head, squeezing the skull within. The mad thoughts weren't real. He never could have harmed the boy. "I didn't!" he declared to the empty bedroom.

What of Elias? his mind immediately asked. *Will you kill him too?*

"No!" His bellowed response echoed around the low, barren chamber. "It didn't happen that way," he huffed, snot blending with his tears. "I won't let it happen that way." Plopping down on the edge of his bed, the Steward attempted to promise himself that Wally had left to find his mother. *I begged him to stay. He wouldn't listen. He... he left.* The memory of his son marching alone out of the cave wouldn't come though. He knew it had to be somewhere in the jumble of his memories. Sift them all he like, however, he could not find it. *He left. I know he left. I ... shoulda stopped him, but ... he left. I wouldn't kill him. I won't kill Elias either. I can't.*

What if the Commander demands it? His vicious inner voice broke through his growing confidence to pose the fateful question. The Steward did not want to answer. The inner voice nagged and nagged, but he refused to look at it.

It won't happen like that, he finally told his pestering moral conscience.

You hope, the conscience quickly retorted with sinister sarcasm.

"It won't come to that! I won't let it!" he screamed back at the silent voice, bursting off the bed and wagging a finger at his empty room.

You're losing it, Steward, the voice told him, mocking his title. *Look at you. You're shouting at yourself. Maybe you ought to hand your duties over to Captain Alvarez after all. It's all for the survival of mankind, right? Shouldn't the best man for the job be the one who holds it? Or was Sagal right? Was this all for your ego?* The sarcasm and disrespect in the tones of his inner voice reached epic levels. *All the bodies the Witenagemot has stepped over in order to get where you are today—was it all to get back at the big mean men who burned you?*

Harclay hadn't the confidence or strength left to defend himself. As he dropped back down on the edge of the bed, the fingers of his right hand sought the faded scar tissue on the meaty part of his left forearm. He tried to remember the pain of Brent Ashly's cigarette grinding its cherry coal into the soft skin there, but like Wally's exit, it too would not come.

Was that what all this was for? Was that puny little scar worth all the lives your Commander has stamped out of humanity's threadbare existence? the inner voice needled. *Aren't you all supposed to be growing the population? Ain't that the responsibility you assigned yourselves?*

"It is growing," Harclay answered aloud.

No, the cruel conscience told him, *you're simply adding meat for the grinder.*

"No," he shot back at himself, as well the empty room, though all the indignant anger had left his voice. "No. We've saved the world up here. Someone had to take firm charge. Billions of people died. Our species was barely hanging on. The rules changed. I did what was necessary."

You keep telling yourself that, the inner voice mocked. *We'll see how long that lasts. Battle is on its way—don't forget.*

The Steward was well aware of the fact that, simple banner bearer or not, he would likely have to fight at least one or two foreigners to death in little more than a half dozen hours. He didn't need his prick of a moral conscience reminding him. That unavoidable event was in fact the very reason he was back on his feet before the inner voice could finish its taunt, heading to his globe once again. He left the earlier tumbler where it lay in the now sticky carpet and poured himself a few fingers into one of the three remaining clean tumblers inside the spherical bar.

He had no fighting skills to speak of, even back when he wasn't ten years past his prime. So he figured being piss drunk when the battle started couldn't make much difference to his chances of surviving. Also, if he pissed himself, no one would be able to tell if it was abject cowardice to blame or simply the ill-effects of booze. There were only upsides to imbibing, as far as he cared to look anyhow. Therefore, he did not hesitate to refill the crystal tumbler anew as soon as he drank it empty. The pattern repeated after that, only stopping hours later upon the jangle of an alarm clock purring from his pocket tablet to announce a morning of destiny.

CHAPTER 12

ARLO

THE BATTLE OF THE BLOODY MEADOW

The hour had arrived. Arlo Bailey had spent all night silently wishing time to cease its cruel and incessant crawl. Wishes weren't granted in the new dead world, though. Soon they would all learn if ten years of scratching and clawing, barely eking out an existence among the cannibal hordes, would all be for naught, despite his naïve hopes. The Bruderschaft, the family that had been forged amidst chaos and carnage, could very well be facing their last day as free men and women. As much as Arlo did not want to face the truth, he knew, just as his other twenty-eight brother and sister volunteers did, that the odds were not at all in their favor. The Bruderschaft did not lack for heroes, nor for experienced survival fighters, but they all understood they could hardly compare to the thirty trained hand-to-hand combat warriors the Witenagemot were sure to muster. Let alone the equipment disparity.

Arlo wanted to lead his people toward the battlegrounds with shoulders square and a confident stride, but the plain truth of their odds weighed too heavily on his heart. Utterly scared for his people as he was, Arlo nearly stumbled as he led his twenty-eight through Morgana 1's belly hatch. The chuckles from the pack of footmen waiting at the end of Nest Gateway to escort them to the Meadow that followed his foot catching the lip of the narrow portal helped to settle his nerves though. They might have hoped it would be intimidating. Instead, Arlo used their ignorant machismo to steady his breathing and lift his chin. He kept the firm, defiant posture for the entire stroll down the wide catwalk.

Captain Alvarez, the self-important asshole who'd traded insults with Arlo at yesterday's meeting, stood in the center of the pack of a dozen or so cross-armed footmen. "Last chance to back out," the officer told them. "I'd take it if I was you. That ratty shit you got strapped to ya'll for armor ain't gonna stand up well at all compared to us. Ya'll might as well be wearing tissue paper for all the good that pathetic shit will do ya."

The man had a point. The Bruderschaft couldn't find much by way of armor, beyond taking their few acetylene torches to some cargo containers and hacking off slats of steel. Most of his people had strapped oblong scraps to their upper arms and thighs with duct tape or had it quickly sewn into their coats and cargo pants. Many had devised make-shift breastplates by gluing lengths of ratchet strap to a square of steel. There hadn't been much time to cobble together enough for all of them, though. The others were simply relying on leather jackets stuffed with padding. Nearly all of them had made their own individual modifications and additions as well. And as for head protection, only Luca Clijsters actually still carried a Kevlar helmet from his Army days with him. If they'd have known, they could have gathered up enough military helmets to supply every brother and sister in the Bruderschaft two or three times over. But they hadn't known. And hindsight being 20/20 was of no help either. Their heads would have to be exposed. That was that.

Just how well any of their half-assed armor would fare in the coming struggle, Arlo did not like to guess, but it didn't take much imagination power to predict scattered steel scraps littering the grassland at battle's end. "You plan on leaving us with our few clubs and knives and hatchets and the like against your fancy steel too?" Arlo sardonically retorted to the cocksure officer. "How many advantages do you people need? Huh? Just how far can you rig this bloody shite and still pretend you've got any honor?"

Alvarez glanced around at his audience of footmen with a petulant grin on his lips that Arlo felt like smacking off and shoving back up the smug buffoon's asshole. Finally, he looked back at Arlo, the grin growing wider. "No, Mr. Bailey, quit pissing your britches. We have emptied our armory. At the Meadow you will find nearly a hundred blades to choose from, as well as hammers, morningstars, mauls, and everything in between. Our engineers crafted each one from AOA's super steel. You couldn't find any to rival them anywhere back on Earth. And you and your people can take your pick of any of it. Hell, you can snatch up it all, if you really think that will help any," he added with a mocking scoff as the footmen surrounding him giggled like twelve-year-old playground bullies.

"Lead on then," Arlo muttered through gritted teeth.

"You sure?" Alvarez laughed. "I'm telling ya, me and my people ain't gonna take it easy on yas. We're gonna fucking massacre you tea-drinking, refined, fancy-ass intellectual bitches. Understand that. If you cross this here threshold," he said, tapping his foot on the end of the rubber walkway a pace in front of him, "there ain't no going back."

"The man said lead on," Barret Hitchens growled beside Arlo. "What's the matter, Captain? You dense as well as sadistic?"

Alvarez managed another mocking scoff, but his eyes told the truth. He wasn't nearly as confident as he was pretending. The look was heartening. Arlo used the revelation as fuel to propel him forward. Without invitation, he marched past the threshold, the gaggle of footmen parting before him in a tense silence.

Elias Sagal stood alone at the far end of the Terminal. His footman's gray blouse no longer draped his shoulders. A breastplate with hasty straps, much like the ones the Bruderschaft devised, lay atop a tight black t-shirt. Whoever had made Sagal's armor either had more skill or more supplies to work with than the Bruderschaft. The slats of steel sewn into his cargo pants and strapped tight around his forearms and biceps seemed to be far more secure and durable than anything Arlo or any of his people now wore. A part of him thought to begrudge the young man his advantage, but another reminded him that Elias was on his side. That part thought not to spurn the edge, but rather revel in the sight of the two wicked weapons poking up over either of Sagal's bulky shoulders.

"You look ready," Arlo told him as he reached Elias' isolated position beside the Terminal's archway.

"I hope I am," the boy modestly responded.

The retort brought a grudging, and much needed, smile to Arlo's lips. Placing a hand on Sagal's shoulder, he said, "Then let's not put things off any longer. Lead the way, kid." Elias smiled and nodded his head at the Bruderschaft's warriors following close on Arlo's heels. "We'll talk strategy on the walk over."

"Very good, Mr. Bailey. From what I've been hearing, we're gonna need one," Elias said, setting off down Branch 2's long alleyway.

"It's just Arlo, kid. There ought not be formalities in a foxhole, figurative or otherwise," he added with a bit of dark cheek as Hitch, Tionne Jepson, Luca Clijsters, Helmut Dittmar, and a few others pressed in tight to join the strolling confab.

Sagal was bright as well as bold, Arlo was pleased to discover. He'd told them of the rumors he heard of the Bruderschaft keeping the engineers up all night making steel shields for all thirty of the Witen's warriors. Elias suggested they collect as many spears and staffs as they could from the part of the Witen's armory they would be allowed to pick from. He surmised that they would employ their protective arsenal like a medieval shield wall, and so the Bruderschaft would need long weapons to keep the wall from closing on them.

Hitch suggested they pass on a directive to go for the feet and legs if the bastards were able to close. "Get 'em off their feet, and it don't matter what kinda steel they wrapped themselves in," the barrel-chested retired airline pilot and part-time primary school teacher said.

"What's our terrain going to look like?" Arlo then asked Sagal. "I know it's going to be a section of mown meadowland, but how wide and long will the field be? What will the boundaries look like?"

"I didn't get a chance to check it out myself yet," Elias qualified his response, "but the Meadow itself is three-hundred-yards wide. If they mowed the section just past the gaming fields, then there is only about a fifty ... or maybe seventy-five-yard stretch before it turns into bushes and shrubs. So that far side will be pretty well cut off, but if we need to, I suppose we can always use the gaming field's side to swing around them or something... if we have to. With their shields and all, I'd say they're likely to be able to span their wall most of the width of the mown patch."

"So I'm sure they'll anchor it on the side with the shrubs and bushes," Arlo had deduced, not liking the picture the young man was painting one bit.

"Are they thick, these bushes?" Luca Clijsters asked.

"It's pretty dense shit. You can move through it, but swinging a weapon won't be easy," Sagal had gloomily reported.

"Okay then, we gather up as many spears as we can and keep the shield wall off of us by going at their legs and feet," Arlo had summed up their simple plan before they even made it out of Branch 2.

It took arriving at the end of Branch 5 and crossing a steel footbridge with a roaring whitewater river flowing beneath to discover the array of weaponry laid out on the Meadow's soccer field before the first puncture point struck their simple plan. There were few slim spears at all among the hundred-odd killing tools. After nearly fifteen minutes sifting through the leftover clubs and blades, all they could pool together were twelve spears and five bladeless staffs, for all the good they would do.

"The cheating bastards knew well enough not to offer what we'd need to beat them," spat Tionne Jepson, a fearless former restaurant manager and current muscle-bound badass.

Arlo held his tongue. Elias caught his gaze and must've read on Arlo's face what he now plainly read in the eyes of the burly young warrior, judging by the sad smile Sagal offered up. He knew their unexpected ally understood their one and only play had been checked. But he'd known too not to discourage his fellow warriors. *The boy's got decent leadership instincts*, Arlo had time to think before Hitch bellowed, "Grab up all you can, lads and ladies. C'mon now. Let's show these bloody American apes we don't fear them. Head down to our end of the field with your heads held high. There, on the desert side, march confident. Let's get away from these honorless thugs and regroup. C'mon folks." One of his hands pointed toward their end of the strip of mown meadow while the other waved the listless mob toward their starting position the whole time he spoke and for long after.

Arlo was testing the edge of his borrowed double-bladed battleaxe against the ball of his thumb when he first heard the drums. His people had made it to their end of the battlefield a few minutes before.

Now many were testing the edge and balance of their own weapons much the same as he. Arlo didn't look around to see how many of them sliced their thumb at the echo of the first pulsing beat as he had, but he swore he heard a few gasps very similar to his own. They appeared beneath the circular chamber's massive archway five or six pulses later. There must've been a speaker in their midst, but Arlo couldn't see one. Standing so close together as they were, shields hung low in their left hands and matching spears slung loose in their right, Arlo could not make out anything beyond the first rank.

The drums were definitely emitting from their dense pack though. The beat grew louder the closer the Witen's thirty got to the battlefield. The rattle of steel shields clanking into one another could only just be heard beneath the ceaseless *boom boom bang, boom boom bang bang* rattling on repeat from the speaker still hidden in the middle of the armored pack. His eyes watched every foot of their flawless lockstep march, transfixed and terrified.

Arlo hadn't even noticed the hundreds of residents who had followed the Witen over the footbridge and were now spreading out down the length of the gaming fields. Even as he watched, two men emerged from the congestion stretching along the boundary of the mown meadow. Captain Alvarez was one of them. His march toward the Witen's steel formation was inconsistent, in a word. Seemingly every ten paces, he'd backtrack five to shout some order or another to the footmen on security duty along the boundary line. The other man was single-minded, determined to reach the still mass of warriors. He wore tight gold pants, tattered at the ankles, and nothing else, save a bushy beard and a thatch of graying chest hair. In a spindly arm, the shirtless man awkwardly gripped two ten-foot steel poles wrapped at the end in black cloth five feet long.

The shirtless wild man arrived before the Witen's tight formation, fifteen paces ahead of Alvarez. At first he merely stood in silence, surveying the deadly crew. The Captain arrived and squeezed himself into the front rank just before a bellowed order from a gravelly voice then forced the formation to spread out into a shield wall fifteen men wide and two deep. Two steel-strapped gray-uniformed footmen dropped out of the rear rank and began to jog side by side toward the gaming field boundary. Clearing the end of the fifteen-man-wide front rank, Arlo finally saw the source of the ceaseless drums. The speaker was a deal smaller than he'd expected, given its volume. *Those blokes must be deaf by now,* he thought of the two dropping the speaker in the end zone of the football field.

As they jogged back to their places in the shield wall, the bearded wild man loosed a piercing howl that somehow sounded like an entire wolf pack baying all at once. He let it fade as all eyes before the bare-chested man locked on him. Though Arlo could make out none of it clearly, he plainly launched into some pre-game, get-your-adrenaline-up type of speech. Nearly every third word was punctuated by the man pumping the twin poles in his hand up and down while almost every sentence elicited a unified enthusiastic cry from the shield wall before him.

The speech ended, but the wails and berserk hoots it had brought out of the formerly stoic warriors across the mown grass remained, even after the shirtless wild man had pushed through the wall and joined up with a warrior in the back row that Arlo was certain had to be the man the Witen called the Steward. The two of them took one of the ten-foot poles apiece and spread out the banner between them, flying their black flag with a finely embroidered Olde-English golden "W" perfectly in the middle of the stretched shield wall. The sight of it taut, yet subtly rippling in the Meadow's fabricated breeze, increased the rabid shouts of the Witen's brave thirty.

"Shall we fly ours?" Mustafa Roland stepped up right behind Arlo to ensure his query was heard above the insane wailing.

"It seems the time has come," Arlo said, turning to face his friends milling around in a loose gaggle. "Hoist the colors, Cora, if you would. Everyone else gather 'round."

Arlo heard the Commander's distinct growl bark an echoing order across the hundred-yard-or-so stretch of grass between them. The drums quit mid-beat. He could make out none of it clearly, but it seemed as the Commander then embarked on the first stages of a rousing speech to his assembled troops. Arlo knew the moment of moments had at last come knocking. He must somehow match that scar-faced despot; that much was plain. The polished-wood shaft of the battleaxe grew slick in his hand. He'd never lacked for words in the past, but the thought of having to try to convince his people that hope of victory was anything more than a child's fantasy was sending him into full-panic mode.

Luckily the sweat had not quite stung his eyes beyond clear sight, for the image of their group-sewn battle flag flapping at the end of the pole in Cora Lindross' waving arm settled his raging turmoil. The panic and fear were still there, but the flag had put everything in perspective. It reminded him of how far they had truly come, of every hard-won mile, of the countless times they had stared down annihilation only to come out laughing on the other end. He had felt just as hopeless many times before, just as certain that they'd exhausted their good karma, and always the Bruderschaft had pulled through. There was no reason they couldn't do it again.

That patchwork quilt might have clashed to some eyes, but to his own, there was no Rembrandt or Van Gogh, nor Caravaggio or Monet that could ever rival that six-foot-by-six-foot flag. Atop the many varied squares, each one a brother or sister of the Bruderschaft's hand-picked tatter of cloth from amongst their few personal items, was sewn a non-symmetrical royal-blue "B." The sight of that "B" flying proud behind his courageous folk reminded Arlo that they had made it through all the darkness before together, and that here and now, they would do the same. One by one, his brothers and sisters turned from the lightly flapping flag to face him. Arlo took the time to look each and every one in the eye. Unsurprisingly, every last one of them smiled back, offering up a small nod too, showing they were with him.

"However this day ends, I want to say that there is no one else I would rather share this field with than you, my friends. We all know that all eighty-five of us would have fought in the end, if these bloody bastards had made us."

"We're proud to stand for the rest," Terry Yves called from the middle of the tightening gaggle.

"And I'm damn proud to have even known you, let alone fight for our freedom beside you," Arlo declared in the wake of the "hoorays" and "here, here's" that followed Terry's assurance. "The Bruderschaft shall not die here today, no matter what happens in the next chaotic minutes of our lives. The seeds of brotherhood, the ideals of freedom and societal cooperation that we embodied so well down on Earth, the care for our fellow man that got us across the bloody Atlantic and half of the goddamn American continent will not perish with us, win or lose. They live on in our surviving brothers and sisters. Every honest and empathetic resident of this station here today," he added, pointing to the hundreds of gathered residents still jostling for a place along the boundary, "despite how thoroughly they've been gaslit and fearmongered, they will see how our care and protective instincts for one another can move mountains and face down death with a smile. They'll carry that example in their hearts. That seed shall take root one day—that much is inevitable. I swear to you all, my friends, my family, this fight is not in vain. It might well have been thrust upon us, but that doesn't mean it's not worth the risk of fighting. Our people are worth risking everything for. All of us have long believed as much. I've seen the ideal in practice on countless occasions. God knows, we all have. And now, here we are, risking it all again. I know it isn't fair. I know I should have never led us into this. I know too that you don't blame me, despite how much I blame myself. But none of that really matters now. All that matters now is us sticking together. These blokes with their fancy shields and spears across the way are hoping to intimidate us right out of this fight. Well, fuck that. Fuck them. Do they really think they're any more frightening than a cannibal horde, than those blood-soaked, gray-skinned demons? How many nights have they fallen asleep with the sick humming of a hunting horde ringing in the distance? Never. They have no idea what fear is. Do they honestly think they could ever frighten us? Really? What pampered twits. I guess they really have lost their bloody minds."

He paused there to let the few chuckles in the crowd relax the rest. "If we stick together, we can defeat these cheating bastards. I know we can. Protect the brother or sister to your left and know that your brother to your right will do the same for you. We shall beat these arrogant bullies with our secret weapon, our one advantage over these fascist thugs: our love for each other, our compassion for our brothers and sisters. There is no loyalty there," he told them, pointing now at the shield wall silently taking in the Commander's grumbling speech. "All they have is fiat and fear. It will crumble when they see us stick together, when we don't just turn and run when they come marching toward us. We shall beat them by fighting for each other. There is nothing that says we have to lose this battle today, my friends. Fight beside me, for each other, for freedom, for victory!"

The burst of concurrent hollering that followed his impromptu speech was everything Arlo could have hoped for and more. The Commander was still in the middle of his own when the Bruderschaft began to shout and pump their borrowed weapons. Arlo turned around to see the Witen's ruler staring at him across the field. Apparently, they'd stepped on his moment. With a chuckle and grin, Arlo waved at the man across the hundred-yard gap.

The Commander started walking. Arlo wasn't sure what the guy was up to until he paused halfway across the stretch of open ground to stand with crossed arms and a serious look on his scarred and scruffy face.

"Parlay?" Rick Powys wondered from behind Arlo's shoulder.

"Probably. They seem to be keen on the old formalities," Arlo concluded.

"Well, you're not going to go stand beside that madman alone," a fairly recent Bruderschaft brother and one-time boxing coach named Turk Skipper exclaimed, clapping a hand on Arlo's shoulder before he could take two steps.

"I'm sure I'll be back," Arlo casually threw off his friends' concern, at least on the outside. "No matter what happens though, everyone stick together," he added before setting off toward the orchestrator of this whole nightmare.

"Finally succumb to reason have we?" Arlo asked as soon as he got within range of the Commander so as he did not have to raise his voice nor lower it, yet none of the other four hundred-some-odd people gathered around that patch of leveled turf could hear. "Are you ready to talk like men and come to an honest and just settlement? If you yield to us now, I know my people would be willing to forget all this. Maybe we can try and remember that eight billion people are dead, or else infected—which really amounts to the same thing in the end—and maybe let's focus on the fact that we few are all that remains. And maybe, with that in mind, we can swallow our pride and greed and selfish madness to come together as brothers and sisters to find peaceful and nuanced and mutually beneficial solutions to our problems."

The Commander's upper lip quivered beneath his bushy black beard. He said nothing in reply, however. Not until Arlo came to a stop three paces in front of him. "That's not why I'm here, Mr. Bailey," the milk-eyed monster said.

"Oh no? Well then, if you haven't strolled out here in no-man's land to surrender to me, then what is the point of this little parlay?" Arlo needled.

The Commander still stood with his arms crossed over his chest, his axe slung at his side and his curly mop of hair flapping in the gentle breeze. Arlo hadn't noticed until just then, but of all the black uniformed officers, only the Commander went without a Kevlar helmet. He wore the vest as the others did, but the helmet was nowhere in sight. *Maybe he left it back at his formation with his spear and shield*, he conjectured. Somehow though, Arlo thought not. He guessed the Commander was the type of man who thought himself invincible and wanted to show off where others took proper precautions. He saw him fifteen years younger and riding a Harley Davidson 60 kilometers an hour down a crowded highway sans helmet or a single care in the world.

"I'm here to make sure the rules are clear," the tyrant grumbled, arms still crossed and brow wrinkled and brooding.

Arlo huffed a good few chuckles as he asked, "You're telling me there are rules here? I suppose equal access to weaponry and armor isn't one of them, eh?"

The Commander didn't take the bait. "Do you want to hear them or not?" he growled instead.

Arlo stopped the short pacing he'd been absent-mindedly engaging in directly opposite the Commander, who now mimicked a martinet as he glowered down at him from his five-inch height advantage with thick veins bulging off exposed forearm muscles crossed over his chest. "Go on then. Have your fun," Arlo prompted. "Run them by me again."

"The appointed time of the battle has come and gone. Both teams are where they should be. The battle is on now, for all intents and purposes. Both sides will come together in the middle of this mown patch of meadow. Once we clash, anything goes. When one side has taken enough damage sufficient to prove whatever stupid point they feel they gotta prove," he elaborated, clearly a bit biased toward the outcome, "their banner bearer screams forfeit and waves their colors until they get the necessary attention, at which point, they lower the colors to the ground, never to be raised again. After that, all those who yielded will be pardoned and welcomed aboard station... pending an oath. Short of lowering the colors, we keep on fighting until one side has no one left to die."

"Why?" Arlo asked, genuine sadness flavoring the question.

"What?" the Commander responded, more than a bit puzzled by just what Arlo meant by the simple one-word query.

"Why?" he repeated the oxymoronically straightforward and ambiguous question. "How, huh? How... how in the bloody fucking hell did it come to this and so goddamn quickly?" Arlo's exasperation was transparent as he turned in a quick circle to indicate the mad scene all about them. "What the hell happened to you?"

The lip began quivering beneath the scraggly beard once more. That aside, the Commander kept his composure. Though he did draw in several large breaths before he finally spoke again. "Life is strange" was all the autocrat had to say for himself.

Arlo could only laugh. Tears right then would in no way serve his purpose. So he scoffed and snorted and said, "Yeah, Jasper, I suppose it is."

The Commander spat at Arlo's feet for an answer. The darkness in his milky eye was a bit chilling, if Arlo was being honest with himself. Luckily, the man turned abruptly to march back toward his waiting warriors. Arlo quickly did the same. Arriving back before his family, he saw Elias Sagal wearing a grin to match those around him. Arlo nodded, and the young warrior returned it after letting out a breath.

"Gather up, people. Those of you with spears, take the front alongside me."

"And me," Elias exclaimed, pulling his hammer and sword from their sheaths across his back before stepping up next to Arlo.

Patting his shoulder, Arlo offered another approving nod as the Bruderschaft's volunteers pressed in tight around and behind them. Across the field, the Commander only watched. The Bruderschaft were assembled, ready for the blood sport to kick off. Arlo didn't know if it would prove wise or not, but he didn't want to be the first to move forward. It somehow still felt vital that the Witenagemot be seen as the clear aggressors. For what felt like minutes, but were probably only a handful of seconds, the Commander would not comply. Finally, he turned from the Bruderschaft's formation to face his own. A few barked words were half snatched on the generated wind by Arlo's failing ears. *The order to move out*, he assumed after the tyrant stepped into place in the center of his front rank, snatching back his long spear and rounded steel shield from a footman beside his open spot. The assumption was confirmed only a beat later. As one, the Witen's wide shield wall began marching at the half-step directly at Arlo and his family.

"Okay, brothers and sisters, this is it," he called over his shoulder, his axe raised high above his head. "Stay together. Keep your heads."

"Keep them off us with the spears," Hitch bellowed from his place in the front rank just to the right of Elias Sagal. "Go for the ankles and shins. Knock the bloody cunts off their feet."

"You ready, son?" Arlo turned to ask Elias.

"We're about to find out, ain't we?" he replied with a lazy shrug that drained the sudden tension from Arlo's shoulders.

Smirking at the honest lad, he waved his axe toward the oncoming shield wall and shouted, "Follow me, my brothers and sisters. Follow me to victory!"

Their collective return roar propelled him forward. The first step proved the hardest, and so he was grateful for the motivating push. Come what may, his people were with him. Holding that thought close to his heart, Arlo kept his team of thirty moving relentlessly forward, but all the while checking their pace to match the Witen's. The gap between them shrank and shrank. Arlo could make out the eyes of his enemy now, fifteen pairs of them peering just above the rim of their round shields. The steel hid everything from mid-thigh to the bridge of the nose. His people were naked by comparison. *We'll have to get around them somehow*, he nervously concluded.

Then, all at once, it was too late for game-planning. The two formations, one arrow straight and spread wide, the other uneven and clumped in tight, came within spear thrust of one another. The blade that buzzed past his head two inches from his face made that clear enough. "Spears!" Arlo ordered, whipping his axe at the retracting blade that had nearly filleted his right eye. "Keep them off us!"

"The legs! The feet! Put them down!" Hitch could be heard shouting instructions between his own spear thrusts.

The first cries of pain reached Arlo's ears just before the copper scent of freshly spilled blood could fill his nostrils. He didn't dare glance around him to see which of his brothers had been struck. Every last one of the Witen's thirty were armed with spears, and they seemed to be thrusting in rhythm, one rank at a time. As a result, Arlo constantly had a spear to contend with, either darting in high, aimed at his neck or face, or one shooting in low, with his waist and groin as target. No way could his people keep up this pathetic defense.

More cries filled the air, the stink of evacuated bowels and fright-loosened bladders joined the bloody aroma. "The feet! The legs! Get them down!" Hitch's increasingly agitated voice rang out over the shouts and moans.

"It's no good!" Mustafa Roland squealed back from somewhere in the melee. "Their boots are plated with steel. The shins too. We won't survive here!"

"We've got to get in close!" Tionne Jepson hollered from right beside Arlo with heartening determination in her voice, especially in the wake of Mustafa's declaration of doom.

"No! They'll knock us off our feet with those bloody shields," Hitch sounded horrified as he slammed his spearhead dead into the center of the shield across from him.

"We're too compact!" Elias Sagal's young voice boomed. "We've gotta spread out and get them to attack us one on one," he reasoned, bashing incoming spears two at a time.

"Outflank them," Luca Clijsters suggested from somewhere to Arlo's left. "Let's swing around the e—aghhh!!!" Clijsters' idea was cut short. Then his awful scream was likewise cut off before climax.

Cruelly, Arlo somehow heard the blood bubble out of his good friend's mouth over the battle frenzy. He would have given much not to. *Poor Luca was right though*, Arlo shouted at himself while shaking his head, trying to wake up his mind to actually think and not simply react. "Move left!" he shouted, at last finding his voice. "As one, swing left!"

"No!" This time the dissenter was Sagal. Arlo looked back in time to see Elias duck beneath one spear thrust and whip back up with his sword to slice a second clean in half. "We can't risk it. They want us to move. They want to divide us up and take us out in small clusters. We have to stay together."

"We can't sustain this," Arlo bemoaned, in tandem with yet another dying scream of one of his brothers or sisters.

"We have to get in close!" Jepson once more insisted. "We have to bust through their shield wall and split them in half. Then we can take them out a piece at a time," she added, darting her spear at the eyes of an enemy crouching behind his shield a few yards across the shorn meadow. The owner of the reclusive eyes ducked them behind cover just before Jepson's thrust could skewer them. "Damn," Arlo heard her cuss under her breath.

"Hey, Sagal!" a nasal voice shrieked out from the shield wall. "Hey, traitor, can you hear me?" the voice asked.

Arlo thought he recognized it. *The asshole from our escort yesterday*, the realization dawned, arriving with a flash memory of the wormy-lipped prick's haughty strut as he led their escort through the gaudily massive station.

The intensity of the Witen's attack slowed as the boy went on, "I hope you can hear me, Elias, you fucking coward fuck."

Arlo still had to be cautious and ever in the moment, but with each word the footman spoke, the less often the Witen launched an attack. Soon the shouting voice had only the moans of the wounded and dying to contend with,

"After we finish slaughtering every last one of your Euro trash pals, we will gut you from chest to balls, you dickless fraud. We're gonna fucking laugh, Elias, as you beg us to help you stuff your guts back inside your stomach and put you out of your misery. We will ... eventually, after you watch all of us fuck that disloyal whore of yours. She won't be able to hide from us long. I'll have your fucking whore in my bed this night. You hear me, Sagal. You're dead... and your bitch is mine!"

Arlo took his eyes off the steady spears a few yards ahead to look over at the talented warrior beside him. Every last trace of fear and self-preservation drained from Sagal's eyes in a flash. A rage so white-hot it burned just to glance at it replaced the focused reticence.

With an ear-piercing shriek, Elias raised both of his weapons high, leaping across the gap between the armies. He jumped into a perfect front kick that caught the shield before him square. The bearer went flying back, taking out the legs of the man in the rank behind. Elias crashed into the gap, swinging his hammer and sword in a controlled spasm of violence, sending other shield bearers recoiling backward to tangle the legs of still others in turn.

"Into the gap!" Arlo heard himself shouting, before feeling his legs carry him into the hard-won opening. He knew Jepson had followed the order, seeing as she had in fact reached the gap a step ahead of him, but judging by the sudden cheer that echoed over his shoulder, he guessed all those Bruderschaft fighters still on their feet weren't far behind. He didn't have time to check. There was no safe footing. The Witen recovered quickly and were fighting like demons to pull their downed people to safety and fill the gap.

Just as he stomped down atop a calf and heard the corresponding howl, a spear blade came slashing in from his left. Arlo used his axe to gain a bit of territory, slashing it in a short arc before him. The woman who had launched the spear slash stepped in close, trying to ram into him with her shield. Just before she reached him, Hitch shouldered into her side, sending the smaller woman flying. Arlo managed to whip his heavy axe at the head of the shaggy-haired man who plugged the gap behind her. The crunch of shattering bone reverberated up his arm as his axe head sank six inches deep into the man's forehead.

My god, it's happened... I've killed an uninfected man, he foolishly took the time to contemplate, forcing Hitch to come to his rescue again. Whipping around, Barrett Hitchens sunk his spear deep into the stomach of the armored gray warrior sneaking up behind him. Hitch only had time to shoot Arlo an ironic side-eye before he was brushing past him to thrust his spear at the next foe. Arlo, meanwhile, hacked at the legs of a lanky teen who'd stumbled into the gap to his right. As the reckless youth went tumbling to the blood-sodden turf, missing his right leg below the knee, Elias was revealed behind him.

The young Bruderschaft ally was fending off two spear-toting footmen with his sword while simultaneously swinging his hammer at the head of a black- and gold-draped lieutenant.

Arlo swung his axe at an oncoming foe as he watched Elias deal with his three enemies out of the corner of his eye. The frog-faced officer interposed his shield just in time to stop Sagal's hammer from folding his face in. Out of nowhere, Sagal spun. The two footmen to his left stumbled forward, thrown by the unexpected maneuver. Elias wasted no time taking advantage of their misstep. His sword pierced the closest footman's neck just as his hammer came clapping down on the other's shoulder. Arlo couldn't make out much in the fray. He felt like he was watching Sagal dance in the dark to a disco strobe light. Each new glimpse showed Sagal in a new spot, wheeling from one of the frog-faced officer's thrusts or crashing his hammer into the skull of the footman with the shattered shoulder.

Arlo had to bury one end of his double-bladed battleaxe in the gut of one footman and then slam the other end into the shield of another in order to step into a gap that offered a view of Sagal hard at work. The man-child faced only the jowly Lieutenant now. Arlo swung his axe in an arc before him yet again to win more space for his people to pour into, always keeping one eye on Sagal. The lieutenant lashed out at Sagal's belly with his long spear. Sagal pirouetted out of danger, finishing the 360 spin with a sword slash at the officer's tree-trunk legs. The jowly lieutenant managed to drop his shield in time to deflect the slash but stood no chance of raising it back in time to stop the hammer from crashing into the side of his face.

Spinning like a top, the frog-man's lower jaw flopped loose. Blood frothed and teeth were spat, but the stout officer did not collapse. His mind wasn't on the fight, however. Dropping both his armament and shield, the man sadly attempted to hold his shattered jaw in place. Elias wasted no pity on the lame. His sword sank a foot deep in the lieutenant's chest before Arlo could blink, Kevlar vest be damned. The last he saw, before the chaos before him demanded all his attention, was the jowly officer dropping to his knees and Sagal disdainfully kicking him off his unnaturally sharp blade before leaping back into the fray.

Arlo did hear their rage-fueled ally's shouts above the din of battle though. "Allanson! Show yourself. Allanson!" Sagal boomed above the chaos. "Face me! You'll die screaming before I ever let you touch her! Show yourself, you fucking coward!"

He did it. The kid did it! Arlo silently exalted. *We've cut them off! We've a chance. We haven't lost too many yet. We've a real bloody chance.* He could not spare much time to glance about him, but the few snatches he had managed showed him as much were true. "Stay together! Get in close! Keep them isolated!" he encouraged his trial-forged family between gasps of breath, hard-snatched inside the tightly compacted and critically noxious confines.

CAPTAIN ALVAREZ

"Reform the wall! C'mon, goddammit! Reform the goddamn wall!" the Commander bellowed, uselessly.

Their formation was fucked. They'd been cut in half. Captain Alvarez knew the Commander needed to give the order for loose skirmish. They'd gone over the procedure with the courageous thirty right after they'd all volunteered, framing it as an unlikely possibility, but one still worth preparing for. Every last one of them understood their roles under the emergency order full well. The Witen officers were all well versed in just about every military tactic ever devised, whether it be close quarters, global nuclear war, trench warfare, pitched battles, tank engagements, aerial assaults, and everything in between. And as for the footmen, they had all long ago learned of the battle procedure in their extensive Integration Program courses. None of them were fools. Even with their advantage, they needed to be able to react to whatever happened on the battlefield. In this case, what to do if their shield wall had been severed.

"Perhaps it's time for loose skirmish, sir," Alvarez finally steeled himself enough to suggest to his irate council chief. "We still have the superior equipment, sir," the Captain hurriedly explained his proposal after the man's mismatched eyes locked on his own. "Let the soldiers pair up and take them out one by one. C'mon, sir, let us have our fun," he tried to add in his most casually confident voice.

"Yeah... okay..." the bearded gorilla growled in response, staring vacantly through the Captain. "Fuck it," the Commander suddenly laughed, tossing his shield to the grass. The spear stayed loose in his right hand, but his now unencumbered left quickly snatched the black axe from over his shoulder.

Alvarez smiled at him. He couldn't help it. Whatever was wrong inside him that made battlefields Captain Alvarez's happy place, as well as that dopey sap before him called Pedro's for that matter, wasn't getting fixed anytime soon. So he leaned in and used it, drawing in a rich, exhilarating breath of pristine meadow air. A beat later, his shield was lying next to the Commander's and his gruesome maul with its five-inch diameter steel ball at the end of a three-foot hard oak staff was held expertly in its place. The Commander smiled back then. It made all the difference in the world. He understood. The Captain was not ill. He was not broken. He was, like his fearless lord Commander, what the human race required. His brutality was something to be gloried in, especially now.

The Commander's battlefield bellow of "Loose skirmish! Loose skirmish! Abandon the wall! Pair up! Protect the man beside you and kill these fucking terrorists! Leave none alive," demanded a return cry.

"The Witenagemot forever!" the warriors cheered back, Captain Alvarez loudest among them.

"Slaughter that gutless fucking fraud," the Commander snarled, catching Alvarez's attention and extending his spear blade at Elias Sagal, who even then was thrusting his stolen sword into Lieutenant Masterson's heart.

"Aghhh!" the Captain's scream just couldn't be contained. The treachery was so heavy and so sinful that he needed the release. *No, killing someone, that's what I need*, his fury convinced him. *Where's the Steward?* The thought prompted a quick glance over toward the last place he'd seen the two bearers of the Witen's holy battle standard. The pudgy little crooked lawyer hadn't moved. He still clutched his flagpole as though it burned him, like the sinfully easy task was too much to ask of him. The Glorifier was doing all the work keeping the golden "W" flying, it seemed to the Captain.

His turn will come, he promised himself. *Sagal first*. Following the Commander into the melee toward the modern-day Judas incarnate,

CHAPTER 12

Captain Alvarez flung his spear at the feet of the comically armored Bruderschaft fighter surging to cut off his immortal giant of a leader. The ill-equipped weakling's legs tangled, faceplanting him directly in front of the Commander. The big man didn't lose a stride, planting a massive boot on the fool's back and driving his face into the soft turf.

The Commander saved his spear until three of the enemy formed up to cut off his relentless trudge. In a microsecond, the spear went from hanging loose at his side to flying across five yards of mown grass to pierce deep into the insufficiently armored chest of the middle fighter of his three enemies. Captain Alvarez lost sight of his king then. The fight had divulged into bands of mini-battles all about him. He saw himself as the Commander's battle buddy in this now loose brawl, and so left the three outnumbered Witen fighters to his immediate left to their own devices, hacking free from their quickly forming scrum to chase after the milk-eyed godman.

Clearing the ruckus, Alvarez saw the Commander had downed the remaining pair of enemies. He imagined it had taken no more than three or four strokes, seeing as how one body was missing a head, cut clean at the neck, and the other was a writhing lump of blood-spurting pain, missing his right arm at the shoulder. "I'm right with ya, sir," the Captain called, catching up to the expert axeman.

"I'm fine, Captain," the Commander growled, whipping his axe at an oncoming foe who managed to dodge over it just in time. "You want to help me, then kill that fucking traitor!" he insisted, this time using his finger to point at Sagal who was right then shouting some nonsense at Footman Allanson that Captain Alvarez could barely make out above the steel-clashing din.

"Yes, sir," Alvarez shouted back after thumping his maul into the side of the enemy who had jumped over the Commander's axe slash.

"I'll be there soon," the Witen's scar-faced ruler assured, hacking another arm from its shoulder. "Put Sagal down and the rest of these bastards will give up the fight. Go now!" he insisted in an earthshaking grumble. "I'll get there as soon as I deal with this." He let his axe show exactly to what he'd been referring.

Alvarez marveled as it whispered like a flash of lightning through the air to drive eight inches deep into the junction of some ugly European broad's head and neck, only to flit back up in time to parry the oncoming spear thrust from one of the five Bruderschaft warriors rushing in to take the haggard crone's place.

"I'm on it, sir. The Ethling will die!" Alvarez shouted, making ten yards of progress toward Sagal before two tall Bruderschaft warriors, half-covered in blood, emerged to cut him off. The Captain feinted left, rather than stop completely. The man on the right went for it. The other held his ground. One was enough though. The man who'd been fooled by the quick deke stumbled into his tall auburn-haired partner. Both of them held one of the crummy spears the Witen had offered up. The long weapons became momentarily entangled. Captain Alvarez wasted no time. His brutal maul found the deked fool's knee just seconds before the auburn-haired fighter felt the steel ball shatter his shoulder. The fool had fallen immediately to the grass to shudder in agony. The auburn asshole had dropped his spear but stubbornly kept his feet. A 360-spin, finished with a backhanded smash of his maul into the side of the asshole's head, became necessary.

Clearing that minor hurdle, the Captain searched for Sagal. Fifteen yards to his left, the ungrateful boy was fending off multiple Witen warriors and infuriatingly getting the better of them all. He had to duck around a few skirmishes, but he made it to within ten paces of Sagal. Unfortunately, the smarmy asshole from the Witen/Bruderschaft meeting, the leader of the ignorant Euro trash responsible for this whole mess, came from nowhere to block his path.

"How are you not dead yet?" Captain Alvarez mocked in a huffed, labored breath. "A fucking candy-ass dweeb like you's got no business surviving more than five seconds of battle. So where you been hiding this whole time, boy?" He snapped the question in tandem with his lashing maul.

Bailey dodged the slash and drew in a hard-claimed breath of his own to reply, "I've been right here, killing off your fascist cunt comrades one at a time, and you're next up, you bloody fucking psycho bastard!" Arlo thrust out his axe, plainly hoping the blood and gore staining its twin blades would be taken as proof of that claim.

"Get out of my way," the Captain said in a quite reasonable tone, given the circumstances.

Bailey only slashed his axe as if he were swinging a cricket bat. Clearly, the man had no formal training. *A mere brawler at best*, the

Captain silently scoffed. Circling, Alvarez let the lucky novice tire himself with an array of slashes every bit as feeble as they were predictable. On the last, the Captain strode in close, leading with the butt of his maul and smashing it square into the hopeless Brit's already crooked nose. Bailey kept his feet though, despite the solid contact. Having suffered a few broken noses himself, the Captain knew the man's eyes had to be watering. He knew the blood flowing out of both nostrils had to be making it difficult for an already exhausted man to breathe. So he allowed himself a moment of respect and only ducked back from the man's wild defensive slashes, leveled to cover his few paces of retreat in order to gather his wits and struggle for a few gulps of flawlessly filtered air.

"I warned you," the Captain said, savoring the panic in the stupid Brit's eyes. Three quick steps and he was within maul range. Alvarez aimed his first swing at Bailey's legs. The man attempted some sort of o' le maneuver along with a last-ditch attempt to drop his axe shaft down in time to parry the blow. The Captain's heavy slash nearly smashed the double-bladed axe clean from Bailey's hand. As he worked to regain control of his grip as well as footing, Alvarez was already twisting around to thump his punishing maul into Bailey's open ribs. The crunching of bones was almost drowned out in the shrieking cacophony all about him, but Captain Alvarez knew he had not just been imagining things when he saw the pained and defeated look in Arlo Bailey's eyes shortly after impact.

Bailey, admirably, still kept his feet. His breath was completely gone now though. The heavy axe in his right hand somehow stayed there as he crumpled around his injured side and stumbled out of range of a follow-up smash. The Captain gave the attempted usurper the few steps and precious seconds to recover. He wanted the pretentious jerk to be clear-headed when the final blow landed. As soon as he saw Bailey manage to draw in his first pain-sodden but otherwise full breath, Captain Alvarez leapt in to finish him. The Brit's eyes were fixed on what was coming. The sight brought a smile to the Captain's lips as he reared back for the coup de grace.

The bulky wiseass who had sat to the left of Arlo Bailey during yesterday's meeting forestalled the fateful moment. Luckily, by the coward's trick of blindside surprise, Barrett Hitchens, armed now with a maul of his own, rather than the spear the Captain had seen the man wield in the first moments of battle, parried Alvarez's swing, knocking it wildly off course.

"Get behind me, Arlo," Hitchens urged in a hoarse voice as the Captain regained his balance.

Bailey didn't argue. Still clutching his shattered ribcage, he limped behind his large, dark-eyed rescuer. The Captain snarled at them both, lashing out with a probing thrust. Hitchens went for it, bringing up his maul to bash it clear, only the Captain's weapon wasn't there to be parried. Quick as a pickpocket at work during rush hour, the Captain abbreviated the thrust and turned it into an upward slash that clipped the larger man in the upper chest. The contact was by no means devastating, but it did cause Hitchens to stumble backward and collide with the severely injured man cowering behind him. This time Alvarez completed the jabbing thrust, smashing it into roughly the same place the previous blow had landed.

The Captain might've expected the pair of revolutionary pretenders to trip over one another and wind up in a tangled heap atop the newly shorn grass. Somehow though, only Hitchens tumbled to the cushy turf. Arlo had not only kept his feet yet again but had somehow managed to anticipate Hitchens' collapse. There was no other explanation for how quickly his two-foot-wide blade was whipping through the newly opened space as quickly as it was. Captain Alvarez simply had no time to flick his maul up and deflect the vicious head slash. The Captain and his people had thought ahead though, and his combat blunder didn't cost him nearly as much as it could have. His Kevlar helmet had cracked in half, and the blade gouged a nasty cut in the top of his head, not to mention the concussion its impact most definitely caused, but he was alive. Six inches of super space steel weren't sunk into the top of his skull. His brain might be a bit rattled and woozy, but it wasn't cut in half. All in all, a success, as far as his scorecard had it marked anyhow.

Still though, now it was the Captain forced to do the retreating and regrouping. His helmet was split down the upper right side almost clean in two—utterly useless now, in other words. Bailey gave him the time to unsnap the chin strap of the lifesaving headgear and rip it off his bleeding head. The Captain even had time to wipe some of that blood from his forehead before it could pour into his eyes as Bailey, still favoring his ribs, helped Hitchens off the grass.

They smiled at him once they'd both regained their feet, confident in a way they plainly didn't deserve. The look made Alvarez scream yet again. His fury was surpassing heights never dreamed of before. Violence was the only thing that could sate the red rage. There was a beast inside him. The taste of his own blood dripping down his face fueled the craving. His thoughts and senses had suddenly never seemed clearer, concussion be damned. Captain Alvarez marched in to destroy both of his enemies, seeing his strikes and their counters before the blows were even thrown. Bailey was easy to keep at bay. The man could hardly lift his massive axe above his waist. So he maneuvered him clear of Hitchens with a few expert jabs and turned to focus his attack on the bigger of the two weaselly Brits.

Hitchens was strong. Alvarez could feel it when their weapons collided. He had a heavy grip with firm control. Even so, the Captain had him set up for a skull-cracking down slash within seven moves. The fresh-cut, dewy-soft grass did him in though. Or to be more precise, a slimy white rope of intestines atop that slick lush grass did him in. The treacherous organ had been spilled by a miserable Bruderschaft bastard who was even then crawling through the frantic melee and leaving a coiled trail of steaming guts to mark his path. The Captain's boot, despite all the great many centuries of combat boot technology poured into its fancy, guaranteed no-slip soles, had simply slid right down the tortured wretch's blood-slick intestine. He had to bail on the head slash altogether in order to keep from crashing down on his ass and doing the splits.

Hitchens and Bailey used the slip to their advantage, putting the Captain on defense. His footing was never stable. With each rushed parry, he came closer and closer to the fatal fall. Hitchens' maul had even managed to land a semi-blocked, but still bone-bruising blow, down on the Captain's unprotected left upper arm, all while Bailey hacked at Alvarez's legs, managing three glancing cuts across his thigh and calves. They would have had him, whether he avoided falling over or not, within another few moves, but fate wouldn't let something like that happen. In tandem, Lieutenant Woodson, along with Footmen Allanson and Erkov, stormed in to save him.

"We got ya, Captain!" he heard Allanson bellow as he came slashing with his battleaxe to win the Captain some much-needed space to recover.

"The Commander just ordered us to seek you out. He and a half dozen or so of our guys have got control of that half of the battlefield," Woodson explained as he jabbed his morningstar at Bailey's chest. "Dirks and Dobechek are with him. They'll wrap the bastards up sure enough. This half is on us," he informed his superior while glancing around, clearly tallying up the remaining Bruderschaft warriors about them. Captain Alvarez couldn't help but count as well. *Twelve*, he self-reported after glancing about his half of the battlefield. *Not good,* he thought, before cheering himself with *Better than the Bruderschaft's nine, though.*

"Yeah, Commander says he sent ya to kill Sagal too," Allanson added. "We're here to help with that for sure. I want to look into that traitor's eyes as he dies."

"I take it these fuckers won't let you pass though," Erkov said, lashing his war hammer toward the two recently outnumbered Brits.

"These usurping fucks need to die too," the Captain managed after a few well-earned breaths and moments to internalize the pain and turn it into rage.

"You got it, Cap," Erkov huffed between wicked slashes and exhausted wheezes.

Bailey's broken ribs significantly diminished his defenses. Erkov and Allanson had paired up to oppose him while the Captain and Lieutenant Woodson focused on Hitchens. Both of the footmen managed to land a half dozen glancing blows and lancing cuts with their respective war hammer and axe. Hitchens, though, was well recovered from the bruising smash the Captain had managed earlier. Woodson and he were having a hard time penetrating his guard. It wasn't until Lieutenant Woodson went low with his morningstar and drove three of the brutal weapon's six blades deep into the Brit's calf that they gained any ground.

Captain Alvarez should have been able to thump his maul into the insolent asshole's skull, but instead the chance came and went. Hitchens crumbled to the ground and rolled clear as Alvarez watched Bailey in the limits of his periphery, from nowhere, whip his heavy blade through the air. The axe only had space for two revolutions before it thwacked into Erkov's chest plate. The Captain had a moment to hope the armor had withstood the sudden toss before the tall young footman collapsed to his knees. Blood poured from the man's mouth a beat later as the wide-bladed axe stayed firm in place in the center of his chest.

Allanson was first to break the unexplained freeze that followed the footman's abrupt demise. His anguished scream was no more intelligible than any of the Captain's had been so far that day. The shriek kickstarted Alvarez back into motion though. In the corner of his vision, Allanson attacked the now unarmed Bruderschaft leader just as the Captain wound up a slash to whip at the head of Hitchens who was only then regaining a wobbly footing. The man's fresh injury told. His parry came a beat too late. It took some of the force from the Captain's bash but not much. The rest landed solid, just above Hitchen's narrow forehead. He didn't have time to see the man's eyes roll up in the back of his head, not with how quickly Hitchens tumbled limply to the turf after the overhand slash landed home, but the Captain knew, beyond doubt, the man's lights were definitely out.

Woodson whipped his morningstar down to finish the job completely when, impossibly, Hitchens rolled to his back and jabbed his maul square into the Lieutenant's nuts before the killer stroke could fall. Captain Alvarez had taken a few strides toward Allanson by that point, intent on helping the boy finish off the Bruderschaft leader who had somehow found a spear to defend himself with and was therefore unable to get back in time to stop the big Brit from sitting up and using all his momentum to crash his maul into the side of Woodson's now helmetless head. The Lieutenant had been utterly exposed and vulnerable, stooped as he was over his smashed testicles. The blow couldn't help but be mortal.

The contact was dull and muted, despite the damage. The sound still pinged around in the Captain's ears, nonetheless. A dozen clashing steel weapons and as many painful moans had no power to drown out the sick noise. Captain Alvarez was screaming again, the trauma transformed to rage once more, as he smashed a front kick square onto Hitchens' chin. He did see the man's eyes roll up this time. The tongue lolling from his mouth and the heavy, unaided way his upper body crashed back to the turf were good indicators as well that, for real this time, the man absolutely had to be good and truly out cold.

Allanson's panicked wail prevented the Captain from making sure Hitchens never rose again. Before he could even lift his maul to strike, he had to dart back toward Allanson and Bailey. The footman's cry clearly meant trouble. And indeed, Allanson was lashing out with his battleaxe as he stumbled away from Bailey, limping heavily on his left leg. Captain Alvarez saw the gash plainly from five yards across the grass. The deep cut had been placed expertly between the two steel sheets of armor over the footman's thigh and shin.

Bailey then chased the footman backward with a few quick thrusts from his fortuitously claimed spear until Allanson bumped into the Captain. The young footman whipped around fast, bringing his axe to bear on what his panicked mind told him was a new foe. The Captain grabbed him by his hastily cobbled chest plate and hauled him out of danger from another one of Bailey's thrusts. A relieved look flooded the footman's chalky blue eyes as he aborted his attack. The Captain won them a bit of space by knocking Arlo's spear shaft so hard it rattled in his hands. "Where's the Ethling?" Alvarez inquired of the limping footman after he glanced around the place on the battlefield where the boy had last been spotted.

"There," Allanson answered in an exhausted huff a few beats later.

Slashing once more at Bailey's inexpert thrust, Captain Alvarez chanced a glance back toward where the footman was pointing. Elias Sagal was only a dozen yards from the Commander now. He'd clearly cut a bloody path straight toward the Witen's supreme ruler. The evidence was sickening to look upon. "Go and kill him before he gets to the Commander. The treacherous fucker is planning to sneak up and stab him in the back," Alvarez told the footman. "Go now. I'll deal with this son of a bitch. Cut him off and I'll be there soon. Just keep him in place until we can kill him together. Go now. I got this!" the Captain insisted.

Allanson nodded after a time and almost reluctantly. It pissed the Captain off, truth be told, but he didn't have time to scold the weak-willed boy. He simply flicked his wrist to dismiss him and turned all his attention to the arrogant and pompous blond twit cowering behind some pathetic spear thrusts. The Captain felt the injured footman limp away behind him as he knocked the spear to the side and strode in to close the gap and eliminate the spear's advantage. Alvarez got so close he actually collided with Bailey, smashing a shoulder square in the man's sternum. Bailey loosed a gasped huff of air as he crashed to his ass atop the blood-slimed grass.

The Captain grabbed the Brit by his thinning pale hair and dragged him a few feet, just to hear the bitch wail. Bailey did not disappoint. He added some feeble attempts to pry free the Captain's grip as well, making the victory all the sweeter. Alvarez regripped the man's short hair and pulled back, exposing the invader's unwelcome face. Setting his maul against his leg, the Captain landed nearly a dozen punches, mangling the man's already ugly face even further.

He might have been screaming too as he battered the interloping Brit, the Captain wasn't sure. No one around could take their attention away from their own personal battles to confirm for him one way or the other. It didn't matter. He'd won. The man had taken his beating. Sure, he deserved far worse, but the Captain still had Sagal to attend to. He needed to end this clown and thus get one step closer to ending this unfortunately necessary and sacred battle. So he released his grip on the man's hair. Bailey crumpled to his knees, eyes on the red and green grass before him. In one fluid motion, the Captain snatched back up his maul only to bring it back down in a whipping smash straight at Bailey's temple. It never arrived.

The knife was in his thigh for a good few seconds before he felt the pain. It had been the sheer shock of spotting Hitchens stumble over and stab him that had forestalled Bailey's deathblow, more so than the injury itself. Somehow the steel-jawed bastard had regained consciousness to a level of enough clarity and presence of mind to pull out a six-inch hunting knife and crawl across the viscera-drenched turf to shove the nasty blade three inches into the Captain's left thigh. The pain's arrival let him know that the knife had even sunk deep into the femur itself. Alvarez couldn't help but scream once again. This one though, if he was being honest, was more pain-induced than rage-fueling.

The Captain fell down on his left knee but still overtopped the now sprawled-out and glossy-eyed Hitchens. His maul had plenty of leverage and velocity thus, as it landed flush between the pesky Brit's dark eyes. A splatter of bone fragments, brain chunks, and warm blood splashed up into the Captain's face as Hitchen's own shattered inward. He saw the fist flash then, in the corner of his vision, but he had no time to react. He tried; the Captain gave the all-time best effort in his lengthy combat history, whipping his head back out of range while interposing his weapon in defense, but none of it mattered. Bailey's fist caught him square on the jaw. There was only enough time to hear the crack inside his skull and taste the first bitter measures of pain from a dislocated jaw before his limbs turned to water and darkness swept in to claim his consciousness.

CHAPTER 13
JORDANA

PRISON BREAK

The muffled sounds beyond her cell door had changed again. Jordana was sure the jailhouse had been abandoned for the evening. Her cell door had stayed closed ever since she'd awoken back inside it again, strapped to the same damn chair, only this time with the zip-ties cinched so tight her fingers were turning purple. She figured its resolute stillness meant interrogations were over, time being. Since then, there had been a melancholy heaviness beyond her door, ceaseless and suffocating. All that changed suddenly. A splattering of sounds, new sounds, strange sounds, hopeful sounds, were now floating down to her end of the cramped and cold prison.

Jordana had not been asleep, not fully; she doubted whether she put more than five minutes of sweet unconsciousness together at any point throughout her agonizing confinement. So she knew she wasn't dreaming. What she now understood to be a swelling multitude of feet dashing all about somewhere near the far end of the jail's narrow hall were no illusion.

Those surprise-lightened and thankful voices can't be illusion either then, her battered mind told her. *Something is up. Something good!* she silently exclaimed, recognizing Maisie Sagal's muted praises above the symphony of pattering feet and joyful wonderings. Her cell door slid open barely a heartbeat later. A pale woman with a bruised face raced in, bearing a pocketknife. Jordana instinctively knew not to fear. She knew the woman was there to slice her bonds well before the woman went about her work. Jordana assumed she was one of the dozen-odd residents she'd heard the Witen toss into cells all around her shortly after Maisie, Sheffield, Sheffield's girl Arlene Fincannon, and Jordana herself had been tossed into individual cells on opposite ends of one another.

Apparently, the bastards had a few questions for them as well, she thought, getting a closer look at the woman's black and blue eye and swollen broken nose as she gave Jordana a hand to the door. Jordana felt ashamed to rely on the help of someone in such a state, but she could not fight off her wooziness. She knew better than to shake her head though, as was her wont. So she leaned. Drawing in a few clean breaths on the short walk while rubbing her wrists, Jordana's legs finally began to feel her own again. "Thank you," Jordana said to the mystery resident once out in the narrow buttercream hall. The woman only smiled and moved on to the next cell. Jordana watched as she simply tapped the keypad once to order the cell door open and darted inside to cut its occupant free.

"Jordana!" Maisie's call spun her around to face the prison's lone entryway. Maisie Sagal was already slow-jogging toward her. Jordana barely had time to open her arms before the brunette beauty wrapped her in the kind of hug that couldn't be faked, the kind that went as quickly as it came but somehow lasted lifetimes. Jordana hugged back, harder, planting a soft kiss in Maisie's hair, still fragrant despite their recent trials and adventures. "Did he hurt you?"

"He tried." Jordana smiled, staring now into the mesmerizing swirl of hazel that were Maisie's eyes. "That thug Commander bloke and his pettifogging sidekick weren't even the worst part of my night."

"What do you mean?" Maisie asked, her beautifully unlined face shifting from something close to romantic infatuation to simple confusion as smooth as faint ripples on an otherwise placid pond.

"I mean him," Jordana declared, her voiced raised over all others and her finger pointing straight at the chest of Nate Novocaine Barker.

Barker seemed pinned by her still and damning finger. He managed a few glances around him, but he didn't flee. Those few recently liberated residents nearest him began to back away, but Cainey stayed where he was.

"What about him?" The question had been croaked from a strained, abused throat. Certainly not Maisie's. So Jordana turned, searching for the speaker. When she spotted Father Boyd hobbling her way, one arm over his wife's sturdy shoulder and Roddy Sheffield lurking just inches away from the other, ready to catch the big man, should he stumble, Jordana knew it was definitely he who had posed it. His appearance alone explained the strain and distortion in his voice. Clearly, of all present, he'd been worked over the most. Then she saw his fingers, knuckles swollen up large and ripe as green grapes, and she knew, however horrible her night had been, she had no right to complain to this man.

"How could you, Barker?" Maisie growled, taking a few predatory steps toward the treacherous worm. "I saw him with them! He gave us all up! The priest and Dolly and Mr. Holderman and Aziz, they are only here because you betrayed us, you fucking jerk," she scolded the wilting weakling. "I knew we never should have trusted you. Everyone told us what fools we were. But we still took you in, made you a part of us, and you fucking betray us... and to people who all collectively hate your fucking guts, no less? How, Cainey? Huh? Why?" All conversation had ceased. Jordana guessed all the cells had been emptied by then, and so every eye in the prison was fixed on her animated condemning plea.

Before Barker could defend himself, if he was even planning to, she spoke, "The sick wanker thought he was going to get me in return."

"What?" Maisie, the priest, Dolly, Roddy Sheffield, and Arlene Fincannon beside him all asked at roughly the same time.

"This delusional bloody bastard thought he'd convince me to give up all I knew about my Bruderschaft in exchange for a life up here with him."

"What?" Maisie asked again, this time with a hearty laugh at the end.

"Why would he think that?" Father Boyd asked, his question a serious one despite the incredulous grin that couldn't be kept from his lips.

"I certainly haven't the first bloody clue," Jordana scoffed. Cainey still hadn't moved yet, not so much as muttered a word, but she could clearly see him begin to subtly search for an exit. "I pegged him as a chauvinistic moron, like so many millions of others, almost the moment we were introduced. I saw him staring at me, but I never so much as returned the gesture. In fact, I did everything within the bounds of good taste to make it clear to the fool that I had no bloody interest in him. But somehow, the entitled buffoon couldn't take the hint. I tried to play him once I realized what he'd done, but the Commander never actually trusted him either. They acted as though they had left the prison unguarded while Novocaine made his pitch to me, but really they were expecting me to play him and expecting Barker to get played. They had two footmen hiding in the hall to waylay me after I got the idiot to cut me loose. I was barely conscious, but I heard them confirm all this to Cainey as they dragged him into a cell."

"You fucking pathetic coward!" Maisie shouted, stepping even closer to Barker, his eyes seeking an exit all the more urgently.

"Toss him back in the cell." The priest spoke up, regaining his distinct and soothing voice. His instruction halted Maisie's progress. She crossed her arms and stood staring Barker down no more than three paces in front of him.

"No," Maisie answered flatly.

"What?" Boyd asked as though he hadn't heard her.

"This traitor deserves far worse," Maisie told him, arms still crossed and eyes still glowering.

"He surely does, Mais," the priest agreed, disentangling himself from his supporters and stepping a firm, unhindered stride toward Maisie. "But if we give him any more than a cell to rot in while we convene a court to duly try him, then that won't be justice. It'll be vengeance. It'll be them. Leave the fleeting gratification of the suffering of those we deem deserving to the Witenagemot."

That reached her. Maisie dropped her arms and turned to face the priest, her face softening by the second. A young girl waddled out of the tight press in that narrow hall to snatch Maisie's hand into her own, drawing her gaze from the priest. "Forget ab-abou... Forget about this guy, big sis. We gotta get going now. Eli can only keep them distracted so long. For all we know he is alrea... he is al-al-already gone. Maybe they all are, the Bru... the Bruder-Bruderschaft I mean. We g-gotta g-g-go now. I promised him I'd make it count. That I'd get us away from here. We gotta go now so I can keep it. Fo-Forg-Forget about Mr. Barker, Mais. Put him in the cell, like Boyd says. He wo-wo-won't starve. Someone will find him, no matter what happens. We can le-le-leave the prison's main hatch itself open in the Grand Rotunda. Someone will c-come for him eventually. We just gotta leave now."

"What about the Bruderschaft?" Jordana picked up on the mention of her people in the child's strange rant. "What's this about them being all gone? Wha... what are... what's going on?"

"It's kind of a long story." A young twenty-something fit woman with flawless bronze skin and a voluminous frock of jet-black hair stepped up alongside the child while answering for her.

"If it concerns my people, I'll hear it now," Jordana insisted.

"We'll have time to go over it all, but like Carrie was saying, we gotta move on to the next phase of this prison break," the statuesque young woman in the gray footman's trousers said.

"Whose plan? What is going on, Carrie?" Boyd asked, catching the young child's eye. "Did Supervisor Addison find you? You're Tessa Rodriguez, right?" he asked the handsome and athletic woman beside Maisie and her baby sister.

"That's me," the woman apparently named Tessa replied with an easy grin, defying the tense mood.

"You helped Carrie put this escape together?" Boyd then asked.

"Yep." She smiled back.

"Wh... why would you... Wait, Carrie mentioned Elias just now. Is he a part of this too?"

"In a way," Tessa Rodriguez answered Boyd, still smiling. Jordana was beginning to find it annoying. Thankfully, the girl turned a bit more serious as she finally elaborated a little, "Carrie, Eli, and me all planned it, but Elias has a much more difficult road to walk," she finished, tossing Jordana the strangest look afterward.

"What road? What the hell is going on? Did Addison find you or not?" Boyd asked, irritated.

"He found Elias," Carrie Sagal answered in a sweet voice that visibly drained the anger from the priest's shoulders. "He told him ab-ab-abou-about your green notebook. We used the li-list and-an-and put a plan together, the three of us. We took a few other items you had hid-hid-hidden away along with us too. We gotta u-use at least one to g-g-get in the Control Room."

"The Control Room?" Maisie wondered. "Why do we need to get back in the Control Room?"

"It's part of the plan," Carrie patiently explained, taking her big sister's hand into her own once more. "Most everyone is down at the Meadow watching the battle. The shifts have been ordered to ske-ske-skeleton crew. There's only t-t-two guards out in the Grand Alleyway. All we have to do is subdue them and then use one's tablet to lure an operator in the Control Room to op... to ope... t-t-to open the hatch."

"But why do we need back in the Control Room at all?" Maisie bent down to ask her sister.

"It's how we are going to get aboard the Bruderschaft's E11. We're going to go out the way you and Ms. Re... you and Ms. R-R-Reve... Ms. R-Revere and Roddy went in."

"You're boarding our ship?" Jordana exclaimed in utter confusion. "What are you talking about, kid? Please, tell me what is happening to my people."

"Your people are safe, Ms. Revere," the bright-eyed child assured, before caveating her declaration, "most of them anyway."

"Twenty-nine of them are at the Meadow," Tessa Rodriguez said, all trace of humor vanished now from her face and tone.

"The Meadow? Why there? Why twenty-nine? What's going on? Please tell me," Jordana found herself pleading.

She even nearly fell to a knee, but Maisie stepped up beside her just before she could buckle. "Whatever your plan is, Carrie," Maisie began, smiling at her sister and Tessa both to set them to ease, "it's gonna have to suffer a short delay while you fill us all in. Logistics are what they are, I'm afraid, kiddo. Just as time is what it is. The only fact that matters in the face of all that uncertainty right now is that Jordana needs to know about her people. So just lay it all out for us, Ri Ri."

"Fine," Carrie said, after locking eyes with Tessa and exchanging a nod, "but it has to be the quick version. We really d-d-do have to hurry."

"Stuff this creep back in his cell, and I'll lay it all out," Tessa said, directing traffic all about her. Two residents followed her instructions and manhandled Cainey back into his cell. The weasel put up little fight, beyond a few petty, whining complaints, and only after they'd tossed him in and were halfway through closing the door. The rest of the freed prisoners heeded her invitation to gather close and listen up.

Tessa didn't waste a breath. Jordana would normally have found most of the recap, as well as the rest of the prison break plan hard to believe, but the dark-haired woman's plain frankness all throughout left no room to doubt her. Certainly, little Carrie beside her seemed to agree with all of it, and Maisie had made it clear to Jordana that her miraculous baby sister was someone to be trusted, always. So, she wasted no time darting down avenues of doubt. Jordana turned her focus to what to do in the face of the insane reality. She didn't come up with much. All she knew was that, whatever Carrie, Tessa and Elias had planned, she was not leaving. Twenty-nine of her brothers and sisters might well be lying dead in a bloody meadow right then, but she'd still be damned if she'd leave them.

These people needed to know her intentions. Maisie deserved to know. So she didn't let the silence that followed Tessa's spiel last long. Almost immediately, she told them, "I'm not leaving. I'll help you all get aboard. I'll talk to my people on that ship and get them to take off with you, but I can't leave my brothers and sisters behind to die in some mad battle. I'm not leaving."

"Me neither," Maisie declared without hesitation.

Jordana smiled at her while Father Boyd spluttered. Finally, the priest calmed himself enough to speak a coherent sentence. "You can't possibly believe you could find a way to safely stay here now! What the hell, Mais? What have we been striving for this whole time, if not a way off this rock?"

"I can't leave everyone behind. It ain't right," Maisie explained.

"We were always going to leave folks behind. You know that. You helped draw up the goddamn plans for our Branch 2 takeover," the priest shot back.

"I know. I know," Maisie allowed, throwing up her hands. "It's different now. It feels different. It feels wrong. We can't run away from the Witen, especially since we will have no clue what we are running in to. We haven't done the surveillance and research to find a suitable settlement location. We aren't ready to just run. And it wouldn't be right even if we were. Every last person in this station, the Witen zealots included, are victims. We've always understood as much. We judged it the lesser of two evils to leave them behind. I'm not so sure that's true anymore, Boyd. I'm not about to judge anyone for getting out while you can. I'm just saying I can't go with ya, and if I'm being honest, I think a part of me always knew as much. I think maybe I was just going along with the plan to lock ourselves down Branch 2 because it felt good to participate in some kind of active defiance of the Commander. But," she said, pausing to look her sister in the eye and wait for the hazel-eyed child's return smile, "I know now what my father would want of me. The Commander needs to be stopped, once and for all. I have to face him. I have to trust that good faith and a desire for fairness and justice flickers somewhere in the heart of everyone who's ever lived, including those traumatized co-residents of ours. If I can tap in to that reason, I know it can burn far brighter in their hearts than the flames of any fear. I need to trust that I can appeal to it. I can't run. I need to face him, for Eli's sake," she insisted, sharing another hand squeeze and grin with her baby sister.

"The way I see it, no matter which side wins this evil battle Jasper Montrois has concocted, the Witen will be diminished afterward. We can take advantage while they're weak. I know we can. All that has happened over the last few days has to be weighing heavy on the hearts and minds of every last person aboard station. They have to have questions. They have to have doubts. If we speak to them, maybe let Jordana tell them about the Bruderschaft and all they've been through firsthand, it will be enough to win them away from Montrois's madness for good. I know it could. Or at least, I have to believe it. We can lock up all the recalcitrant Witen agitators and dissenters in these very cells after we all agree to act sanely and collectively. Then we can let Jordana's people aboard, all of them, and live in peace, for Christ's sake. We can do it. We can restart AOA and my father's vaccine research. We can get back to the people we once were. We can turn the nightmare of this past decade into a faint memory, no more than urban legend. But we have to act now. We can't run."

"I presume all our guns are still somewhere on our E11?" Jordana cleared her throat to inquire.

"Don't even think of it," Boyd exclaimed.

"Think of what?" his wife Dolly beside him asked.

"Wellllll," Jordana began by dragging out the word and collecting her thoughts, "instead of us using the VLSE suits to clamber aboard our E11, we could instead use them to ferry all our firearms aboard. We've more than enough guns, as well as the ammo to go along with it, to arm everyone here fifty times over. If we all rush the Meadow and subdue them while they're busy trying to club each other to death, we probably wouldn't even have to fire any shots."

"*Probably* being the keyword in that sentence," Boyd condescended. "We have no idea what we will find in the Meadow. I'm sure the Commander would not have proposed the battle if he didn't have a strong conviction in his side's overwhelming victory. The man is a lot of things, but an utter fool ain't one of them, unfortunately. He knows the Witen can only risk being weakened so far. I'm sorry to say, Ms. Revere, I truly am, but I do fear your people in that meadow are already long dead. And he'll be coming to wipe all of us out next. We have to leave now while we still can. Don't forget about the team of footmen still manning the PRZVL33 in the Terminal. They hear gunshots in the Meadow and bring that thing in response, this station goes up faster than flicking on a light. We've long begrudged the Steward and the Commander their wisdom in destroying all the firearms up here. Although, I do wish the bastards woulda done the job properly and blown both of their damn PRZVL's into scattered atoms. The motherfucker that remains might well be viewed as a WMD up here, for all intents and purposes. Same goes for smaller guns too really. Just one stray bullet from any of them, be they automatic-rifle or simple revolver, can set off a catastrophic chain reaction that would doom our species for good and all. They're just far too dangerous, Jordana. I'm sorry. They won't save your people now. If we storm the Meadow, shots will be fired. The Witen will resist. Something vital will get damaged. And then everything, everyone, all of us, all of everything, will be gone forever."

"Forget the guns," Maisie said, taking control of the conversation. "We don't need them."

"There isn't enough here to stop them if the priest is right and most all the Witen's fighters survived the battle," a freed prisoner pointed out.

"The people will join us. I know it," Maisie persisted.

"They'll never fight the Witen, especially not after they've all just watched them slaughter thirty of the Bruderschaft's best," Jordana's former rescuer, Larry Holderman, flatly stated. She searched then among the prisoners, hoping to spot the lined and handsome face of Jed Redding towering somewhere above the rest. Jed was nowhere to be found, however. She wanted to ask Larry about his absence, but something in the way the pot-bellied sot was carrying himself screamed of heartbreak. The instinct not to pry into fresh trauma kept her quiet.

"Why would they? They weren't with us at the protest. Anyone with the balls to face the Commander and his gang is right here in this jailhouse," a young female prisoner added.

"I'm going to the Meadow," Jordana told them all, daring someone to argue her down.

"Me too," Maisie said, taking Jordana's hand.

"I was always headed there, regardless," Tessa quipped.

For a long time, no one else spoke.

Finally, the priest sighed and stepped up beside Maisie to place a hand on her shoulder. "Okay, ladies, okay," he said, slowly nodding. "We'll go to the Meadow. But," he added when Maisie started to smile, "I insist we take the Control Room first. We should follow little Carrie's plan and take it over. That way, no matter what happens at the Meadow, at least we have that big ace up our sleeves."

"They'll just threaten whoever we leave's family or friends again," one of the oldest of the recently freed prisoners quibbled, unconsciously staring down Arlene Fincannon all the while.

"Well, we'll deal with that problem when we come to it," Boyd said, dismissing all other concerns with a wave of his hand. "For now, its benefits outweigh the risks. We need that bargaining chip, so we ain't just running in there empty-handed. It'll help in getting the people on our side as well."

"Okay then, we'll take it back," Maisie said, smiling at Jordana and then Roddy Sheffield in turn. Roddy and Jordana both smiled back. Arlene Fincannon flushed red.

"Guards are on their way back now," Carrie Sagal called from beside the prison's hatchway. Jordana's view of the monitor before the little girl was obscured, but she guessed it displayed a video of a slice of the Grand Alleyway beyond the hatchway. "Wh-wh-whatever our plans are, we gotta take care of these guys first." Exactly when the child had hobbled on one forearm crutch to the small console, Jordana wasn't sure. Whenever though, Jordana was impressed that the child, alone among them all, had the presence of mind to monitor the guards while the adults bickered.

"Do they both have their tablets on them?" Boyd wondered.

"Looks like it," Carrie answered in an uncertain voice.

"Okay then, come on, people, let's get 'em," he said, shoving through the crowd to join Carrie at the hatchway, only slightly hobbling now.

"If it is security we want," Jordana began a thought as she set off to follow the priest, "then we ought to bring the rest of my people aboard to join us. The more people we have confronting the Witen, the better."

"It might take too long, Jor," Maisie said, stepping up alongside Carrie. "We need to get down to the Meadow as fast as we can. We might even have to hijack some repulsion trolleys, if we can. This station is massive. We won't have a second to waste."

Jordana acknowledged that point with a begrudging nod before Boyd instructed Carrie to "Hit it!" and "Open the hatch now!"

The portal before them swished into the wall. The two footmen caught flatfooted just beyond stood no chance. Two twenty-something male prisoners assisted Jordana and Maisie with clamping a hand around the two guardsmen's mouths and dragging them into the prison's narrow hall. They were hogtied with their own plastic straps and had their own socks jammed into their mouths within twenty seconds of being thrown to the buttercream slab floor. Carrie Sagal had withdrawn one of the footmen's tablets from a cargo pocket, pressed the bloke's thumb to the screen, and was ready to send a message to the Control Room from it no more than fifteen seconds after that.

Carrie, her brother Elias, and his girl Tessa's plan to take over the Control Room proceeded fairly smoothly, save one minor hitch. The operator was at the hatchway shortly after Boyd had instructed Carrie to send her message, but the man only planted himself in the portal's threshold, hollering for the footman. He never actually stepped out. He was plainly confused, expecting to find the guardsman right outside the hatchway and was obviously wary to instead discover a seemingly empty alleyway. Why, if the man was as cautious as he was, he opened the hatch at all after looking through its small porthole and not seeing the footman, Jordana couldn't say, or even if he had checked the porthole at all. She saw none of it, pressed tightly as she was to the silver wall beside the hatch, waiting there to pounce on the operator as soon as he stepped out.

Luckily, Maisie had acted fast. Jordana, Tessa, and the other three prisoners on snagging duty all hesitated. Maisie had understood the operator was too suspicious. She saw clearly that he would not step out and search for the wayward footman who had so strangely pinged him. And just before the wary man could slam close the hatch and foil all their plans utterly, the amazing woman had abandoned cover and darted in to subdue the man inside the Control Room itself. The remaining operator, a pudgy-necked blonde female with a face like old leather, had not even left her seat before Tessa was tossing out a shock disc into an empty corner of the expansive room. The woman's hands were in the air the instant after the arching voltage fizzled out of sight. A dozen seconds later, she too was hogtied with the footmen's bindings and the Control Room was once more their own.

Arlene Fincannon had been the first to notice the odd stockpile beside the external hatchway. "Hey, ain't those VLSE cannisters?" Jordana heard her ask from across the chilly room. "I thought you said there would only be four or five in here, Carrie?"

Jordana hopped up on the viewing platform to gain a sightline on just what the distraught freedom fighter was going on about. The loose clump of a dozen or more cannisters piled together just beside the hatchway keypad was immediately noticeable. "That's what

"Father Boyd's contacts said in that gr-green book of his," Carrie Sagal defended herself as Jordana hopped off the platform and jogged over to the fortuitous find.

"There's gotta be at least a dozen here," one freed prisoner marveled from beside the stockpile.

"Fourteen," Carrie corrected the man.

The girl couldn't have done a proper hands-on counting already, but Jordana trusted her tally, nonetheless. "What the hell are they all doing here? Something is up. I don't like it," Maisie said in a rush while keeping an unconscious wary distance from the discovery.

"The Steward ordered every set in the station brought to the Control Room right after they took it back from ya," the hogtied female operator told them from her seat atop the cold white floor.

"Why would he do that?" Boyd asked.

"Stuff a sock in the bitch's mouth already," a freed prisoner directed another nearer to the operator.

"No. Wait," Boyd barked. "Why did he want them all in here?" The woman hesitated, darting glances at the escapees surrounding her. "Sit her in a chair," the priest commanded the man the prisoner had tried to direct moments earlier. He followed the priest's orders, pulling out a chair from beside the central terminal and hauling the operator up and into it by a hand on her upper-arm. "Tell us what you know, and the cuffs come off too," Boyd said, after she'd made herself somewhat comfortable.

"I'll tell ya anything you want. You can slice 'em off here and now," she exclaimed, holding out her zip-tied hands. "I've never been a fan of these misogynistic, arrogant pricks. I just did what I had to do to stay alive. Ya'll can fault a girl for that, if ya want. I don't give a damn. Alls I'm saying is, I ain't got no allegiance to the Witen. I'll help ya'll if I can. My partner there," she added with sarcasm thick in the sweet melody of her unique voice, "you'd do best to keep that creep tied up though. Or better yet, toss him in them cells ya'll somehow escaped. He's the Witenagemot through and through. Not me though. I'm willing to help, if I can. Ya'll can cut me loose here and now, really."

"Tell us why the Steward wanted all the suits brought here," the priest broke through her rambling to prompt.

She didn't like it any and made a big show whining about her bound wrists, but eventually the leather-skinned computer tech elaborated for them, "They didn't want anyone from the E11 that showed up to sneak aboard the same way ya'll got in here the first time. They had two footmen out on patrol out there for a few hours after, but they gave up on that in the end. Instead, one of us in the Control Room was to always keep an eye on the Lunar Dock. If we see anyone coming, we were to alert the Steward and initiate an emergency protocol that sends every available Witenagemot associate to the Control Room to don VLSE gear. Once fourteen of 'em show up, they depressurize the room and head on out to intercept the raiders. He said he was going to make it SOP from here on out. Said he wanted every last vacuum suit in the station in this room at all times. Said it would be good for overall security no matter what happens with the Bruderschaft."

Her partner began to squirm on the floor and bark, "Traitor!" and "Bitch traitor!" and "Whore!" and the like at the female operator.

The freed prisoner who had directed the female operator be gagged now performed the duties himself on her squirming counterpart, using the man's own sock.

"This is great!" Jordana exclaimed. "We can get all my people aboard in no time."

"I wouldn't get your hopes up quite yet," the cooperative operator warned.

"What do you mean?" Dolly Duchesne-Boyd was the first to ask.

"The Steward had us install a failsafe."

"What?" Jordana and a handful of others around her incredulously asked.

"A program was uploaded into the system of each suit," the woman in the chair explained, plainly annoyed about still being bound and therefore not fully trusted. "They'll start up just fine, your gauges will all read full and charged, but unless a secret passcode is entered into the central terminal, the suit will stop feeding oxygen thirty seconds in, and the helmet will latch in place. Whoever is wearing the thing won't be able to get it off. You see, a failsafe. Means no one can use the things without the Steward or the Commander knowing about it."

"They're the only ones with this secret passcode, I take it," Boyd said, sounding as if it all were just inevitable.

"Yep," the woman confirmed, trying not to grin.

"Well, shit," Boyd huffed.

"Whatever. We gotta get down to the Meadow right now anyhow," Maisie said, throwing up her hands and turning to march out of the cold, wide room.

"I could probably hack through the failsafe," the leathery operator added in an offhand manner.

No matter its flippant delivery, the casual statement stopped Maisie dead, even turned her back. "How fast?" Maisie crossed her arms and asked.

"I dunno," the operator said, shaking her clasped hands in bewilderment. "I do know the two operators who was on duty when the Steward ordered the program designed pretty well though."

"So? What of it?" Boyd prodded.

"They ain't terrible programmers, I guess, if I'm feeling generous," the operator shrugged, "but I'm willing to bet I can slip past any slick bullshit they might think to use."

"And why would you do all this for us? Just out of the kindness of your heart? You just been waiting for your chance to rebel this whole time? Is that it, Ms. Balfritz?" Boyd asked the leathery operator with the strange last name apparently of Balfritz.

"Please, Boyd, call me Cheryl," Ms. Balfritz invited him with an out of place smile.

"What do you want for this service, Cheryl?" Boyd demanded.

"Just some trust," she assured, batting her nonexistent lashes.

"Best get to it then," Boyd said after a time, sporting a sharply arched and skeptical brow.

It was a long minute before Cheryl Balfritz said she was through the failsafe program's security. Maisie had spent every last one of those sixty seconds impatiently pacing. Jordana had wanted to go to her and take her into her arms. She wanted to utter soft words and bring comfort to a tumultuous heart. But she didn't think this the right time and place. Jordana was ninety-nine percent certain Maisie felt for her as she did for Maisie, but there was still that pesky one percent. It was enough to keep her firmly in place the whole time

Balfritz worked her magic. "I think I got it," the operator eventually informed them.

"You *think*?" Boyd and Maisie asked together in the same dubious tones.

"Well, yeah. I'm pretty sure I skirted the firewall easy enough, but I can't say whether or not they installed some booby traps along the way."

"Booby traps?" Jordana joined Boyd and Maisie in their vocal incredulity.

"There could be a tripwire somewhere, a sort of last-ditch defense for the firewall against subversion," Balfritz explained. "Could be everything seems hunky dory, and twenty seconds in, the air cuts out and the helmet latches firm. No way to know, short of testing the damn things for ya'll selves."

"We need a guinea pig then? That's what you're saying?" Boyd asked for clarification.

"Well, yeah. If you wanna use them suits, I s'pose you do."

"Novocaine!" Maisie and Jordana proposed in tandem.

The priest tried to think of an argument against their suggestion, clearly, but apparently drawing a blank after a short moment's thought, he agreed with a simple stiff head-nod.

"Wait," one of the twenty-something male prisoners cut in. "We can't put that little snake in a vacuum suit. He'll just run off to the Bruderschaft's E11 and sell 'em some lie and convince them to take off without us."

"Not if we only put a few minutes' worth of oxygen in his suit," Boyd settled the dissenting complaint. "Cheryl, you say the helmets on these suits can lock in place?"

"Sure can."

"And you can control each suit from here?"

"Sure can."

"Okay then... we put Barker in a suit with a couple minutes air and leave him alone inside this room. We disable the passcodes on the hatchway so we can get right back in. You can do that, right, Cheryl?"

"Sure can," the operator supplied her simple answer for the third time.

"Good," Boyd said, plainly focused on his train of thought and not really hearing the woman. "So we leave Barker in the suit with limited air in here. We have him follow our instructions, or he'll suffocate in the suit. We tell him to switch his suit on and depressurize the Control Room, and then we watch through the porthole. If he starts writhing and kicking for air, we'll know we can't risk using the suits."

"Sounds good," Maisie and Jordana said in tandem again, satisfaction plain in their voices, even to Jordana's own ears.

"This ain't vengeance though, Mais," the priest warned. Though the caution was somewhat undercut by the grin tugging at the corners of his mouth.

"No, Boyd, it's only practical," Maisie answered, matching his grin. "We do gotta act fast though. I'm talking right now," she added, instantly growing serious as the pressures of time once more tapped her on the shoulder.

"Go get him, Aziz. Take Marcy and Riley there," Boyd said, pointing to two freed prisoners beside the saturnine mechanical engineer. Patel only nodded, once at Boyd and once each at the two beside him, before striding swiftly out of the Control Room.

Maisie's patience was a threadbare thing by the time Novocaine had finished slipping into the VLSE gear they'd siphoned most of the air from. The delusional perv grumbled all the while, each excuse more feeble and contradictory than the last. No one really paid any attention either way. Boyd did most of the talking, and ninety percent of that was just yelling at the swinish traitor to hurry up. Maisie had started to pace almost the second Patel had gone to drag Barker out of his cell. Her path had grown longer, but the time it took her to make each revolution had stayed the same.

The brunette wonder was nearly sprinting back and forth now. They were all milling in the Grand Alleyway just in front of the Control Room's entry hatch. Maisie paced at the back of the crowd while the rest of them squeezed in tight, fighting for a view through the hatch's tiny porthole at Cainey Barker suited up in an orange set of VLSE gear inside the otherwise empty Control Room.

"We don't have time for this," Maisie was saying at the back of the crowd. "We have to get down there now. It could already be too late."

"Turn on your suit and depressurize the room," Boyd loudly and slowly instructed, not knowing if his words could travel to Cainey on the other side of the thick sliding hatch.

Barker gave no direct indication that he had understood, but he did tap his suit's wrist controls a beat later, right before stepping up to the hatchway keypad. The lights inside the Control Room cut out a second later, the emergency red ones instantly kicking in to take the place of their bright yellow brothers. Cainey stepped away from the keypad and stood square in the hatchway threshold, staring them all down through the tiny circular porthole. The only noise for a half minute was Maisie's persistent assurances that they had to leave right then. Everyone else only stared back at the small man, waiting for either panic and pain or a safe shrug of the shoulders.

"Is your suit still working?" Boyd asked, still loudly enunciating. "Any problems? Barker, hello?" he asked even louder when the man only looked down at his right wrist. Strapped overtop his orange life suit was a cracked-face wristwatch with a ratty green strap. "Barker, is your suit still operating? Hello? C'mon, you fool," Boyd growled, taking a step toward the hatch and pounding one of his meaty fists against the small glass porthole. "If you want to survive another minute, you better give your report. Otherwise we will just leave ya in there to suffocate."

Cainey Barker looked up from his watch with that, a grin plastered to his face, one so utterly unexpected as it was disconcerting. Jordana couldn't say why exactly, but the little traitor's smirk actually seemed to hurt her to look at it. Shameful as it was, Jordana cowered from that grin. Her eyes fell to the parquet floor, so she only heard what happened next. But it was well narrated by the many dumbfounded voices who watched Novocaine bolt toward the exterior hatch clear across the Control Room. The man was bounding across the lunar surface within ten heartbeats of her eyes hitting the floor.

"What the hell does he think he's doing?" a voice cried.

"Seriously," Larry Holderman concurred. "He ain't got enough oxygen in that thing to get anywhere."

"Fuck it," Boyd cut off the array of similar conjectures that filtered through the small crowd. "It don't matter where the fool thinks he's off to. The suits work. That's all that matters. Let's get to work getting the Bruderschaft aboard. We don't have a second to waste."

"I don't think we even have those seconds to waste, Priest," Maisie said, resolute but still discombobulated too.

"Okay, Mais, okay," Boyd said, after looking the brunette beauty square in her hazel eyes. "You go on. We'll be right behind. Matter of fact," he added, snapping his fingers before pointing a thick and gnarled index digit at two freed male prisoners just in front of Maisie, "you two go with her. There should be three trolleys parked outside the hospital. Mais, you take one down to the Meadow now. Try not to get yourself killed before we arrive," he directed with a shared smile. "You boys bring the other two down here. Once we get the Bruderschaft aboard, we'll race down to the Meadow on those two trolleys. Hell, we'll ride on the roofs if we have to."

"I'm coming with you," Jordana said after Maisie exchanged a solemn head nod with the priest. Jordana was in the middle of the pressed gaggle just then. She tried to extricate herself from the group still watching a distant Novocaine Barker bounding out of sight as politely as she could. The decorum caused her to place a foot in a precarious spot. Her balance went, and just before she could stumble to a knee, Father Raymond Boyd grabbed her arm and held her firm until she stabilized. "Thank you," Jordana instinctively said. She was still feeling the odd discomfort from Cainey's sneer and kept her eyes on the floor.

"Don't mention it. Everyone needs a hand to hold on to," he said while wearing a smile that totally reversed whatever Cainey's had done to her.

"Is that from the Psalms, Father?" she asked. "I'm afraid I'm not familiar with that passage."

"It's from the gospel according to Cougar. John Cougar Mellencamp, more precisely," he explained. The randomness of it all, along with the priest's warm presence in these dark and cold times, plucked at her heartstrings. She couldn't fight the chuckle, nor did she want to. The priest added a huffed giggle of his own before clapping her on the shoulder and gently ushering her off toward Maisie.

"I'm coming too."

Jordana wasn't expecting to hear another voice, much less one so young. That would have been surprising enough, but Carrie had declared her intention from directly beside Jordana. She hadn't even known the child had been there. *She's everywhere she means to be*, Jordana admiringly thought of the wise young Sagal's movements.

"Well, you ain't going without me," Tessa said, stepping up alongside Carrie.

"Don't be ridiculous, Ri Ri," Maisie demanded of her sister, her brow furrowed and hands on hips. "You aren't even gonna come down to the Meadow with the priest and everybody else. You're gonna go back to our quarters right now, or better yet, your clubhouse. And I mean right now. You did great, baby sis, but the rest of today won't be kid stuff."

"I promised Elias I would be back for him," Carrie offered in her defense, hobbling up alongside her sister. "If we aren't going back to Earth, then I'm going to fulfill my promise right now. He needs me. He needs us. Whether or not he or you real-re-realize as mu-much. I'm coming," she finished, mirroring Maisie with her own hands on her hips.

"We don't have time for this, Ri. I don't got time to argue."

"So, don't argue," Carrie said, logical as ever. "Let's get moving," she finished, strutting past her sister with Tessa keeping pace beside her.

"C'mon, Jor. You too, guys." Maisie waved for Jordana and the young prisoners to join her in catching up to Carrie and Tessa. Her shoulder shrug and eye roll were there but not as prominent as they might have been. Carrie had a presence of character and strength of will with which one could not argue. Maisie knew it. Her shrug said it all. Carrie Roxanna Sagal was going to the Meadow, with or without their permission.

CHAPTER 14
HARCLAY

THE BATTLE OF THE BLOODY MEADOW

Woodson's death had failed to reach him. It had pissed the Glorifier off something fierce, but Harclay Aponyaschefski was numb. He barely even felt the flagpole clutched loosely in his left hand. The odd tug and jounce resulting from the bare-chested prophet's wild gesticulating and hollering was all that remained to remind him of his duty. It was a simple enough task: hold one pole of the Witenagemot war banner, but Harclay had no taste for it. He had told the Commander he needed to be on the battlefield, to be seen. The Witen's foot soldiers needed to see both of their titled officers sharing their mortal danger. Once it started though, his conviction abandoned him completely.

It was the screams. The stink of blood and shit was bad enough, but the cries, the wails, the pleas for mercy, those were the hardest to endure. They had sent a man named the Steward running for the woods, for a dark, hidden cave. That confident legislator was long gone now. Harclay Aponyaschefski was all that was left. And that man knew well the art of cowardice. Harclay had known what to do in the face of the violent horror: nothing. Just stand in place, still as he could, and hope no one noticed him. It was working so far. No one in the melee had the time to notice the scowling distaste behind his thousand-yard stare. No one, save the Glorifier, anyway.

The golden-legged zealot was well aware of Harclay's desire to pretend it all away. With every shout and cheer he shrieked above the steel-clanging clamor, he'd look over to the Steward, expecting him to echo the encouragement. Harclay had no cheer inside him though, no fire for victory, not even after he and the Glorifier both watched Arlo Bailey knock Captain Alvarez unconscious with a wild right hook before collapsing atop him. The wild-haired prophet was incensed by the event, even as it unfolded ten yards across the shorn red grass. He'd even taken two paces toward the unconscious combatants. If not for the fact that he was still clutching his war banner pole, the Glorifier might well have darted in and tried to kill Arlo Bailey himself.

Harclay had nearly lost his grip on the banner after the Glorifier's sudden charge, but he managed to grab firm hold of it after a few seconds. The Glorifier stepped back to stand even with him once more. Harclay did not fail to note the furious disgust and incredulous disdain emanating from every ounce of the opportunistic performance-artist's sycophantic being as he stared him down. His cowardly persona, Harclay "Schef" Aponyaschefski, Esquire, was still in control just then, and so he shamelessly averted his eyes from the Glorifier's. What they found was no easier to watch. The battle was winding down. Half of the combatants were now casualties. Half of those were lifeless and still while the other half writhed and shrieked as best their injury allowed as they bemoaned the loss of a limb or a puncture wound deep in the belly or chest.

Among the living and still physically capable half, Lieutenant Dirks hounded a lone Bruderschaft warrior, his chintzy breastplate now hanging limply over his belly and obstructing his ability to defend himself against the knife-faced officer's probing spear thrusts. Not far from her, Dobechek traded slashes and jukes with a tall barrel-shaped woman with long arms and no chest plate. A skirmish between four Witen footmen and three Bruderschaft fighters, all armed with steel shields along with a blade or maul, were squared off in the center of the thin-spread melee. Beyond them, the Commander was hammering his axe at two cowering and retreating Bruderschaft warriors armed with mauls, each of whom was at least eight inches shorter than the Commander, as well as seventy pounds lighter. But the hardest patch of that gore-speckled mown meadow to watch were the five square yards where Elias Sagal currently fought. Even though the boy seemed to be getting the better of the two footmen who were attacking him from either side, Harclay still found the event painful to look upon.

Intuitively, he had known that should his eyes find his protégé in the midst of the carnage, a cruel and treacherous memory would flash in his mind. And sadly, he was right. A morningstar came looping in to crack Sagal's skull. The Ethling had avoided the smash with a quick head dodge, but even still, watching his brush with danger extracted the memory flash...

"Why?" Wally had managed to ask after Harclay had pulled the knife from his son's belly. No, *he tried to assure himself.* That ain't how it happened. He left. The Damned got him. *It was no good though. The comforting lie had dissolved. Truth was reigning now in Harclay's mind.* "Why, Dad? Why?" *he heard his son ask with his dying breath. Harclay didn't have an answer for him then, but he did now:* Fear. Just fear, Son. I was afraid you'd bring them to the cave. I had to stay alive, *he silently told the dying boy at his feet in that damp darkness nearly a decade past.*

He saw Wally's eyes. They looked up at him. They hadn't done that day, but now, in the hallucination, they captured him, holding him firm as his son's voice rattled around in his fear-pervaded mind. "Coward. Murderer. Coward. Murderer," *Wally accused him on repeat.* "Look at them all, Dad. Look at the grass," *his son's voice demanded.* "See the red. Look at it all. So much ... you could fill a pool. And it's all your fault, Dad. This is all your fault. Your vengeance is to blame. AOA started the genocide, and you finished the job. Coward. Coward. Murderer. Coward. Murderer."

"Nooo!" Harclay shrieked, falling to his knees. Instantly came the tug from his banner mate. The Glorifier was yelling something at him as well, but Harclay Aponyaschefski could not hear it. If he was screaming aloud at half the volume that he was currently screaming inside his head, surely the noise would've pierced through even the focus of men and women engaged in a life-or-death struggle. It seemed, however, that the Glorifier alone was aware of his collapse. The battle raged on, oblivious to the emotional state of its ultimate creator. Elias dodged away from three slashes, each time only milliseconds from catastrophe. The Commander had finished one of his outmatched opponents and was currently at work bashing through the other's ever-weakening guard.

"Stand up, goddammit, man!" The Glorifier's words finally penetrated his anguish. "You're embarrassing yourself. You're embarrassing the Witenagemot!" the man shouted as he bent to drag Harclay to his feet.

The banner was bunched up behind them as the bearded bastard slapped him twice and thrust his flag pole back in his hand. Harclay knew he'd been slapped. He was hearing the prophet just fine. But he somehow did not feel the smack, nor the impact of the words. He was numb. He'd thought he'd been before. He'd thought the screams had taken him away. He was wrong. There was more to take. There was further to go. But surely, that was all. This numbness was final. It had to be. Harclay Aponyaschefski could take no more. Another un-felt slap from the Glorifier was encouraging on that end.

"Our people need you!" the shirtless performer told him after the slap. "I know you're a phony fucking coward. I've always known. Me, the Captain, Woodson, Masterson, Dobechek, Schwambach, and shit knows how many supervisors, we all know. But the people don't. They need to see the power. The people are right there, you pussy-ass bitch," the Glorifier shoved his face toward the line of residents along the gaming fields on the heels of the insult, "and they need to see a regime in control. They don't need to see your fucking pussy-ass weeping like some fucking child. Straighten yourself the fuck out!" He added a slap to his demand once more. "I'm not letting our great Witenagemot suffer just 'cause your cowardly little punk-ass can't handle a little blood."

"*I* built the 'great' Witenagemot," Harclay heard himself answer. He had no idea why he was bothering, but the words were indeed rolling off his tongue. "Whatever it is, I made it. It can't exist without me. Now, get your fucking hand off me," he added, shoving the man's grimy paw off his shoulder.

"The Witen will know what a coward you were here today. They'll not only hear it from me, but from the lips of all them goddam gossiping residents whom you've just put on this pathetic show for," the Glorifier assured him. "But until your fucking bitch-ass is gasping your last breath beneath a gibbet in the desert for treason and cowardice, you're gonna play the role of a man of the Witenagemot. So, stand the fuck up straight. Hold the goddamn banner firm and don't you dare cry another fucking tear." He leaned in close then.

Harclay felt the bunched-up banner fall on the back of his head at the same instant the zealot's scraggly beard scratched up against his own face. Adding to the indignity, the Glorifier clapped a hand on his chin and pulled his face until their eyes locked.

Holding him firmly in place and washing him in his stale breath, the man then asked, "You got me, Steward?"

Harclay said nothing. He did tighten his grip on his flag pole though, as well as sidestep a few paces away from the Glorifier to spread out the golden "W" on the thickly woven black wool war banner. He heard the pretend prophet tisk and scoff as he stepped away, but after a brief and unbidden emotional interlude, he was righted once again behind the refuge of numbing banality, and so they had little more effect than the man's slaps. Harclay understood that it would surely try his cold zen to watch more of the horrible battle still clashing hot before him and was thus tempted to keep his eyes on his shoes, but he also held the simultaneous counter understanding that the Glorifier would be returning with his scorn and slaps should he keep his tortured eyes on the ground. So, after a breath and a deliberate and exhaustive attempt to empty his mind of memories of days and moments gone by, as well as any postulations of future ones to come, he lifted his gaze to take in the violence his blind genius and petty vengeance had wrought.

The numb emptiness persisted in the face of the horror, though, ironically, it was a struggle. Dirks finishing off a teak-skinned thirty-something woman with shoulder length dreadlocks by way of a spear thrust between the eyes tested his apathetic resolve. So too Dobechek hacking into the back of some poor snot-nosed, pale-skinned, pimply teen boy's legs and sending his rusty morningstar hurtling unguided through the rotten air rife with lamentations. Although following the discarded weapon on its somber plummet, Harclay spotted a sight that he was pleased to have penetrate his numb shield. The morningstar had buried itself in the turf, spike-end first, right beside the corpse of one of his earlier enumerated enemies, Lieutenant Steve Schwambach. The Lieutenant's face was already turning black, all the blood drained from his corpse through the gaping wound the spear that even then still jutted up and out of the man's groin must surely have caused.

    Harclay didn't smile at the sight. At least, he thought he didn't. He'd deliberately tried not to. Humor could crack the cold numbness he was trying to affect as easily as violence or trauma. Regardless, whatever he'd done or however he now felt, the sight he turned back to as he followed Lieutenant Dobechek after she beheaded the poor British teen and stormed after her next opponent would have pierced his distant numbness anyhow. Elias Sagal was down to one opponent now. Blood covered nearly every inch of the Ethling. How much of it was Elias' own, Harclay could not even guess. A good deal though, that was for sure. Sagal had lost his war hammer and was now using a two-handed grip on his longsword, hacking his enemy down in much the same way Harclay had watched the Commander attack his foes. The threat of the battered opponent at Sagal's feet wasn't what had caused the lurch in Harclay's heart. It was Lieutenant Dobechek and Footman Allanson arriving nearly in tandem behind Elias, their razor-sharp weapons aimed for the back of Sagal's head.

    "Nooo!" Harclay screamed at his maddening creation once more.

    This time though, by the grace of some god or karma to which Harclay Aponyashcefski was entirely undeserving, someone other than just the Glorifier heard him. Elias himself was, in fact, that other someone. The shout reached his ears just in time for him to arrest a downward thrust that would have finished off the battered footman at his feet, as well as catch a quick glimpse of the twin battleaxes swinging in to decimate and decapitate. Elias Sagal was insanely talented, it must be said. It wasn't just the trials of a hard life that had forged him into a formidable warrior with lightning speed and quickness, along with uncommon strength and stamina; rather, it was innate to the boy. He'd always been impressive. Harclay had noticed long ago. He was a rare talent. And he used those uncommon skills to drop to his knees and let the wicked weapons pass harmlessly through the air a few inches above his head.

    He was back up and squared off against Dobechek and Allanson in a flash. The lieutenant and footman barely had enough time to regain their own balance after their wild slashes caught nothing but air before Elias was sending his bright sword looping down at them. Whether it connected or not, Harclay could not say. It was then that the Glorifier reclaimed his attention. The prophet didn't step to him this time. He held his distance, keeping the banner stiff and proud, but he was hollering up a hellfire, naming Harclay a coward and a pussy and now a traitor as well. Harclay Aponyaschefski knew the scantily clad preacher was saying those things, but somehow they weren't what he heard. Instead, it was Wally's voice echoing inside his head. They were Wally's words rattling around his mind on repeat, calling him a *Coward* and a *Murderer* over and over again.

Harclay turned his gaze from the angry zealot, hoping that would halt Wally's repeated assessment. It didn't. Instead, it continued its loop as he watched Elias duck beneath a wild slash from Dobechek only to pop up fast and drive a shoulder into Allanson's chest. The footman went tumbling backward, tripped up by the foot placed expertly by Elias behind him. Sagal used the room opened up by the footman's tumble to dodge out of the path of two more looping axe slashes from a rebalanced Dobechek.

Murderer, Wally silently called Harclay as Elias parried a jab from Dobechek and then used the momentum to spin behind her. *Coward*, the accusation silently boomed as Elias went on to aim a thrust down at Allanson trying to climb back to his feet. The footmen's chest plate had torn at one shoulder and was now hanging loose off his chest while his left thigh plate and right shin guard were missing altogether. The faltering gear encumbered the man to the point where all he could do to avoid being skewered on Elias' sword was to drop back to the ground and roll out of range.

Elias thought to chase the scrambling footman, or so Harclay read in his pause, but then thought better of it, turning back just in time to interpose his sword before one of Dobechek's arcing slashes could cut him in half.

Coward, Wally called his father yet again. *He's right. You are. You could do something. You could help him*, Harclay urged himself, hoping the invocation alone would summon the courage to intervene on Elias' behalf. But he only watched on. Impotently, meekly, pathetically, he only took more of the silent scorn from his son and simply watched, still as a stump, as his protégé, his surrogate child, escaped death from one breath to the next.

The numbness had thawed. He was feeling. He was remembering. The weight of each day he had lived and every word he'd ever spoken, of every action either done or undone, of lost hopes and unrequited fantasies, of decisions and compromises, of a lifetime of loss and struggle, all of it, it all came back at once to slam down upon his shoulders. The pain of that little world, his own unique universe, pressing its mighty weight upon him was white hot, but he could not remove his hand from the theoretical stove. Instead, he held it down, watching on, even smelling the metaphorical skin start to burn.

Allanson was back on his feet now. Elias had the footman to his left and Dobechek circling him to his right. A few other skirmishes remained engaged in an exhausted struggle, but the Commander had destroyed everything that had once drawn breath in his small patch. Harclay saw him marching straight toward Elias, his black axe now painted red. The bellow did not make it through the chaotic din of the battlefield, but Harclay clearly saw the Commander scream something as he pointed his axe at Elias once he'd got to within twenty yards of where Sagal fended off Allanson and Dobechek. Elias heard it though, that much was plain. Even Allanson and Dobechek heard it. Nothing else explained why all three of their heads darted toward the Commander in the instant after the bellow.

Knowing the man, Harclay understood the Commander had issued the shout as a way of intimidating his opponent, a useful tactic ... on certain occasions. However, Harclay figured the Commander's rage might well have been more useful put into an axe swing just then. All the shout seemed to do really was distract Elias' pair of foes and warn him that, if he didn't act fast, he'd soon have three enemies to contend with. Before Allanson could even whip his head back to face him, Elias had his sword past the footman's guard. Allanson tried to flick his battleaxe up in time to parry the thrust, but Elias' sword point was through his eye before his weapon even made it halfway there.

If the Commander's bellow wasn't able to reach Harclay's ears through the pervasive steel song, then surely Allanson's piteous screech that followed Sagal withdrawing his sword and taking Allanson's right eye with it couldn't have made it to where he stood holding a flag pole at the edge of the chaotic scene either. Harclay still heard it, nonetheless. Perhaps it was pure imagination. The footman's scream had, after all, momentarily silenced Wally's condemnations. Whatever the truth of the matter, Harclay was happy to see Elias still alive and his opponent seriously crippled. He nearly smiled, despite his guilt and shame, despite his resolve to remain numb to it all, despite everything. Dobechek's axe looping in to back Sagal off from Allanson's deathblow after the tormented footman had fallen to his knees to clasp his blood-pulsing eye socket forestalled the unreasonable impulse before it could properly manifest.

Sagal refused to give the ground Dobechek was trying to claim with her wild slashes. Elias planted his feet and deftly parried each blow as it came. When the lieutenant switched to a downward hack, Elias dropped spryly to a knee, releasing his two-handed grip to lash out with his right hand and catch the shaft of Dobechek's axe just before the blade could plow into his skull. Using her momentum, he tugged on the weapon while simultaneously twisting at the hips, sending Dobechek and her axe flying over his shoulder to crash on her back atop a patch of relatively unstained green grass.

The Commander was sprinting now, Harclay noticed out of the corner of his vision. Both of Sagal's enemies were on the ground and vulnerable. Clearly, the milk-eyed goliath Harclay had helped raise up as some sort of demigod wanted to reach Elias in time to prevent him from finishing them off. So, Harclay shouted again, in words a bit more intelligible than his earlier emotion-laced shriek, "Elias! Watch out! He's coming!" Elias gave no indication he'd heard this time, beyond never hesitating. Harclay was certain, though, that his protégé would have behaved the same regardless of what he had or hadn't heard.

The Glorifier, for his irritating part, had definitely heard. And again he answered with insults and threats and demands to hold the banner tight and not embarrass the Witen. The prophet's words were still drowned out by Wally's ceaseless accusations, however, and so, easily ignored. Harclay's eyes stayed on the battle. Elias had not wasted a single motion or millisecond. After he'd heaved Lieutenant Dobechek over his shoulder, he had whipped around to slash at the footman still on his knees beside him, both hands pressed firmly to the red weeping socket. The lightning slash took Allanson's left arm off at the elbow. Sagal's blade was so sharp that it took Allanson spasming the remaining nub of his left arm and the upper part dropping slowly away from the footman's face before Harclay realized the damage. Allanson did not have long to contemplate his severed limb before Sagal had the sword whipping back in to claim his right as well. Elias did pause a beat then, waiting for the right upper arm to tumble slowly to the turf and for Allanson to get a good look with his one remaining eye at the ruin of what once had been his strong young arms.

The left stump spurted blood up into the footman's face just before Elias thrust his war-slick longsword deep into his chest. Even from where he now stood, twenty yards across the battlefield, Harclay could plainly see a trickle of blood leak out of the corner of Allanson's fat, wormy lips. Elias let gravity help extract his blade from the chest of his bitter foe, allowing the dead man to drop like a stone to the cushy turf while he clung to the hilt.

Harclay didn't scream another warning. Not because he was numb or dazed or crippled by guilt or fear, though all of that was so, but rather the axe slash Dobechek aimed from her knees from just behind Elias and the running jab the Commander launched as he closed the gap came so suddenly and so quickly that he simply didn't have the time. Elias Sagal was not the slow, weak fool that Harclay Aponyaschefski was, however. He somehow felt Dobechek's swing without ever turning to face it. Rather, he allowed the Commander's jab to do the job for him by rolling out of range of both swings at the last possible second. The Commander's jab not only halted Dobechek's slash, but it sent the pair colliding into one another, shoulder into shoulder.

Elias shuffled away from them, regrouping and drawing in some clearly needed breaths. The Commander and lieutenant gave him his space. Dobechek used the time to claim a few deep breaths of her own. The Commander though, used the time to bellow something else, the last few syllables of which coming only faintly to Harclay's ears. All he knew was that once the Commander was finished shouting and his hands came back to his sides and his eyes fell back down from the brightly speckled wonder beyond Stargazer Ceiling, he shoved Dobechek away and then used his axe to point to a skirmish a few yards away between two Witenagemot footmen and three Bruderschaft fighters. It seemed he was directing the lieutenant to lend her help in that battle while he handled Sagal. When the lieutenant shook her head and took two steps toward Elias only to be grabbed by the collar and shoved toward that other skirmish by the Commander, Harclay figured it was a safe assumption.

Dobechek went sullenly, but she did trudge off toward that precarious and stagnated skirmish. The Commander pointed his axe at Sagal then. His back was to Harclay, but he assumed his handcrafted king was issuing some threats to his adopted son.

Coward! Wally shouted in his head. There was no real sound, but he still felt as if his eardrums had popped. Wally's silently loud and percussive calls of *Murderer* and *Coward* that followed relentlessly as time itself afterward disabused him of that sweet release.

Out on the red grass, the pair began to circle one another: his creation and his redemption. Harclay watched on, Wally's silent voice never wavering. All about the battlefield, each individual skirmish in their own good time, abandoned their private struggle to watch the legendary one now set for imminent kickoff near the edge of the widespread battle, with thorny hedges and thickly woven grapevines serving as both boundary and backdrop only five yards behind them. Even Dobechek, now standing beside Lieutenant Dirks and Footman Childress, had eyes fixed on the Commander and the Ethling. Even the Bruderschaft warriors lined up across from them, as well as every last one of their remaining seven or eight battle-capable brethren spread across the breadth of the killing grounds in various states of health and vigor, stopped to watch the circling pair.

Harclay's eyes were fixed on that cruel patch of spongy turf. The Glorifier's were fixed on him. Harclay never turned to verify that, but he knew. He felt their scrutiny. But he could no longer veil his turmoil. His frosty distance had thawed, thrusting him into the here and now. Harclay knew the Glorifier could read quite well every spasming emotion and counter emotion as each rippled across his face, as well he could decipher the cause of each bead of sweat that trickled down his neck and cheeks. Harclay couldn't absolutely say he didn't care anymore what the Glorifier might think, but he did have a hard time right then of allowing such theoretical and distant concerns stemming from the prophet's current scrutiny to override his primal reactions to witnessing his surrogate son face a challenger Harclay did not think he could defeat. The walls were down. The spotlight was on him. His future was over, one way or another. All there was now was the *now*, the present moment. So Harclay lived there, emotionally, in a place where the son he murdered shouted condemnations in his head as he watched the son he tried to redemptively apotheosize fight a death duel against a superior opponent. And in that place, rightly, or at least understandably, he was a mass of nervous frustration and fear. He could not calm himself now out of a mere sense of embarrassment before the eyes of the Glorifier.

Harclay was still holding his end of the banner, after all. The golden "W" was still soaring over the carnage, bright and proud. The Glorifier really couldn't say much. He tried. He yelled his piece. But the nuisance wasn't very impactful, to say the least. Especially after the Commander ended the wary circling with a sudden charge. Elias was caught flat-footed by the quickness of the larger man. Harclay's heart was in his throat as the boy only just managed to duck and roll under the arcing slash the Commander launched at his eyes. A quick somersault and Elias was back on his feet. The Commander halted his first empty slash and came back with a rapid backhand, but his back was still partially facing Elias. Sagal ducked low beneath the backhand and thrust out with his longsword toward the small of the Commander's back. The big gorilla man managed to show off some more of that unexpected quickness, avoiding the fatal puncture. Though even his legendary agility couldn't spare him the foot-long gash that Elias' blade tore across the council chief's unprotected back.

The Commander snarled as he darted clear of any follow-up slash, gaining ground to press his hand to his lower back and discover the extent of his wound. He spat toward Elias after staring at the blood from the gash that covered his hand. Apparently, this meant that wound was nothing to him because he immediately charged back in, leading with another devastating slash. Elias had to be delicate trying to parry a heavy axe with his long thin blade. The sword was extremely susceptible to shattering should he pit it against an axe in a straight hacking contest. So, instead, he flowed with the deflection, allowing the axe's own momentum to work against it. This time, the tactic spun him around so that he wound up with the Commander's full back to him.

The Witen's ruler was no fool; his instincts in battle were as attuned as a spawning salmon's sense of direction. He was already twisting back around to dodge and deflect another thrust aimed at his back. Only thing was, Elias decided to go low. Sagal's longsword hacked into the Commander's calves, catching more of the right than the left. The scarred goliath roared in pain and rage, whipping his axe back savagely to forestall any follow-up cut. Sagal backed off, perhaps to gauge the damage he'd done or merely to catch his breath, or even both; Harclay couldn't say for sure. The Commander took the respite to snarl back up at the stars. He stood straight and tall while blood sheeted from his right calf and dripped from a smaller gash in his left.

Pumping his axe toward the heavens, the Commander bellowed on, and now that the fighting had ceased everywhere but between the Ethling and Commander, and Harclay's ears had only the moans of the dying to contend with, he heard his creation say, "You cannot hurt me. You cannot *kill* me! No man can kill me. I am the Witenagemot. I am the chosen. Bow, traitor. Fall to your fucking knees. Bow to me, right now. This is your last warning. You've proven your strength. Bow and be forgiven. Bow now... or I'll hack your fucking head from your shoulders just as I did your old man's."

Elias' expressions were barely discernable beneath the layer of blood and grimy sweat that caked his handsome young face. Harclay could not tell what the boy might be thinking. He did pause though. He stayed stock still for a good ten count, giving Harclay and, judging by the tense, unsure groans from the assembled residents, every other witness to the current calamity plenty of grounds to wonder if he was contemplating the offer. Perhaps Elias knew all that and was only playing up the moment. Or perhaps he was just tired and summoning up a last burst of strength.

Either way, after he stretched out his arm and pointed the tip of his sword straight at the Commander's chest and said in a loud yet easy voice, "You die today, Jasper. Good luck explaining all this to

Carrie and Roxanna in the next life," any doubts about whether he was wavering or not were put to rest.

The names shook through the Commander, physically. Harclay saw it from yards away. The man actually shuddered as Elias' words washed over him. Then, with a snarl and any care for some small thing like a sliced calf muscle tossed to the wind, the Commander charged once more at the boy he'd once named Ethling. Elias calmly shifted to a ready stance, seeming to eagerly anticipate the larger man's arrival. Only, the Commander's axe unexpectedly preceded him by a good five paces. He'd been sprinting with the nasty black weapon held ready for a down slash above his shoulder when suddenly he'd flicked the wicked tool at Elias, sending it flipping expertly through the clean recycled air, end over end. The shock of the axe's arrival ahead of its former bearer revealed itself in Sagal's feeble last-second parry that only just knocked the heavy blade off course before it could slam home dead into the boy's sternum.

The Commander finished his charge a mere second behind his axe. Elias was still dealing with deflecting and dodging the throw and trying to avoid becoming entangled and so was wholly out of balance when the Commander crashed his shoulder into Sagal's belly like some highlight-reel quarterback sack. Elias folded around the tackle, landing hard on his back with the Commander on top, driving all 270 pounds of his massive, muscled frame down onto him.

"Nooo!" Harclay might have screamed again. The Glorifier certainly gave the banner a good few tugs and hurled up a few more insults, but Harclay still couldn't be sure. Wally was screaming so loud inside his skull he could not hear his own voice over the silent insults and accusations.

All of it mattered little. His fate was sealed by then anyhow. So, he allowed himself to scream again. It remained unheard in his own ears, and if the Commander heard it, he paid no attention. It had no benefit beyond the needed release. The tension radiating inside was set to burst him into a thousand pieces, otherwise. Whatever the case, the scream, whether silent or shattering, certainly didn't stop the tyrant Harclay constructed from wrenching the sword from Elias' weakened grip as he planted himself atop the boy's chest. Nor did the useless plea stop him from working to trap one of Sagal's now flailing arms while bashing hammerfists into the boy's battle-grimed face between efforts.

When the Commander finally captured Sagal's right arm, clamping it tight against his chest, Harclay knew the end was near, just as he knew it was a righteous punishment that he should be forced to witness his protégé's demise. He felt himself shout, "Nooo!" one more time, as opposed to hearing it.

Across the bloody grass, the Commander took advantage of the now opened gap in Sagal's defenses to drop a half-dozen firmer and more precisely aimed hammerfists into the boy's exposed face. Harclay found it hard to keep his feet after seeing them land. Sagal's nose warped and shattered under the pummeling. The blood pouring forth to cascade across his cheeks and into his mouth seemed to herald the end of everything.

Elias Sagal, however, did not agree. Rather than allow the big man sitting on his chest and his shattered nose and blood-filled mouth to do their work and suffocate him to death, Sagal let his need for a clean breath of air fill him with a ludicrous strength. Elias suddenly bucked his hips, over and over. The Commander abandoned any further hammerfists to focus on maintaining his balance. The Ethling kept up the effort until the Commander finally fell off his chest. Unfortunately for Elias, the wily gorilla man kept a hold of his arm. Sagal tried to scramble free, but all his panicked jerking achieved was for the Commander to firm up his grip on his arm while swinging his legs over Elias' chest.

With Sagal's arm trapped firm against his body, the Commander then bucked his own hips, much the same as Sagal had done moments earlier. This buck, though, snapped Elias' right arm at the elbow. The boy's wail was evidence enough, even if Harclay hadn't heard the bone crack from twenty yards away. He had though. The sound pinged around in his mind in between his son's ever-present condemnations. The crack and wail brought a smile to the Glorifier's face, Harclay saw as he averted his eyes from the catastrophe. He thought the man might toss a few more insults his way, but instead he let a victorious and sinister grin do all his taunting for him.

Harclay couldn't face that smirk. He turned back to the field of red-stained grass. The Commander had kicked Sagal away and climbed back to his feet. Elias was up on one knee, cradling his broken arm close to his chest. His face was even redder and dirtier and far more battered than when this fight had begun. Regardless, Harclay could easily read the pain in his eyes. He was sure the boy was all through. He had to be exhausted, as well as in a world of pain. Whether he even realized the Commander had sauntered back to his axe and was even then charging back at him, a looping slash ready to strike, no man could say. At least not until he suddenly leaned to the side and whipped out a straight kick that connected flush into the Commander's knee long before the big man's looping slash could finish its wicked arc. The weapon, in fact, went cartwheeling through the sky the instant after the kick connected.

Now it was the Witen council chief's turn to wail in pain. Elias' kick had sent the man's left knee bending backward in the exact opposite way for which its joint was designed. Surely all the tendons and ligaments inside were torn and useless. The way his lower leg flopped around below the knee as he hopped in place certainly spoke of utter destruction. The initial shocking pain seemed to be wearing off fast. The Commander was hopping on one leg, but that one leg was already gashed earlier, and now that wound was telling. Harclay dared to believe his creation might actually fall to his ass soon. There were few other options for him.

It was Elias who used the writhing of his recently injured enemy to recover his weapon this time. He'd scooped it from the turf with his left hand, leaving his injured right still cradled tight. The Commander had watched him the whole time, snarling in pain and hopping around, desperately searching for a way to put pressure on a leg that wouldn't result in excruciating agony and failing miserably. Elias made it to within three paces of the hopping gorilla. He paused there and said something to the Commander that Harclay wouldn't have been able to hear even if Wally wasn't shouting *Coward* and *Murderer* louder than ever inside his head. The Commander spat for answer, trying to play unaffected and unintimidated, but Harclay caught his quick glance over to his black axe now laying atop a dead Bruderschaft warrior a few yards to Elias' left. Elias caught the glance as well, or so Harclay assumed after he watched Sagal's battered face stretch into a wide grin.

The cocky smirk didn't last long. It was there as Elias, sword held strong in his left hand, lashed down a cut aimed for the junction of the Commander's head and neck. Had it landed, the sword would have sliced a foot deep into the big man's torso and Sagal's grin would've stretched, Harclay was sure of that. Sadly, the slash did not land, at least not where Elias had aimed it. The Commander had suddenly stopped his feeble hopping to plant all his weight firmly on his slashed left calf. The impossibly strong ruler even burst up off that leg to snatch the sword from the air before it could work up much momentum. The blade did sink fairly deep into the Commander's palm, nearly to the wrist, but no further. The hand remained intact enough to squeeze around the blade and rip it clean from Eli's grasp.

Sagal was stunned by the casual nature of the sudden maneuver. He only watched as the Commander grabbed the hilt of the sword with his right to rip the blade from the meaty palm of his left. Elias kept right on watching as the Commander snarled and bayed once more at the milky wash of blue and white speckled stars and was thus caught off guard when the monstrous man cut short the snarl and slashed out with the sword. The blade ripped a bloody tear across Sagal's face on an upward diagonal from lower left cheek to just below his right eye. Elias reeled back, bringing his uninjured arm up to staunch the blood sheeting from the nasty gash.

The Commander hounded the retreat, snatching a clump of Sagal's hair in his hacked left hand only to yank on the clump and send Elias tumbling down to his ass. He could have ended it then and there. Elias had his back to the man. One good slash at the boy's neck would settle the matter. The Commander had other plans though. He wanted the Ethling to suffer a bit more before he supplied the mercy of death. Nothing could be clearer. Especially after the Commander plunged the sword, point first, into the turf beside him, freeing up his right hand to bash home another half dozen jabs square into the boy's blood-soaked face.

"I told ya to bow! I gave ya a chance! You fucking traitor! We gave you everything!" the Commander shouted at Sagal just inches from his battered visage. "I gave you all a chance!" Harclay's creation said, addressing the silent fighters and residents all about him. "You didn't want to take it. So ... now you die," he finished, releasing his grip on Sagal's hair and letting him fall limply to the cushy turf.

Harclay saw where the Commander was headed and knew what was coming next. His black axe was still propped atop an unnaturally splayed corpse only ten paces from the man. He'd soon have it in hand and then too Elias' head only a few moments after that.

Murderer! Coward! Wally silently shouted. Then, breaking the repeated accusations, his son's voice suddenly echoed something new inside his skull, *Do something, Dad,* Wally said simply, his voice reasonable and measured as though nothing in the universe could be more plain or obvious.

And, for whatever reason, the simple, obvious suggestion spurred him. His legs would move at his command, he knew somehow. There was no more paralytic panic pinning him in place. He *could* do something. Hadn't he said something similar to Elias last night when the boy had called him? Harclay thought that, yes, indeed he had. Elias had said, "I'll ... do what I have to," and Harclay had answered, "So will I." At the time, he hadn't known what the answer implied. Now the promise was clear.

Harclay darted a quick glance at the Glorifier. The man had eyes only for the Commander. He scanned the field and saw that the same was true for every man, woman, and child present. Acting on impulse, with his son's encouragement rattling inside his head, Harclay chucked his flag pole at the feet of the Glorifier. The prophet reacted from surprise, making his first step unwise. The great black banner tangled up in his feet as he lurched to grab hold of Harclay and instead crashed bodily into him. Somehow though, Harclay didn't go down. The wild zealot did have a hold of his arm now though. Harclay tried to shake him off, but before he could complete the job, the Glorifier had a four-inch hunting knife scything in to skewer his stomach. Harclay stepped back from the blade and used the banner itself to aid in his defense. *Now, just where the fuck did the bastard have that thing hidden?* he asked himself with a bit of out of place dark humor that for some reason added an extra jolt to his churning determination. Meanwhile, the Glorifier's struggles only furthered his entanglement until the banner finally tripped him. Using the man's off-balance tumble, Harclay wrestled free the four-inch dagger. The

Glorifier was on the ground with the black banner obscuring his face when Harclay drove the blade into what he guessed was the man's chest.

He didn't wait to see if he'd aimed correctly. Harclay simply ripped the dagger free of the Glorifier's flesh and set off sprinting. Wally's voice was now full of pride, cheering him silently on. Harclay ate up the yards, closing fast. The things he trod over did not merit contemplation. He stayed on his feet. He kept his balance. That's all that mattered. With the knife held out and leading his way, Harclay bolted past Dobechek and Dirks, past a stirring Captain Alvarez and the pain-weary Bruderschaft leader sprawled atop him, past two still and silent skirmishes, past moaning amputees and wailing belly-wound victims, past maimed and blood-soaked corpse upon maimed and blood-soaked corpse, undaunted by any of it. Not one of the still breathing and upright warriors he passed, regardless of what banner they bled beneath, made the slightest move to stop him.

Alvarez's groaning confusion did grow louder and louder as the man's mind slowly recovered from its recent British fist-induced vacation. Harclay was halfway to his target when they suddenly cut out altogether. He chanced a quick look back and saw that the Witen's number three man had struggled out from under a severely injured Arlo Bailey's grasp but was now on all fours, frozen, voiceless, eyes fixed on Harclay's back. It was then he realized the cavernous Meadow had grown silent, utterly. There were only his breaths and Wally's private cheers now, nothing else. The Commander made no sound as he raised his axe high over his sprawled and beaten nemesis. Harclay might have expected some banshee war screech, or at least a warning shout from Captain Alvarez. Instead, there was only Wally, the wind, and his labored breaths.

That was, right up until he made it to within a single stride of the Commander's back. The Witen's champion and tyrant had only just begun to bring his axe back down to claim the son's head the same as he'd done the father's. Harclay had been frantic about whether he could plunge the knife home before the cruel black axe could fall to its ultimate ends, and so, he screamed again. There were no words this time, no battle cry nor apology, just regret, just shame. And exactly what, one might ask, does shame sung honest by the shameful sound like? Sorrowfully, Harclay now knew. Its bitter melodies were revealed in the shriek he'd loosed just before sinking a false prophet's hidden dagger to the hilt into the junction at the Commander's neck and shoulder.

The Commander jolted back to his full, towering height with a bemused growl, causing Harclay to lose his grip on the knife. The black axe fell harmlessly to the grass as Harclay stepped back a pace. The Commander did not turn to face him. It was almost as if he knew but would rather not receive the confirmation.

How fitting, Harclay reflected. *He'll get to indulge in one last self-deception before the end.*

The Commander's hand slowly moved to the dagger in his neck. It soaked red almost the instant after coming within range of the wound's spurting shower. Harclay thought he might try and pull it free. His fingers even brushed the wooden hilt. Instead, he whipped the hand down while sidestepping one pace to his right to snatch Elias' sword still wobbling point first in the soft turf. Over two-thirds of that priceless blade were then jammed through Harclay's gut before he could even think to react.

A cord had been cut. Suddenly, he had no legs. Harclay crashed to the grass, landing on his knees. The sword had run him through. He felt both the entry and exit wounds tear deeper from the jouncing impact. The pain had been there from the start, but only a shadow of itself. The true breadth of his agony was now unveiling its epic majesty. Harclay could not speak. He could barely look up. The Commander's eyes met his. His sick creation fell to his knees before him. With the Glorifier's dagger still quivering in place, the Commander reached out a hand. At first, Harclay was afraid. He thought the man meant to twist the steel stuck firm inside his belly. The hand cupped his cheek instead.

Elias slowly staggered to a knee in Harclay's periphery. Before him, the Commander stared down with watery eyes. Harclay knew the tears were not there from pain, not a physical pain at least, despite the mortal stab-wound in his neck. Jasper Montrois huffed and scowled a few times, but his eyes stayed locked with Harclay's all the while. Neither spoke, but pages of understanding passed silently between them. Elias made it to his feet just as the Commander's bloody hand finally fell from his cheek. His wound still spurting, the milk-eyed despot hobbled back up on his one halfway good leg to lock eyes with Sagal. Neither were armed, but Harclay doubted a blow would have been struck even if they had been. The Commander seemed to nod. It was a small movement and might have been purely from pain, but Harclay thought he saw it just before Montrois hopped away three paces to a somewhat open patch of battlefield.

With a huff and labored growl, the big man crashed back down to his knees. His eyes went star-ward. Harclay was just on the edge of earshot, and the man was speaking slow, not to mention the buzzing pain and his own thumping internal heartbeat, but he thought he heard Montrois call out his wife's name. He thought he heard "Forgive me" pass the man's lips as he reached once more for the hilt of the dagger in his throat. Jasper Montrois, the Commander of the Witenagemot, was a strong man indeed. The knife was almost completely out of him before massive blood loss and shuddering pain combined to steal his life away.

Elias had fallen to the ground beside Harclay by then, cradling his head in his lap. Both of them watched on as the man who'd named himself the Commander of the human race flopped lifelessly forward to fall face-first into a meadow he had ordered shorn no more than twelve hours earlier. Their eyes met after that, Harclay's and his protégé's. Elias muttered apologies and regrets. Harclay groaned, hoping it was enough. It was all he could give. The world was going dark at the edges. Wally's voice no longer rattled about his mind. The pain was still there but diminishing by the moment.

Harclay Aponyaschefski knew what it all meant. The boy's tears couldn't save him, nor any wondrous new medical procedure in Newton Hospital. He was dying. *It's as it should be*, he thought as the tunnel of darkness shrank to a single pinpoint of light. The pain was over. All he knew were the boy's arms holding him tightly. He actually felt warm just before the end, and though he was sure he didn't deserve even that much peace, he accepted it with a thankful heart all the same.

CHAPTER 15
MAISIE

AFTERMATH

They were still on the footbridge when the man collapsed, too far to know for certain, and Maisie was weary of cognitive bias and wishful thinking, but she still would bet that the man they'd all just watched fall to his knees and then faceplant in the turf was Jasper Montrois, the Commander of the Witenagemot. *He's dead,* she tried out the news silently to herself first. Finding each step she took closer to the eerily paused battle only confirmed, more and more, that her eyes hadn't been deceiving her, Maisie tried the words aloud, "He's dead."

"Was that him?" Tessa asked, huffing slightly from their sprint.

"The Commander?" Jordana wondered through a huff of her own. "My god, there are so few left..."

They had only started running at the Meadow's archway, the trolley had taken them the rest of the way, but still, they were all worked up, so sure they'd be too late to make any difference. Maisie heard the panicked pattern of breaths in her own voice as she ignored Jordana's last comment to answer the first. "I think it's him."

"How come everybody is just standing around?" Carrie asked, her voice alone among the four of them even and unlabored. Of course, she was being carried.

Maisie had insisted once they'd leaped off the trolley, scooping her up before her sister could argue. Maisie was asking herself pretty much the same question. She didn't have an answer, so said nothing, just kept sprinting for that mown patch of meadow.

"Hey, it's Elias!" her sister screamed into her ear.

Maisie spotted him a beat later. She'd been staring straight at him for yards now, but it took Carrie's pronouncement before she recognized her kid brother beneath his slashed mask of grimy blood and yellowing bruises. He was no more than five yards from the Commander, kneeling on the ground and cradling the Steward's head in his lap, the former lawyer's scrutinous eyes now motionless and vacant. *They're both dead?* Maisie didn't dare to believe it. Her heart skipped a beat. *I have a moment here. There is a chance.*

It was almost as if Captain Alvarez had heard her thoughts. His voice screeched out before Maisie could catch her breath and speak sense. Orders for her brother's head and for the remaining Witen fighters to kill the man across from them pierced every ear inside the monstrous structure. A blond Bruderschaft fighter was struggling to prevent Captain Alvarez from regaining his feet. The man was clearly injured, cradling his side, and so Alvarez was up and free within Maisie's next three sprinted paces. Thankfully, none of the Witen's fighters seemed in any great hurry to follow his maniacal orders. This fact only incensed the corridor regent further. With a fascist finger fixed firm on Elias, Alvarez hurled insult after insult upon him, then switched to his recalcitrant footmen and the Witen's two remaining officers.

Dobechek, apparently sufficiently shamed by her better, finally lifted her axe and took a step in Eli's direction. All around the disgusting battlefield, Witen fighters stirred. The injured blond man rushed Alvarez, knocking him wildly off balance. Diminished as the man was, however, he could not take advantage. He tried to trip the Captain back down, tried to grapple him into submission, but it was no good. Alvarez easily disentangled himself, adding a backhand smash across the blond man's chin after wrenching his last hand free.

"Kill the traitor! Kill them all! This battle is not over, you fucking cowards! Fight! Kill! For the Witen! For glory! For the Commander!" Alvarez shouted as the blond man toppled over.

"Noo!" Maisie screamed just as she reached the battlefield's boundary. She stopped to set her sister down as gently as haste permitted before continuing her sprint straight for her brother. "This fight is over!" she told them all, still running. "This war is over! It was his!" Maisie declared, her finger pointed straight at where the Commander lay face first in the bloody turf. "It's over!"

"Nothing is over," Alvarez turned to snarl at her. "No one listen to this terrorist, this prisoner. Fucking gag the bitch. Tie her up until our duty is done."

Tessa darted past Maisie. Not saying a word, she barreled into Alvarez, sending him sprawling back to crash on his ass. The blond man lurched toward the tumbled pair, clearly looking to aid Tessa.

"Arlo, no!" Jordana screamed, coming up behind Maisie. "You're hurt. I've got him," the pilot told her leader before diving atop the wrestling pair.

An uneasiness gathered as the two women pinned the Captain to the turf and secured his arms behind his back. No one had dealt another blow, but Maisie knew one was imminent. Dobechek especially looked ready for further combat.

"You!" Alvarez snarled at a footman with whom he'd managed to lock eyes. "Kill these two fucking prisoners on my back right fucking now, son. That's an order!" he added the screeching command when the footman hesitated. The shout shook the man into action. Alvarez was trying to shout more encouragement at him before Tessa clapped a hand over his mouth. The footman came on, shakily yet also resolutely. His eyes were everywhere, but his axe was rearing back to strike.

Maisie strode four firm paces to cut him off. The boy, for he was barely more than that, a wide-eyed, impressionable boy, locked eyes with her but did not halt his trudge. Alvarez's muffled orders goaded him on. Maisie had not known she launched her slap until her palm smacked loud against the boy's pimply cheek. It stopped the kid in his tracks though. So she didn't second guess herself. Instead, she turned from him, spinning all the way around in the middle of that horrible patch of fertile soil. The tension about her settled. It didn't leave, not completely, but she thought she could at least get a few moments to speak with their full attention.

When she finally started, her voice was as reasonable as it was exhausted. "Throw down your weapons, please. It's all over. Let the madness they created die with them," she pleaded, pointing to the Commander and then the Steward in her brother's arms. Maisie strode close to where Elias knelt. She hoped the smile on her face and the warm blush in her cheeks were enough to show him how happy she was to see him still alive and how very much she still and always loved him and how she held no grudge for the mad past and how she hoped he could forgive her someday for her part in their estrangement and that all she ever wanted was for them to be a family again. She couldn't tell if he read all that with her eyes as watery as they were, but when he reached up from his knees to clasp her hand, she knew nothing else need be said between them.

So she once more addressed the crowd, "No one will be punished for any of it. I swear this. Throw down your weapons, and everyone goes home free. Let the past stay there, I say. Let's move on together. Toss away the steel these vengeful, misguided, broken men placed in your hands. You don't need it. It was not your choice to take it up in the first place. Set them down. The fight is over. This unnecessary conflict was no more than the deliberate construction of a vicious and tormented mind. Let's allow this day to fade away, remembered only as the last act of a desperate man, if ever. It had nothing to do with any of us. Let it all fade, everything. C'mon, people, please, let's move on. Throw down your weapons. Come back to reality, to decency. Let us all tend to these brave dead today and then forget this nightmare past and instead work to build a bright future, a true future. Let's all... let's... hell, it's time we all went home. Let's get there together. Please throw down your weapons."

"Throw them down. It's over!" Bailey shouted through his pain. Those few folk of his that remained standing complied with their leader's order almost immediately.

"He's right. It's over."

Every head in the meadow, Maisie's included, turned the speaker's way. Maisie's eyes arrived just in time to witness Lieutenant Millicent Dirks toss her spear to the turf. A shocked murmur rolled through the gathered spectators. It increased when two footmen in the skirmish beside her followed suit. Alvarez bucked and bellowed his muffled bellows, but they could not stem the tide. Maisie watched in awe as, one by one, each combatant left standing tossed their weapons to the turf.

"Lower the colors, Cora," Arlo Bailey instructed in a strong voice despite his wince while climbing back to his feet once more. "We're just one people now, the last people... but not the *final* people."

Maisie turned to beam at the man. The Bruderschaft's quilted flag disappeared from the starry skyline. Warriors stumbled from the field or collapsed in place from exhaustion. A collective sigh escaped the lips of the gathered crowd. *It's over*. Maisie smiled. Carrie came hobbling up a few seconds later. Sweeping her kid sister up, Maisie and Carrie shared a giggle as she kissed her brow. Then they bent low beside their brother, who only then was gently setting the Steward's head down on the grass. Elias looked up. This time it was his eyes filled with tears. Both of the sisters wrapped their arms around him tightly. Elias sobbed, begging Maisie for forgiveness. She only shooshed and squeezed harder. He didn't need to say a damn word. She hadn't been feeding the crowd a line. She really wanted to leave the past where it was and focus only on the future. Maisie could taste the dream of home, the dream of Earth. It was so close now.

Carrie began to explain to Elias in a muffled stutter how sorry she was about failing to convince the prisoners to leave and that she hoped he wasn't mad at her. Elias lifted his head from Maisie's shoulder and paused his huffing tears long enough to smile at his baby sister. His hand went to his back pocket then, and when it came back, it was tugging an old blue ball cap on top of Carrie's chestnut mop. The girl could only smile back and dive back into his chest to squeeze him tightly.

The other two trolleys arrived then. The remaining prisoners and Bruderschaft members all rushed together across the footbridge. Some faces wore smiles, many of the Bruderschaft's wore somber visages, but all of them sprinted. Clearly, they could tell some paradigm shift was in the works and wanted to be a part of it. Maisie heard the crowd fill the newcomers in, just as she heard many of the Bruderschaft members scream in discovery of a killed or maimed loved one. *So much tragedy*, she thought. *So much to heal*. Maisie, still hugging her family tightly, turned her head then to lock eyes with Jordana. The gorgeous woman was still holding a squirming Captain, but she found a smile for Maisie nonetheless. The hope that filled her soul then was equivalent to an entire civilization's lifetime supply. They'd done it. The Witenagemot was dead. She was happy.

The laugh put an end to that. It started off quite distant and faint, but still she hated the sound from the moment it first reached her ears. It somehow penetrated every reunion throughout the Meadow, whether they be informative, joyous, or devastating. She felt all heads turn toward the sound. It wasn't some straggling prisoners, nor lost Bruderschaft members on the steel footbridge now. Crossing over the rushing rapids this time were the AOA. From this distance, Maisie only really recognized Harrington and the cold-eyed woman who'd spoken for him concerning the satellite platforms all those years ago. She searched for President Rafferty as the peculiar gaggle drew closer but saw no sign of him or any other government head.

The footmen who'd been manning the PRZVL33 in the Lunar Dock stood out in the strange group though, as did the fact that each of the five guardsmen's wrists were strapped tight behind their backs. The PRZVL itself was likewise conspicuous, as was Cainey Barker, none the worse for wear and still donning his VLSE gear with the top half tied around his waist. The towheaded man with smooth, unblemished skin pushing the PRZVL33's dolly too was noticeable, though, oddly, she found she could not place his face, nor those of the twenty or so other impossibly fit and handsome people surrounding Harrington and the satellite platform woman.

Every last one of that mystery score was dressed to the nines, each suit, skirt, and blouse among them tailored perfectly to their athletic and sleekly powerful physiques. The laugh had come from among that group of strange and unknown twenty. The chuckler was a tall, dark-complected man with a pot belly and an exquisitely lined black beard. He bore a self-assured smile that did not reach his still and lifeless eyes.

Questions like, *How did they capture those five footmen and steal their PRZVL*, or *How did Cainey make it back inside the station before his O2 ran out?* were irrelevant next to the two supreme questions. Those being: *Who the hell are these people and how the hell did they get here*? Maisie had no answer for either. She felt her jaw on the floor the entire time the group of fifteen or so AOA execs and the twenty-odd finely dressed newcomers strode their merry way to the battlegrounds. The big pompous bastard led the way all throughout in the center of the gaggle, periodically shifting between giggling and guffawing as he scanned the scene.

There had to be close to five hundred people in the Meadow just then, yet not a one of them made the slightest sound when the obnoxious man with the flawless skin and beard finally abandoned his demeaning laughter after halting his group's march on the edge of the battlefield no more than ten yards from Maisie and her family.

At length, Harrington stepped up beside the immaculately dressed condescender to break the silent tension. "What do you think you're doing here, Arlo?" the CEO asked the bent and battered Bruderschaft leader.

Maisie's mind was awash in a sea of confusion, but still she had the presence to think both the casual delivery of the question, as well as whom it was directed toward were very surprising. She might've expected the aging executive to address her first or perhaps Eli even. It took her a minute to remember that Arlo Bailey had once worked for AOA. Somehow though, Maisie had pictured him as a lower-level employee, at least not one whose face the company's CEO would know. Also, the tragedy and triumph of the past few minutes seemed to Maisie the sort of somber event that demanded a measure of respect and reverence from anyone who cared to speak just then. The casual off-topic accusation was almost offensive in light of all that. Bailey seemed to sense as much. He only straightened up as best as his broken ribs allowed and glared at Harrington.

AOA's CEO had no sense of propriety, however. "I asked you a question, Mr. Bailey. I believe we fired you, sir, long ago. So just what in the hell do you think you're doing trespassing on our property?" Harrington asked, clearly enjoying himself.

Still, Bailey, like the crowd, stayed silent.

Harrington only scoffed at his glare. He waved off the nuisance of his former employee and appeared as though he were preparing to address the crowd when the burly, handsome laugher among the unknown twenty cleared his throat. Harrington instantly cut short whatever he'd been working up. His head even seemed to bob down in deference as he whipped around to face the elegantly dressed and imposing man. The chuckling had apparently run its course, but the man's thin black beard still framed a grin. A certain menace lurked beneath the playful façade though. It was as obvious in his cold gray eyes as it was well disguised beneath that wide, handsome smile. "Won't you introduce me?" the man prompted. His voice was deep, much as Maisie suspected, but his accent was strange. She hadn't been exposed to a great many over her short life, but she was sure she'd never heard any other quite like it.

"Certainly, sir," Harrington said. His head stayed bowed until he had fully turned away from the big man with the strange accent. Maisie watched, rooted to her patch of grass, as the other nineteen strangers standing behind him, along with the satellite platform woman, began to spread out. They moved through the still and silent crowd, and even among the surviving fighters, their dead gray eyes roaming over everything and everyone. Harrington let the silence stretch as the newcomers went about their inspection until he heard the handsome man behind begin to impatiently stir. "Mr. Bailey, might I introduce you to the true owners of this station... and the planet itself, for that matter? This is Virgil Datalis, Advancement Operations Alliance Chief Executive Officer. The well-dressed folk strolling about you now are Mr. Datalis' fellow board members. They all hail from Corporate Zone 7. I'm told it's what's called a Mega City built atop the decimated ruins of what once had been named the South American Continent."

"What the bloody hell are you talking about, Hubert?" Bailey managed to ask through his clear befuddlement. "Who the hell are these people?"

Arlo looked over to Maisie after Harrington only grinned at his question. Maisie could do no more than shrug her shoulders. She was as confused as Bailey, if not more so.

"Look," Arlo restarted after a shake of the head, "I don't know what the hell you think you're doing just now, Hubert, but the rest of us have just had one right good shit of a morning. So, why don't you and your little Super-City-Corporate-Zoney place friends, or whatever the bloody fuck you muttered, just go away for a while? I promise we can all come together and hash out whatever knob-headed power grabs you've in mind then. For now, have a heart. Read the bloody room, for Christ's sake. Just go away. Let us bury these people in peace."

Maisie might have said much the same to Harrington, had she the use of her voice just then. She desperately wanted to know who the hell these twenty strangers were and where they came from, as well as how they captured the PRZVL and rescued Cainey, but more desperate right then was her desire to bury the dead, to bury the Witen. Her mind wasn't ready to deal with whatever the hell Harrington and his strange friends had in mind. She needed a rest. They all deserved a break after the Witenagemot's fall. Harrington was an unwelcome nuisance. She would have given much to see the back of him just then. The CEO, of course, did not care about either her exhaustion or confusion.

"Mr. Datalis and his board members commissioned this station from three hundred years in the future. It's theirs, all of it, right down to the last bolt," Harrington said, smiling at Bailey's incredulous demeanor. "In their wisdom and righteousness they learned to master time itself. And now, finally, gratefully, they have arrived from their dead world to claim what they deserve: a healthy, pristine Earth to etch their glory upon."

"Jeez, M-M-Mr. Harrington, you sound like the Glorifier. I n-n-never thought that would happen," Maisie heard her sister say from just beside her.

Harrington was not pleased. She remembered how angry he'd been when Alice had refused to make her leave that impromptu meeting all those years back. Clearly, the déjà vu irked him. He tried to ignore Carrie, but after he'd stayed silent for too long to be just some dramatic pause in his speech, Maisie knew her little sister's accusation had rattled him.

Polly Dobechek actually wound up being the first to speak after Carrie. "What the fuck you talking about time travel and shit right now for? The fuck does some sci-fi story got to do with anything?" she asked, her brow furrowed so one could almost read each of the churning emotions brewing within her. "Enough of the fucking stupid games. C'mon now, just tell us, where the fuck you been hiding these friends of yours?"

"Yeah, Hubie," Dirks agreed. "We ain't got the patience for any bullshit just now. Who the fuck are they? And don't give us no *Corporation Zone 7* shit, whatever the fuck that is."

"It's *Corporate* Zone 7, actually. And it's where I'm from, born and raised, to use a colloquialism of your time. It was my old fiefdom, one might call it. I'd love to tell you all about it, in fact, but first..." he added, pausing there to show off a grin that was somehow simultaneously malevolent and congenial, "I'll need you all to bow."

"What? You... you want us... t-t-to... to *bow*? Can that truly be what you just said?" Bailey asked Datalis, indignant and disbelieving. "Get the hell out of here," the Bruderschaft leader barked, waving his arm in dismissal before the man could answer. "I mean... truly, how dare you? Have you any idea where you're standing just now? These are my brothers and sisters lying dead around you. Have some bloody decency. Take your nonsense somewhere else."

"Why the fuck would we ever bow to your fancy ass?" Dobechek scoffed.

"Enough with this bowing talk!" Maisie shouted, finding her voice at last. "We just ended that nonsense, Polly. You threw down your axe. It's over. Just ignore these jerks. There won't ever be any more bowing!" She screamed this last at an undaunted Datalis, still wearing his bright, evil smile.

"Yeah, sod off, you bloody fucking nutter. Take your bonkers fairytale somewheres else," a muscular British woman bearing evidence of the morning's battle in the form of bruises, stains, and gashes from head to heal told Datalis, before she too dismissed his nonsense with a wave.

Datalis kept his creepy grin the whole time he strode toward the battle-weary British woman. It was even there when he suddenly lashed out to wrap a lanky hand around her throat. The woman did experience a moment of shock, probably over both the sheer speed of the move as well as its unprecedented nature. She was fighting to free herself from the grip within a heartbeat though. None of it seemed to do her any good, sadly. She was a big woman too. Her neck was as thick as most bodybuilders'. Somehow though, none of that mattered. Datalis' grip held firm. He even lifted her off the ground with just his one outstretched arm.

That display of strength, impressive as it was, paled in comparison to the show he put on for the crowd next. Just before the British woman passed out, Datalis reared back his arm and chucked her across the grass. The bulky fighter flew no less than ten full yards across the shorn meadow, landing hard on her back in a pool of blood collected from at least three nearby corpses. Maisie's eyes were off the man for a few seconds, but she was still certain that Datalis' smile had not left his face for a single moment. The grin was even stretching when she turned back to it.

"Bow, please," the immaculate man instructed. He was still smiling as he clasped his hands behind his back and began to stroll around, deliberate in his aimlessness.

"Fear will never rule us again," Maisie's baby sister defiantly shouted at Datalis as soon as his wanderings swung their way.

"My dear child, I don't wish to rule anybody," Datalis assured in a voice that begged to be doubted. His strange accent seemed to add to the man's obvious falseness. "This is our station, however. You all are more than welcome to stay, but I'm afraid I do have a few house rules. Number one being, I need you all to bow. Anyone who can't follow my simple house rules will be asked to leave. Mr. Barker knows of an airlock close by you are all free to use. Isn't that right, Mr. Barker?" Datalis turned around to ask the man whom Maisie and her fellow prisoners had left for dead no more than an hour ago.

"I'll show 'em the door, Mr. Datalis. Whatever you want, sir," the traitor answered, his hands on his hips and an equally irritating smile of his own plastered to his pig face.

"Why did ya bother doctoring your evacuation data, Harrington?" Bailey's odd question abruptly drew all gazes his way. "I don't understand. Was it just for me? Really? I mean... I don't want to sound egotistical, but truly nothing else makes any sense. Was it all just subterfuge? Could it really have been just to get me up here in the off chance I managed to survive and find the means to follow after you?" Arlo Bailey still cradled his injury, but the pain in his voice seemed to have a more subtle and bewildering cause.

"You were a loose end, yes," Harrington answered. "We had people looking for you since the very day you hacked into the mainframe after your termination. You proved one elusive son of a bitch,

Bailey. My hat's off to ya. If you hadn't eluded us in the weeks before the infection, we might not have thought the deception necessary. Who knows? But since you had managed to escape us, we figured if you somehow managed to escape the infection too, that, one way or another, you'd recover our doctored data. We knew you'd see your chance in it. You knew about the alternate site in Wyoming, after all. And so, the very reason we needed to find you and considered you a loose end in the first place, we turned into the tool that would bring you straight to us. And what a fortunate bit a subterfuge it was. Not only did it bring you here, but you brought the very thing Mr. Datalis and his people needed for their return. You brought the blood of an alpha straight to us. We had begun to worry that we'd never recover one. Then you show up all unexpected bearing gifts. It's kismet, Arlo. You're our goddamn savior. Thank you," Harrington explained, ending with a full-on belly laugh. "Like I say though, Bailey, I really didn't ever believe you could survive the infection, not for this long. Really," he added, catching his breath between laughs, "hats off. Good show, sir. Ain't that what you Brits say?"

"I can't believe you bothered," Bailey said in a low voice, almost as if he meant it only for himself.

"AOA had a great many failsafes in play, Mr. Bailey," Datalis said, reclaiming the spotlight. "Heck, Mr. Bailey, the infection itself was only one of a hundred plans we devised for our return, all of which had a mountain of failsafes and protocols to go along with them. Our corporation is quite thorough, I assure you, and our triumphant return was quite important. It was certainly the biggest thing on our calendar, anyway," he added, giggling. "We left little to chance, Mr. Bailey, as little as possible." Datalis strode toward the hunched and weary Bruderschaft leader as he spoke. "We are right where we were always meant to be," he told Bailey, placing a massive hand on the blond Brit's shoulder. "So, don't be a fool. Bow."

Bailey wanted to protest, obviously. His face ran the gamut from hostile to resigned, but he said nothing. In the end, he simply yielded to Datalis' unnatural strength as the man pressed down on his shoulder. Bailey crumpled to a knee beneath the pressure, and when the man's hand left his shoulder, he stayed where he was, bent and submissive before a finely dressed and unsettlingly handsome monster.

Nooo! Maisie silently screamed. *This can't be happening.* "Noo!" she screamed again, though this time it burst free her lips. One by one, as Datalis' gaze fell upon them, the residents and warriors in the Meadow fell to their knees and bowed their heads. "Noooo!" she screamed again. "Get up! We can't just trade one tyrant for the next. Get up!" Maisie spun, screaming at the sea of kneelers around her, begging them to see sense. None rose. In the end, only her brother and sister standing beside her kept their feet. Abruptly, Jordana gave up holding down Alvarez to come stand alongside them. Tessa then shoved the Captain in the back as she popped up to take her place beside Elias. Their examples inspired no others though. Even Alvarez stayed frozen in place, despite the absence of his captors.

The five of them stood proudly above the rest, uncowed by Datalis' petulant menace. The other nineteen exquisitely attired strangers and the satellite platform woman were left standing as well, scattered here and there around the shorn patch of meadow. Their roaming studies had ceased for the moment, however. Every last one of them seemed to be standing still with crossed arms and staring right at Maisie and her family.

For his part, the handsome newcomer only held his smile and nodded his head. "The airlock then?" he casually inquired through his smarmy grin.

Jordana's hand sought Maisie's. The pressure of their soft palms nestling snugly together sent a shot of warmth and comfort straight through to her core.

"Well," Maisie answered the AOA CEO from the future, her voice hoarse but firm, "we ain't bowing to you."

"Very well then," the mysterious monster sighed, "Mr. Barker, show these brave folk the door, if you would."

"Yes, sir, Mr. Datalis," Novocaine said, untying the VLSE gear from around his waist.

Maisie had an insult set to devastate Cainey, but it never made it beyond her mind. Elias had clapped his hand on her shoulder just before it could be loosed.

"I'm sorry, Mais," her brother was saying as he pushed her and Carrie down to a knee. "I just got ya both back. I'm sorry, Mais. We gotta kneel." He began to plead with her when she bucked beneath the pressure of his hand. "Kneel, Mais, for Carrie. You too, Tess. All of us. We have to, for Carrie."

That got through to her. Maisie's eyes went to her little sister. Carrie was staring back, innocence and confusion radiating from her every molecule. No fear though. Carrie was too brave for that. She would demand to go out the airlock with them. *He's right*, she bemoaned in silence. *Oh, god, he's right. We've freaking lost again. I'm sorry, Alice. I'm so sorry. Please forgive me, Stevie. I have failed you all. Forgive me, Daddy. I beat your monster, I did... but... but... but a new one's come, Dad. I'm so sorry, Daddy. I lost. A new one's come.*

She was on her knees by then. Datalis held up a hand to stop Cainey.

"Good. That's a wise decision, I think," he said softly to the five of them, still wearing his obnoxious smile. Raising his voice, he then told the collection of kneelers around him, "You've all made a very wise decision today. You'll soon see the truth of that, I assure you, a very wise decision, indeed."

She was technically on her knees, but Maisie's head had stayed unbowed. So perhaps she alone watched the man spin slowly in a circle while his smile stretched wider and wider as he surveyed the submissive masses dotting the tarnished meadowlands, and perhaps too, it was she alone among those average masses who bore witness to Virgil Datalis pausing in place after the circle was complete only to raise his arms toward the milky darkness twinkling high above. "I'm home," she swore she heard him say just before her heart shattered in a thousand pieces and the last ember of her hope was snuffed out forever and the burning weight of her tears grew heavy enough to drag her eyes down to join with all the others now staring at the bloody grass out of deference to yet another despot.

The End... of the Witenagemot... and the dawn of the Age of AOA...

BOOK CLUB QUESTIONS

1. Twist end aside, did you find the climax a satisfactory ending to wrap up the trilogy?
2. Who were your favorite characters and why?
3. Which characters did you have the hardest time relating to?
4. Were there any "villains" in the story you could empathize with?
5. What moral lessons can be taken away from the series?
6. Are you excited about how the AOA universe can open up, given the ending?
7. What other genres would you like to see the author write in?

AUTHOR BIO

Andy T. Hanson is an author of science fiction, general fiction, and dystopian horror. After driving Abrams tanks in the U.S. Army, Andy settled into life as a regional-stage actor. He parlayed that passion first into playwriting—most notable of which is *Molly's Chamber*, his modern-day take on the old Irish folk song "Whiskey in the Jar"—then graduating to screenwriting, with *Paradise Valley*, a former Los Angeles Film Festival quarterfinalist script. On the strength of their modest success, he tried his hand at the ultimate goal: sci-fi novels. His first foray into that magical world was *The Despot Chronicles*, a dystopian three-part epic series, the first of which, *Calamity*, released on 10/26/24 by 4 Horsemen Publications, Inc. Andy is thrilled to occupy a slot among their fantastic stable of authors.

Residing in Bay City, Michigan, Andy is an avid Detroit, and Michigan in general, sports fan, and somehow finds time to write in the midst of a busy life packed with Lions games, golf, a healthy love of film and television of all genres, grilling and chilling with his big family, in particular his lovely wife Lauren and son Teddy, and devouring science fiction, historical fiction, and fantasy novels.

He's inspired in large part by George R. R. Martin, Stephen King, Bernard Cornwell, Lee Child, and Sara Rosett, with a bit of Stephen Fry, Richard Dawkins, Kurt Vonnegut, Neil Gaiman, and Craig Allanson for spice.

Andy is attracted literarily to well-fleshed out characters, especially gray characters, while his favorite part of writing is simply being present as the story seems to grow of its own volition.

Discover more at
4HorsemenPublications.com

10% off using HORSEMEN10

www.ingramcontent.com/pod-product-compliance
Lightning Source LLC
LaVergne TN
LVHW041747060526
838201LV00046B/931